The One That Is Both

The One That Is Both

A Novel

L. E. Maroski

iUniverse, Inc.

New York Lincoln Shanghai

The One That Is Both

iUniverse books may be ordered through booksellers or by contacting:

iUniverse
2021 Pine Lake Road, Suite 100
Lincoln, NE 68512
www.iuniverse.com
1-800-Authors (1-800-288-4677)

This is a work of fiction. All of the characters, names, incidents, organizations and dialogue in this novel are either the products of the author's imagination or are used fictitiously.

ISBN-13: 978-0-595-39490-6 (pbk)
ISBN-13: 978-0-595-83887-5 (ebk)
ISBN-10: 0-595-39490-6 (pbk)
ISBN-10: 0-595-83887-1 (ebk)

Printed in the United States of America

Acknowledgements

First and foremost, I thank and acknowledge my Accountability Group, Jerry Thomas and Helen Kessler, without whose support this book surely wouldn't have happened. I thank the following people who contributed to the content or gave me feedback on early drafts: Hector Sabelli, Wilbur Dillman, Steven M. Rosen, John Scott-Railton, Andreas Quast, Alla Milikovsky, Darlene DeMille Baker, Theresa Wood, Netza Roldan, Joy Boggs, Kathrine Myers, Philip Andrews, Fred Hecker, Ashok Gangadean, and Allan Teske.

I thank Lucius Outlaw for letting me write a story for that first philosophy paper and fostering that Socratic tendency to explore ideas in dialogue.

Chapter 1

"Hey buddy, can I wash your windows?" came a voice from the front porch. Through the screen door, Jerry saw a young man with longish blonde hair wearing a torn but clean red T-shirt that said, "Ask me." He carried two buckets full of soapy water, a mop, and a squeegee, and he sported a hopeful grin.

Jerry was glad for some company, any company. "How much?"

"For the whole house, twenty bucks and dinner."

"Deal." Jerry stuck out his hand to close the negotiation. *What a bargain,* Jerry thought. The young man had a mop in his shaking hand but that didn't deter him. The mop head, however, tipped the buckets, sending sudsy water all over the porch and into the foyer.

"Never mind. I'll get…" Jerry mumbled as he went to get towels.

He returned to find the mess gone, cleaned up, and so was the young man.

The window washer had set his equipment in front of the big bay window and had begun soaping it. Jerry shut the door and mentally noted the man's diligence. Now there was the problem of dinner. *What do I have to cook?* He nosed through his cabinets full of trail mix, power bars, canned soup, and breakfast cereal. Toward the very back was a jar of tomato-basil spaghetti sauce. In the refrigerator he found a few slightly limp carrots, an onion that was sprouting, and some old kalamata olives, the kind that gets shoved to the back of the refrigerator for a special occasion that never seems to occur, and a hot dog. He rejected the hot dog for the spaghetti sauce.

The young man arrived for dinner cleaned up, although he hadn't asked to use the bathroom. The observation flitted through Jerry's mind so quickly it almost didn't register.

"I don't believe I got your name," Jerry said, motioning him to sit.

"Tom Byrd," the young man replied. And after an awkward silence, "And yours is?"

"Jerry Fowss." They both burst out laughing.

"After you," said one.

"No, after you," said the other, recreating an old cartoon about a couple of too-polite gophers whose good manners get them nearly eaten by a cat in every episode.

Each sat behind a mountain of spaghetti and sauce, waiting for the other to say something first. Jerry twirled his fork in the spaghetti. "What brings you to these parts?" he asked.

"The short answer is 'just wandering around seeing where I could be useful,' but I doubt that's a satisfying answer. It wouldn't be for me, anyway," Tom said, putting a large forkful of spaghetti in his mouth.

"So what's the long answer?" Jerry took the bait.

Tom chewed the last of the spaghetti bundle while considering how to answer. "How does anybody get to where they are? Through a series of reactions to circumstances, the most important of which is the family you're born into. However, I won't bore you with that."

"If it's so important, I think you should," Jerry countered.

"Point taken." He took a big bite of pasta to fortify himself for the explanation. Still chewing, he continued, "My parents were older when I was born. I came along after they had given up on the prospect of having any children. So you can see the inherent conflict right there."

"Sorry, I don't. What's the big deal?" Jerry asked.

"They were at once delighted but had grown so set in their ways that a child was a tremendous imposition on their comfortable, familiar lifestyle. I grew up feeling dearly loved, the apple of my mother's eye but always underfoot, in the way. I learned how to breeze in like the wind, do or say only what was necessary, and then breeze out just as quickly." He took another bite of spaghetti.

"Where did all this wind take you? You must have traveled a lot. I'm the exact opposite. I tend to find someplace that I like and plant myself. I've been here six years now."

"Like all kids, I wanted to please my folks. Dad was a plumber and wanted something better for me than what he had, so he sent me to medical school. I figured I could be a good doctor because you don't have to stay very long with one patient."

Jerry grunted in acknowledgment; his mouth was full of the long starchy threads.

Tom continued, "Although I might have made a good doctor, I hated medical school and left in my third year."

"Why?"

"It was so stressful that I had a nervous breakdown and was then treated by the very people who were teaching me. What a horrible experience being on the other side of the examining table. I realized that my teachers, who had taught me all this wonderful information about how the body works ultimately didn't respect the miracle that the human body, my body, is. All they wanted to do was cut and drug, cut and drug. They weren't interested in what caused it in the first place or in helping me deal with the stress that brought it on. They weren't concerned with healing the whole person. They just wanted me fixed and back doing rounds."

"And it was painful seeing yourself in the mirror?"

"Yeah. I didn't want to be like that. I wanted to really help people heal, not just drug them up and go on to the next half-naked body."

"So what did you do after you left?"

"You're looking at it," Tom said triumphantly, stretching his arms out with the dramatic flair of a performer in a Broadway musical.

Jerry managed a quick smile then guzzled some water to avoid saying what he was thinking.

Tom pulled his extroverted mannerisms back in quickly and said almost to himself, "I was disillusioned." He put another fork full of spaghetti in his mouth, chewed a few times, and continued, "Not to sound too sour—you have to balance the negative with the positive you know—I learned a lot about immunology because it's a key component of the healing process. That to me is the most fascinating system because it's all about adapting."

Jerry looked at him quizzically. "I thought it was about fighting off germs."

"It's a shame that our most powerful healing force has been characterized by a war metaphor, like there's a battle going on inside your body, with bad guys and good guys, foreign invaders, and defenses. Odd thing is, most of the bacteria that give us infections already live in and on our bodies."

"So why don't we have infections all the time?"

"Thanks to the immune system. The bacteria are organisms trying to eke out a living just like you and me. Look what happens with people: everything is fine until resources get scarce, then crime goes up. We live with potential murderers, crooks, and terrorists day in and day out, but the police aren't 'activated' until one of them does something harmful. Similarly, if you're not giving your body enough resources, like good nutritious spaghetti with lots of veggies in the sauce, the residents are going to get rowdy. Crime will go up. Cells will get damaged and there won't be enough resources left over to fix them up and clean up the mess. Immune responses happen when something, foreign or domestic, gets rowdy on you."

Jerry sat fascinated and perplexed as he attempted to figure out whether this talk about healing answered his original question about what had brought Tom to these parts. Jerry digested that deluge of opinion and information in silence for a few minutes. *Why did a wandering window washer, med school dropout show up in my life today?* There were obviously more pieces to the puzzle of this young man's identity, but Jerry didn't care, really, about uncovering them. Tom's openness and generosity, his seeming lack of care about what people might think about him made him easy to be with. Jerry found it easier to talk to Tom than to people he knew well, and so he took advantage of what seemed like a diamond dropped in his lap, a conversational partner who didn't shy away from the big questions. "You seem to know so much about the human body," Jerry began tentatively, "and I had something happen to me as a kid—I don't know how to explain it. I haven't been able to fully understand what happened."

"So, what was it?" Tom had finished eating and pushed his chair away from the table to take a more reclining position.

Jerry felt his insides knot up. He hadn't told anyone but his mother what happened to him one night when he was a child. Telling her had ruined his life, or so he thought. Now, however, it felt oddly safer to tell this complete stranger than it had been to tell her. Jerry took a deep breath and his face rearranged itself, like a squeegee had wiped away the wrinkles, cares, and age.

"When I was about 10 years old, I woke up one night, right at that magic time of night, just before the sun makes the horizon glow. I felt it right away—something was different. I looked around my room. It was mine all right; I hadn't been whisked away by a tornado or teleported to an alien space craft (my secret wish). I sat up in bed and pulled the sheet up to my chin. Out of the corner of my eye came the clue. Where my left hand held the sheet, I couldn't see where my hand ended and the sheet began. They blended together where they touched. I sat motionless, afraid to move. Only my eyes moved as they scanned the room. Although everything was in its proper place and nothing was moving, it all somehow seemed alive. I detected a faint light—but the sunrise wasn't for another half hour—that seemed to be emanating from inside everything. I could see my room clearly: the desk in the corner with the banker's lamp on it, the antique Star Trek models on my dresser, the no-longer-hugged stuffed animals heaped next to the dresser, and the poster of Stargate SG-1 signed by Richard Dean Anderson hanging on the wall across from my bed.

"Mustering all the courage I had (I always dreamed of having something paranormal happen to me, I just didn't think it would be like this), I lowered the sheet and looked directly at my hands still holding the fabric. I could feel the pima cotton; I just couldn't see my hands apart from the fabric because they had become part of the fabric. Startled, I dropped the sheet and stared dumbfounded at my glowing hands. It was as if there was a fog or a mist around them, around all of me as I looked up my arms and down my legs. Next I touched the tips of my fingers together. The same thing happened: the fingers of my left hand merged with the fingers of my right hand. It was spooky and thrilling at the same time."

"Cool, man!"

"It is now. It wasn't then. I was wide-eyed and numb. I had no idea what happened, and I didn't even know how to ask. The memory dogged me, and as I grew up the desire to find out grew along with me. Of all the things that ever happened to me, that experience set the course for the rest of my life. I needed desperately to understand it, to tame it, so I wouldn't feel so different, so abnormal. First I studied physics to learn about energy and matter and the boundary between them. What happened to me seemed so contrary to how it 'should be' that I had to find out why it was so atypical. However, since it wasn't replicable, my experience was dismissed by most of my colleagues as a hallucination or a child's fanciful memory. Around that time some Buddhist monks came to our departmental lectures. I think some of them must have read *The Tao of Physics* and decided to check out the physics on their own. Most of the department tolerated their presence but didn't want to hear about the parallels they thought they saw. Nevertheless, I was impressed not only with their decidedly immaterialist stance but also their eagerness to understand. To make a long story short, I quit my job and left school because my boss assigned me to write up a proposal to study ways to turn our results into fodder for the Department of Defense. The ideas that he had for bombs were beyond sinister. I couldn't do that. I hadn't gotten my answers yet, but I couldn't continue trying to get them in the context of finding ways to destroying others. So, after an internal wrestling match in which my future values won over my past values, I decided to study metaphysics with some of those monks. However, they didn't have the kind of technical answer I sought either. Caught between those two ideological extremes, I gave up trying to explain it all. That was six years ago. Now I'm a computer programmer. Six years of slavery to the corporate machine has numbed my mind, erased all memories of a higher purpose to my life, and left me contentedly unhappy."

"You need an ulcer, my dear Doctor Faust," Tom told him.

Jerry stared at him, dumbfounded.

"You heard me correctly. You need an ulcer. It will shake you out of this self-imposed living death you've gotten yourself into. You'll be forced to take stock of your life, look at what isn't working, and get to work on it. You and me, we're not so different—to a point. We were both pursuing something that didn't work out the way it should have, but I have a great life and you, well, you're in suspended animation. You're not living at all anymore. You had a great purpose there, man. Why did you give up on it?" Tom leaned forward across the table and looked at Jerry imploringly.

"I don't know. I was too devastated, I guess. I had spent so many years chasing a ghost, getting no closer to understanding, and it was time to settle down and have a normal life."

"Normal? You call this normal? It's pathologic! Who the hell would want you to sell yourself into slavery to the corporate machine? Your friends? No. Your family?"

"They're dead."

"Well, dead or alive, I assure you that no parents want to see their child working as a slave."

Jerry stewed in silence and the color came back into his face, like the heat was indeed being turned up. Finally he reached the boiling point. "I couldn't do what you do, wandering around, depending on the kindness of strangers. That's pathological! There's no security. What do you have to show for your life? I have a home, a car. I have money to pay wandering window washers. I'm not so bad off." Jerry's voice trailed off, as if he couldn't really stand behind what he just said.

"Friends?" Tom pushed a little more.

Jerry pushed his empty plate aside and put his head in his arms on the table. He wanted to cry, but wouldn't allow it, not in front of a stranger.

"Look man, I'm sorry I..." Tom began.

"Don't be sorry. You're right," Jerry lifted his head back up. His jaw was clenched tight.

Tom stood up and took his dishes to the sink. "Look, there's hope for you. If you were really a goner, you wouldn't have had such a powerful reaction. You would have brushed if off with more resignation. Right?"

"Yeah."

"So harness that energy. That's what you're all about, right? You've just been looking out there for answers. It's all in here," Tom said slapping Jerry on the back. Tom picked up Jerry's plate and rinsed them off.

Jerry got up and cleared the rest of the table and put everything into the dishwasher. "Want a beer?" he offered.

"Sure."

When Jerry handed him the beer, Tom looked him in the eye and said, "We got a little side tracked, eh? You were telling me about your experience as a kid. That was the troubling part to you, not the business at the end."

Jerry nodded, still discombobulated by the confrontation. "Why was I telling you that story?" he said to himself out loud. "Oh yeah." Jerry took another deep breath. He could hardly spit it out. "You were talking about healing and about how the body works. What happened to me back then doesn't fit into anything I know about physiology. What do you think happened?"

Tom looked down at his beer then sat in one of the threadbare armchairs. He began slowly, choosing his words carefully, still focusing intently on the brown bottle in his hand. "Okay, first we must ask, what is the body? Is it simply a collection of cells artfully arranged, or not, by the genetic code? And what are cells? Molecules that function cooperatively. And what are molecules? Artful arrangements of atoms. And what are atoms? Positive charges and negative charges with lots of space in between." He looked up and looked hard at Jerry. "Charges are energy. That's a good game, I think, energy passing itself off as matter. But now we're into your territory. I have no idea how that could have happened. Sorry I can't be more helpful," Tom said taking a swig of his beer.

"It was worth trying," Jerry replied. "You're the first person I've told in a long time. As you can imagine, that experience sparked the need for me to understand what is matter and what is energy, how what is usually discontinuous in space, my hand and the bed sheet, could become continuous. I wanted to know how the equivalence between matter and energy that Einstein identified is parlayed into everyday life, not just studied in the nuclear physics labs. Every high school kid knows that Einstein showed that one can become the other, well certain types of matter, anyway. However, there is an equals sign between the E and the mc^2, so why do we continue to act as if there's a one-way arrow instead of an equals sign?"

"Two different words," Tom offered. "Since matter and energy are different names, we seem to think that they are distinct entities."

Jerry lifted an eyebrow and looked at Tom obliquely.

Tom continued, "Not many people consider the importance of language in structuring the way you think your world is, like a fish not knowing the importance of water. It's always just been there, almost imperceptible, almost unnoticed, though always used. As a scientist, you were trained to look outward, to measure and manipulate things. You weren't trained to examine the words coming out of your mouth."

"You're right. But it's not very accurate to say 'we think they're different things because we have different words.' After all, there are plenty of things in which the same word identifies two different things. For example, 'iris' identifies a flower, a part of your eye, a part of a camera, and it's even a woman's name."

"Why is it so important to agree to call a tomato a tomato and deadly nightshade something else? At the very least, for some survival value. But we've gotten way beyond survival. It all probably boils down to convenience at this point. Maybe tomorrow night we'll talk about verbs. That'll keep us going until 3 or 4 in the morning. I'm bushed for now," Tom said yawning and pushing himself up off the chair.

"You can crash here tonight if you want." The words surprised Jerry as they tumbled out of his mouth. He hadn't had a guest the entire time he lived there. Jerry gave Tom his bedroom, and he slept on the couch. As he lay on the couch unable to sleep, he savored the feeling of fullness, not the satiation of hunger, but a fullness of being. After six years of feeling like he was contracting, he felt tonight like he began to expand again. Jerry was more awake now than he had been all day. As he lay there watching his mind spin, he made three promises to himself—to be more outgoing and meet more people, to recommence his study of matter and energy, and to have more fun.

Next morning, Tom the Window Washer was gone when Jerry knocked on the bedroom door. The bed was perfectly made, not a trace of evidence that he had been there, except for a small piece of paper left on the nightstand. It read, "Thanks for the great conversation." He hadn't even collected the twenty dollars.

Jerry thought it strange, but stranger things had happened to him. Instead of making pancakes, he poured himself a bowl of cereal.

◆   ◆   ◆

The next day a postcard arrived in the mail. It was from Tom. The scene on the front was of Niagara Falls, which was over 1000 miles from where Jerry lived. The postmark was Toronto. It read, "Dear Jerry, Sorry I had to bug out so quickly. I was needed up here IMMEDIATELY. Please send the $20 to PO Box 122, Ore Station, WV. Thanks for the great conversation. Tom"

There are unpredictable things in life, such as hippie-like, med school dropout window washers showing up on your porch, and there are predictable things, such as how long it takes the post office to deliver mail across country—at least 4 days. It is conceivable that Tom caught an **early** morning flight to Toronto and mailed it from the airport. But according **to** the laws of mail delivery, a letter never gets to its destination on the day it was mailed. Now all the little details that Jerry dismissed previously were rounded up for analysis. Every word of the conversation was recalled and reprocessed. It didn't add up to a theory. Who was Tom Byrd, really?

Chapter 2

◆

Helen's Journal

I met this guy today, Jerry Something-or-other. I like him, but I don't know if I want to like him. He's not particularly good looking—sort of plump around the middle with light brown hair that looks like it was cut by a butcher not a barber—but he is amazingly nice. (I hate that word, but it fits, fortunately or unfortunately.) He helped me change a tire, except that my spare was flat too, so he waited in the car with me until the tow truck came. Actually, we waited in his car because the air conditioning worked and because it's a hybrid. With gas over $10 a gallon, it didn't cost as much to sit there and run the air conditioner.

Most guys in that situation either would hit on you or, worse, try to impress you with their mechanical prowess. He did neither. We sat there and talked and talked like we had known each other for years and were catching up. He told me that he had been a metaphysical physicist but now was writing software code. That's the boring part. He started the conversation in a most unconventional way, by asking me if I had ever thought about language. (!) Me, of all people to be asked that question. If that isn't synchronicity, I don't know what is. Language is my element, words my currency. Ever since high school, I've been eating at the language buffet. I've done a smattering of poetry, a dash of fiction, now I'm experimenting with journalism. I'm not sure yet, which language is my language, which style, genre, form suits me best because I love them all.

As a physicist, Jerry didn't think about language much, but this guy named Tom showed up in his life by coincidence and opened his eyes to it. Now Jerry said it is like having another color added to the visible spectrum, one that he couldn't see before. I asked him how he couldn't think about it much if he was programming computers for a living. He thought that writing code wasn't using a real language; it was more like putting a puzzle together using predefined pieces, a puzzle that did something very specific like spit out paychecks or inventory merchandise.

"Do you think flexibility is what characterizes human speech and writing then?" I baited him.

I assumed he'd just say yes, but he didn't. For someone who had not thought much about language, his answer was insightful. He said that language can't be entirely flexible; otherwise we couldn't understand each other. However, if we didn't all agree to call a chicken a chicken, you might be really surprised by what you get for dinner some nights. We laughed about all the exotic foods that "taste like chicken."

Sometimes I think that language has become too flexible; I don't understand kids these days. They seem to have perverted words to mean their opposite, like using "healthy" to describe someone who is fat, taken words from one context and thrown them into another, like "half-past seven" to mean crazy or stupid. It seems like they are devolving language, breaking the conventions that have made it functional, useful, and relatively unambiguous.

Jerry told me that philosophers of science wanted for many years to have an unambiguous language. They thought that would make science more objective. The project failed. Of course it did! It's like having a blow-up doll as a lover.

"Yes, that's the joy of language. It can be as precise or imprecise as you want it to be," I said.

"What's the advantage of such ambiguity, though?" he asked.

"To confuse your opponent."

"Mumbletygook," he said, or something that sounded like it.

I laughed.

Jerry made me feel so at ease, like I didn't have to hide or pretend anything. He is such a sweetie; I didn't think guys like him still existed. It felt safe to share some of my poetry with him, so I pulled out my notebook and read him one of my poems.

Oh to be like a pond unperturbed
Always in motion
When disturbed
The ripples fade in time
Always returning to a similar state
But not to the same location

"You sound like the yogis I used to study with." That was his response. Was it good? Was it beyond him? I didn't know how to take it. Ambiguity. He got me.

We had just started a heated discussion about whether the speaker conveys the meaning (my position) or the hearer makes the meaning (his position), when the tow truck showed up. My car needs not only a new tire but a new axle, which is going to take a week to fix, so Jerry offered to drive me to work and pick me up while it's being repaired. I think I should marry this guy now. Men like this—gallant and thoughtful—don't come along every day. So why isn't he already married? What's wrong with him that some other woman hasn't scooped him up? Maybe now the synchronicity has shown up in <u>my</u> life.

Chapter 3

Day 1

Jerry pulled up in front of Helen's house and honked his horn, an anemic bleating. *Just because this car is friendly to the environment doesn't mean it shouldn't have a real horn. This one's pathetic.*

"He is always on time, and I am always running late," Helen muttered to herself as she slipped on her heels, grabbed the coffee from the counter, and stuffed papers into her briefcase almost simultaneously.

Jerry honked his horn again, longer this time to get more emphasis from it. It sounded like a sheep in excruciating pain.

"I'm coming, I'm coming!" Helen shouted out the screen door. *Where did the keys go? They couldn't have disappeared. Metal does not disappear that easily.* Then she spotted the unusual lump under the dish rag and swooped up the rag and the keys like a peregrine falcon nabbing a rabbit in the brush.

Holding one shoe in her hand and the coffee in the other, she flew out the door and down the walk to Jerry's car, which was double-parked illegally.

"Sorry. I'm not a morning person," she said slamming the car door on her skirt.

"I don't like my job either, but I have to be there by 8," Jerry said.

"I know, and I appreciate your picking me up and everything. I hope I don't get you into trouble because I'm not as organized as you." *Why would he assume I don't like my job?*

Jerry drove on in silence, a little faster than usual. Helen put her other shoe on and sipped her coffee.

"What's your beat?" Jerry asked her.

"Huh?"

"What kinds of things do you write about? Politics? Metro news? International news? The Sunday book section?"

"Oh, um, I handle the social news, you know, who gets married, divorced, celebrates their 50th anniversary. Yeah, I know, really exciting stuff. Sometimes I get to cover real stories, but they all seem to be downers, you know, bad stuff happening to good people—isn't that a shame. It's sickening, but it sells papers."

"Shows you what kind of society we've become," he replied.

"What about you? How goes the programming?" Helen asked, to steer the conversation away from her.

Jerry hesitated, as it stung, knowing he was still an unemancipated slave. "I'm still doing it even though…I don't know. I used to enjoy the challenge."

"What happened? Is it too easy now?"

"Yes and no. It just seems…irrelevant." His voice trailed off.

"Irrelevant how?"

"It doesn't solve anything or alter the big picture in any tangible way. People are still starving, corporations are still corrupt, and half the population is still depressed. Nothing changes."

"But it keeps you fed…"

"…and it keeps a roof over my head, but that's not enough anymore. It's not a life. It's not…"

"So quit. Do something else. They don't own you. I'm sure you could find a better job."

"I'd love to. I just don't want a job anymore."

Aha, this is why he isn't married yet, Helen realized. "Well, this is fine timing. Just when things start getting interesting, I have to leave. Thanks for the ride, Jerry. And if there's anything I can do…"

"Yeah. Have a great day. I'll see you tonight."

She got out and shut the door but leaned back in through the open window. "I'll find a way to put some spark back into your life." She winked at him and strutted off.

Day 2

Helen heard the distinctive honk of Jerry's horn outside. *You'd think that getting up 30 minutes earlier would have given me enough time…*

"I'm coming!" she yelled out the open window.

A passerby jogging down the street heard her, looked at Jerry in the car waiting, and said to him "Way to keep your sheila happy, mate."

Jerry rolled his eyes. Helen flew out of the house with her laptop bag on her shoulder and make-up case in hand. She had on a gray business suit with pants and flats. On her mad dash to the car, one by one the make-up fell out of her case, the lipstick rolled into the flowers, the powder blush spattered all over the sidewalk, the mascara bounced into the grass. Helen stopped abruptly when she realized it, slapped herself on the forehead, and returned to gather the spilled cosmetics.

"No businessman should be without his war paint!" the Australian shouted back to her.

"Bugger off, Ian," Helen parried back.

"I'm sorry, Jerry. I got up 30 minutes early today so this wouldn't happen…" she said while climbing into the car.

"No sweat. I was 10 minutes early. We're actually on time today. Put your seatbelt on, please."

"I thought we women were supposed to be the devious ones. You're putting us to shame." She slapped him playfully on the arm.

Day 3

Jerry honked and Helen opened the door immediately, as if she had been waiting there for him. She walked confidently, almost smugly, down the stairs and across the sidewalk to his waiting car.

"Casual Wednesdays?" Jerry asked, noticing the jeans and sweatshirt Helen wore today.

Her self-satisfied grin evaporated. "Didn't you notice that I'm not late today?"

"Yes, as a matter of fact, I did. Congratulations, you win."

Helen scowled at him. *Win what?* she wondered.

Jerry remained mute.

"Are you going to tell me what you're talking about?" she asked. He shook his head.

Jerry turned right when he should have turned left to take her to work. Helen looked sharply at him, but he just grinned and ignored her. He pulled up in front of a grocery store, put the car in Park, and instructed her, "Wait here. I need to pick up some things." He ran into the store and came out with two bags, one of which he threw into the back seat and the other he handed to Helen. "Don't open it here. Wait till you get to your office."

Day 4

Jerry honked. The door didn't open right away.

"Could you give me a hand?" she shouted from the front window.

Jerry walked to the door. "It's open," he heard her say from inside, so he pushed it open. She was standing next to a large cooler, the kind you take on picnics or to tailgate parties. Jerry grabbed the handle on one side and she the other.

"Company picnic this afternoon. Would you like to join me, if you can get off, that is?"

"I'll see if I can." They loaded it into the trunk.

"Thank you for the flowers yesterday," Helen said when they were under way.

"You're welcome."

"Why?"

"Inspiration."

"Huh?"

"When you write poetry, doesn't something inspire you to write—an event, a moment of sublime beauty, an odd juxtaposition?"

"Oh, you're a poet of gracious acknowledgment and noble actions?" she asked but wondered to herself, *What happened yesterday that sparked it?*

"Unlike you, sometimes words fail me, so I must resort to other media," he said hoisting the cooler into the trunk.

Helen studied him out of the corner of her eye as he drove. *Uh oh, could he be falling in love with me?*

Day 5

Jerry honked. Helen emerged with two cups of coffee, balancing them carefully as she walked down the stairs. She handed one to Jerry through the car window. As she got in, he reached over to take the other one from her hand, so she could get in more easily, but she didn't see him and he knocked it into her lap.

"Aaagh!"

"Oh god, I'm so sorry."

Helen jumped out of the car faster than a startled rabbit. "I'll be right back."

Five minutes later she re-emerged with a different suit on, looking a little harried.

"Helen, I apologize. I'll get the cleaning bill."

"That's not necessary. You've been kind enough to chauffeur me around this whole week. I should be paying you."

They drove in silence.

"My car should be ready this afternoon," Helen said to break the awkwardness. "I've enjoyed riding with you."

"Mishaps and all?"

"Mishaps are the jokes of your poetry of action. If you can't laugh at them…"

He smiled, relieved.

"However, now that you have me getting up early and getting to work on time, my coworkers and boss expect it of me. I won't be able to forgive you for that."

"Helen," he started.

"What?"

But it wouldn't come out. Words failed him yet again.

"See you later?" Helen said as she got out.

Jerry smiled and nodded. He reached his hand out to her. She took it and gave it a squeeze.

Chapter 4

"I have a granddaughter I'd like you to meet," said the woman standing in front of Jerry in the grocery store check-out line. She was short and plump and had long gray hair in a single loose braid. Her soft brown eyes kindly embraced him, telling him that there was no need to worry.

Jerry looked about nervously, hoping the old woman was talking to someone else. No one was within earshot, only an elderly couple choosing pears. "Thank you, ma'am, but…"

"Good then, you'll come to my house tomorrow at 4 PM sharp."

"But, I don't know…"

"I live at 430 Rio Rancho. Not far from here, a little to the north." And off she went with her plums and macaroni.

Why does she want me to meet her granddaughter? Is this the way old yentas work these days? Or is this the universe conspiring to have me meet more people? he wondered, recalling the promise he made to himself the night he met Tom the Window Washer. Much as he didn't want to go, he felt compelled to. She reminded him of his own grandmother but more so, like she was the incarnation of the archetype Grandmother. There was something wise about her, something endearing, and something commanding, in the warm way that only grandmothers can pull off.

When he arrived at the small wood frame house nestled back in the woods, a few cats scattered to the trees. He wiped his moist palms on his pant leg and knocked on the front door. A stunning young girl with long charcoal hair answered the door, looked at him, blanched, and slammed it shut. "Grandmother!" he heard her call from inside. Jerry wanted to bolt immediately, but he took a deep breath and asked himself, *Now what?* When the door didn't open back up in a few moments, Jerry walked back to his car. He was quite taken with her beauty but knew that she was too young for him—16 maybe 17 years old. *Surely she didn't ask me here to hook me up with her granddaughter. But why then?* he wondered as he walked back to his car. As his key entered the lock on the car door, the old woman opened the front door.

"Come back, please, come back. She meant no harm. Dear me, I should have said something about your coming, but she wouldn't have believed me. This way she saw it for herself," the old woman said as she bounced down the front stairs toward his car.

Jerry was uneasy knowing that he had something to do with the "it" she was referring to.

"Oh don't run off. There's nothing to be frightened of my dear boy. Come in. Come in."

He sensed that, despite her sweet grandmotherliness, she would run him down and drag him in if he didn't go willingly. She wasn't pleading with him, she was ordering.

"Have a seat while I get some refreshments."

Jerry sat on the edge at one end of a love seat. The granddaughter sat sideways in an overstuffed arm chair with her legs draped over one arm. She looked away from him, defiant but poised. She was more beautiful in profile, he thought, as she had the look of a not-yet-broken filly.

"This is my granddaughter, Penelope. Penny, dear, this is, um…"

"Jerry."

"Why don't you tell him what you told me," she said and then left the room.

"Hi," Jerry said extending his hand.

Penny didn't take it, but she turned to face him. "I'm sorry my grandmother put you in such an awkward position. She does this all the time…" After a 10-second-which-seemed-like-50-year pause, she continued. "I had a dream the other night, and I, um, we think it was your dream."

Jerry shifted his position. *This is weird. How can she dream my dream?* he thought.

Penny shut her eyes and saw the images again dancing in her mind. "In this dream, I'm walking in the woods behind the house, and I come to a stream. It's all dried up, but I can still see my reflection when I look down. Across the stream is a dark-haired man in jeans and a red and black flannel shirt, motioning me to cross. He has a can of cream of mushroom soup in his hand."

Jerry recognized why he was there. *Would she mention the half-gallon of milk too?*

She continued, "I tell him 'the water is too deep.' And he says, 'The mountain is too high.' Then the man sees a bear that has just come out of hibernation. The bear is wearing a wooden mask with slits for eyes and a curved beak like an eagle. The bear is hungry and comes to a tree with apples that are still unripe, but that doesn't seem to bother the bear. He stands high on his hind legs and reaches up to a branch and shakes it. A few apples fall to the ground. The bear eats the apples but the man does not. He sits on a nearby rock and watches the bear. Then I saw the blue moon sky." For the first time in this conversation she looked directly at Jerry and asked him, "Do you know what the blue moon sky is?"

Jerry shook his head.

"It's the prophetic image for the end of the world. The sky is very colorful, with deep reds and dark purples, occasionally yellow. The moon isn't literally blue, but it is reflecting all the colors of the sky."

"So that was my dream. Grandmother was right. This was your dream. I am pleased to meet you. And I apologize for slamming the door in your face."

Jerry glanced toward the kitchen, where he could hear the clattering of dishes. "That's a very interesting dream. I wonder how you could have dreamed about me so specifically without having met me before now. Do you know what it means?"

"Although I dreamed it, it is not my dream. It is your dream because clearly you are the man in the dream. I have this gift, Grandmother calls it, although sometimes I think it's a curse. I dream the dreams of people who—don't take this the wrong way—need to receive a message but who don't pay attention to their own dreams. You must determine what this dream means for you."

Jerry shifted nervously in his seat. "I don't know. I haven't a clue about dream interpretation. You're right. I don't pay much attention."

"Don't be intimidated by the dream world. If you watch a dream like it was a movie, then it might make sense. If you were trying to make sense of an avant-garde movie, what would the symbols mean to you?" she coached.

Jerry took a deep breath. "First, I'm in a world of paradoxes. I see that I am asking you to step into the unknown or at least the uncomfortable."

"One more thing," Penny interrupted, "consider that all parts of the dream, the man, the bear, the dried up stream, and even me, represent you."

"Okay, so I'm asking myself to step into the unknown but making excuses not to do it, saying the water is too deep when there's no water there. Then I come across a bear, who is masked, which means he might put on a different appearance to the world. So I might be wearing a mask to hide my identity. I want people to think I'm an eagle when I'm not. The bear doesn't care about whether he's stealing someone's apples. If they are there and he can get them, they are his. Then there's the end-of-the-world image. Maybe that means that if we keep taking without regard to the consequences, we will bring our own destruction. There's one thing I don't understand yet. If the bear also represents me, then what am I taking? What do apples represent?" Jerry asked.

"Knowledge."

Grandmother came back into the room with tea and raisin cakes, offering them to Penny and Jerry. Penny shook her head and got up and left. She had fulfilled her obligation, and Terrah knew not to make her stay and socialize. Terrah sat next to Jerry on the couch so that she could feel his energy and so that she wouldn't have to talk loudly.

"My dear boy, don't you see? If you are Bear, then Bear is the answer to the fear in the first part of your dream. Our lives are like the flowing of a stream, taking the path of least resistance. But your stream is dried up. Your life is not flowing. But here I go doing it for you. Heaven forgive me. Have you ever met a bear?" she asked.

"A real one? In the wild? Noooo."

"Then you should. They're not takers in the malicious sense. They just go after what they want, and they usually get it. Perhaps that's what the dream is teaching you. You need to go after what you really want. This Saturday come by at 6 AM. We will visit the neighborhood bears. But before then, go to the zoo and watch the bears there. Get familiar with their habits and get comfortable being around them. Imagine that there is no deep moat separating their habitat from yours. There's nothing to be afraid of. There are things to respect, but that's different. Honor their teachings. We tend to think that animals in the zoo have lost their nature, but they haven't. They're just not in a context that allows it."

Jerry looked at her with a mix of incredulity and reticence. *What is the point of all this?* he thought.

Terrah sipped her tea and continued filling the void left by Jerry's silence. "I worry about Penny sometimes. She is a lovely girl and has a great gift, but she thinks that her life is her own. Part of it is her age. Teenagers, like 4-year-olds, have a strong sense of me-my-mine, but now it's not 'my toy,' its 'my life.' She has yet to realize that her life is not her own. Your life at least belongs to your fellow creatures of all shapes and sizes, like your finger belongs to your hand and your hand to your body. So I am teaching her how she must use her gift. Gifts are not yours to keep. You must give it away, otherwise it wouldn't be a gift now, would it?" Terrah smiled up at him.

"I know what you mean. My life feels like it belongs to the company I work for. They must tap into that innate sense of your life not being your own, and they steal it from you or at least convince you to give it all to them."

Terrah's face went ashen and her tone of voice deepened. "You must get out of there. If that is what is happening, then you are like a tumor on the body of life.

You must find the gift that you are to all of humanity, not just the usefulness you are to a company."

Jerry startled at the seriousness of her charge and wondered *What might my gift be? I wasn't raised to believe that I had a gift. I was taught to work hard.*

"You'll know what your gift is," she said, almost reading his mind, "because you too have hidden it. We all do. It's the thing that makes us stand out from the crowd, makes us different. Surely you don't think that I wanted to accost strangers in the supermarket and bring them to my house for tea and cakes, do you?" she said with a twinkle in her eye.

"I can see how that could be unnerving for you because I'm sure you know how unnerving it was for me to be told to show up at your house when I didn't know you at all," Jerry said.

"Yes, you were brave. I commend you for that. You can probably imagine that I wasn't always this way. I had to learn to get over the feeling that I was imposing on people, to talk to people with authority so that they would listen, and to create the space for them to trust me. Gifts don't show up fully built, no batteries required. Instead, they show up as a kit with no instruction manual, and you have to put the pieces together. Just know that you can't fail. You can't put the pieces together the wrong way, but some pieces might not be what you think they are."

Jerry's mouth opened but nothing came out. Questions about his gift, stories about his childhood, and his search for understanding matter and energy all wanted to be spoken but remained stuck in his throat, unverbalized.

"If you have a girlfriend, take her to the zoo with you," Terrah said while pushing herself off the couch.

Jerry was being ushered out as abruptly as he was summoned.

"Thank you for the tea and cake and conversation, Mrs., uh?"

"Call me Terrah. See you Saturday, 6 AM sharp!" she said waving him off.

Jerry got in his car and caught a glimpse of himself in the rear-view mirror. There was something different. He looked again but couldn't put his finger on it. On the drive home his mind swam with thoughts of stepping into the unknown, taking, and giving. He thought of Tom, wished he could tell him how crazy things had gotten since his visit. Jerry was so preoccupied he missed his turn and kept driving blithely on. Finally the road dead-ended at some train tracks, and he realized he was lost and turned around and headed home.

Chapter 5

◆

Helen's Journal

For being such a smart guy, Jerry used one of the lamest pick-up lines I've ever heard. He said, "I have to go to the zoo. Want to come with me?" What middle-aged, single man without kids "has to" go to the zoo? Anyhow, that was our first date. Or maybe it wasn't really a date. Maybe it was just a "let's be friends and do something together" thing. I don't know, but it was fun. I have since revised my prejudice that the zoo is just a place to take little city kids to see animals other than the various species of that ubiquitous denizen of the city—the rat and its relations: rats with wings (pigeons) and rats with furry tails (squirrels).

When I was young I saw the animals in the zoo from the eyes of "oh this is what was in the picture books." Now that I'm older and the novelty has worn off, I found myself seeing them more from the eyes of an ethologist. I watched their behavior, how they interacted with the other animals in the exhibit and with their environment. I know that the zoo is a fake environment, but they develop behaviors for that too. A wild animal certainly wouldn't sit and watch someone prepare his lunch, but those animals did.

We spent a lot of time watching the bears. Jerry had some sort of dream, and an old lady he met in the grocery store told him to watch the bears at the zoo (What is that about?!).

One bear paced incessantly, nervously, back and forth, back and forth. It was hard watching him (her?) because you could feel the frustration. The other bear was oblivious to all that and sat there seemingly daydreaming. I don't know what Jerry thought he could learn about bears from that.

Jerry remarked that it was sad that their food was just handed to them, that they didn't have to hunt for it. He thought of bears as takers—they just roam around and take what they want. What satisfaction is there in having it handed to you if your nature is to go after it and take it? I thought that we humans aren't much different. Yeah, we learn not to take our younger siblings' toys, but we take practically everything else, even the bears' territory. We take resources with no plan to replenish them, and we call all this thievery "economic growth." If my mother had been Mother Earth, we all would have gotten our butts whacked a few times!

Hmm. Do I think of replenishing what I take? Do I even think of asking permission to take something? No. Well, maybe if it's from another human, but I don't ask anything that can't verbalize a "yes." Since a plant can't say anything, I pick a flower without a second thought. I pull weeds as if it's my right to exterminate them. There's the language thing again—that linguistic arrogance we have built into the culture. Who are we to assume that the plants and animals don't understand our language? Maybe they do.

I remember being at a bookstore while an author was giving a talk. She was an herbalist, and she told a story about wanting to collect some herb to use to treat a sick patient. Part of her practice was to meditate by the plant and tell it why she wanted to pick it. Then she would ask the plant's permission to cut it. (I thought she was nuts.) For the first time in her life, a plant said no. So she went back the next day and the next, and it kept saying no. Finally she asked the plant why not. She said that the plant told her (how, I don't know) that if she wanted to use it to treat this person she'd have to pick it on a sunny day. It had been cloudy for the past three days, and that had diminished its potency.

At the time, I thought she was nuts, but maybe she isn't. Maybe there's something to language beyond the words in English or Spanish or Swahili or whatever—something universal perhaps. Or maybe there's something communicated in the intention one has, the intention to express something, and the words themselves are simply the icing on the cake. Like all the times I'm thinking about Jerry and he calls, just like that, out of the blue. And the times I'm thinking about going to a specific restaurant and he suggests the same one. It's spooky how often he takes the words right out of my mouth.

If that's the case, then why do we have so many different languages, so many different flavors of icing? What really happened at the Tower of Babel? Is that a just-so story, or did something terrible really happen? I couldn't remember the story exactly, so I looked it up in the Bible to refresh my memory. There was a line that had escaped me before. It reads: "If now, while they are one people, all speaking the same language, they have started to do this [i.e., build the Tower of Babel], nothing will later stop them from doing whatever they presume to do. Let us then go down and there confuse their language, so that one will not understand what another says." Whoa! If that's God talking, then why the use of the plural in the second sentence? Does this indicate that there are many gods? More importantly, however, is the indication of God being threatened by man's initiative. What kind of all-powerful being would be threatened by some men building a big ziggurat (especially since ziggurats were usually temples used to worship this same God)? Why would God, who created us in His image, need to cut us down, prevent us humans from building a tower? Why didn't God want us getting closer to Him? Is it a story about our arrogance? If that were the case, I'd imagine God would be up there laughing at us rather than finding ways to thwart us. Surely we are laughable creatures. Of course I'm probably thinking too much, just like the author of this tale, who felt compelled to say something other than "I don't know" to his child's question about "how come they don't talk like us?"

Chapter 6

Jerry arrived at Terrah's house promptly at 6 AM. She had a lunch packed and two walking sticks waiting. "Where are we going?" he asked.

"You'll see. Can we take your car?" she said as she handed him the backpack and a stick.

What am I getting myself into? he thought. *Why am I doing this? Because of someone else's dream? This is nuts! What if we do encounter a bear? Damn, I should have told Helen what I was doing and where I was going, just in case I don't come back.*

They drove for 35 minutes until the dirt road abruptly narrowed to a footpath. Jerry parked the car there and followed Terrah on the footpath, which became a steep trail speckled with rocks that looked stable but gave way under his weight. The climb left him huffing and puffing after 10 minutes.

"Let's have some water," she said when they reached a small clearing. Whether she really needed water or was allowing Jerry to save face didn't matter; he was grateful for the rest. He sat on a boulder that was still cool from the night air. The trail had ended in this clearing, which might have had a log cabin in it ages ago. Why else would the trees and undergrowth not have reclaimed it? Terrah motioned for him to sit in the cover of the woods, near a small dug-out area, not in the open. It had an unobstructed view, which wasn't important for listening to the symphony of birds, cicadas, and squirrels but might be necessary to keeping an eye out for bears.

There was no guarantee that bears would show themselves today, so they sat in the shade of a large oak tree. Squirrels played in the branches overhead, and beetles crawled on the ground below. Butterflies flitted around them, and birds sang to each other. "Everything really is alive out here," Jerry said. "Very different than being in a cubicle where almost nothing is alive. Sometimes even I feel that way, just on this side of death. But out here, out here I feel so energized. I feel my heart pumping. The sounds are crisper, and the colors are bracing."

"Yes, when you live and work in high-rise buildings you can easily forget that the earth is alive, and in forgetting, commit great atrocities."

Terrah watched Jerry's curiosity jump from centipede to crow to saw grass to wind to ant to flower to fly to bee to moss and back to her. *It is good to see this innocence in a grown man.* "Let's try something, a game of sorts, to make the waiting pass quickly. See that beetle?" she said pointing to a brown beetle whose shell had tones of iridescent green. "Put yourself into that beetle's perspective. See through his eyes—mind you, they aren't very good, that's why you have those long antennae, to pick up the changes in air quality, temperature, and so on. When you are that beetle, that oak leaf looks like a bridge to cross. You are in search of something to eat all the time. The smell of fresh deer scat is perfume to your senses. Okay, try it now."

First Jerry watched it, watched how its legs moved, watched what made its antennae twitch. Then he closed his eyes and saw the world from the perspective of the beetle. Coordinating all six legs wasn't that difficult; it came naturally even. Seeing the world in black and white horizontals and verticals was more difficult, or perhaps it was the lack of depth of field that made it hard to see. He could see in almost 360 degrees, but it was like seeing the world as a flat picture. It got really hot inside the hard exoskeleton he wore, so he sought out some darkness, which was cooler. The antennae sensed that it was even cooler below him, so he tried to get under whatever he was standing on. Ugh. It didn't want to budge, so he walked on in search of coolness.

Terrah's voice broke his trance. "What's it like experiencing the world from a perspective that's not your usual one?"

"Wow," he said, opening his eyes, "it's amazing. I don't know why I've never done anything like that before."

"It's not part of your culture. In my culture, the elders taught us to learn about the world that way, not by cutting it up and searching for smaller and smaller bits, but by becoming another piece of it, another perspective from which to view the rest, through the power of shifting consciousness. All the things you see before you—the trees, the bugs, the birds, me—have a unique perspective, which you can access. You can learn not only about what's out there but also you can learn about yourself. How are you like the lowly beetle? What can you learn from the beetle about living here? What's the beetle's gift to the world?" Terrah raised an eyebrow and cocked her head to the side.

"I don't know. Let me think. I'll be dinner for a bird or lizard some day!"

"That's a good thing to realize, that you are part of the food chain. Others depend on you for their nourishment. What else?" Terrah asked.

"As this beetle, I clean up the debris in the world, the dead and rotting things. So I guess the beetle teaches us about recycling, that even things that are old and rotting have value. I guess everything has value. I never would have imagined I'd be saying that after seeing through the eyes of a bug."

Terrah stuck her two cents' worth in: "Here's how I like to think of it. Consciousness is like light passing through a prism that we call matter and spreading out like colors into the myriad of perspectives, which we call by different names—humans, beetles, horses, bears, and even things we in the West don't normally attribute consciousness to, like dirt and rocks, moss, trees, and so on. So if you consider yourself the pure consciousness before it gets refracted by matter..."

"But that's not possible," Jerry interrupted, "because my consciousness is necessarily embedded, or I should say embodied, in matter, in my body. Although you could keep my body alive when my consciousness is absent, you couldn't keep my consciousness alive if my body died."

"Right. When your consciousness is unencumbered by your body, we call it death," Terrah said, "but really, life, death, it's all the same thing, just viewed from different angles."

"Like seeing a glass as half full versus half empty?"

"It's both half full and half empty. The people who see the glass as half full will always congratulate themselves on their superior perspective, as its pretense is optimism and positivity. But it is equally as warped as the pessimist's perspective which has a pretense of negativity and cynicism. By seeing both ways, you get the reality of the situation. And there are probably perspectives beyond the unification of opposites that take interdependence even farther."

"So are you saying that our individual perspectives are wrong, that we shouldn't choose to see things a certain way?"

"Well, yes and no," Terrah said with a twinkle in her eye. "You are your perspective, which makes you the unique person you are, and you are not your perspective. You are your living body and you are not just life stuffed into a body. You are solitary and you are part of everything else. Your interconnectedness with the world you live in makes you that world, you and everybody and everything else. My native language expresses that. It is implicit when I say 'I see that mountain' that I am that mountain. This imported language unfortunately does not."

Jerry looked at her as an athlete looks at a coach after having just gone through a tough workout. Indeed, every metaphysical muscle in his body was just exercised, and he was tired.

Terrah brought the workout down a notch, to a practical level, allowing him to catch his breath. "For example, take the air you breathe. The oxygen goes to your blood and so it becomes you on a physical level. The car you drive pollutes the air you breathe, thereby polluting your own body. Why would you want to do that to yourself? Have you so little respect for your own body? If you still think of things out there as being separate from you, well, they're not. They are yourself. Ugh. I cannot stand this language we use. Just to say 'they' puts it outside yourself. To say 'it' puts the Thing you're referring to outside yourself. There is no outside. The world is like a big dynamic Klein bottle—you know what that is?—it's a shape that only seems to have an inside and an outside. But when you look closely, one becomes the other, and vice versa, on and on.

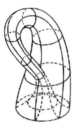

Klein bottle

It's a limited perception that only sees one but not the other. The world takes the form of a paradox, and somehow this imported language has taken the paradox out of the world. Oh, I've exhausted myself. It is so hard, so very hard to talk about this properly." Like a geyser, she gushed and shut off. Terrah leaned back against the rock and closed her eyes.

Who is this woman? Jerry wondered. *Why did she show up in my life now? Why not ten years ago when all this would have been useful?* Ancient memories of unexplainable events resurfaced, along with life-long frustrations. *When the student is ready, the teacher will come,* he recalled. The buzzing and tingling from recognizing a kindred spirit coursed through his body. Gone were his doubts and misgivings about her. Present were excitement and anticipation. His muscles twitched from the amplification of those feelings in his chest, from how his lungs wanted to burst forth from their cage, and from how his heart beat like he had just run a mile. A life-force long dormant in him awakened. He felt attracted to Terrah in a way he had never felt attracted to a woman before because the attraction had nothing to do with physical beauty and nothing to do with intellectual compatibility. It occurred on a level previously unknown to Jerry, and it was magnetic.

Jerry remembered his own feelings of not being able to verbalize thoughts because there was a paradox at the heart of it. His research into matter/energy frequently had left him feeling like a pretzel. Terrah pointed out something that

Jerry had only vaguely sensed: the structure of language had created a huge rip in the fabric of reality between opposites, such as inside and outside, body and mind, male and female, and me and not-me, energy and matter, that had to be repaired, like gluing the two sides of a coin back together again. It is as if we lost the ability to hold two "seeming opposites" simultaneously in our minds at once. In losing that ability to live in a world of both/and, we were thrust into a world of either/or. Maybe that was the proverbial fall from grace. Jerry experienced the merging of inside and outside in Terrah's words, because they could very well have come from him. It was like she was inside him, speaking his mind. Inside/outside dissolved in that brief moment.

It was Jerry's turn to speak now. "I searched for that paradox by studying physics. But mathematics is the language of physics, and so it wasn't there, because matter and energy, stuff and nonstuff, actuality and potentiality could all be discussed using equations. You are the second person to show me that the source of the problem is in the common words we use. I don't know the first thing about language. I use it everyday, but I don't understand it. I feel out of my league, like I wouldn't know where to start asking the questions that might give me a solution to the problem."

"Oh it's a problem, now, is it? Something you think you can solve?" she said without opening her eyes.

"I guess I have been trained to look at everything that way. From grade school on, I was given problems to solve. And the problems are more important than discovery through play because you are graded on how well you solve them. From about second grade on, play was removed from the learning process. So as students, we start seeing our world as a field of problems to be solved. Just look at the assumptions of popular books and shows: relationships are a problem, jobs are a problem, the economy is a problem, even your health is a problem to be solved. Inventors invent from a problem to be solved. Some composers even compose as if they are solving a tonal problem."

"Consider this," her voice was firm, "what if there is no problem, yet invention is to occur? Can you create from nothing, from the pure pleasure of creating?"

"I don't think so. We create by rearranging already existing somethings."

"Oh come now, I'm sure you did that as a kid—invented a game on the spot, invented a private language between you and your buddies or you and your imaginary friend, built something out of scraps, made things for the sake of making them. Don't you ever create simply because it feels so good to create?"

"That's still all re-creating. It's not creating from nothing."

Terrah got a mischievous twinkle in her eye. "Didn't you even try to procreate simply because it feels so good?"

"Well, yeah," he mumbled, then diverted attention away from that. "But creating something from nothing is a paradox." Jerry refused to budge.

"Indeed, it is the central paradox by which this world began, whether created by God or big banged into existence." There was triumph in her voice.

"Are you saying that we should look to paradoxes to solve the problems we face?"

"Jerry, do you not get that there are no real problems to be solved? There is what there is, and that's it. If no one messed with what is, it would still be just so. The problems that most people concern themselves with are fake problems that they invent and then take ultraseriously so that they can keep themselves employed, occupied, or to avoid being bored."

Jerry looked away from her, took himself out of the conversation. He felt chagrined because that had been his life. Although he knew she wasn't insulting him, he was embarrassed for having done that for so long.

"My dear boy, I'm not picking on scientists or computer programmers or you in particular. From my perspective, alone here on the mountain, people have given up living for being employed."

That statement, like a lance, pierced through his ribs and into his heart. His life had become exactly that, and so predictable—well, until now. He couldn't have predicted that he'd be sitting in the woods with a woman he barely knew yet was drawn to like a bear to honey, waiting for actual bears to wander by. Nor had he seriously considered the possibility that it might actually occur; bears might indeed pay them a visit. And then what would he do? Run? But that would defeat the purpose of his coming out here. Could he possibly just sit and watch? Hardly.

"What do we do if we actually encounter bears?" he asked.

"Considering that they can outrun us, outclimb us, and rip us in half with a single swing of a paw, we should probably sit as still as possible so as not to draw attention to ourselves. If they don't smell food in our direction, they probably won't come this way. Bears don't generally care about things that aren't food or threats."

"I take it you have done this before."

"I have been around bears. Usually I don't go looking for them. They find me, if they want to."

Terrah and Jerry looked at each other simultaneously when they heard the crunch of twigs breaking in the distance, the distinct cracking of dead wood underfoot. Jerry's heart leapt into marathon mode. Something was rustling leaves on the forest floor and breaking branches with every step. They crouched down even further. Only their eyes and foreheads were visible behind the boulder that was their shelter. Though he sat still and silent, any animal with sensitive hearing could pinpoint Jerry's location by the loud "thum thump" emanating from his chest cavity.

As the animal got closer they heard it snorting. Jerry felt the adrenaline flood his bloodstream. His muscles twitched and contracted, ready to sprint. He could barely contain himself. The rustling got closer and closer. His breathing got louder and more labored like he was gasping for air. The animal stamped its foot and snorted. Terrah knew what that meant—it had caught their scent, so she put her hand on Jerry to calm him. His whole hyperalert body twitched when she did that.

Then it came into view off to the right. It was a young buck. Relief and disappointment shared a fleeting moment. *At least it wasn't a bear. Too bad it wasn't a bear.* And in that same fleeting moment, the deer was gone.

"Perhaps it's good you got a trial run with a deer," Terrah teased. She stood up and stretched. "Deer teaches us to be gentle and compassionate."

Jerry could barely hear what she was saying through the blood pounding in his temples. He was glad his pants were still dry.

"I think you've spent too much time in cubicles or whatever computer programmers live in during the day."

"Perhaps," Jerry said, wiping his brow with his shirt sleeve. "I can't believe I was so terrified by a deer."

"It had nothing to do with the deer. You would have been just as terrified if it had been a raccoon or even a mouse. You were terrified of your own fears and expectations."

"Yeah, I guess so."

"Where else does that happen in life?"

Jerry could barely concentrate. "With my boss, sometimes."

"Not too much…" Terrah winked. "Let's keep moving."

Jerry's adrenaline-soaked body was at once hard to move and grateful to be moving. He shook the stiffness out of his legs and swung his arms around a few times to loosen the shoulders. They walked in silence deeper into the woods. The biting flies swarmed around his head, attempting to land and snatch a bit of flesh. Jerry shooed them away with his hands.

"Before I realized that the animals can read us, I used to get annoyed with the flies, too," Terrah began, "but then I realized that they're as vulnerable to appreciation and flattery as we are. Just send them love. It works, you'll see. I once spent some time up north, where they have black-faced hornets. Curious creatures. They'd circle my head three times—I don't know why three—then fly away. One got a little aggressive with me, so I sent him love, saying 'I love you too!' and off he went. Fear seems to pull them in closer. Interesting, isn't it?"

"That wouldn't be my instinctual response," Jerry said.

As he stepped over fallen branches and walked into spider webs trying to keep up with Terrah, Jerry saw where his studies with the monks had lacked practical application. He had learned the ideas and concepts but had failed to see how they worked in the world. Terrah didn't seem to have any theory, but she certainly applied the principle of benevolent compassion, or love your neighbor as yourself, even if your neighbor is a hungry deer fly.

"Of course I'm not afraid to kill one, if I get stung, for example, and I reflexively hit it. Nothing really ever dies; it just changes state. But still, you can't use that as a justification," she said to herself as much as to Jerry. "Ironically, since I've started sending them love, I haven't even been remotely tempted to kill one. I wonder if that would work at a broader level…"

"How do you mean?" Jerry asked.

"Let me show you my garden when we go home."

They came to a small stream, not more than three feet wide and a foot deep. It gurgled happily over rocks and branches, not letting them get in the way of where it was going. Terrah leaned her walking stick up against a tree and slipped her backpack off. Jerry followed suit. They sat in the soft moss and had some bread, cheese, and peaches. Terrah dipped a cup into the stream and drank. Jerry looked aghast at her. "You think it's safer if it comes out of a faucet?" she said handing him the cup. He dipped it in and drank.

"I've been thinking," she looked at Jerry sternly, "maybe you should become bear."

"Become what?"

"You know, get naked," she winked.

Jerry feigned covering his juicy bits.

"Like you did with the beetle, imagine being the bear, so you know the bear's perspective. That way, if and when you encounter a bear, you will know it as a brother rather than as a projection of your fears. Here, sit. Get comfy."

Jerry leaned against the trunk of a tree. He closed his eyes and took a few deep breaths to relax himself. Terrah instructed him, "Use whatever technique you like to release all cares from your mind, all tension from your muscles." She paused and gave him time to do that. "In your mind, see the following scene in front of you, the trees and the brush, the mountain in the background. Hear the cicadas and the breeze blowing overhead. Imagine a brown bear coming into this peaceful scene. He finds a patch of bearberries and sits and eats them. While he is eating them, you walk up behind him. Don't worry, you are invisible to him. Your spirit walks into the bear's body. His body is now your body. Take a moment to get used to it. Look at the big paws. Feel their strength. Feel how clumsy they are and despite their size how much dexterity you still have. Stand up in your bear body and notice how high you are. Try walking. Yes, it's much easier on all fours. Notice your acute sense of smell, your poor hearing."

Jerry became the bear eating each little berry, one at a time. The bear now rolled over and scratched his back on the ground. He let out a big yawn then rolled over onto all fours. The bear lumbered off and found a nearby tree and stood up and clawed it, communicating "I was here." Then he left without looking back, in search of more food. He came to a fast-running stream. He waded into the water and stood, watching. It wasn't easy catching fish because they were hard to smell. You have to watch for them, and the water plays tricks on your eyes. The little ones are quick, but he took a swipe anyway and missed. Big dark wavy motion, that's how fish looked. Several more misses, then he spotted a much bigger dark wavy motion and waited patiently. As it swam in front of him, he swooped a large clawed paw down into the water. The claws didn't stick in the flesh but sent the fish flying through the air where it landed with a thud on the stream bank. He chased after it, with heavy limbs weighted down from the water soaking his fur. The fish flopped in agony on the shore until he sank sharp teeth through the scales into the soft flesh.

"Okay, step backwards out of the bear's skin," Terrah instructed. "Bring your attention back to your own body, its thinness, its lightness."

Jerry opened his eyes, which widened and sparkled with the excitement.

"Thank you, Terrah."

"What did you experience?"

"Innocent power."

She looked at him quizzically.

"The bear has so much power in reserve. Most of the time there's no consciousness of it. But when it is necessary—to catch dinner or chase off a threat—it's immediately accessible."

"Do you, Jerry Fowss, have that?"

"I guess I do. It's never been tested."

"When it is, just remember the bear," Terrah said and got up. "Enough for today. Do you know how to get us out of here?"

Jerry froze. He had put his complete reliance on her.

"If I didn't have to get home for my granddaughter, I'd make you take us out of here. But you're off the hook this time. Next time, be aware of where you are and how you got there."

She picked up the knife, buried the peach pits, and swept the area with a tree branch to erase obvious evidence that they had been there. She picked up her walking stick and followed the stream a ways.

"You can jump across or walk through it, depending on how dry you want to keep your feet." She jumped. Jerry took a long step across. She picked up a well-trodden deer path that led back toward the car.

When they reached her house, the cats were waiting on the porch. Terrah reached down and scratched each one, as glad to see them as they were to see her.

"You were going to show me your garden," Jerry reminded.

"Oh yes, this way." She led him to the south side of the house, where nearly a full acre was blooming, fruiting, and bursting with deliciousness. The cats followed along.

"What did you want me to see?" Jerry asked.

"Look around. Tell me what you see."

While Terrah picked up and held each cat one by one, Jerry walked around the perimeter, occasionally bending down to inspect leaves or the size of a vegetable. Many were much bigger than normal. There was a salad for 20 people in her garden, with lettuces, tomatoes, radishes, carrots, and herbs like basil, parsley, thyme, rosemary, and sage. The plants were scattered in and about one another like a cocktail party, not in neat rows like a school room. They seemed to thrive this way, the way people also thrive when not constrained by artificial order and structure. "It's pristine, flourishing, except for that one corner," he said arriving back full circle.

"Why do you think that is?"

"I don't know, different soil perhaps, different plant species."

Terrah smiled and said, "That's their food, this is my food."

"Whose?"

"That section is specifically planted for the insects and rabbits and deer and whomever wants to feast. I give them that so they don't eat mine. This way I don't have to poison them or myself with pesticides."

Jerry was silent as he processed the data. Yes, that one corner seemed to have an infestation of bugs, but the rest of the garden was free of them. "How do you do that?" he asked finally.

"Whenever I explain it in public, people think I have lost my mind, which I suppose I have. And I don't miss it! How? you ask. It's really quite simple. You talk to them, acknowledge that they were here first, honor them because they have as much a right to exist as you do, then explain the deal, and ask them if they accept. I said, 'I've planted this portion just for you. It is filled with all the things you like—tender lettuce, juicy tomato, savory herbs. The rest is for us; please leave it alone. Deal?' You'd be surprised at how cooperative insects are."

"You're not kidding, are you? They actually stick to their side of the field?"

"Yes, of course. They're simple creatures. They understand simplicity and fairness."

"Wow. That does have some potential." Jerry pulled on his nonexistent beard while thinking. "I can see how people think you're nuts. So, to convince the doubting masses, we'd have to do something a little more normal, like set up a scientific test of your plan. We could plant two fields for comparison, a field of love and a field of hatred and killing with pesticides, and see how the crops faired."

"Don't waste your time planting the second one. Those are planted all over already!" she said dismissing the idea with a wave of her hand.

"Yes, but the scientists and the skeptics need proof…"

"All right, all right! I suppose there's a method to your brand of madness as well. If you must temporarily perpetuate the war with the insects in order to show its fruitlessness…but I don't believe you have to nor do I believe that your experiment will be as successful if you do. You know as well as I do that your intention influences the outcome. Trying to remain neutral is self-delusion and won't get you the results you want!" Her conviction was persuasive. She was practically shouting. The cats had taken cover in the brush. "The whole culture is grounded in the assumption that war is the only option, whether it's with insects or other humans. Well, it's not. We have just gotten accustomed to it because we have chosen to live that way throughout most of recorded history. Why is it that times of true peace are treated as the anomaly in the history books? Why don't we name them, like The 100 Years' Peace or The 50 Years' Prosperity? Why do we only name the tragedies?"

Jerry had not seen Terrah this agitated before. "Maybe you're right," he said, "It would be more efficient to start this type of agriculture with people like organic farmers who are already on your side of the tracks. Once it has been shown to work there, maybe the ball will keep rolling all the way to the big agribusiness."

◆   ◆   ◆

On the drive home, Jerry felt a stirring inside, like he had been awoken from his slumber, his hibernation from investigation, of the past seven years. Faculties he had shut down in order to survive in the corporate world were put back online in a most unusual way. *If I could do that with bears, I could do it with anything. I could investigate the properties of light by becoming light. I could study the behavior of subatomic particles by becoming one. I might even be able to figure out what happened to me when I was 10 years old.*

Chapter 7

From a block away, Jerry saw her sitting al fresco at the only coffee shop in town. Helen's long dark hair obscured her chiseled features—the strong square chin and thin nose, the piercing brown eyes. His pulse quickened as he hid the bouquet of flowers, fresh from his backyard, behind his back. They met here after work on Friday evenings. She read a book while she waited for him. This "Friday After Work" coffee ritual was becoming a predictable thing in their lives. They had imposed one rule only: no bitching about work.

Helen had ordered two lattes. Hers was half gone, and his was half cold. Jerry snuck up behind her and blindfolded her eyes with his right hand while he put the bouquet of pansies, lilacs, and daisies in front of her with his left. She put the book right in the froth of her latte when Jerry blinded her but didn't miss a conversational beat. "Hi Jerry. Did you ever notice how the little words in English are the ones that make the biggest difference in meaning?" Jerry frowned, not knowing where this was coming from.

"No 'hi, how are you? How was your day? It's so nice to see you'?" he mocked being crushed.

"I can't see you; you have your hand over my eyes." Without waiting for an answer, she plowed on, "I was talking about prepositions. Just consider the difference between…"

Jerry kissed her on the back of the head. "Your book's in your latte." he said, releasing the mask and retrieving the book from the steamed milk. The flowers fell to the ground.

"Oh, yikes!" She grabbed the book from him and wiped it off. "I don't like that preposition. I would have preferred 'under' or 'beside' my latte. It's all your fault," she teased. Jerry picked up the flowers, presented them to her, and sat beside her and kissed her lightly on the cheek.

Helen took them and admired them. "Thank you, Jerry." The note read "Pancetta for my princessa." Her face twisted in panicked appreciation. He usually wasn't this affectionate. *What's going on?* She stuffed her face in the pansies, pretending to smell them, to hide her expression from Jerry and to muffle her laughter. When her composure was back, she put them in her water glass.

"I was just reading about the importance of using the right word, like pansy not pancetta." She jabbed him in the ribcage.

Jerry gave her a forlorn look. "I couldn't think of anything else to rhyme with princessa."

"It's sweet of you to bring me flowers rather than charcuterie." She pecked him lightly on the cheek and continued describing her Aha moment. "Listen, Jerry, you have to hear this. It's incredible. I'm reading about the language of the beginning of the Old Testament. There aren't any vowels in ancient Hebrew, so the meaning has to be interpreted. One way of interpreting the first words of the Bible, which are spelled, "BRSHT" could be bereshit, which means 'in the beginning'; however, it could also be bareshit, which means 'in a beginning.' That one tiny article—the versus a—could completely change our notion of creation depending on whether it's definite or indefinite, couldn't it?" Helen said.

"No vowels? Interesting. Hawaiian has mostly vowels. A desert-residing people with a written language lacking vowels versus a lush island people with an oral language with few consonants, and mainly soft ones at that. Hmm, what do think about that contrast?" Jerry added his own twist to the conversation.

"You missed the point," Helen said.

"No, I think I got the point. I just went off on a tangent. Your point is that what I just said, had it been written in ancient Hebrew using just consonants, could have been interpreted as," he thought for a moment, "ni, u thonk u gat thi pent."

"Well, yeah, but that makes no sense. So you need the context to help you determine which vowel is correct," Helen added.

"Except that the first words of the Bible don't have much context yet."

"Yes! Exactly." Sometimes she loved arguing with Jerry, and sometimes she loved when he saw it her way.

"Except their cultural context. How much influence did the Jews have from the Mayans, who believed the creation cycle begins again every 5200 years?"

"Very clever, Jerry. Very clever." Helen was not pleased. She thought he was joking, and she wanted to be taken seriously. But then she looked at the flowers and let go of her drive for one-upmanship. *What's more important, looking smart or being content?* Jerry was, she had to admit, a lot smarter. That's one of the things she found attractive about him.

Jerry sipped his cold latte. "Perhaps it was left ambiguous because it's both."

"What's both?"

"It's both 'in a beginning' and 'in the beginning.'"

"How could it be both?"

"Just supposing."

Helen furrowed her brows and turned her gaze inward as she struggled to conceive of the possibility of the ancient text being left ambiguous because multiple interpretations were all correct. "I suppose it could be. There are modern poets who leave meaning ambiguous by playing with homonyms and force the reader to choose an interpretation. But the writers of the Bible, why would they do that?" Then inspiration hit her. "If there was no vowel there in the first place, what if none was intended? What if it's neither?" she countered.

"What do you mean neither?"

"Perhaps it's a modern propensity to use articles. Many languages don't use them at all. Maybe 'the beginning' is not like an event kind of beginning, but how you start: in beginning, you start by doing this, as in, this is what comes first, this is what gives genesis, birth, to a new world. Maybe the Old Testament is a how-to guide to creation: How to Bring Order Out of Chaos. How to Create Something From Nothing. It all starts by speaking, 'let there be…' and whatever is named and brought into being is distinguished from what was. Light is distinguished from darkness, earth from sky, water from land, and so on, bifurcation after bifurcation until you get the ten thousand things. And all these years we thought it was a history book, when it's really a guide to creation."

"Watch out. You'll get yourself killed for saying such things," Jerry warned.

"Yeah, right."

Jerry sipped his cold latte, its bitterness distracting himself from the eerie feeling of synchronicity happening. *What if there are no problems to solve, yet creation is to occur?* he remembered Terrah saying.

Chapter 8

♦

Helen's Journal

I think I'm falling in love, except that I don't want to. I don't want to risk it. I've fallen in love before, and right after you felt like life couldn't get any better, the ground comes up to meet you and bang, now you know why it's called falling. So you get up and bandage your wounds and try to prolong the airy, weightless feeling a little longer next time and maybe the thump won't be as loud and hard. But falling in love feels like a spring day when the flowers burst into bloom and the air smells fresh. And I want it to go on and on and on and never stop. Right now my heart is just starting to get fluttery, the knees are crackling, and I'm gushing. Yup all the signs are there. Love is definitely in the air.

Jerry looks like an ordinary guy, but he's not slick and doesn't use the usual bag of male tricks, so he is not an ordinary guy. First, he's smarter than most, but he doesn't try to show that off. Second, he doesn't have that macho edge of insecurity. Most importantly, he's someone I can really talk to—no, wrong preposition—talk *with*. So I guess what I'm saying is that he listens. He really listens. And when you have six other siblings, there is such competition for being heard that it feels like paradise when someone actually listens, intently, just to you. So much for all those romantic notions about what love is. I found out what it really is: love is listening, it's being heard, like your words, no, your meaning, your very essence was embraced. When it happens, it's magic.

So why am I resisting it?

Chapter 9

Kttkkttkkttkkttkkttkkttkkttkktt. Kkttkkttkkttkkttkkttkkttkkttkk. Jerry awoke to the harsh grating of a jackhammer outside his bedroom window. He scowled and pulled the sheets over his head, but that didn't stop the awful racket. *What could they be doing on a Saturday morning?* On and on it went, tearing up concrete. Buzzing. Vibrating. He lay in bed floating in and out of sleep, listening to the vibration not with his ears but with his body, feeling the reverberations as he drifted in and out of consciousness. It was so close and so loud that the vibration felt like it came from inside his body. His heart rate quickened and synchronized with it, and the nerves in his arms and chest vibrated sympathetically. The vibration had become him. He felt larger than the boundaries of his physical body. *I am sound now. I am that vibration.* The annoyance was gone when oneness was present.

There was no more chance of sleeping, so Jerry got up and soaked in the shower. The pounding, pulsating water cleared the sleep-cobwebs from his mind. Coffee sensitized his heart to feeling the vibration directly, from the inside. This was the same thum thump that the deer had aroused. Thum thump. Thum thump. This was the primordial vibration, the one that all others are measured against—the beat of life itself, the beat of rock and roll, the beat of time. This simple beat of the heart was the vibration that gives rise to all other vibrations.

With that the caffeine kicked in, the world lit up, and more thoughts poured into his freshly scrubbed, early-morning mind. Vibration, as in sounds, light waves, electromagnetic radiation, is energy. Even matter has vibration. The earth and its atmosphere, Jerry recalled, has a base frequency, a heartbeat or breath, of about 12 Hertz, which is called the Schumann resonance. The Schumann resonance is a standing wave that propagates between the Earth's surface and the ionosphere. It depends on the temperature of the atmosphere and frequency of lightning strikes. Unlike the jackhammer outside Jerry's window or the sound of birdsong, it's a very slow vibration, not perceptible to the human ear. Curiously enough, the human brain's alpha waves are in the same frequency range. In comparison, our eyes see vibration in the range of 400 to 700 nanometers (10^{14} Hertz). Our ears hear in the range of 10^6 to 10^7 Hertz. We can use instruments, such as X-rays in the range of 10^{16} to 10^{21} Hertz. What about all the rest of the frequencies, the ones that are infinitesimally small or infinitesimally large? How do they fit into our reality?

As he mused about the different forms that vibration took: music, light in its variety of colors, speech, that feeling you get inside when you are certain about something, like when you meet the person you know you will marry, knocking at doors…his reverie was interrupted by a loud banging at the door.

Helen nearly knocked him over when he opened the door. She bounced into his arms like a superball in a rubber room.

"What happened?" he asked.

"I *finally* got a real story to cover! No more 'Miss Beautiful Marries Mr. Handsome' and 'A Marriage Made to Last.' Finally, I get to cover something that's really newsworthy!"

"A little more coffee than usual today, huh?" he said, pouring himself another cup.

"Oh hush, Mr. Sleepyhead," she said, tousling his still uncombed hair.

"Well, how did this happen, and what is this story to end all stories?"

"Doug, the regional news guy, is out with a bad case of stomach flu, so I get to cover a UFO crash 300 miles west of here, now that we can officially report such events. I have to leave immediately. Want to come along? If you do, we have to leave right now."

In the previous administration, President Manuel Rodriguez led the government of the United States to come clean about the Roswell incident and thousands of others since then. Legislation was passed that made public all investigations of nonterrestrial life. It was speculated that President Rodriguez needed to boost his public opinion ratings, so he opened up those "closed" files and proclaimed "openness and honesty between the politicians and their constituents." To many it seemed like a moot point, as there was so much other information available because the encounters with other beings had become almost commonplace. As it turned out, most of the Roswell information had been leaked out long ago. But for purists, it was a sign that finally the government was done pretending that something that happened didn't happen. The transparency that the government had imposed on the lives of its citizens by monitoring their every transaction and phone call was boomeranging back onto itself. Now real strides could be made in research and in establishing legitimate contact with these visitors. The government didn't have to hide its treaties and dealings with extraterrestrials anymore. Despite the ultimate lack of novel information actually released, there was a sense of national relief when those classified documents, which had been withheld for such a long time, were finally opened for inspection.

A new breed of politician who had done the internal work necessary to bring integrity and justice into his own life and work, President Rodriguez won the election based on a platform of "healing the past for a healthy tomorrow for all." With enough people like him in Congress, they could begin to do that for the country. Trust needed to be restored, and the only way he could do that was to uncover the lies that had been told for centuries, from the JFK cover-up to the 9/11 deception, the real reason for the invasion of Iraq, and even the truth about the pyramids. But like the ancient Egyptian ruler Akhenaton, the power-hungry beta wolves were trying to eat their leader for lunch. It was unclear which would prevail, an ugly but relief-filled truth or a beautifully spun saccharine placation.

Jerry scratched his back and looked skeptically at her. "You really want to wade through the hordes of nutcases that follow UFO sightings like groupies?"

"Keep up that cynicism and I'm going to rescind my invitation. Whether I want to or not, I have to. It's a hot story, and it's my job."

"All right, all right. I'll go. It might be more interesting than watching football all weekend."

"You don't even watch football!"

"Yeah, I know."

"You facetious little..." She whacked him playfully.

"Don't say it," he said, covering a sensitive body part where it looked like she might strike.

Jerry packed quickly, and they drove all day in Helen's newly repaired car to the site of the crash.

"You really like your job, don't you?" Jerry asked Helen, noticing her light demeanor and cheerfulness during the long drive.

"When I get interesting projects like this I do. The rest of the time it's just a job. Why?"

"I don't know. I'm envious, I guess. I never seem to get projects that break the monotony and boredom. Sometimes I get caught up the minutiae of some little subroutine and lose the sense of what the whole program is trying to accomplish."

"Sort of like life, huh?" Helen added.

"What do you mean?"

"Each one of us is like that subroutine. We get caught up in the minutiae of our own lives and forget about the big program—life as a whole."

"Are we even able to comprehend life as a whole?" Jerry wondered aloud.

They drove on in silence.

The crash site was 50 miles outside a small town, which had now been over-run with the curious and the serious. The locals all saw the crash, but nobody wanted to talk. *Strange behavior for a small town*, Helen thought, *usually people want their 15 minutes of fame.* It seemed like they were protecting a secret. Quickly she learned to stop saying that she was a reporter from the *Morning Sun*. She donned a bandana and became just one of the crowd. Jerry had a harder time blending in. His height notwithstanding, he had a bookish look to him that just didn't say "UFO chaser." So together they did more eavesdropping than talking.

At The Waterin Hole, which was the local hangout, the out-of-town gawkers gathered. One young man who was drinking whiskey on the rocks (one too many) was recounting his encounter:

"It was about 11:00 and I was jus drivin home from work (he winked and held up his drink). That's when I noticed somethin lightin up the sky 'most like it was daytime. It just hung there above some scrubby trees over near the Mason's ranch. I slowed my truck and watched. It didn' move for about 15 minutes. Then I heard a loud noise, like a pipe bomb goin off, and it crashed to the ground. Straight down, like someone cut the wire it was hangin from. I high-tailed it outta there cause I didn' know what might be gettin out of it and I didn' want ta find out."

"Mike, you been drinking too much you sorry s-o-b. This is just another one a them damn government experiments. Look how many we seen already, that black thing, the one that bounced up and down like a ping-pong ball, the 'Flying O' remember that one? Naaah, this is just another one of their goofy-assed test planes," replied a large burly man who looked like he could have been an ex-marine. His presence was imposing enough, and he certainly did a loud job of imposing his opinion on the gathered crowd.

"I smell some foul play," Helen leaned over and whispered to Jerry.

"Like how?"

"Like someone shot it down."

"Why would they want to do that?"

"I don't know, but that's what we have to find out." While Jerry kept listen-ing, Helen uplinked her Personal Secretary and got the address of the Mason ranch. She also tried to find out whatever she could about the Masons from a background check and police reports.

"Let's take a ride out there tonight," she said as she got back to their table.

"Now? It's nearly 3 am. We can't go knocking on their door asking for an interview at this hour."

Helen rolled her eyes and grabbed his sleeve and pulled him out of the bar. "Hey look at that broad. He's gonna get lucky tonight!" Jerry overheard someone say. The others looked at him and laughed.

"Why are we doing this? What did you find out?" Jerry asked when they were safely outside.

"I'm still checking. I should know by morning. I just have a hunch…Let's go."

"Where?"

"The crash site."

It took nearly 30 minutes to find the Mason Ranch. It was north of town and south of a big no man's land. For a ranch it had hardly any vegetation, no water to be seen, just a desert rabbit or two. What could otherworlders possibly want with this area of the country? From the road it looked like there were lights on at the farmhouse. On any other night that would be surprising.

"What now, Sherlock?" a sleepy Jerry chided.

"We fake a flat tire."

"Ugh," Jerry groaned, "you've got to be kidding."

"We need to see who comes and goes here tonight. Keep a pen and paper handy to write down license plate numbers. Jack up the side that's not facing the road. Put the hood up, and make it look like you're working."

"Something I'm good at, finally."

Jerry got out the jack and the spare tire, jacked up the car and put the tire on the ground as if he were going to use it any minute. Then he lay down with his head just under the car and tried to catch a few winks of sleep. Helen, meanwhile, was on her cell phone. A state trooper drove past and slowed to ask if she needed a tow truck. "No thanks, I think he almost has the tire changed," she replied. The trooper looked confused but relieved, as Jerry was not in a position to be changing a tire, and drove off. She noted his license number.

Little by little information trickled in. This ranch was one of the biggest in the state. They raise some cattle, but not enough to justify all that land. One of the Masons had been convicted of extortion 30 years back.

A large black car with headlights off whizzed past. It was going so fast she didn't get the full license number, only the last 4 digits, D10Z. She watched it snake its way up the long driveway to the lit-up house.

More information trickled in. Apparently the *Wall Street Sentinel* had reported some earnings irregularities with a company known as Energy Technology Assistance, Inc., of which the Masons were principal shareholders. Back when this was reported there had been a rash of earnings irregularities in the energy business. As she was saving that to a file, another car drove by. She almost missed it, as it was very quiet and it, too, had its headlights turned off. Fortunately it wasn't traveling quickly, so she got its plate number and checked it out. It must have been a hybrid car because it didn't have the same kind of noisy engine, just a subtle whirring. "I need to find out what that Energy Technology Assistance, Inc. makes. Oil? Nuclear? Alternative?" she said to keep herself awake.

Helen kicked Jerry's sneakers to wake him up. "We've been out here long enough. If they get suspicious, we're likely to be in deep doodoo, given what I've learned so far. She rolled the spare tire back to the trunk. "Jerry, help me put this back."

Jerry didn't stir.

"C'mon. This is heavy."

Helen leaned the tire against the rear bumper, went over to Jerry, and poked him. He didn't wake. Her heart leapt. She pulled him out from under the car and shook his shoulders. His head slumped down onto his chest. She slapped his cheeks. He didn't wake. She felt his pulse; he had one, but it was faint. After laying him back on the ground, she stood up and paced. *Oh my god, is he dead? Did he get carbon monoxide poisoning? What do I do now? If I call 911 then I'll miss getting my story. If I don't get help for him soon, he might die. Where could I get help around here anyway?* She knelt in front of him, threw his arm over her shoulder, and hoisted his limp body up off the ground. His weight and height nearly knocked her over backward, so she laid him back down on the ground, dragged him to the back door of the car, and maneuvered him into the back seat. Carefully, she laid him in the long way, and bent his knees up so that he'd fit. She released the jack, got in, and sped to the Mason Ranch, leaving the spare tire along the side of the road.

Helen banged on the front door, wheezing out "Oh my god he's going to die!" in between breaths and sobs. "Answer the door, dammit." She could hear voices inside. They sounded scared and confused. She kept pounding, no longer caring about being scared of what might happen if someone actually answered it.

Finally, the door opened a crack. The state trooper who had driven by and asked whether she needed help peeked out.

"I need help now. He's not conscious. I don't know what happened. He was working on the car and then stopped…He's barely breathing."

"Don't panic, Miss. Where is he now?"

"He's in the back seat."

The trooper carried Jerry into the house. Helen spied around, but could see no one else. He took Jerry into the living room and gave him CPR and mouth-to-mouth resuscitation. As the state trooper was working, another man of very large, muscular build quietly entered the room and stood and watched until the trooper finished. As Jerry revived, the large man moved forward and pulled something out of his coat. Jerry woke up to a gun barrel pointing in his face. He looked around for Helen.

"Don't move," instructed the man with the gun. "Harry, what should I do with this creep?"

"Put the two of them in the bedroom until I hear from Jack," the state trooper replied.

"Okay, get up now. Lady, you get over here with him. Walk down that hallway on your left. Open the door on your right. Not a word from you two, or I'll shoot first."

Helen tried to listen to the conversation through the door, but couldn't hear anything clearly.

"Where are we?" Jerry whispered to Helen when he had regained some wherewithal.

"Inside the Mason Ranch."

"Why the hell...?" Jerry whispered loudly at her.

"Shhh." Helen didn't want him revealing their purpose.

"What a fine mess you've gotten us into, Ollie," Jerry jibed.

"Me?! Why the hell did you pass out like that? I was afraid you were dead!" Helen was half in shock and half furious.

"Look, I don't know what happened there. Maybe your car has a carbon monoxide leak. One minute I was perfectly fine and conscious, and the next minute I wasn't aware of anything in particular. I just had this vast oceanic experience. I was still conscious; I simply wasn't conscious of anything out there."

"What are you talking about?! You were totally unconscious. I tried everything I could to bring you back."

Jerry put his arm around her to calm her down. A hysterical woman would not be an asset at the moment. "Let's look at our situation." *Why, of all places, did you choose to bring me here? Why didn't you take me to a hospital?* he thought.

"We're trapped at the Mason Ranch is what our situation is. The Hulk is probably guarding the door. They have guns, and we don't." Helen sounded despondent, about to give up. This was not what she had bargained for when she accepted the assignment.

"We're not trapped," Jerry said, pointing to the room's one window. Jerry opened it, and in doing so triggered a silent alarm at the police station. He motioned to Helen to follow him. He jumped to the ground first.

"I can't jump. I'm scared," she said.

"Hang over the edge, and I'll catch you down here," Jerry told her. Helen turned around and went out the window backwards, holding on to the ledge with her hands. Jerry grabbed her calves and told her to let go. As she did, he slowly let her slip through his arms down to the ground.

"Come on, let's get out of here." Jerry said, heading toward the front of the house, where the car was.

"No, not yet! We have to check out this spacecraft. Where do you think it is?"

"Hell if I know."

"Let's look in the barn."

"No, Helen. Bad idea. Let's get out of here." He grabbed her by the arm.

"Let go of me!" She twisted loose and glared at him. "I have to get this story," she said with steely conviction in her voice. "I'm not willing to settle for mediocrity."

To get to the barn, they would have to walk right past the room in which the men who had driven here in the middle of the night were gathered. It had a big picture window facing the direction of the barn.

"Get down." Jerry told Helen, as he crawled on his belly as close to the house and under the window as he could. His heart beat wildly. *Why did I let her talk me into doing this? Why didn't I just bolt for the car? Oh yeah, she has the keys.* Helen reluctantly got on her stomach and crawled in the dust behind him. They could hear the conversation going on inside the house.

"We gotta get that device out of here," said one of the men.

"How? We can't take a zero-point energy collector just anywhere," said another.

"Who the hell is going to know what it is? Why, I reckon that you could set it up in a circus and charge folks money to come see a 'spook deminimizer,'" said a third.

"A what?" said the fourth.

"What I'm tryin ta say is that you could tell people just about anything. They'll believe you. You could tell 'em this here thing sucks ghosts right out of the air."

Jerry stopped cold.

"Did you hear that?" he whispered to Helen.

"Hear what?"

"They have a zero-point energy device here."

"A what?"

"Shhh."

When they were safely past the house, Jerry stood up and brushed himself off, then helped Helen up, and they ran the rest of the way to the barn. The main doors were locked. They walked around the barn looking for another way in. Jerry couldn't contain his excitement.

"Wow, it's incredible! I didn't think there were any functional zero-point energy devices in the public sector."

"What is a zero-point whatchamathingy?" Helen asked now that they were safely out of sight on the far side of the barn. She sunk down to a squatting position with her back against the wood as she caught her breath. Jerry kept looking around for a way to get in.

"It's a technology that can generate energy from the quantum fluctuations. Maybe that's why the OWBs, other-world beings, were sniffing around here," Jerry said as he tried to pull open a window that had been nailed shut.

"Jerry, for chrissake, I don't know a damn thing about physics. The closest I got to physics in high school was some equal and opposite reaction with the captain of the basketball team."

"Oh," his eyebrows went up and he turned to face her.

She shook her head and rolled her eyes.

"Let me see if I can explain it. I haven't thought about it much lately. Zero-point energy is an offshoot from quantum electrodynamics and the Heisenberg uncertainty principle."

"The what?"

"Oh, never mind. Can you check that door over there?"

She pulled on the handles of a cellar door, but it didn't budge. "You don't have to explain it now. We have more pressing things to handle at the moment."

"There's our way into the barn." Jerry pointed to a window at the second-floor height. If I give you a boost up, see if you can push that window in."

"Oh no, I'm not climbing all the way up there. You won't be there to catch me this time," she complained.

"Do you want to get your story or not? Because I'd be more than happy to just leave right now. There's something weird going on here."

"Okay, okay." Helen climbed on Jerry's shoulders like a circus performer. Standing on them, she just barely reached the bottom of the window. She gave the window a hard push, which nearly caused her to fall off his shoulders, but the window swung open. "Can you get me up just a little higher? I can't get a good grip."

Jerry stood on his toes.

"Higher. Just a little more. Oh shit, it's a long way down!"

"I'm going to have to try to lift you up," he said as he pushed the bottoms of her shoes up. It was awkward, but he managed.

Helen had her torso over the bottom ledge of the window. Jerry gave her one last push, which sent her over the edge. "Oh no!" She lost her grip and fell headlong into the barn. "Jerry!"

Outside, Jerry heard the thud of her hitting the ground. "Are you okay?"

"Nothing's broken. Ow. But my ribcage hurts like hell." Then her tone changed abruptly. "Oh my god."

"What?"

"Oh god. Oh god. Oh god." There was fear and excitement in her voice.

"Helen, what is it? Helen, let me in!"

Chapter 10

What did it look like? wondered Martin Matz, one of the men who had been summoned to the Mason Ranch. He didn't believe in anything he couldn't see or touch, and he certainly had never seen a ship from another galaxy, even though he had read about them in the newspaper. The knot in his stomach surprised him, but he didn't show the anxiety in his face. He had defended some of the most dangerous people around—serial killers, rapists, and terrorists—and didn't have a trace of fear around them. He knew their type, knew what made them tick, knew how to manipulate them. But how do you manipulate something (someone?) that isn't even human?

These men—Martin, the lawyer; Harry, the state trooper; and Sam, the owner of the local newspaper—were Jack Mason's inner circle, the ones who took care of things politically, civically, and financially. In exchange for their loyalty and "help," Jack granted them this opportunity to see what they would have to make disappear in the minds of the public.

Although these were powerful, well-connected men, today there was nevertheless a common feeling of concern hiding sheer panic. Nerves were twitchy and tempers short. Their usual camaraderie, grounded in bawdy commentary, was absent.

"Let's go," Jack said. The four of them went to the barn to see what they had come to see—the fallen OWB ship.

"Why don't we destroy it," suggested Sam.

"How do you suggest we destroy something that managed to get light years across space, enter the earth's atmosphere, and still not burn up?" Jack countered.

"You really should ship it to the nearest air force base," suggested the state trooper. "I know some guys from my old navy days who probably know some guys who could take care of this for you. With a little encouragement," Harry rubbed his thumb against his fingers, "they'd keep it secret for you."

"God, no, Harry! They'd be able to tell from the forensic analysis that this puppy didn't just fall out of the sky. You left a big hole in it with that anti-aircraft thing of yours. They'd be able to analyze the trajectories and pin the location of the strike to right here. Shooting a poor, defenseless OWB craft right out of the

52

sky probably violates some intergalactic treaty. Then the government would come snooping around here, and that is what I don't want to happen because it wouldn't be good for business right now, would it? For now we need to make it look like this energy is being generated by conventional techniques."

"Why do you suppose it was messing with the device?" asked Sam, the newspaper man.

"Maybe it needed fuel and was doing the OWB version of siphoning from the gas tank," Harry suggested.

"Hardly, you idiot," Jack said. "It was *increasing* the output of the device, far beyond what even a nuclear plant is capable of. And things around it started disappearing—the computer control panel it was hooked up to, the carpeting in the room, my coffee mug—gone. Can you believe it? We were generating *too much* energy. The regulatory agencies would have been sniffing around here in minutes because it is simply not possible to generate that much energy by conventional means. God, it kills me. Like having to rein in a horse that just wants to tear across a field, I had to shoot down that contraption because it was causing too much of a good thing."

"Perhaps we should try to keep it, not bury it," Martin said. "Maybe in the future we could use it to do just what it was doing—and make us all very rich men."

"That's a huge risk, Marty. Why should we take it?" Jack shot back.

"For our future, when the grid fails, we can step in and, shall we say, 'save the day' with an enormous profit margin." He grinned and rubbed his palms together.

◆   ◆   ◆

Helen staggered to a window on the ground floor level, unlocked it, and opened it enough for Jerry to slip inside. There it was—what all those people in the bar were there to see but probably never would. The OWB ship was about 25 feet in diameter and about 8 feet high in the center. It had lights of some sort encircling the fuselage, but not lights or bulbs as we know. The exterior looked like so many that Jerry had seen in pictures and on videos on the news that being so close to it was rather anticlimactic. *These particular other-world beings must have a strong presence here on earth, for as often as their vehicles have been sighted and photographed,* he thought. There was a large hole near the outer edge, probably where it had been shot. The hull looked like it had melted but didn't burn. Helen walked all the way around it while Jerry stood rooted to the ground.

"Shall we have a look inside?" Helen asked.

"You're not really going to go in there?"

"Yeah, sure. This is what I'm here to cover. Why wouldn't I?"

"What if there are still OWBs in there? What if they think you're the one who shot them down?" Jerry cautioned her.

"Are you coming or not?" Helen demanded.

Jerry shook his head and stepped toward her. He didn't know whether she was brave or just plain foolish. She put her hand in his and they walked toward the hole in the fuselage. "No fear, no fear, no fear," she repeated as they moved closer to it.

They got within 10 feet of it and were stopped short by a powerful wave of energy, a type of force field around the ship.

"Whoa, what was that?" Jerry staggered backward.

"It sure feels good, whatever it is." Helen was standing inside the radius of this energy field. "I've never felt so good in my entire life."

Jerry ventured closer, a step at a time. The wave of energy hit him again but he walked into it this time. He inhaled sharply, as it took his breath away.

Jerry and Helen stood there as if mesmerized, with beatific looks on their faces. It wasn't an ordinary electrostatic energy field. Whatever it was, it dissolved any fear they had. It felt good like a mother's hug, hot chocolate on a cold day, your first kiss.

Anxiety melted away. It was a paralyzing kind of bliss that eliminated any motive to do harm. Jerry looked at Helen and felt such fullness in his heart, pulsating with each beat, expanding beyond his physical borders.

"Do you feel it too? What is this?" she asked.

"I don't know, but it's incredible."

They looked at each other then walked toward the opening in the fuselage, where the ship had been shot down. They peered inside and saw three sets of eyes peering back. They were eyes filled with compassion, big eyes that wanted to swallow you, eyes that spoke to them.

The OWBs' "defense" system consisted of sending out powerful waves of love that neutralized any harmful intention. To most people, whose own defense system consisted of the projection of fear-based energy, the two clashed like oil and water. So when fear met such love, it would be repelled. In contrast, when love met this love-based force field, it was allowed through, the way some light is allowed through a polarized lens and some is blocked.

Without words, the OWBs welcomed Jerry and Helen, and Jerry thought he detected some surprise on their part. Their method of communicating caught

Helen off guard. It wasn't linear, with one word or concept coming after the other; it was instantaneous, so they grasped the whole picture all at once. At first it was like watching a conceptual slide show. You would get a fully formed, all-details-included picture. It was like a mental image, where you see a picture in your mind's eye, only it was more complete, like you also understood an entire argument in one word, like if you comprehended *The Critique of Pure Reason* instantly. As Jerry and Helen caught on and could process such complete, complex, and intense messages, the "slides" came more and more quickly, more like a movie or an orchestral piece being played directly into his mind. *How thin and wan our one-word-after-another language seemed compared with this broadband communication system of theirs!* Helen reflected.

Jerry and Helen learned by being shown mental images that their ship had indeed been shot down with a hand-held anti-aircraft missile. They obviously had the capability to escape, as their vehicle could outmaneuver all of our technology, but they chose not to because they hadn't sufficiently intercepted the zero-point energy operation. When Jerry thought back "Why?" the answer he got was an image of a young child playing with a match and setting the rug on fire, which caused the house to burn, which spread to the neighborhood, and then the entire city. Many lives were lost, and the devastation was widespread. People lost their jobs, parents lost their children and children lost their parents, and the entire city suffered morally and economically. The next image was of earth shrinking or imploding, which twisted the fabric of space, causing havoc in the solar system as planets and stars spun out of orbit affecting the entire universe. The next image was of them taking the lit match from the child's hand before any of that could happen. The child bore a striking resemblance to Jack Mason.

Those images showed Jerry and Helen that zero-point energy is fundamental to the structure of the universe and as such must be approached with respect, reverence, and caution. To use it from the motivation of greed and hoarding is a violation of the energy and will destroy not only all those using it that way, but potentially many others as well. We treat nuclear energy with respect because we have seen the devastation that it can cause. We have not yet seen the devastation that can happen if we misuse zero-point energy. The OWBs "explained" through more images that these men were attempting to misuse it to further their own gain, without regard for the whole of humanity, let alone the rest of the universe. They did not intend to give it; they intended to sell it and hide its source. They had an elaborate scheme for selling it to power companies and making it look like it was coming from a conventional fuel source. The OWBs made it clear that their greed and desire for power are unsuited to the use of zero-point energy. In pictures relayed mentally, the OWBs showed Jerry and Helen how the military had stolen this technology from them years ago and developed it in secret, and then these men had in turn stolen it from the military. Because our civilization isn't capable yet of using it properly and ethically, they conveyed that it was their responsibility to prevent its misuse, for the good of the universe, not just the good of Earth.

How would one use zero-point energy ethically and properly? How is that different from how we use energy presently? Jerry wondered. Those questions stuck him in the ribs and wouldn't let go. As he thought about it more, he realized that if you try to use zero-point energy without the understanding that everything in the universe is One and comes from one life energy, especially that you ARE that life energy, the misuse of zero-point energy technology could destroy life. In a rather gruesome image of a man who cut off his own arm to use in a fire to cook himself a hotdog, these compassionate beings showed Helen and Jerry that zero-point energy is the fabric of the universe, which supports all life everywhere and is not to be used for running refrigerators, TVs, and other mechanical devices. The next image was a question: what if the man in the mental image had instead used his heart or his brain instead of his arm to cook the hot dog? What if that zero-point energy device just happened to tap something essential, thereby destroying it and destroying that which it was meant to serve? The OWBs emphasized that zero-point energy is the energy that is the foundation of all life in the universe, and to use it as a source for simple electricity would be like using a guided missile to light a candle. Furthermore, they showed Helen and Jerry through a rapid-fire slide show of images projected directly into their minds how every technology that humans have encountered or developed has been turned into a weapon, from gunpowder to genetic engineering to anti-gravity. To use zero-point energy as a weapon would wreak havoc not only on Earth, but in the universe. They showed Helen and Jerry how humans do not have sufficient understanding of their connectedness to the universe. In images of government leaders, scientists, and religious leaders all saying or implying that humans are alone in the universe, the OWBs showed Helen and Jerry how the cultural institutions keep people believing that the inhabitants of this planet are the only ones who exist, despite sufficient evidence to the contrary. They even showed how such separateness and aloneness has been built into the structure of language. For example, that much-touted phrase of connectedness—I love you—exemplifies how I and you are kept separate, not allowed to merge, even by the most powerful connective force of all—love. That's why they had to show the interconnectedness in images. It couldn't be done adequately in language.

"You must warn others," one of the big-eyed diminutive beings said out loud, although how he said it was a mystery because he didn't have a mouth. Whereas the images were more informative, this command was simple, direct, and couldn't be misinterpreted.

Jerry stepped back. His eyes got big. Helen stepped closer to and slightly behind Jerry. It was one thing to be carried away in a mesmerization by the mental images; it was something else entirely to be given a command directly.

Sensing the fear that was activated, the OWB sent out another smaller wave of love. There was no harm meant, no cause for alarm.

"Warn them about what? Zero-point energy?" Helen asked.

To answer her, they communicated a new vision telepathically. This time, the image split in three segments. In the middle segment was the primary scene, in which a mother standing over her child says, "Eat your broccoli." In the left-hand image, in which the exact same scene occurs, you get the sense of the mother lovingly caring for her child, making sure she grows up healthy and strong. In the right-hand image you get the sense of the child being persecuted by this demanding, controlling woman who makes her do something abhorrent. From there the image exploded into a multiplicity of images, as if seen through a fly's eye, in which there was a different interpretation of that same scene hundreds of different ways. The difference in experience between the perspectives jolted Helen's nerves because it struck close to home. In a flash of insight she saw her tendency to take a simple comment and amplify it, either positively or negatively, according to what suits her, and then react to the interpreted meaning. Jerry's helpfulness when her car broke down, for example, she interpreted as "he's interested in me" and she reacted accordingly. If she had been in a sour mood, his helpfulness might have been interpreted as "the poor girl can't handle automotive breakdowns" and her reaction would have been "go away, I can do it myself." Everything has its basic data of what's so, which can be interpreted in almost any way you please.

"Wow, that was intense," Jerry said to Helen.

Helen wiped the tears from her eyes, but Jerry had seen them nonetheless. "Are you okay?" he asked.

"Yeah. But I still don't know what they want us to warn people about."

"All of it." Jerry said. "I think your story just took on an agenda."

"I can't put this in my story."

"Then you'll just have to write a book."

Helen turned and looked at Jerry and smiled.

Chapter 11

"What the hell do we say to them—why were you fucking with our device?" Martin asked.

"I don't care what you say. Do you want to see it or not? I'm not running a circus side show here. Your chance is now or never," Jack Mason answered.

"Okay, okay."

"Let's go then."

"What kind of weapons do they have?" asked the State Trooper.

"Hell if I know, Harry. Everybody have theirs ready?"

"I'll be right back. I need to get something from my squad."

Martin pulled his out of his shoulder holster. Sam held his open hands out. Jack threw him a piece. Sam held it gingerly. He believed the pen was mightier than the sword, but in this instance, he might feel safer with a gun despite his inexperience in handling weapons of the non-ink-bearing variety. Harry came back in with an automatic. The four men walked to the barn.

"Here's the strategy. I'll push the door open, and two of us will come in from each side.

Don't shoot unless you're attacked. We've got enough of a mess on our hands as it is."

◆　　　◆　　　◆

"They're coming! What do we do?" Helen said in a loud whisper as she looked around for a hiding place.

"Up there." Jerry pointed to the hay loft. They climbed the ladder and laid face down on the wooden planks. They could only see parts of the area through the cracks between the boards, but they could hear everything.

The OWBs retreated inside their craft. The barn door slid open, aided by a push from Harry's gun. Sunlight rushed in and reflected off the fuselage. Four faces peered inside. A couple chins dropped.

"Jesus, Mary, and Joseph," Sam said, making the sign of the cross more out of habit than belief that it would actually protect him.

"I never would have believed it," Martin said shaking his head. "Never in a million years. In fact, Jack, when you called, I thought you were playing one of your pranks again, making excuses to have a private party, if you know what I mean, so the missus wouldn't suspect anything," he elbowed Jack in the ribs.

"How did you get it here?" Sam asked.

"Tractor, you fool. Hell, it's lighter than a wagon full of hay. Ten guys could probably lift it."

"What are you going to do with it?" Sam continued.

"Take it apart and figure it out," he glanced at Harry. "There's some incredible technology in that bucket o' bolts. What we could do with that..." Harry glared at him to shut up. "But that's enough questions for now. The reason I brought you here is to show you what you must not let into the hands of the public. There might have been amateur photographers who snapped pictures of it, made movies of it, sketched it, whatever. If such things show up, discredit them. Do whatever it takes. Don't let it get printed, Sam. Got it?"

"Got it."

"This never happened."

"Can we take a closer look?"

"Sure, but watch out..." Jack warned.

Sam and Martin moved closer and were hit with a wave of energy that knocked them on their backs. Jack rushed to help them up and got knocked back as well.

"What the...?" Martin said as he shook the shock out of his head. He struggled to his feet and brushed himself off, saying, "Okay, I've had enough. I don't know what we're messing with here, but I'm leaving."

"Not so fast." Jack stuck his gun in Martin's ribs. "I'll tell you when you can go."

Harry hadn't moved. He covered the door with his automatic weapon both protecting them from the OWBs and keeping order for Mason. "Jack, lower it. This is nerve wracking for all of us. We brought guns in case they did something, not to use on each other."

Jack lowered his gun.

"Did any survive the crash?" Sam asked.

"I don't know. Haven't seen any," Jack replied. He didn't like so many questions. "Let's get back to the house. We have some work to do."

As they walked back, a squad car made its way up the meandering driveway. The guns got put back in hiding, and the state trooper ditched the automatic in a bush.

"What is this all about? Did any of you call these ninnies?" Mason was furious.

"Hell no," came the replies.

Jack tilted his head toward the house, which is where Sam, Harry, and Martin went, while he strode to the driveway.

The police car stopped, and a young man with a crew cut stepped out of the car.

"Everything okay, Mr. Mason?" the rookie asked.

"Yes, sir. Everything's under control." Jack folded his arms over his chest, stood with his feet wide apart, and glared at the rookie officer.

The young cop had heard the rumors around town and was more than eager to be sent to investigate. "Your silent alarm went off, so it's protocol to come out and check. Mind if I take a look around?"

"I assure you that everything is okay. I'll do the check myself." Jack Mason stepped right up to him, physically cutting him off from going any farther.

The rookie stepped back, nodded his head, and got back in his patrol car and drove off.

When he was out of site, Jack fumed on his walk back to the house. "Where are they?!" He strode to the bedroom and kicked down the door to the room where Helen and Jerry had been put for safe keeping. It was empty, and the window was open.

"Find them!" Mason commanded.

Chapter 12

Helen rolled over and took a long, deep in-breath. Jerry stood up and brushed himself off. "We have to get out of here now. These men are dangerous," he said.

Helen burst out laughing.

"What's so funny?"

She doubled over with laughter, gasping for air in between. The tension combined with his flippant statement of the obvious triggered the emotional release.

Jerry climbed down from the loft and walked toward the spacecraft.

"Hey, come here. Look at this."

"What?" she said regaining her composure as she climbed down the ladder.

"Look where the hole was."

The fuselage was growing back, healing itself. "How is that possible?" she asked.

"I don't know, unless the ship itself is somehow alive," Jerry replied.

"How can metal be alive?"

"We don't know it's metal. It could be a bio-crystalline life form. Whatever it is, I doubt they're going to hang around when it has grown back to its original shape. We may be able to use that to our advantage."

"Cover me as I open the door," they heard Martin say from outside the barn door.

"Yes, sir," Harry replied.

Jerry hid behind some bales of hay, and Helen ducked behind a tractor.

The big barn door swung open, and instead of walking through it, Martin and Harry flew 20 feet backward through the air like human cannon balls. Their guns discharged into the air. Harry skidded across the stone driveway, the clothes and skin being ripped off his back by the jagged edges of the limestone rocks. Martin landed on his shoulder, dislocating it. He writhed in pain.

"Force field hit us like a bomb. There must be an intelligent being in that ship. I'd reckon it's protecting our two fugitives," Harry told Jack Mason as he stumbled, bleeding, to the house.

"Time for Plan B, huh?" Jack looked at him sideways.

"Hell no, I'm not sticking around for Plan B."

◆   ◆   ◆

The hole in the fuselage had nearly grown closed.

"It looks like they're just about ready to go home," Jerry whispered to Helen. "I suggest we do the same thing."

They crawled along the barn wall to the open door and Jerry peered out. Martin was still in a fetal position holding his shoulder, screaming for Jack, Harry, or Sam to get him some ice. Sam came out with an ice pack and got Martin up on his feet, with his good arm over Sam's shoulder. The two of them went into the house.

Jerry motioned to Helen to run for some tall bushes near the driveway.

"What was that?" Sam had heard them.

"I don't care! Get me a doctor. My shoulder is broken." Martin bellowed, self-centered especially when in pain.

"Hey, look, Jerry, an AK-47," Helen said pointing at an automatic weapon that Harry had ditched in the bushes.

"That's not an...but who cares, we might need it," he said picking it up and nearly dropping it. "I didn't know these things were so damn heavy."

"Shhhh." Helen pointed toward the barn. A light was starting to glow from inside.

"This is our chance." Jerry motioned for Helen to ready her car keys by making a hand gesture for starting the engine by turning the key.

"Damn, where's my purse?"

A look of horror crossed Jerry's face. No keys, no escape.

A bright flash of light caught their attention. The OWB ship emerged through the top of the barn roof as if it wasn't there. The four men inside saw it, and three of them came running out to the barn.

"Now. Run!" Jerry and Helen sprinted to Helen's car.

Harry, who was still bleeding despite having the wounds cleaned somewhat, shot at the spacecraft as it rose silently into the sky, about 300 feet up. His puny bullets had no effect on it. They just ricocheted back. The ship's lit aura dimmed, and it took off toward the north with lightening speed. Gone. Sam came out when it was safe, after the ship had departed.

Martin, Jack, and Sam stared at the sky in shock and disbelief. It was gone so quickly that the whole situation seemed unreal.

◆   ◆   ◆

Jerry got to the car first. "Your purse is in here." He turned it upside down on the passenger seat and fished out the keys. Helen jumped in the back seat on the driver's side as Jerry started the car and sped down the driveway.

"How the hell did that happen?" Martin shouted. "It had a big old hole in it from the anti-aircraft missile. How could you let it get away like that?"

"Shut up, Martin." Jack snarled.

Harry slapped him on the back. "Look at it this way, Jack, one of your problems just flew away."

"Just because it's gone doesn't mean we still won't have work to do," Jack reminded them. At that moment he caught sight of Helen's car speeding down the road back to town. Control was slipping away. "Harry, get them!"

Although he knew it was pointless, he got in his squad car, turned the lights and sirens on, and sped off.

◆   ◆   ◆

"Do you remember how to get out of here?" Jerry asked Helen after it seemed like they were a safe distance away from the Mason Ranch. "It was so dark when we arrived that I was completely lost."

"No, just go fast. I think that trooper's coming," she said. "Damn, I never found out where those OWBs were from. How am I going to write a credible article if I don't know the origin of my source? Actually, how am I going to translate those images into quotes? Damn, this is going to be hard."

"Quotes?"

"Yeah, right. Maybe I shouldn't reveal that part. Stick with eyewitness fabrications, I mean, descriptions, eh? Okay, so where are we?"

"That's what I was asking you," Jerry said.

Helen hadn't a clue, but she said anyway, "Next major intersection make a right."

Chapter 13

Jerry wanted to lock himself away from people for awhile until he could process the events of the weekend and not feel so overwhelmed. But he didn't. He went to work Monday morning, as usual, pretended nothing happened, even looked up the football scores so that he might appear to have had a normal weekend. *This is what I hate about the life I have—I have to pretend that weird things that happen to me didn't happen. I have to pretend that my life is normal like other peoples' lives, but it's not. And it's because they're the one's who can't handle it! Ugh. I hate it. I'm tired of hiding.* But down deep Jerry knew that he wouldn't trade his weird life for a "normal" one.

The following week he visited Terrah. Though he barely knew her, he trusted her and suspected that she wouldn't think he was crazy, on drugs, or lying to get attention. Indeed, there was something nonordinary about her. Despite her sweet-little-old-lady appearance, she had passion and resolve to live and do what she wanted rather than what others expected. *Maybe she can help me understand what happened with those other-world beings, the implications of zero-point energy, and how I fit into this strange web in which I find myself.*

Jerry arrived unannounced at 430 Rio Rancho on Wednesday after work. "I need to talk to you," he said when she opened the door.

"Why don't we take a walk? I want to check on the spring that feeds the stream that nourishes my land. Kind of like taking your own pulse," she explained.

When he saw the stream they were following, Jerry felt an electric chill run up his spine. There was a moment of recognition. "This was the stream in my dream, the one your granddaughter dreamed, isn't it?"

"There's water in it now. Good thing, eh?" she said.

As they tromped this way and that, following the stream up to its source, Jerry told the story from beginning to end. Terrah didn't say anything immediately, but she looked deep in thought, even mildly disturbed, as if sifting through the rubble of words for the important ones. Finally, a faint smile appeared on her lips. "It seems you stumbled into the bears' den, doesn't it?"

"Huh?"

"The bear's den. Those men are all bears. Did you learn from the bear how to deal with those…those…beasts?"

Bears? Them? How? Jerry thought about the dream Penny had and his last trek into the woods with Terrah. The Mason clan were takers. They took without regard for others. They were big and clumsy and didn't realize their own strength. Like the bear that wants and apple (he doesn't pick a single apple, he shakes the tree, and twenty might fall), Mason shook the wrong tree, causing a cosmic immune response to halt the harvesting of energy from the universe's infrastructure.

"You saw OWBs at the Mason Ranch, huh?" Terrah looked at him out of the corner of her eye.

Jerry wondered whether her askance look meant that she really didn't believe him. "People never believe me" was the conclusion he had reached at age 10, when he saw how his mother reacted to his extra-ordinary experience. Already his world felt smaller, more constrained.

"They were sabotaging a zero-point-energy device."

"Oh, my," she said.

More ambiguity.

"They said we weren't ready for it yet—still too much greed and lack of awareness of our interconnectedness," he said.

"That is true."

"And they told us to warn people."

"About what?" Terrah asked.

"About the dangers of using zero-point energy, I suppose. I don't know why they want me to do it. And frankly, I'm afraid to. I don't want to look like one of those nut cases hollering about the apocalypse."

"Uh huh."

"Terrah, you're driving me crazy. I can't tell if you believe me. Do you or don't you?"

"Oh Jerry, dear boy, I very much do. I wanted to hear your account without any commentary from me. You know how I can get sometimes—or perhaps you don't. If I'm not careful, I'll be telling your story for you because I can't contain my excitement and impatience. You can, however, count on me to listen without judgment."

Jerry saw his own inner workings for what they were. He had come to her because he knew that she wouldn't scoff at his experience, yet his old expectation of not being believed, formed from his childhood trauma, kicked in automatically nonetheless. They walked on in silence, which was unusual for Terrah. She always seemed willing and anxious to talk. "Is everything okay, Terrah?" he asked.

"Huhm?" she said, having been deep in thought.

"You're awfully quiet. Is everything okay?"

"Oh, I suppose I must. You'll never get past this point if I don't spill the beans."

"What are you talking about?"

She stopped walking forward and turned around to face him. "Harry Timbres, the state policeman you met, is my ex-husband."

Jerry stood in shock, barely able to form the words, "I'm sorry to hear that."

"I moved here to get away from Jack Mason. He poisoned Harry. Harry used to be a good man. He was a good father to our kids, but Jack Mason—she said his name with the venom of a cobra in her voice—turned him against me, against what I stand for.

"What happened?" Jerry asked.

"Oh, at first Jack would come by and they'd sit in the kitchen, maybe have a beer, and talk the usual guy talk—hunting, local politics, weather. You know what I mean. Then they started going to the Moose Lodge to talk, I suppose because Jack realized that I was sitting in the next room knitting and hearing every word. Jack, you know, is a very wealthy man, and Harry was just a patrolman. We lived quite modestly. Then things started showing up, a new gun, hunting trips to those fancy game preserves, then a set of golf clubs. I knew Harry had turned when that happened. He used to think golf was a sissy sport. Now there he was in those stupid pants and frilly shoes. He'd have extra work to do for Jack in the evenings. That's how I developed the ability 'to see.' I wanted to know what he was up to instead of being home helping me raise our children, and I couldn't follow him because we had one car and he had it. I certainly couldn't hire someone to follow him. So I started 'watching' him intuitively, with my third eye as some might say."

"I can't believe that goon was actually your husband. He was the one who shot it down, I gathered."

"Jerry, you must be careful. If they know who you are they will come after you. And warn your lady friend too. He has become ruthless. I don't know what kind of elixir of power Mason fed him, but he's drunk on it."

Jerry saw a mixture of sadness and fear in her eyes. He understood how hard it was to see those who supposedly love you turn against you. To lose something that seemed so stable and so nurturing, like a teat whose milk has gone sour, brought such a stew of emotions with it, grief, longing for what once was, then anger and bitterness, followed by self-recrimination, and finally pained picking up the pieces and moving on.

The young gurgling stream added its say to the conversation. They were getting near the source. Terrah knelt by the stream and cupped her hands in the cold, fresh mountain water and took a drink. She could tell what is going on inside the mountain by how the water tasted. "Have some. Tell me what you think."

"About what?"

"The water."

Jerry cupped his hands and drank. "Fine nose. Crisp entry. Fresh. Full bodied. Slight metallic aftertaste. A very good year."

Terrah rolled her eyes and shook her head. She got up and walked on, higher up the mountain, to the spring, the source, the heart that pumps blood through this mountain's arteries. The spring was no more than four feet in diameter. Its dark water bubbled like it was boiling; however, if you plunged your arm into it, its coldness would send shockwaves rippling through your flesh.

"Jerry, would you leave me alone for a few minutes. I must nourish that which nourishes me."

Jerry wandered twenty yards or so away and found a mossy spot to sit. He leaned his back against a tree, closed his eyes, and listened to the song of the forest. The gurgling spring provided a steady base line, the cicadas provided the melody and chorus, with one group high up in a tree calling and another group in a different tree responding, and the bird calls provided the percussion, the way the triangle does in a symphony. It calls total attention to itself, no matter how many violins are playing. None of these creatures was causing harmony: the cicadas were talking to each other and the birds to themselves. Jerry realized that he was the unifying factor, the one hearing the simultaneity of voices and turning them into a symphony and letting that symphony carry him away. He had just started drifting off, lulled to sleep by the Forest Lullaby, when Terrah called out "Jerry, where are you? Let's go!"

His head snapped to attention, but his senses took extra time to catch up. He looked around but saw no one.

"Jerry!" Terrah called again.

He joined her, and they began the descent.

The birds aren't conscious of their contribution to the whole, neither are the cicadas. It seems that I am the only one conscious of how all the parts fit together. With what responsibility does that leave me? he thought. To Terrah, he asked, "How do you suppose we can gain better understanding of our interconnectedness? How will we know we're ready for zero-point energy?"

"When we don't have to ask questions like that. Your question betrays your lack of connectedness."

"How does it do that?" Jerry frowned.

"If you were truly present to your interconnectedness, you wouldn't need to ask whether we'll gain better understanding of it. Your experience would show you, day to day, minute by minute. That's how we lived when I was a young girl. The spirits of the trees and the rocks and the corn on lived among us, and we interacted with them just as you would a sentient human being. You talk to them directly rather than talk about them like they're not there."

"People would call you crazy if you did that today."

"They can call me what they want. I know my connection, and no one can take that from me. I think it's crazy to pretend we're so superior."

"Okay, but how do we do it? What do those OWBs know that we don't know?" Jerry asked.

"That I don't know, but look at the way you treated the water—as a thing, a commodity to be analyzed. I realize that you don't know how to tell how the water is doing by its taste, just as I don't know how to look at my blood under a microscope, but they're the same—a diagnosis of the circulatory system. This mountain is me; if it gets sick, so do I because its blood becomes my blood. Water is unique among the elements because it can change form. It can go from not flowing to flowing in one direction to expanding and filling all directions as steam. Think about how you could be present to your interconnectedness if you transformed yourself from being water that flows to the lowest point to being water that expands and fills space."

"Water needs fire to turn to steam." Jerry said aloud as he thought about her challenge.

"It is easier to see interconnectedness from a mountain top. When you're in the woods, you see what is in front of you; you can't see how it relates to something 10 miles away. So let's sit on an imaginary mountain top and look at we silly human beings who are barely able to cope with differences, our own human differences, not to mention the differences between us and nonhumans. This group with black hair can barely cope with that group with blonde hair, and these people who worship a god named Yahweh can barely cope with those people who worship a god named Allah. How do you think we silly humans would react to a race that knows how to use their bodies as a laser to send pure love—love amplification by the stimulated emission of radiance? We'd want to steal that ability to use against our enemies! It's crazy. No, we're crazy. We crucified a guy who told us to love your neighbor as yourself. They must know that pure love can neutralize anything, weapons included." There was passion in her voice as she delivered this sermon to Jerry.

"How do you know all this?"

"I have some weird friends."

"You must have had contact yourself."

"I did."

"Tell me all about it. I'm fascinated."

"You be fascinated, then. You've had your own experience; you don't need to live off mine. Yours is for you. It's unique. If you knew mine, you'd start comparing, wondering why your OWBs didn't tell you such and such that my OWBs told me. You'd be all over the differences like a wolf on a deer. It's natural and human to want to compare. We want to see if our experience was 'better.' Not till you see that there is no 'better' will I tell you. There's only different."

Jerry thought she was done, but before he could speak again, Terrah continued, "We tend to think that things are either different or they're the same. However, difference and sameness coexist. We have songs and games for children to teach them to recognize differences and similarities, but we don't have games yet to teach them to see both at the same time, the yin and the yang, the light and the dark, the body and the mind. Oh there we go, that's an idea to put on the shelf to work on—a children's game."

"Actually," Jerry interrupted, "the Beatles wrote a song for adults about that."

Terrah squinted her eyes, questioning.

"Yeah, they wrote some lyrics that go something like this, and pardon my singing, "I am he as you are he as you are me and we are all together."

"Yes! Yes, that's perfect."

"Unfortunately, I think it was lost on most people, especially since we don't expect profoundness in pop culture, particularly from a band under the influence of drugs and yogis."

"Okay." Terrah looked at Jerry as if to ask, may I go on? He said nothing else, so she continued, "These states of sameness and difference are sacred. What I mean by that is, when you work through them, you have access to the divine. The sacred state of difference occurs when you recognize that you are just different—not better than or worse than, just different. That enables you to see that the meaning you gave to being different gives you access to the sacred state of sameness, in which you recognize your utter sameness with all of creation. You're just another carbon-based life form trying to survive on this planet too—albeit while being different and unique. That sacred state of sameness is your divinity, but your only access to it is through the *sacred* state of difference. So, how do you get to this sacred state of difference? First you must recognize the difference and the meaning you gave it, such as 'good' or 'bad'; for example, being a teacher is good and a lawyer bad, being employed is good and unemployed bad, being a career woman is good and a stay-at-home mom is bad, being male is good and female, well you get the idea. After you realize how you give simple differences such charged meaning, in order to get to the sacred state of sameness, you must then make amends with other beings that you judged as better or worse than yourself. You have to acknowledge that you were putting meaning where there was none."

"When would I do such a thing, make being different mean something?"

"We do it all the time. You just did it. You made my experience with the OWBs mean that it was better than yours—that's why you were 'fascinated'—and so you wanted to find out what your experience lacked compared with mine or how your experience was better. Your experience wasn't better and it didn't lack anything. It was perfect for you in the situation you were in."

"So am I supposed to then say to you, 'I'm sorry, I made my experience be less than yours'? That doesn't sound like the type of thing to apologize for," Jerry said.

"Maybe not to others, but you might want to apologize to yourself for devaluing your own experience."

"Oh, yeah, I do that a lot."

"You're not the only one. We all do it," Terrah reassured him. "Let's take a common everyday thing, for example. Say you're at work, and a coworker makes a mistake on an important project. In your head, you decide that he is stupid; you might say to yourself 'what an idiot.' You say it in a specific context relating to a very particular thing. Then almost unconsciously you generalize that judgment. His supposed 'idiocy' starts showing up everywhere—in what he wears, in his political opinions, in his choice of sports teams, and so on. How could you have missed it before? So now you start treating that person with less respect because you're convinced he's an idiot, even though you never said it to his face. And on down the road, he says something to you and, without thinking, you flat out insult him. It could go on and on. He reports you to the boss, who gives you a disciplinary warning, and all of a 'sudden' you're the victim, and life is miserable because the people at work don't respect you now. Funny how your judgment turns on you that way. If you really looked hard, you could see that it all started with you making a simple difference—that person made a mistake and you didn't—mean that you were better than him. And it got cemented when you thought it but didn't tell him that he was an idiot. You gave him an unfair trial. He might have had a good defense. The supposed mistake might have been a brilliant innovation if it had been given a fair hearing. Look at how many failures or accidents have turned out to be tremendous successes—the glue on Post-It notes; the potato chip, which was invented in a fit of pique after an unhappy diner sent back soggy French fries; Teflon; Krazy Glue; microwave ovens; and many more. Now don't misunderstand me, I'm not saying you should tell people all your judgments about them, but just think what awesome relatedness could happen if you went to that person and said, 'look, when you made that mistake, I made one too. I decided you were an idiot. I know you're not an idiot, and I apologize for thinking that about you.' You'd be amazed at how willing people are to forgive you. In that moment of apology and forgiveness, you'll experience a kind of togetherness, a connection where you both get how human you are—your sacred sameness. Kind of ironic, isn't it? When you truly are present to your humanity, you have access to your divinity. It all happens in conversation, not in your head. The thoughts and judgments occur in our heads, but the connection comes when we bridge that gap between me and you, when we're aware of our differences and our sameness."

Jerry stroked his chin as he thought. "So this kind of connectedness is not like the yogi-sitting-on-the-mountaintop-meditating type of oneness and dissolution of boundaries."

"Absolutely is and absolutely is not."

"Touché," Jerry said, pointing his finger at her like it was a fencer's foil.

"For us humans who are so trained in difference, the access to oneness is fleeting, momentary at best. The love that occurs between people when this momentary oneness happens is powerful. And your OWBs have a technology to harness that power."

"They do? How?"

"Oops, there I go again. I got so carried away I forgot where I was and got way ahead of myself. Okay Jerry, I'll spill some beans. I learned that they set up a resonance between the root and crown chakras. If you know how a laser works, the energy from the energy source bounces back and forth in something like a garnet or argon gas, and because the wavelengths are in sync, when they collide, they are amplified. Well, the body can amplify coherent electromagnetic energy, such as love, which can then be discharged through the heart chakra. It has to be pure, coherent energy. If it gets mixed with a little doubt or a smidgen of envy, the coherence is gone, doesn't work."

"Hold it, I think that's what happened to us in the barn. Can this coherent love energy be set up as a force field too?" Jerry asked.

"What happened to you? A force field? What are you talking about?"

"Didn't I mention that when we approached the vehicle, I got knocked back from a force field? Well, I did. And when I stopped being fearful, I could walk into and through it, and it felt like, like, I don't know how to describe it. Helen could do a better job than I can."

"There you go judging and comparing again."

"Achh. You got me. It happens so automatically. I never realized how judgmental I am."

"Okay, enough. How did it feel?"

He thought for a second and smirked, "It felt like a dog."

Terrah let out a chuckle, showering confetti laughter, light and sparkly, on the conversation.

"You know," Jerry explained, "that feeling of pure happiness when you come home and your old mutt is wagging his tail and jumping up like he hasn't seen you in months—that kind of unconditional love. That's what being in this force field felt like. But you should have seen what it did to Jack Mason and one of his cronies. It knocked them twenty feet back with some force, too."

"You're taking delight in their suffering. There's a judgment there of 'I'm better than you.' Be careful, Jerry. Whenever you find yourself making yourself better than another or making them wrong and you right, most likely it's trying to cover up your own feelings of not being adequate."

"You're right, again. I was totally oblivious to it."

"Be gentle on yourself, too. Careful not to redirect the judgmentalness at yourself," she said with a playful sternness.

"Okay, okay. I really am in this judgmentalness like a fish in water. So where was I?" Jerry scratched his head. They were in some dense underbrush now, so the going was slow and measured. "If these OWBs exist in a perpetually more connected state than we do, is it basically telepathic? Do they know what the others are thinking?"

"There are no others," Terrah explained. "If they are thinking it, it is likely that so-called others are doing so as well."

"Then it seems as if their individuality disappears. That might be fine for them, but what about us? How does one stay individual while being, how would you say it, united in oneness? I like my individuality, and I don't want to give it up. And if that means continuing to make judgments and be right, then I'll do it," Jerry said with playful impishness.

"This is exactly why zero-point energy is still so dangerous."

"Huh?" Jerry spun his head around. Terrah had an uncanny knack for letting a conversation wander all around, but just before it spins out of control, she nails it right back to the center, exactly where it's supposed to be.

She continued, "So long as we stay individual, unconnected, and judgmental, who's to say that we won't use you, or any marginalized minority, for our energy source—since the energy is the same everywhere, in rocks, coal, uranium, feathers, and humans. Instead of using lots of energy to electrocute criminals, we could use them as our energy supply."

"I hadn't thought of that."

"Don't spend too much effort thinking about it, Jerry. Intellectuals, blondes, old folks, even computer programmers, anybody could become the target. History has shown us many times that it can happen, and I certainly wouldn't want that again. Because zero-point energy is the common denominator of the universe, there are ways to use it responsibly, and there are ways to abuse it. That's probably why your OWB friends wanted to destroy the device—to stop the abuse."

There's that question again. It is sticking to me like a flea, biting me when I least expect it, Jerry thought. To Terrah he posed the question on the tip of his tongue at the moment. "What constitutes abuse? How do you use zero-point energy responsibly? I mean, we're in an energy crisis. Our oil reserves are about to run out, and soon after that our gas and coal supply. The multinational energy conglomerates tied up alternative energy development in the courts for so long that we won't have the capacity to meet current demand levels until 50 years from now. It is imperative that we have a viable, reliable alternative energy source."

"You don't need to play devil's advocate with me, Jerry."

"I'm curious to know how you would answer Everyman's question. It's fair, I think."

"Fair enough, except that Everyman doesn't necessarily ponder the difference between the energy that he uses and the energy that he is. Chew on that one for awhile."

They walked in silence while Terrah let Jerry digest her comment. The terrain became steeper downhill as they approached a ravine where the stream ran down the mountain. Terrah stopped and sniffed the air. Jerry wondered what she was trying to smell. He walked to a large boulder that had been carried here on the stream's back when the ice had melted long ago and sat, watched, and waited for her.

"Here we go," she said as she jumped down to the rocky stream bed below. She felt the water, for its coolness, its hardness, and its eagerness to get downstream. She listened to the sweetness it spoke to the rocks, like a xylophone singing to the trees. "How do we use zero-point energy responsibly, you ask. How do you use anything responsibly? Let's start with something innocuous, like paint. How do you use paint responsibly?"

"You put it where it's supposed to go. If it's house paint, put it on your house. If it's oil paint, paint a picture with it," Jerry answered.

"Using it as intended. That leaves little room for creativity. Jackson Pollock didn't use paint as it was intended, and in doing so he took painting to a whole new level."

"Yeah, I get the analogy, but who are we to know what the intended function of zero-point energy is?"

"Indeed, who are we? Or more to the point, who are *you* to know such a thing? Perhaps that is your gift, Jerry."

Jerry froze as if he ran into a wall. There was that knack of hers to lead you down the primrose path and then, wham! drop a truth-bomb on you. He stood there immobilized while the shock wore off. "The first time I visited you, you told me that I'd probably want to hide my gift. If that is indeed my gift, I want to hide *from* it."

"Hide it from others, hide it from yourself; either way you're not honoring who you are. It takes someone who has integrity and responsibility to give such a gift to humanity. If the universe thinks that highly of you, why don't you think that highly of yourself?"

"But how do I know that's…"

"You know it in here," she touched her heart, "not up here," she touched her head. "Wrap your heart around the question of purpose. Stop siccing your mind on it."

These were not the kind of words that Jerry was used to hearing. They were too soft. They lacked the firmness and definition that scientific words have. When you try to grab them and wring the meaning from them, they squished through your fingers. "How do I do that, wrap my heart around it?" Jerry asked.

"Your mind is still trying to be king. Turn it off and move your awareness to how you feel. What is your true purpose? You know it, in here," she said tapping his chest.

Jerry thought about it, and while thinking realized that he was still thinking rather than feeling. He shut his eyes, and immediately the memory of his experience of having his hand merge with the bed sheet returned. He brought back little details, like the pattern on the sheet itself. It had a picture of the universe printed on it, with swirling galaxies and colorful supernovas. There was a big red arrow pointing at a dot in one of the arms of one of the galaxies in the Milky Way. Next to that arrow was a sign saying, "You Are Here." Jerry had wanted to be a space traveler back then, an explorer of unknown worlds.

After re-experiencing the memory, he then looked at it as if watching a movie or reviewing a dream. He saw his little 10-year-old hand merging with the fabric of the universe. *Aha! That's what zero-point energy is—the fabric of the universe. I'm not separate from it, no different than it.* The meaning of the experience that shaped the direction of his life finally crystallized clearly. His eyes bolted open, and he told Terrah about his vision and then gave her a big hug.

"It was no coincidence that you ended up at the Mason Ranch," she told him. "Now remember, be careful."

They headed back into the woods to complete the journey home. Jerry felt the excitement of his realization being pushed aside by a loud and intrusive thought: *Now what?*

Chapter 14

When Helen walked into the office Monday morning, she received a standing ovation. The room with the reporters' cubicles was decorated with little green men and a life-size blow-up doll of the character from the movie *Alien*. There had been a Frisbee-decorating contest to see whose looked the most like the real thing. Helen was to judge that contest. When she lied and told them that she hadn't actually seen it, there was great disappointment and tossing of Frisbees. Several of the guys had played Ultimate Frisbee and were good shots, throwing the Frisbee so that it hovered over someone's cake and then dropped on it.

When the festivities were over, the Editor called her into his office. He was a short man who had grown plump from sitting at his desk for 12 hours a day for over 20 years. When he looked over his reading glasses, he seemed a kindly old man. But like the gentle ocean breeze, he could turn typhoon. "How did you like your first real assignment?" he asked, motioning her to have a seat.

Helen took the stack of papers off the chair in front of his desk and put them on the floor.

"I'll take them," he said, standing up and reaching out.

Helen noticed that the top one was a government document, "Summary Findings of Investigations into Unidentified Flying Objects, 1943-2000" from the Department of Defense. "Can I borrow that?" she asked, handing it to him.

"Oh that. Um, not right now. Not for this article. Keep this one to the facts, no history. Where it was, who saw it, what did it look like, that sort of thing."

"I don't suppose you want me to reveal what the OWBs told me."

He stopped mid-movement, frozen, contemplating what to say next, staring at her.

"You saw them?"

"Yes."

"But you said…" he pointed out to the office space where the party just happened.

"I know. I lied. Those guys can be brutal."

He guided his corpulence into his chair as carefully as a signal man guiding a just-landed jet to the gate. His eyes had that faraway look when you're shuffling twenty thoughts at once and trying to pick the right one to win your hand.

"Miss Donellyn, you are a fortunate young woman," he began. "I shouldn't have been so foolish as to send you on that assignment alone. But I'm glad you're back and that you didn't have any, um, unfortunate incidents with the OWBs?" he asked, peering over his glasses. "No loss of time? No unexplainable scars?"

"No, and I wasn't so foolish as to go alone. I took my boyfriend with me."

"Good, good. I knew you had good sense." His head bobbed up and down as if on a spring. "I should very much like to hear about what they had to say, but not now and not here. I have a certain curiosity about such things." He tilted his head toward the government document. "You have a story to write, quickly, I might add. Remember, just the facts and a few eyewitness accounts—not yours—lights in the sky, that sort of thing. Let me ask just one little thing before you get started. A juicy bit. Although you might not know."

"What?!" She hated when he stalled like that.

"They're so much more advanced than us, you know. It boggles the mind that they crash at all. Their technology is so far superior…"

She cut him off. "It didn't crash, it was shot down."

"Oh my heavens."

"It was messing with something called a zero-point energy machine. I don't know. Jerry, my friend, overheard the guys who shot it down talking about it. There's obviously something going on there," she said, "something big. Jack Mason, the guy who had it shot down, has an energy company, and I think it might be under the radar."

As she spoke, the Editor's eyes lit up, like he was counting hundred-dollar bills. In his currency, he was—at least two more stories that he could see right here.

"What is this zero-point energy? How does it work?"

"I don't know. Jerry seems to know. I could ask him."

"Good, that's your next assignment. Go. You have lots to do."

◆   ◆   ◆

Helen's Journal

You'd think that with all the information on OWBs that has been released into the public domain since the government declassified it I could find something on the vehicle that crashed on the Mason Ranch. I searched the internet; I searched government documents; I put in Requests for Information to the Air Force, Army, and even the National Weather Service, hoping that one of them would at least have it on radar. Nada. It's as if it never happened. I'm beginning to feel like I hallucinated the whole thing.

While searching, however, I found out all sorts of other tidbits that I suppose I could turn into a story. For instance, there are 57 known species from other worlds who have visited here at some point. 57! Some were involved with the government as far back as 1954! We have traded human lives for weapons technology. The government was spending gazillions of dollars on the search for intelligent life in the universe, for evidence of life on Mars, and for evidence of the seeds of life in Halley's comet when other life forms were landing right here the whole time. How gullible people were back then. "No, UFOs don't exist," said the government to people who saw them in their back yards, over Mexico City, even in Washington, DC, "but there might be some bacteria out there that are alive!"

I want so badly to tell someone about it, but it's almost as if Mason has me in his grips and his intention to make all evidence of it disappear has affected me. I shouldn't let it affect me. I should say something to someone, my boss for instance. He's obviously interested. But I'm afraid someone will find out and think I'm nuts. I don't want to risk my reputation, the possibility of being a serious journalist.

Despite the widespread acceptance of the fact that OWBs are real, not many people have actually seen one up close and personal, let alone have them communicate with you. Every day, I still see those images in my head—of taking the lit match from the baby, of the guy cutting off his arm to cook a hot dog, of the multitude of interpretations of a single event. They're such powerful images, I can't let go of them. But what can I do with them? They told us to warn people. How? Warn them about what? Not to use zero-point energy?

◆   ◆   ◆

Mystery Crash Near Springfield

By Helen Donellyn

Springfield—At approximately 11 pm, many residents of Springfield noticed a bright light hanging in the western sky. "I didn't know what it was, because it just sat there," said local resident May Binchey. It was so bright that it woke people up and brought them out into the streets to gawk and hypothesize. Some thought it was a UFO; others thought it was another one of the military's experimental planes. "Sometimes we see new military aircraft flying around here. There's a base south a piece. But I don't think it was one of theirs. It just hung there. It wasn't flying," said Bob Hale, an ex-Air Force officer. He was referring to the Peacefield Navy Station, which is home to some of the Navy's most advanced aircraft. Consensus agreed with Mr. Hale—this was no regular aircraft, as it was silent and much brighter than anything these residents had ever seen.

About 15 minutes after it was first spotted, there was a loud noise, "like a pipe bomb going off" as one resident put it, and then the light crashed to the ground and went out. That was enough for most residents to head back to bed; however, the word was out: a strange airship had crashed in a remote area near Springfield. The sleepy town rapidly filled up with professional UFO hunters and the just plain curious.

There were no reports of alien beings sighted in the vicinity of the crash. In fact, no ship nor any debris has been found. Local law enforcement officials declined to comment on whether they were investigating this incident.

Chapter 15

"Your performance has been slipping, Jerry. This month you've only written 1500 lines of code. Your average for the past year was over 2000 per month."

Jerry's boss was an anomaly. He looked like he should have been a linebacker for a professional football team. He worked out daily and probably took illegal steroids. He had muscles. Not many people in the computer programming field had muscles—either skinny and bony or obese were the norms. Some ate coffee and cigarettes whereas others ate anything else. His physical presence alone was intimidating, regardless of what words came out of his mouth.

"I see." Jerry lowered his eyes and stared at the folds in the fabric of his chinos.

Jerry's boss looked out the window as he spoke to Jerry. "If there's a problem with the concept, take it to Marketing and rework it with them and the customer. But if it's something personal, get it out of here. Leave that at home. When you're here, we get all of you. That's what we're paying you for. Anything else?"

"No, sir. I'll get my numbers back up."

"Good. Ask Sheryl to come in here on your way out, if you would."

"Yes, sir." Sheryl was on the phone, so he tapped on her desk and pointed at the boss's office. Sheryl hung up immediately and sprung out of her chair. Jerry walked down the corridor to his office in a daze. *It's all about numbers to them. Are all companies so devoid of compassion? Doesn't he care that my life was in danger? Oh yeah, I didn't tell anybody.*

Jerry slumped back into the chair in front of his monitor. Thoughts of quitting flitted through his mind but were immediately censored. Unable to concentrate, he watched the mesmerizing motion of his screen saver, a fractal-generating program, and thought about the conversation with Terrah about his purpose, his gift. The shapes on the screen saver arose are grew and repeated themselves over and over but never were exactly the same. *What could I do in the area of zero-point energy? It's been so long since I've done any physics. I probably couldn't get a job in that area, except maybe as a low-level technician. That might be better than this. Anything might be better than this.* The question still haunted him: how would one use zero-point energy ethically and properly? He didn't feel the clunk when his head hit the keyboard.

On the other side of the cubicle partition, Rob heard the thud and sent Jerry an instant message, "Everything okay over there, buddy?" When Jerry didn't reply, Rob walked over to Jerry's desk to find his head typing an endless string of jjjjjjjjjjjjjjjjjjjjjjs.

"Hey, Jerry, wake up, pal."

Jerry didn't stir.

Rob shook his shoulder. The line of js turned to lllllllllllllllllllllllllls. Jerry still didn't wake up. Rob lifted his head off the keyboard and slapped his cheeks, as if trying to wake him from a hangover. When he lifted Jerry's eyelids and his pupils didn't respond, Rob hoisted Jerry up in a fireman's carry and took him to the corporate medical office.

"Faint pulse, shallow breathing, no pupil response, blood pressure 80 over 50," the doctor read off his signs. "Before we do anything drastic, let's try some old-fashioned measures. Nurse, get some smelling salts."

They had no effect. "I'd really like to use the paddles on him, but if that doesn't work, I don't have the facilities here to revive him," the doctor explained to Rob. "I'm going to have him transported to the hospital."

"I'll break the news to the boss. Thanks, doc, for all your help," Rob said.

"Do you know who the next of kin are?" the doctor called out to Rob. "Let me know, so I can inform them of the situation."

"Sure thing."

The ambulance rushed Jerry to the nearest hospital, St. Althea's. The ER physician read his chart as he was hauled off the bus and scratched his head. "Coma?" he said to the ambulance driver.

"Don't know doc, I just drive."

"Get me full bloods, an EEG, and an MRI, stat."

◆   ◆   ◆

Helen rushed to the hospital as soon as Rob called her. She was in his room when the doctor came in with the test results.

"Good afternoon, Mrs. Fowss, I'm Milton Stanley. It looks your husband here has a case of syncope."

"Thank you, Dr. Stanley. I'm Helen Donellyn. There is no Mrs. Fowss. What is syncope?"

"I'm terribly sorry. No next of kin?"

"Not that I know of. We were friends."

"I see. Anyhow, syncope is a temporary loss of consciousness and postural tone. It's relatively common, especially in people with low blood pressure."

"His coworker told me that he passed out at his desk. What is going on? Why does he keep passing out?" Helen asked.

"He's done this before?" Dr. Stanley asked with keen interest.

"Yes, just last week."

Dr. Stanley jotted notes down on his chart. "And what happened then?"

"Well, he was getting ready to change my tire. I thought he just fell asleep under the car, because it was late at night and we had been driving all day. When I couldn't wake him, I panicked. I thought he had carbon monoxide poisoning or something, from being under the car. I took him to a house. And, um, eventually he came to."

"He left the car running while he was under it changing a tire!?"

"Oh, no. It was off," Helen reassured him.

"It probably was not carbon monoxide poisoning then. Did he wake up naturally, or did you use some method of waking him?"

"I think someone gave him CPR and mouth-to-mouth, but I don't remember exactly."

"How long was he out then?"

"Maybe 15 minutes."

"Hmmm." Dr. Stanley offered no further information. "Thank you, Helen, was it? Please register with the nurse's station so that we can call you as soon as we know something or as soon as something happens." He turned to leave the room.

"Hold it. How long will he have to be here?" Helen asked.

"I can't say for sure. He's sedated right now from the MRI. When he wakes up, we'll have to see whether his vitals remain normal. We'll start by giving him a high-sodium diet to get his blood pressure up."

"Thanks." Helen was alarmed and disgusted at the same time. *Is this place in the dark ages? A high-sodium diet might help this for the short term, but it could cause worse problems in the long term.* She shook her head.

After the doctor left, Helen went to Jerry's bedside and took his hand. "What is going on, Jerry? Why didn't you tell me this about you? Is this a disease? What's going on?"

He lay there quietly, while the machines attached to him beeped and hummed rhythmically. Helen stroked his head, then sat in the chair next to the bed and rested her head against her hand. The machines lulled her to sleep.

When she awoke, someone else was in the room with her, another doctor, judging from his scrubs. He was feeling around Jerry's gut. He didn't seem to notice her. Occasionally he would take Jerry's wrist and hold it up, like he was feeling his pulse. He shut his eyes, and held down different fingers, as if he was playing Jerry's wrist like a violin. Then he put it down and put his fingers on other places, like Jerry's face, arms, and legs, murmuring to himself. He opened Jerry's mouth and looked at his tongue on both sides. He held his hands over certain places on Jerry's body, not touching it, and closed his eyes. Every few minutes he'd move to a different spot. He massaged the bottoms of Jerry's feet, blew onto them, then came over to Helen. He bowed slightly to her. "I Dr. Wu. Who you?"

"I'm Helen Donellyn, a friend," she said extending her hand.

Dr. Wu nodded but didn't shake it.

"What were you doing to Jerry?" Helen asked.

"Traditional Chinese Medicine. Listen to body," he said holding up his own wrist, as he had done to Jerry's.

"What did you hear?"

"Ohh, traveling shen."

"What does that mean?"

"Patient not sick. Patient okay."

"What do you mean he's okay? He's unconscious."

Dr. Wu held his hand up to cut her off. "When he ready, he come back. Be patient." He grinned, pleased with the little joke he just made in a language that was not his first. "Patient okay," he kept repeating as he walked out of the room backwards, bowing the whole time.

Helen rubbed her temples, then looked at her watch. 1:30 AM. She had been asleep in that chair for almost four hours. No wonder her back was so stiff. *Traveling shen. What the hell is that?* she wondered. She pulled out her new Personal Secretary with Universal Roaming capabilities and typed "traveling shen" into the search engine. Many hits came for shen, which, she learned, is the Traditional Chinese Medical term for a type of life force, the one that is responsible for consciousness and mental abilities. It is often translated as "spirit" or "soul," but so are jing and qi, which are different forms of life force, so the English words don't adequately capture the differences in meaning. Shen resides in the heart/mind, and it manifests in various ways, including personality, awareness of self, and sensory perception. *Yup, that's what was missing at the moment.* Unlike the western understanding, in which there's one spirit or soul, and if that's gone, you're dead, the three treasures of Chinese Medicine worked together but can also work separately. So while Jerry's shen is 'traveling' the jing is the form of the life force that was keeping his body alive.

Dr. Wu came back in carrying a box of acupuncture needles. He bowed to his patient in that quick dipping way. He worked quickly, rechecking the points and inserting needles in various parts of his body.

"If he's not sick, why are you treating him?"

Dr. Wu kept working on Jerry. When he was done, he came over to Helen and bowed to her. "Patient need to be called back. Gone to lunch too long." He chuckled again at his own joke.

"Where is he?"

Dr. Wu inhaled deeply. How to explain it? "Okay, you me here," he said motioning around the room and holding out his left hand, palm up. With his right hand he pointed at his left hand. "Here." He put his right hand about six inches above his left. "Death here," he said, moving his right hand. Patient not here (moving his left hand) and not here (moving his right hand). Patient on vacation in between."

"On vacation?"

Nodding vigorously with his whole upper body, he said, "Yes, yes, on vacation. Escape life, escape death. Deep meditation. Special people go vacation."

Behind them, Jerry moved. Dr. Wu jumped to his side and felt the pulses in his wrist. Jerry's breathing deepened.

"Vacation over. Coming home." Dr. Wu pulled out some of the needles and put them in a red biohazard waste container. He put his fingers on three spots on Jerry's forehead and made a sucking sound. Jerry opened his eyes. Dr. Wu pulled out the remaining needles. Helen was at his other side. Wu motioned to her not to speak and left, bowing at the door.

Helen mouthed "Thank you" to Dr. Wu as he left. She held his hand as he got oriented and realized that he was in the hospital.

"Water," he whispered.

Helen got some water and propped his back up so he could drink it. He lay back down and fell asleep. She could tell it was sleep from the rapid eye movements and his eventual snoring, so she sat back in the chair and fell asleep herself.

Dr. Stanley came in the next morning, early. He checked the chart before he checked on Jerry. "Well, Mr. Fowss, I see that Dr. Wu treated you last night and that you're ready to be released."

"Good," Jerry replied, "but why am I here to begin with?"

"Nothing serious. You just passed out at work and were rushed here by ambulance. Turns out you have syncope. Nothing serious, but your regular doctor might want to give you something to keep your blood pressure up a bit. In the meantime, eat all the salty snacks you want. I never thought I'd see the day when I had to tell a patient that! The nurse will have some paperwork for you to fill out. Thank you for visiting St. Althea's. We hope you choose us again next time you need skilled medical care." And out the door he went.

"Who was he, the walking advertising department?" Jerry asked Helen.

"No, your doctor."

"I hope he didn't cut anything open."

"No, he was a formality. Dr. Wu was the one who pulled you back."

"Pulled me back from where?"

"From that space between life and death." Then she turned to him and asked in earnest, "What was it like Jerry, wherever you were for the past 16 hours?"

"I don't know. I have no memory past staring at my screen saver, thinking about work, and wishing I didn't have to be there anymore."

Chapter 16

"…This is Jerry. Please leave a message."

"Jerry, help! I've been researching zero-point energy for my next story, and I am getting nowhere. These text books are too complicated for me. I don't understand them. They have too many equations and not enough words. I need your help. Can you come over for dinner tomorrow? Please? Thanks, hon. Bye."

◆   ◆   ◆

Jerry arrived at Helen's house with a dozen pink roses and a bottle of chardonnay.

"I hope you're hungry, because we're eating right away," Helen kissed him then ran back to the kitchen. Jerry followed her to get a corkscrew.

She found a vase, and he arranged the flowers in it. As she sautéed the scallops, Helen noticed how Jerry took the time to arrange them, even inserting the delicate white baby's breath into the center of the arrangement. Another reason to keep him around. Despite his artistry, Jerry seemed to have something heavy on his mind. His attention was turned inward and so he was uncharacteristically quiet.

"What's on your mind?" she asked.

"Oh, you can tell, huh?"

"Yes, Jerry. There's something bothering you."

He fidgeted while he considered which approach to use to tell her. "I saw Terrah the other day, and she warned me about how dangerous Mason and his gang are. We need to be careful."

Helen balked. "Do you think they will come after us?" she asked, while serving the scallops and linguine in a garlic-butter sauce.

"After all, we know that they have a zero-point energy device there. We're a wild card in their poker game, and they know that they can't afford that. We could bring down their whole operation, if we wanted to," Jerry said.

"But they don't know that we know that. They only know that we know about the OWB ship."

"That's enough for them to still come after us. They don't want that information out either because it might lead to discovery of the ZPE activity."

"Jerry, I don't mean to rain on your paranoia, but I can't think about that right now. I have a deadline, and I'll be in more immediate danger from my boss if I don't get this story done. If they haven't done it yet, they probably won't. That's my hope anyway."

"Well, we should be careful anyway. They're dangerous."

"Sure, but I don't know what we can do about it. If they're that dangerous I doubt I'd be able to outsmart them. You might be able to, but not me." Her voice had a tone of finality, like a teacher who doesn't want to answer any more questions.

"Okay, so what do you want to know about zero-point energy?" Jerry filled their glasses with the chardonnay he had brought.

"First of all, what is it?"

"Basically the idea behind zero-point energy is that there is always energy available from atomic particles because they never come completely to rest, even at a temperature of absolute zero, which is when they stop moving; that is, there's energy even when there shouldn't be any. So the idea is to tap into that energy. Hence, this energy is everywhere, only we can't see it because it is the same everywhere—whether inside our bodies, outside our bodies, in air, or in rocks. We perceive differences, and with there being no differences, we don't perceive it."

"So how do we know it's there?" Helen asked.

"It began as a theoretical prediction. Now they have been able to measure it, miniscule amounts of it anyway." Jerry sounded proud, as if he had done it himself.

"Well Mason and those guys must have figured out how to get a lot of it, because they seem like the type who are in it for the money, not the scientific kudos. And if those idiots could do it, why hasn't it been done before?"

Helen certainly has her own brand of logic, Jerry thought. "Those idiots stole the technology, remember?"

"Oh yeah. But if it's already known among physicists, why couldn't they make the same kind of device?"

"Well, at first physicists didn't really believe that there could be much energy produced by these phenomena, so they dismissed it, subtracted it out of the equations. Then a few tried to produce some devices, and they were shown to be frauds, so that turned most reputable physicists away from the field. However, when some people eventually did make some devices that worked, weird things started happening to them. Their houses burned down, their devices and supplies for making them were stolen, they got cancer—it became very dangerous to be a zero-point energy physicist. It wasn't the energy itself that was dangerous, but some folks—powerful folks—were threatened by it."

"Okay, I get the drift. How dare you have zero-point energy when the rest of us still have to rely on oil or gas."

"Worse than that," Jerry added. "Rather, the issue is: how dare you destroy the world's economy and our wealth by enabling people not to be dependent on fossil fuels. Oil and coffee are what fuel the world economy, believe it or not. The oil companies certainly don't want every person to be able to generate their own energy forever. One country certainly wouldn't want another country not to depend on them for fuel. There are many people with a stake in keeping this technology hidden from the rest of us. Rather, a few very rich, powerful people. The irony of that is beautiful." Jerry chuckled as he realized, "The very people who were destroying the zero-point technology are the ones who absolutely should not have it anyway. They were doing us all a favor by keeping it from themselves. If they would have sweet talked those designs and devices from their inventors, we probably wouldn't be here right now. They could have made toast of us all."

"As for understanding how it works, I don't even know where to start asking questions," Helen said.

"Why don't you tell me what you have found out so far."

"Let's see." She twirled her fork in her linguine. "Zero-point energy has something to do with quantum physics, but it's not part of mainstream quantum physics yet. It's still a fringe area. There are a lot of skeptics." She flipped through her file on her Personal Secretary where she kept all her research notes. "Oh, here's something else. Zero-point energy is a sea of energy around us, like the water a fish swims in."

"Well, it's more than that," Jerry interrupted. "It's not just outside of you. You yourself are part of that sea of energy. Just as we stand on the shore and look at everything in the water, including the fish and the plants and stuff, as 'the sea,' now imagine someone standing in space and looking at the universe as if it were the sea. Everything in it, including you and me, is that 'sea of energy.' It's everything, not just your physical body but probably even your thoughts, considering that they consist of energy pulses in your neurons and synapses. It's a perspective that requires you to be able to be two places at once, both the viewer and the viewed, the one looking at the sea and one in the sea."

"Both subject and object. So if it is everywhere, how do we know it's there?"

"That's an excellent question," Jerry said taking a sip of wine.

Helen straightened up, smiled, looking pleased with herself.

"We know when energy is flowing because we can measure a differential, a difference between here and there or between time A and time B. With zero-point energy it's rather difficult because it is so omnipresent, it's hard to get a differential. But a man named Casimir managed to do it."

"Oh yeah, I saw his name. Helen flipped through her notes. He did an experiment with two metal plates, or something? I didn't get it."

"Not quite. He predicted the presence of a force produced by quantum particles popping in and out of existence, but other people showed the presence of that force between the two plates that were really close to each other, like a micron apart."

"Is that how zero-point energy was discovered?"

"Not quite," Jerry corrected. "Theoretical physics works backwards compared with most science. First you derive the equations, then you look to the 'real world' to see if it corresponds with what you predicted in the equations. So this energy was first 'discovered' in the equations."

"Why do they do it that way?" Helen asked.

"Working in the mathematical world of equations lets you see more, so to speak. Just as we metaphorically jumped out of the universe in order to look at it in its totality, it is a technique that can be used to explain phenomena that have been unexplained. In math, you can work from a higher dimension. This is what happened, for example, when the shift was made from the belief that 'the world is flat' to 'the world is round.' By adding a third dimension, roundness, ships no longer fell off the edge of the world, they got smaller and disappeared because of the curvature of the surface of the earth. That third dimension, a round earth, explained the observations more completely than belief in a two-dimensional flat earth could."

"Okay, I get that, but just barely. I feel like I have to go back and take Physics 101 and then get a PhD in order to understand this stuff." The exasperation in her voice was apparent.

"Did your editor give you a slant for your article? That might help you focus your research."

"No. He has no clue. He didn't know what zero-point energy was, so he sent me to find out for him. He's just lazy," Helen complained.

"I think he chose the perfect person for the job."

"But I'm not a scientist."

"True, and that's good because the only way to make this intelligible is to turn it into poetry."

"My editor wants facts, not poetry!" Her exasperation returned.

"The way people can understand it, however, is through metaphor. You can't talk about subatomic particles in your story, but you can describe what it's like in other terms."

"Like how?" she challenged.

Jerry straightened in his chair, looked into an empty corner of the dining room, scrunched his eyebrows and scratched his nose. "Let's look at the idea of a boundary. What is a boundary? Do they exist for real?"

Helen nodded, as she had a mouthful of linguine.

"Yes, there are boundaries, but they might not look the way we think they look. We think we see a clear line of demarcation between, say, this wine glass and the surrounding air, but if you look more and more microscopically, first the boundaries that seemed so crisp become more jagged; the glass looks more like Swiss cheese than smooth. It's a wonder it even holds the wine inside. When you get to the atomic level, there are just electrons and protons and neutrons and lots of space in-between. Where does an atom of the air begin and an atom of the glass begin? They don't line up nice and neatly. Then even below that, at the quantum level, there are subatomic particles and waves popping in and out of existence so quickly that it creates an indistinct foaminess."

Helen looked confused, so Jerry clarified.

"When you stand on the beach looking at flat seas, the boundary between water and air seems fairly crisp. But when the waves crash against the rocks, the foamy water doesn't look exactly like we think the boundary between air and water usually looks; its color isn't blue, it's white, its form is different—it's broken up into drops, not smooth flowing water any more. Well, that was a crude analogy, but this sort of thing is happening at a subatomic level. It's occurring everywhere, even in the empty space inside of atoms. Because those particles are constantly popping into and out of existence, they give off energy and so there is energy for the gathering everywhere. It has been assumed that the amount of energy that is released is negligible, which is why some physicists dismiss the attempts at harnessing it. Think further of how foam is. The foam on the top of a pint of Guinness takes up more space than flat beer, right? Same thing applies to the quantum foam. It has a kind of springiness to it, a kind of expansive quality which forces empty space apart. So this quantum foam that's everywhere just might be what is causing the universe to expand."

"Okay, but what does this foaminess have to do with zero-point energy?" Helen asked.

"Well, what happens at the subatomic level is the foundation for everything up the ladder. It's not a separate world, it just behaves differently than things that are bigger, like the atomic, molecular, microscopic, macroscopic, and galactic levels. It applies to everything! The quantum vacuum is becoming the common denominator in physics by being used to explain all kinds of effects from gravitation to inertia to potential space travel. Zero-point energy might be the rock-bottom stuff of the universe—well, as far as we know right now. Who knows what's on the other side of it. It's like the point of an ice-cream cone. The whole cone, which is our world, rises up from it. Maybe there's an inverse cone on the other side of ZPE." Although Jerry hadn't talked about such things in years and so his knowledge base was a bit out of date, he thoroughly enjoyed this exchange. It felt good to imagine again, to speculate on what might be, to talk about things that could make a difference in the world.

"If ZPE is so all-pervasive, then why don't we know about it?" Helen asked.

"First, it's like I said earlier. You have to be able to be both the viewer and the viewed. That's not easy. Then you have to be able to measure a differential in order to detect it. We simply didn't have the technology until recently. Second, if you think you have a hard time understanding it, think of your average Joe who dropped out of high school. What does he want to know about it for? If it doesn't enhance his ability to watch football and drink beer then it doesn't matter. The media cater to the lowest common denominator, so they don't touch it. By writing this article, you are a gem among rocks.

Helen smiled at the compliment but pushed on with her questions. "So how might we be able to make enough?"

"It's like making glass out of sand. You can't make anything useful if you are fusing only a few grains together. You need a pile of it, and we just haven't figured out the process for scooping up piles of it. Furthermore, science has gone underground with it. As with any new idea—although this one isn't terribly new—there's the camp that believes and the camp that doesn't. Usually the ones in the camp that doesn't believe are the ones in power. They say 'show me.' So you show them, but because they haven't opened their minds to it at the theoretical level, they won't believe what they see with their own eyes. They think you're pulling the wool over their eyes, doing some sleight of hand because their beliefs don't allow for your experimental results to happen. So then they set out to discredit you because you are a threat to them and their sources of money."

"It always boils down to money, doesn't it?" Helen interjected.

"As with anything that is potentially as earth-shaking as this kind of energy, there are people looking to prevent it from being used. It has become common lore that many of the inventors who developed zero-point-energy devices died mysterious deaths. Those who took it to their local newspapers and TV stations had bad things happen to them shortly after they gained some publicity. So the inventors themselves are in hiding. That's why our friend Mason had it so well hidden and had people paid off to keep it secret."

"I hope this article doesn't lead him right to me." Helen got very worried. "I hadn't thought about what fallout to expect from it."

"You haven't asked twenty questions yet. Are we still playing that game? Any more questions, Ms. Reporter?"

"Jerry," she got deadly serious now, "what do you think was really going on at Mason's ranch?"

"Sorry, Helen," he finished off the wine in his glass, "I stick to physical theories. I don't do conspiracy theories." There was an edge to his voice that hadn't been there all evening.

Helen read the discomfort in his body language and didn't ask any more questions. Instead, she digested all the information that Jerry had just given her and scribbled some notes into her Personal Secretary.

Jerry stewed in some emotions that were still indistinguishable. All this talk about a topic so near to and yet distant from Jerry's heart gave him a kind of spiritually upset stomach. He just didn't feel right inside. As soon as he finished talking, he wiped his mouth, folded his napkin, and announced that he had to leave.

"But Jerry, I had a special dessert planned," she said, winking.

In a previous time, he would have welcomed the come-on, but the temperature of his feet had decreased precipitously. Talking about zero-point energy shifted something inside him. Old almost-dead embers in his heart were glowing again, making it beat strongly again with the passion and corresponding discomfort of having a cause. That flickering drive clashed with his timid choices of late, his passive way of being. The message from the OWBs about approaching ZPE with love, reverence, and caution was not found in the cavalier attitude of the scientists who developed and refined it. Their approach was all wrong. He wanted to take up physics again, investigate zero-point energy, but what was the right approach?

"Thanks, but I...um...have to go." He grabbed his jacket and dashed for the door. When he got into his car, he sat there and pounded his forehead on the steering wheel. *What am I doing?*

Chapter 17

Jerry woke up at 5:45, 15 minutes before the alarm, and didn't remember where he was because the dream was so vivid. Jerry rarely recalled dreams, and so only fragments of it came back to him. He was at a place that seemed like an amusement park. There was a clown who looked like Albert Einstein sticking his tongue out. He went on a "ride" which spun him around through a coil in a donut shape. It spun him in circles in all three directions, making him dizzy and nauseous. Perhaps, he speculated, this dream was showing him how disconcerting life had been lately. It was uncomfortable, like something was missing, except that he couldn't pinpoint what it might be. *I panicked at Helen's house last night. I don't even know why. I have to call her and apologize today, but what do I say?* And he could no longer tolerate the routine of going to work every day. Writing code that routes employee pay to their various banks and retirement accounts seemed pointless compared with finding ethical ways to use of zero-point energy. The expansiveness of the universe that the OWBs had shown him had not trickled down into his everyday existence. Instead his every-day world seemed to be self-destructing, falling apart.

While he prepared a bowl of cereal, the door bell rang. *No one visits at this hour. Maybe Helen came to chew me out.* He opened the door to find a young man with longish blonde hair carrying books.

"Hey Jerry! Good to see you again. How have you been?"

"Do I know you?" Jerry wasn't quite awake yet, and might have had too much wine the night before or too long a ride in the dream-world amusement park.

"Sure do. Do you mind if I crash here for a couple days or weeks?" said the young man as he picked up his suitcase and started to walk into the house. Jerry stood in the doorway, blocking him.

"Are you sure I know you?" Jerry was still baffled.

"Hey man, I knew your name, right? I'll give you a clue: After you," he said in falsetto with a sweeping bow, as the gophers in the cartoon used to do.

"Tom! So good to see you." They embraced like old friends. "Hey, sorry I didn't recognize you. I wasn't expecting to ever see you again. The hair, or something, it's different. And I am definitely not awake yet," he said massaging his beard stubble.

Tom had a way of weaving himself into people's lives when they needed the unexpected.

"Yeah. I hear you had an adventure lately," Tom said as he put his suitcase in the living room.

"It was nothing." *How in the world does he know?* "Come on in, I was just cooking breakfast. I hope you like scrambled eggs."

Jerry had dumped the bowl of cereal back into the box and pulled out two eggs each. He was searching for the frying pan when Tom joined him in the kitchen.

"What brings you back to this godforsaken town?" Jerry asked him.

"Work."

"Washing windows?" Jerry turned a skeptical eye toward him while whisking the eggs.

"That's just a way to meet people, like you. That's not my real work."

"So what do you *really* do?"

"That's what I came to talk to you about."

Jerry looked puzzled. *What would he need to talk to me for?*

"It's hard to say, exactly, what I do. It might be more accurate to talk about it in terms of who I am for people," Tom answered.

Jerry looked up from whisking the eggs and raised a skeptical eyebrow, "You're an enigma, that's what you are."

"I suppose so." He smiled a self-satisfied smile. "I don't try to be mysterious. It just turns out that way."

"So how do you try to be?"

"Like a T cell in the social immune system." Tom replied.

"T for Tom. What do T cells do? And what's a social immune system?"

"T cells help the physical body heal. Society, like individuals, has its own ills. Sometimes a whole culture can be depressed or have a collective heart attack, figuratively speaking, of course. I like to think that I help the body of humanity heal," Tom answered.

"That sounds like a tall order. How do you do that?"

"I don't do it all by myself. There are lots of us who have taken on targeting something specific, via local intervention. What I do depends on what's needed. Some people need a kick in the pants, others need to see what's missing."

"What is it for me?" Jerry asked, cringing slightly, almost imperceptibly.

Tom took Jerry's wrist as if taking his pulse, pretended to listen, and said, "Ja, fur you, all of ze above. Und zumzing else—levity."

"Thank you Herr Dr. Freud," Jerry said as he stirred the eggs. "I didn't realize I had something missing in my life."

Tom laughed loudly. "Are you sure about that? If I had a magic wand and could dissolve the lie that nothing is wrong in my life, what would we find?"

Jerry tilted his chin to the left and stared at Tom, unsure of how to answer the question. "I can't say anything is missing. I have a job, a house, a girlfriend, I think." *Maybe not any more, after I ran out so quickly last night.*

"Great, so your life is totally joyful?"

Jerry shook his head. "No, I wouldn't say that, but now that you're here, definitely nothing is missing," Jerry said, thinking he was catching on to Tom's game. "If not joy, you certainly bring puzzlement to my life." Jerry contemplated asking him how he managed to send a postcard from so far away and have it arrive the same day, but Tom pushed on.

"I guess it's hard to see what's missing if it's not there. Our perceptual system is tuned to perceive what's there and whether it's dangerous, not what's not there. So you have to try to look in the gaps, the spaces in between, to see what's missing."

"How?" Jerry asked.

"Hmmm. Let me think."

"Can you pour some coffee while you think? Breakfast is ready," Jerry announced.

Tom poured freshly brewed coffee into two mugs, the pungent odor nourishing his thoughts. "Every one of us, at some point, creates a void in his life, mostly in reaction to a great disappointment. For some, it's the loss of a friend, family member, or a true love. For others it's from being pushed into a career that they didn't want. For me it was recovering from the failure of dropping out of med school, disappointing my parents, then finding something I was better suited for."

"How do you create that? Those things just happen; they're not the kind of thing you go looking for in life."

"True," Tom answered. "You create the void because your survival mechanism gets activated. Let's say the love of your life leaves you. Your survival mechanism says, 'That's painful. I'm never going to let that happen again.' So, to prevent feeling the pain of losing a true love again, your survival mechanism reins in the love you express. Your next relationship, because, face it, we still seek the company of other people, occurs at a more superficial level because you've decided not to love so deeply any more. If that pattern continues, you are missing love in your life, not because of others but because you elected not to love fully in order not to get hurt."

Jerry ate his eggs and looked at his watch. "Yeah, okay. I've created some voids," he said after a long silence.

"If you don't get through the void, then it eats away at you, and you look for something to fill it, hide it, or destroy it. Some people turn to alcohol or drugs, others to religion, some to sex, some to television or reading. Lots of people turn to food. None of those things could ever fill the void."

"So what do you, Mr. Human T Cell, do to heal people of their voids?"

"I don't want you to fill it. I want you to enter it. Going into the void initiates the healing cascade."

"Is that why you're here, because I'm an unhealthy cell in the societal body?" Jerry asked.

"You tell me," Tom said. "How's your life going right now? If you could live the life of your dreams, what would it look like?"

Jerry looked suspiciously at Tom. Jerry's grip on his own life had been loosened by the encounter with the OWBs. He felt less in control, as if having a routine is control. Predictability was not control. Just because the sun rises every morning doesn't mean that you have any control over it. Similarly, just because Jerry went to work five days a week doesn't mean that he had control over his life. Jerry's mind tossed and turned trying to figure out what might be missing in his life.

When they finished breakfast, Jerry seemed to be in another world, trapped in his mind, which was racing with worries, doubts, and questions, on a treadmill, round and round. *Why is he here telling me there's something missing in my life? How would he know? He probably doesn't. He's probably just here because he needs a roof over his head and I was a sucker last time…I don't want to have to figure out what might be missing. And I don't like the idea of going into some kind of void. This is not what I need right now. How can I make him go away? But what if he's right? Maybe that's why I've been feeling so uncomfortable in my own skin lately.*

Jerry cleaned up robotically, barely aware of Tom's presence any more. He put his sport coat on and got in the car. Tom watched silently as Jerry left for work, without even a wave goodbye.

The morning was cloudy and the air heavy with moisture. The wind that brought all the warm moist air up from the ocean turned on itself, shifting to the north. As Jerry reached the half way point on the drive to work, rain began to fall, lightly at first. As he passed by the shopping mall it came down harder and harder. He turned his windshield wipers on to the fastest speed and still couldn't see out the window. The rain pounded on his car, beating its random beat on the roof and smashing like kamikaze pilots into the windshield. To avoid accidentally plowing into the car in front of him, he backed off the gas pedal slightly but kept going. He hoped the person behind him had the sense to do the same. The rain kept coming even harder now. It was like driving blind. Hard work. Jerry felt dizzy and light headed. He slowed down more, hoping the person in the car behind him could see his break lights. *Is the umbrella still in the trunk?* he wondered.

When the rain slowed enough to see again, he took his eyes off the road briefly to gauge where he was, but he didn't recognize the buildings on this street. *Damn I must have missed a turn!* The neighborhood looked completely unfamiliar. The street names weren't ones he recognized. He looked around for anything that might seem familiar. Seeing none, he turned around and drove in the other direction. Still nothing looked familiar. Jerry pulled over and looked for a map in the glove compartment. Finding none, he leaned back in the seat and let out a heavy sigh. *I'm lost.* The words hit him like the stinging raindrops blown into your face by strong wind. He stared out the window and the tension turned to tears, which are the rain falling inside cleaning the emotional dirt out of the gutters. Jerry sat in the car with the seat belt still restraining him, trembling because he was alone this time. Neither Helen nor his coworker Rob were around to save his skin and take him for help. *I'm lost and alone and clueless.* His body began to shake, unable to flee from the frightening prospect of possibly having a mental illness so severe that it causes him to lose his way in the world. *Maybe this the syncope again. Did I just have another blackout? How did I get here? Why do these strange things keep happening to me?* At ten years of age, his experience hadn't been strange or unwelcome when it happened. It had been fascinating. Now, however it carried a negative emotional charge. He shut his eyes and leaned his head against the head rest. *Just go with the flow,* he thought, *go with the flow.* He shivered from being chilled by the damp air.

◆   ◆   ◆

In a house on that street, in front of where Jerry had pulled over, a woman watched an unfamiliar vehicle stop in front of her house. The man inside didn't get out of the shiny blue metal capsule. He sat there, unmoving. *Could this be the one, the Visitor we were told would come? Why isn't he moving? I wonder if he's hurt or dead.* She watched and waited to see what he would do.

Finally the rain stopped, but the sun was not out yet. The gray brooding clouds hung low to the ground, siphoning the color from everything and threatening to burst open again anytime.

Jerry jumped in his seat, eyes bolted open, startled by the sound of someone tapping on his driver's side window. "Are you all right?" the woman from the house shouted through the glass.

He opened the window. "I'm okay. I'm just lost."

"Where do you want to go?"

"I don't know anymore," he said rolling the window down. "I was on my way to work. Everything seemed normal until…the rain. Where am I?" he asked.

"You're at 300W 150N Rastonney."

She could have been speaking Portuguese, for as much sense as that made. "No, no, what town is this?" he clarified.

"Sagrada."

Where the hell is Sagrada? How could I get lost in my own town and end up somewhere I've never heard of? This is the epitome of being lost. Although he attempted to keep up the appearance of remaining calm, his heart raced wildly, and breathing became so shallow he should have needed CPR.

The woman saw the panic in his eyes and said, "Why don't you come inside? We can figure out your predicament much easier in the house over tea. Besides, it might start raining again."

Jerry got out, his leg muscles stiff from the adrenaline, and locked the car. As he looked more closely at the houses nearby, they sparkled like jewels from the raindrops in the intermittent sunlight, like they themselves were alive. Something about them appeared uncanny, but it was difficult to tell what. Most of the houses, like modest debutantes, revealed only an ankle or a bare shoulder briefly from behind a silky fabric of tall trees and flowering bushes. The trees themselves seemed to be the pillars holding up the roof, their branches forming the arches of doorways and windows. Perhaps it was the lingering moisture in the air that made it hard to tell whether the curves were concave or convex, whether angles stuck out or receded in. It was disorienting in the way that happens in dreams, where your experiences seem real and fantastic at the same time.

How could I have done this? My boss will surely fire me now. Jerry tried to call the office on his portable phone, but its display was completely scrambled, like a virus had gotten into the software.

Inside the front door of this woman's house, which wasn't really a door but simply an elaborate archway with wisteria-like flowers hanging down, pillars like tree trunks held up the interwoven lattice of branches that formed the roof, but there were no walls, only arches, so he could see into a beautiful garden filled with blooming flowers. In what appeared to be the living room, a tall tree grew, providing a canopy of leaves for the ceiling. It was difficult to tell whether he was inside or outside in her house. One blended and merged into the other. *I wonder what happens when it rains. Oh, it just did. Hmmm. That's odd; it's not wet in here,* he thought.

She led him to a cozy breakfast nook which bordered the kitchen on one side and yet was in an outdoor patio. There was a small round table and two chairs. She motioned for him to sit.

"My name is Maria."

"I'm Jerry."

"Like the fruit? You must be sweet then." She smiled coyly.

Jerry blushed and looked away.

"You are a traveler, no?" she asked while putting some dried leaves into a pot.

Jerry didn't know how to answer the question. He didn't think that driving to work, as he did every day, made him worthy of the distinction 'traveler.' "I'm as confused as you are right now, ma'am. All I know is that I was driving to work in the pouring rain, and when the rain stopped, I was here where you found me."

"I didn't find you, you found yourself."

Jerry looked at her quizzically.

The sun began to show itself fitfully through the clouds and the leaves, like it, too, wanted a glimpse of this strange visitor to its world. The flowers released their fragrance to celebrate the sun's return. The warmth and aroma melted Jerry's anxiety, and he smiled at Maria through the clouds of his own anxiety.

"Did nothing else odd happen?" she asked.

"No. Well, an old friend, or maybe just an acquaintance, I'm not sure what he is exactly, showed up this morning, rather unexpectedly."

"Were you glad to see him?" she asked.

"Yes, I think so."

"You think so?"

"He said some things that…" Jerry drew in his breath sharply.

"That upset you?"

"No. Not exactly."

"Here, perhaps this special tea will bring clarity." She poured the tea into delicate china cups and handed one to him. She put some cookies on a plate and put that in the middle of the table then sat across from him. His eyes followed her hand up her arm to her shoulder, then across the neck to her face. She had soft wrinkles in her skin and black but graying hair. Her features looked like they had once been chiseled, but age had eroded and sedimented them elsewhere. Arroyos formed where laughter poured from her eyes. Her eyes met his. Although it felt like someone had found him and pulled him out of the quicksand, he still squirmed about being so completely lost.

"So where in the world am I?"

"You are here," Maria replied playfully, pointing to herself rather than to him.

Why would she say that? I'm here, she's there. Is this a game? Is she teasing me? "I don't get it. I'm not you. Where is 'here'? Don't play games with me. I want to know where I am, what state or country or world I am in?"

"It's not that simple, Cherry, and there's nothing to be afraid of," she reassured him.

"It's Jerry, with a J. My name."

"Oh, okay, Jerry. Correct? You're not in a different world. Well, not really, although it might seem like it. You are on the other side of the infinite continuum."

"The other side of what? Am I dead? Is this the afterlife?"

"No, you are not dead," she reassured him.

"Then what is the infinite continuum, and how can I be on the other side of it?" Jerry demanded, the aggravation showing in his voice. This whole encounter seemed real and unreal, like a dream. The tea, Maria, the chair and table had their familiar liquidity and solidity, but the conversation spun him in circles. Jerry was exasperated at his inability to understand. *Is my shen out traveling again, only this time with full consciousness? Is this that place between life and death?*

The sun emerged fully from its hiding place behind the sky-water, warming the air and nourishing the plants. Jerry removed his jacket and loosened his tie.

Maria kept an even, unfluttered stride to her voice as she answered Jerry's increasingly agitated questions. "Although there is only one reality, sometimes it can seem like there are different sides to it. Here seems to be on the other side of where you were, where you came from, but it's really not. It's not a place like you are used to, but it is real."

"How can I be 'here' if it is not a place? Here and there refer to places relative to where I am." *What is she not telling me? Why don't words mean the same here? What did I get myself into?* Despair fluttered through his consciousness.

"Jerry, think of it this way. Imagine that all your life you were living on the face of a coin, and you were so close to the edge—however, if you are climbing around on a two-dimensional surface, you don't perceive the 'edge' that you could only see if you were in three-dimensional space looking at the surface from outside of it—so you ended up on the tail of the same coin. It's still the same coin, only you're looking at a different part of it, an unfamiliar part. The only difference, the inaccurate part of this analogy, is that there aren't two sides to reality. It's more like a Möbius strip; although it looks two sided, it really has only one side. However, if you are standing on part of it looking at another part that is upside-down in relation to you, you'd think that it was a different part and even a different reality."

"So I'm in a big optical illusion. Is that what you're saying? I'm here looking at myself as if I was over there."

"No, not really," Maria frowned. "I guess I didn't explain it very well. But don't despair. There's really no need to understand this intellectually." Maria reassured him. "Would you like some more tea?"

"Please." Jerry offered his cup for a refill. *It seems that whenever Tom shows up, my nice, stable, predictable life gets turned topsy-turvy. Is that part of his plan? Did he do this? What does it have to do with that social T cell business? This time it has gone too far. I don't even know where I am anymore. What the hell do I do now?* Panic paralyzed Jerry. Like a wild animal that wakes up from the stun gun shot in a cage, his daze wore off gradually, and he realized he wasn't dreaming. Automatically, his defenses went up, and he pushed the tea away that Maria had just poured. Jerry closed his eyes and heard the voice of his former yogi, in his head saying in a classic Indian accent, "Now it is time to turn the brain off and just be. There are some things that the brain is not meant to process. You must learn to process those with the heart. The heart does not have logic." As Jerry sat there, he expected to feel a great yearning to go home, like he felt as a child away at summer camp, but it never happened. Instead, he felt agitated and still, like the air just before a tornado forms.

"Please tell me about yourself, Jerry," Maria said, startling him from his reverie.

Jerry blinked his eyes open, got his bearings, collected his thoughts, and robotically rattled off where he was from, what he did for a living, where he was born, how he had been a physicist then studied metaphysics. He rambled from one topic to the next, in no particular order. She listened persistently, scouring his words for clues as to whether he was indeed the Visitor. The events of his past provided no clues about the shape of his future, so Maria tried a different tack: "What do you want to accomplish in life?"

Jerry blinked again and stared blankly at her. "I don't really know anymore. You are asking me to describe something I can barely see through murky water." He took a heavy breath, as if mourning a fond memory. "At one time I was determined to uncover the matter-energy link in a way that made it real for people, not just an abstract concept frozen in a famous equation. But then Reality cut in on my dance with Idealism. I hit a wall in my research. I left academia for the corporate world."

After telling her all that, he was left with a hollow feeling in his chest and a nagging worry that he was sure to lose his job now. Ashamed and embarrassed by his lack of purpose, he stared into his tea cup. Maybe there would be a white rabbit in it, anything to distract him.

"I know why you're here." Maria sounded triumphant. Jerry cocked his head. "You are lost," she proclaimed.

"Yes, I know I'm lost, but that's…"

"No, Jerry, you—it is a shame that English does not have reflexive verbs—you are not just physically lost, you are lost to yourself, to your purpose, your very being. That is a great accomplishment, as it opens the door to getting unlost, to discovering, to creating, a way, your way, out of the confusion, to find yourself, to be yourself, finally. You no longer have to be who you have been pretending to be. Usually when you think you are lost it's because you took a wrong turn somewhere, going from familiar roads to unfamiliar ones. Perhaps, however, you took a wrong turn which turned out to be right, because the only way to get someplace different is to take unfamiliar roads." She smiled reassuringly. "You are now totally lost, internally and externally. Nature prefers coherence. Now you get to live the mystery instead of just thinking about it." Maria beamed as she spoke this. She understood the awesome journey ahead of him, the wonderful position he was in, even though he didn't quite see it that way.

Jerry took a cookie from the plate and chewed on it to stall having to answer. *I'm lost.* As the words sunk in, their heaviness dragged his heart down to his feet. Jerry noticed that if he said "loooooooooooost" and held the o open for a long time, he could feel the void open up and swallow him. *Hi, my name is Jerry, and I'm looooooooost in spaaaaaace,* he imagined himself saying to a group of other lost 12-steppers. Like the recovering addicts of all varieties, he had hit the bottom of the barrel. Tom's words that morning—*was it that morning? It seemed like ages ago*—came back to him: "I help people get through the void." *Where are you now, dammit? If this isn't the void, I don't know what is!* He swallowed the last bite of cookie, which snapped him out of his reverie. Maria sat patiently waiting for him to be present again. "What do I do now?" He looked directly into her eyes, desperate and pleading for an answer.

With the intensity of a laser beam, she aimed her energy from her eyes to Jerry's eyes and said, "Absolutely anything. What would you like to do? Who will you be from this point on?"

Jerry seized. To have all possible choices open to him was as paralyzing as having no choices. "Anything? What do you mean I can do anything? I could run away and join the circus?"

"Of course. Why would you think otherwise?"

"I don't think anyone has ever in my entire life told me that I could do whatever I wanted. My options were always circumscribed."

"Not here. So stop stalling. Name it. What would you like to do?"

If this was the equivalent of getting one wish from a genie in a bottle, he didn't want to squander it.

"You see, Jerry, what you want to do is where you want to go is who you want to be. Where you are and who you are are one. You don't find that by looking in your back pocket."

◆   ◆   ◆

That night Jerry slept in the living room under the protective branches of a tall fatherly tree. Before drifting off to sleep, he sized up his situation. *When I was 10 years old I wanted to explore new worlds. Well, here I am in another world, without the help of stargates, warp drives, or transporters. Although I have no idea how I got here, that won't stop me from exploring. I feel like a 5-year-old who wandered off and was found by nice people in a gingerbread house. But what became of my previous life? Is it possible to go back? Is this a parallel universe, and am I essentially in two places at once, but unconscious of my own experiences in the other place? What do I want to do?* Question after question rolled through his mind until they finally became so monotonous that they lulled him to sleep.

Chapter 18

"The Visitor has arrived," Maria told Jorn. "He came yesterday with the rain and is staying with me right now. He calls himself Jerry, but I like to call him Cherry, because he's so…"

"Inexperienced?" Jorn, the current leader of the Sagrada community, was a tall husky man with broad shoulders and a quiet demeanor. "He was wise to find the one who is known for sensitive listening and kind nurturing."

"Thank you." Maria bowed her head slightly, and continued, "He is concerned about where he is and how he got here. I don't know how to explain to him without…"

"Don't. Let him get used to being here. With enough time, he will stop wondering and simply accept his situation. Once he is Welcomed, those concerns will vanish."

"Jorn, I'm not sure he is enough mu-ishi-wa for the Welcoming Ceremony."

"Prepare him then. We shall Welcome him in three days." Jorn beamed with anticipation and love. "This will be as much an adventure for the community as it is for Jerry."

◆　　　◆　　　◆

With a walking stick in hand and an enthusiastic spring in his step, that morning Jerry went out to explore his new world. *Maybe,* he thought, *if I could see the big picture, I might be able to figure out what happened, where I made a wrong turn, how I got lost and ended up here.* The practical part of him didn't entirely believe Maria's explanation. Jerry walked down the dirt road that Maria lived on. *It hadn't seemed like a dirt road yesterday, but perhaps the rain played with my perception.* The terrain was hilly, and there were many small footpaths that led straight up the hill, like shortcuts between switchbacks. He took one that was heavily grown over with a lavender-pink wisteria-like vine. The perfume of the flowers seemed to decrease the strenuousness of the climb, but the terrain caused a giddy sensation similar to vertigo. When he reached what he thought was the top, he felt refreshed rather than exhausted and found himself looking, rather, from the bottom of a valley up to higher hills and mountains. Even though he knew he climbed up, he had the sensation of going down. Physically he felt like he was going up, but all visual cues led him to believe he was going down. In this valley he passed houses that were more fanciful than Maria's. The term "quaint" came to mind but did not fit exactly, as each house seemed to be a structure made of optical illusions. The road became serpentine and sloped gradually downhill. Old trees provided a shady canopy over the path. Eventually the road turned and the canopy parted overhead so that Jerry could see a vista. At the end of the street, he emerged along a high cliff, where he could look over the town.

From there, above the town of Sagrada, he could see that the houses in the valley were arranged in a rough semicircular pattern around a central barn-like building, probably the community house that Maria had mentioned, with the straight side of the semicircle facing east. That central building looked like it was used for games. A wheel-like structure made of stones was embedded in the grass in this field. The inner circle and the outer circle were made of big stones, and the spokes connecting them were smaller stones. At the center was a small, perfectly round reflecting pool glistening in the sunlight.

In line with the east-west orientation of the central wheel but on the outside of the semicircle boundary of the town was a stone structure hidden among the trees. It seemed to be just large stones arranged in a double parabolic pattern. Although it didn't look like Stonehenge, he wondered whether it served a similar religious or astrological purpose.

Jerry saw the road he came in on and followed its path, hoping to see from which direction in came, but lost sight of it because of a fold in the landscape. He saw no roads leading to or from Sagrada.

He walked down a steep staircase cut directly into the side of the cliff. At the bottom was the outermost row of homes. On the east side, near the straight side of town were abundant fields and gardens. Mostly they grew vegetables, not corn and wheat. There was a natural fruit tree forest with many kinds of fruit trees, such as apple, cherry, and plum, growing not in orderly rows yet not randomly either, as if the trees themselves chose where to grow. A meandering river ran through the fields and orchards. From where he stood, Jerry could just barely see rivulets that likely irrigated the crops. With no visible trade routes, Sagrada seemed to be a completely self-sufficient agrarian community. Low mountains crouched in the distance. *What lay beyond them? Were there other such communities? Did they feud with each other?* It seemed unlikely, as there were no defensive structures—no walls, no lookout towers, nothing to suggest that they feared attack.

As he gazed in the direction of the sunrise, his stomach gurgled for breakfast. *Should I pick some fruit to eat on the way back?* He decided not to take something that wasn't his. When he returned, Maria had breakfast prepared.

"You are still trying to figure out where you are," she called to him from the kitchen.

"Yes."

"I will tell you."

Jerry hurried to the kitchen. He didn't want to miss this. "I'm here. Please tell me. No pun intended."

"You know that the light you send and the light you receive merge to form what you see, hear, feel, all those things with which you can interact."

"Yes, but why do I have this strange feeling that you are going to tell me that this place is a figment of my imagination?"

"It is not that simple. Do you think the world you lived in before you came here was a figment of your imagination?"

"Oh no. It's real."

"How do you know?" Maria asked.

"Well, when you injure yourself, you really do feel pain; when you kiss another, you are kissing someone, not nothing. You know it's there because you can see it, feel its wetness, coolness, softness against your body, smell its lusciousness."

"And your senses are perceiving this world equally clearly?"

"Yes," Jerry said, "this world is just as real as the other one."

"Perhaps the key difference between here and there is that we know that whatever is causing that sensation of coolness or wetness is a different aspect of our true body, our Source being-body, which is much greater than this small individual body. Just as my finger perceives itself as being different than my belly button yet part of the same body, so are we different from each other but still part of the same Source being-body. We believe that it is a fallacy to think that the world is 'out there' and is subjectively impenetrable, i.e., objective. Do you see your own subjectivity in the so-called objective world?"

"I can't say I do." Jerry's memory flashed back to a time sitting in the woods with Terrah. *Is this what she was trying to get me to see?* "So Maria, are you saying that being in this world is like being psychotic—not able to tell the difference between what's in my real reality and what's simply my own subjective delusion?"

"Interesting. I never would have thought to equate mental illness with being able to exist in the realm of the one that is both."

"What do you mean, the realm of the one that is both?"

"Here, where the objective is subjective, where my internal reality co-creates my external reality so that it is my experience, and it is unified—neither solely external nor solely internal and both external and internal."

"You're speaking in so many paradoxes that it's hard to understand you, Maria. Our language prefers one or the other, not both."

"I know of no other way to use your language to explain these things. We have our own way, which you might want to try. We're so much more than just one or the other or even both. We are like multi-layered cakes. Perhaps you just forgot about your other layers and came to believe that you only have one layer, the physical layer. At that level there appears to be duality—good and bad, right and wrong, hot and cold, up and down. Your entire existence is structured around such dualisms that are based on the orientation of the physical body, starting with left and right, up and down, in front of and behind. You relate to your physical world from those three dimensions, which intersect about right here," she said pointing to the area between the heart and the navel. "This is (0, 0, 0), the starting point for your physical existence. It is because of the asymmetry of your physical body that you have evolved primitive rules such as 'what is in front of you cannot also be behind you' or 'what is up cannot also be down'; they are mutually exclusive unless you switch to a different distinction, such as 'surrounded by,' which encompasses all three dimensions. That is functional, to a point. But to get to the next layer, which is nonphysical energy and therefore not confined to the body, you must relinquish those particular oppositions and those three planes. The quantum physicists had to relinquish notions of position and direction and invent different oppositions, such as spin, charm, and beauty. Similarly, this layer still has a sense of opposition in the form of being 'separate,' because my energy is not your energy on this layer."

"You mean the energy that we are rather than the energy we use?"

"Why, yes of course." Maria was pleased that he understood and so continued, "Since our energy states are still separate on this level, we can feel when someone else's energy drains us or energizes us. This energy layer is what keeps the parts of your physical layer from falling apart. This is why everything does not dissipate. This is why your law about entropy only seems to be half true. The next layer on this cake pulls all that 'separate' energy together so that there's no separation, just different vibrations, frequencies, amplitudes of the same energy that holds the physical in stasis."

"Yes, scientists and mathematicians are beginning to see that," Jerry added.

"However, without making it part of your day-to-day consciousness, not just your while-I'm-at-work consciousness, this layer will not be recognized or honored for being the basis of all else, which it is."

"What does this have to do with knowing where I am?" Jerry had been expecting a different kind of answer.

"I'm getting to that. Patience, my friend. You must look at the whole map first to see where you, in particular, are."

Chapter 19

At her desk in the city room of the newspaper, a bustling nerve center that ran on caffeine and deadlines, Helen hit speed dial 7, Jerry's office. No answer. She hit speed dial 8, Jerry's home. No answer. She ripped off her headset and threw it on her desk, nearly spilling her coffee. Her deadline was that evening. The story on zero-point energy was to run in Thursday's Science section, and despite the conversation over dinner the concepts were still pudding to her. She had padded the story with "expert" opinions about the validity of the technology, but she knew that she had failed to explain it well enough. Now her primary source was blowing her off. Helen had enough of his game and decided to track Jerry down and get some answers, including why he hadn't returned her calls for the past two days.

When she arrived at his house, the lights were on. She let out a short grunt, like a bull getting ready to charge. Helen slammed the car door shut, marched up the driveway, pounded on the door with her fist, and stood there with her arms folded across her chest. She played her greeting over in her head: *Why the hell haven't you...*

As the door opened she started into her tirade, but only got the first three words out when she noticed that the person who answered the door was not Jerry.

"Why the hell what?" Tom fired back.

"Who the hell are you and where is Jerry?"

"If I knew where he was, I don't think I'd tell you, with an attitude like that."

Helen bristled at losing that exchange. "I'm just very worried. He hasn't returned my phone calls and e-mails or, or..." Her tough-girl persona was cracking and the truth seeping out.

To sidetrack the oncoming emotional train wreck, Tom explained, "He's not here. And I'm as clueless as you. He left for work two days ago and never came back."

"Okay, so who are you and why are you in his house?" Helen's tone flipped from concern to accusation.

Tom wiped his right hand on his pants thigh and stuck it out. "I'm Tom. I came to visit, then Jerry left. I haven't heard from him either. But I'm not taking it personally."

Helen felt the sting. She had made up the interpretation that he didn't want to talk to her. In her wildest dreams she would not have thought he would just disappear. "I'm Helen, a friend."

"Uh huh." Tom intonated in such a way that he knew she was implying more than a friend. "Well, Miss Helen, why don't you come in and maybe we can put our heads together and figure out what happened to our mutual friend Jerry. Would you care for some tea?"

"I would, thank you." Perfect. That got Tom out of sight so Helen could look around for clues. She checked the closet; most of the coats were there. She checked the bathroom; toothbrush was still there with a half-used tube of toothpaste. She quickly checked the bedroom. Although she felt uncomfortable opening up his drawers, they yielded the same information. Wherever Jerry went, he didn't intend to go for a long trip. She hurried back into the living room.

Tom brought out some freshly brewed Earl Grey. "Do you think we should notify the authorities yet?"

"First let's put all our information out on the table and then create a strategy," Helen advised. They sat in the living room, with Helen perched on the front edge of a high-backed chair with frayed upholstery, and Tom stretched diagonally on the unmatching couch to face her. "All I know is that recently he seemed a little down. We had a traumatic situation awhile back, and it put him in a funk. He didn't want to play the game anymore, hated going to work, seemed disconnected from his own life. Maybe he needed to get into the deep woods for awhile."

"Jerry, a woodsman?" Tom asked.

"Touché."

"What did you say your name was?"

"Helen Donellyn."

"And why are you here? You were obviously very upset…"

"I'm writing a story—I'm a reporter—and Jerry was my source. I needed to check a few things with him because my deadline is tonight. And he's been avoiding me…" she realized at that moment that she had invented the reason for his absence. Shifting gears, she asked Tom, "So how long have you been here? I'm surprised Jerry hadn't mentioned anything about having a guest."

"I got here that morning, um, Monday."

Helen was a little shocked. Coincidence perhaps, that this guy shows up and Jerry disappears? "So what happened?"

"Now that I know he was in a funk, nothing out of the ordinary happened. He did seem a little down, and he mentioned that he wasn't very satisfied with his work, but then, like a robot, off he went to work and never came back!"

"This is so weird. People don't just disappear. It would seem, then, that he never made it to work. I'm sure I tried calling him on Monday," she said as she checked her Personal Secretary call history. "Yup. I called him five times. No answer each time."

"I'm sure he didn't just disappear. If he died, we'll find out. If he flipped out, they'll find him. If he…" Tom tried to sound reassuring, but it evidently wasn't working. Helen blanched. Tom stopped before he upset Helen. Her outer cool didn't fool him.

Helen froze. "Uh oh, I hope he didn't pass out again. He has a condition called syncope. One of the symptoms is temporary loss of consciousness. We should call every hospital in town, then if he's not there, the police. Start talking to all his friends. Could you do that?"

"Whoa, I'm not going to track him down like he's a criminal. I'm sure everything is just fine."

"Well, I am going to track him down. Here's my card." She stood up to leave. "Call me if anything important happens—you hear from him or hear news of him. I presume I can reach you here if necessary?"

Tom studied her business card intently while she spoke to him.

"Uh, yeah, for a few days anyway."

"Great, I'll be in touch if I find anything," she said with the air of a professional. *If he's not going to help me, I'll do it myself.* "Thank you for the tea," she said on her way out the door.

◆   ◆   ◆

Helen's Journal

That guy Tom who was at Jerry's house is a character. At first I wanted to think that he was to blame, but I now I doubt it. If he had anything to do with Jerry's disappearance, he wouldn't have been so blasé. Then again, if he knew ahead of time that Jerry was going to disappear, then he has every reason to be blasé. If that were the case, I could have gotten some information out of him, but I don't think he had any. I can't stand his sit-and-wait attitude. What if Jerry's in trouble? Tom just says "when you realize that there is no such thing as time, then waiting doesn't really matter now, does it?" No such thing as time? Uh uh. Not buying it. Time is my master, and her deadlines are my commands. Without Time's arrow pursuing me, I'd be lost and lazy.

Tom says that time is a made-up construct, an artifact from our moving through space at nowhere near the speed of light. If we were light, thereby moving at the speed of light, we would not have a sense of time. Instead, we made up the concept of time, according to Tom, because as we became matter and our vibration slowed down, we lost the sense of being in the Garden. We lost that feeling of euphoria and timelessness that comes when we're all connected, and in losing the connectedness, we started dividing everything up, making pieces to satisfy our sense of the missing whole. That leads to the question, if we could get back that sense of connectedness, would we lose the sense of time?

I've never heard anybody talk like that. I thought he was cracked at first, but then I read an article about relativity, and it made more sense. Tom is one of those rare individuals who doesn't seem to care about what others think about him. In him I can see how, by being yourself, even if you are weird, people still like you. They even like you for your weirdness. Isn't that weird?

I am if
I am why
I am I
What's that?
I am that I AM
So what?
Goodbye.

I have to admit that sometimes I do lose a sense of time when I write poetry. It's great not to have a deadline. I don't think that's what Tom was referring to, however. I imagine that each person experiences time differently according to the situation and their role in it. So of course it will seem like forever until Jerry returns if I keep playing the jilted lover. If I get out there and have fun with other people, time might just fly by.

Chapter 20

"When you got so lost to yourself," Maria continued her explanation to Jerry, "you weren't lost in the usual way, from carelessness or not being present to where you are or where you are going. That wouldn't be enough to get you here. Instead, I think that you, Jerry, were existentially lost."

"What does that mean?"

"You ran into the edge of your existence."

Jerry cocked his head to one side, bewildered.

"We all have personal beacons, like little lighthouses, that remind us who we are, where we're going. Sometimes they're things, sometimes other people, sometimes an idea. When you lose sight of your beacons, you get pulled back into the void, the place of no particular perspective, like a wave crest that sinks back into the vast ocean. You're still connected to everything; you just don't have the singular perspective of a particular wave from which to view everything. To get waves, you need wind blowing steadily in one direction." She gave Jerry some silence to let the idea sink in.

"Before I got here, my friend Tom told me that he helps people get through the void. *Through* the void, he had said, not swallowed up by it. Although it felt like a satisfying answer to my hungry belly, to my rational mind, it still doesn't make sense. The void is supposedly the absence (or the presence, depending on which way you look at it) of All That Is. Certainly this place doesn't appear to be absence of any sort, but it also does not appear to be the presence of All That Is. In certain philosophies, the void is the basis of all possibility or potential (rather than actuality). It is the realm of the not-yet-manifested. Although in physics, it certainly is not called the void, there is the same concept of the not-yet-manifested from which all things can manifest, called the implicate order. When the implicate order becomes explicate, we have our reality. So am I simply in a different explicate order than my normal one?" Jerry asked.

"If so, you would indeed be through the void, wouldn't you? Through the void and into another explicate order."

"Poof, like magic, just like that? I don't think so," Jerry said. "That's not the way things work."

"Your first-layer self usually keeps your explicate order orderly. It determines what is possible or not possible in your world. This tends to give you your sense of identity, which is your sense of where you are and how you are different from other human beings and definitely different from all the other beings—your unique waveform, if you will. The first layer is the space of things and attributes. It is where fish are scaly, moss is soft, and girls are sexy. It's where I am female and you are male. Who is your first-layer self, Jerry?"

"Well, I'm male, a computer programmer, a fan of The Doors. I wish I could say 'tall, dark, and handsome' but I'm missing a little something in the tall and handsome departments, I think. I'm a half-hearted football fan. I'm a Democrat. Ummmm, I'm single, but I was dating someone a little. I have no religious affiliation. I'm shy. Let's see, what else?"

"That's a good start. If you added all these characteristics up, do they really add up to you, to who you really are?"

"No. I don't even know if I could tell you who I really am, especially now. And Maria, what does who I am have to do with where I am?"

"Almost everything. You called yourself a 'democrat.' Well, we don't have those here. Are you still a democrat when you are here? Those labels aren't who you are because they give a fragmented picture, a bit here, a bit there, an approximation but not the whole picture of your explicate order, and they don't even begin to touch all the possibilities of your implicate order that haven't popped out yet. We could use every word in the dictionary, and still it wouldn't be the whole, real you. Right?"

Jerry nodded.

"So next, let's look at the third-layer self. At this layer there is no duality, no good versus bad, no me versus you. There is no fragmentation here because there are no attributes because there is no distinction between subject and object. In order to give yourself attributes, the real you has to look at a version of you as an object in order to describe the various characteristics. And so you become artificially split within yourself as subject and object. In the third layer, there is no subject and object, no split."

"Is this real, or is this a theoretical construct?" Jerry asked.

"It's a different kind of space, not the three-dimensional space that we're in now. It would be more like infinite-dimensional space. But that is hard to imagine, I imagine, when you're only a material being. So think of yourself as being in the space that Christ, Buddha, Mohammed, Krishna, Fools Crow, or any other of your enlightened ones occupied. Imagine knowing yourself as All That Is, so that when you encounter something that seems to be an object, something distinct from yourself, another person, say, you know that that other being is part of your own subjectness. Embrace it and dissolve the embrace. Now you are not only here but also there, so here and there together are now just 'here.' And you can expand that even to things that aren't physically right here right now. You can expand it to people, places, things you've never met, seen, or heard of. That is how 'who I am' and 'where I am' are the same yet different, one that is both."

"This is what the yogi tried to teach us. I never did fully understand it back then."

"It's not an easy thing to understand, because the first-layer self thinks that it *is* you, and it has you believe that if you lose your sense of separateness, you'll die. So it works very hard to prevent you from realizing your true self, your non-dual, non-fragmented self. The first-layer self becomes very good at managing the fragments, making up excuses why part of you can say in church on Sunday 'it's wrong to kill' and another part of you can enlist in the army, why yet another part can lobby for first amendment rights and another part can yell at your child not to talk back. Your first-layer self can't see the irony in that. It feels fully justified in all its irreconcilable behaviors because it has fragments to fall back on, and each fragment has its own separate infrastructure."

"It is pretty ironic, isn't it, when you look at it that way," Jerry admitted. "However, there's still something that confuses me. How can you have a space of total subjectness without it all becoming soup? Can you have otherness in this third layer, without the other being an object? To me, otherness implies object-ness."

"The key is to hold two perspectives simultaneously, to look at the whole painting while seeing each brush stroke, to consider the whole body when just the foot hurts, to be here now and to be everywhere everywhen. Babies sometimes do not know that their toes are part of their body. They will chew on them, bite them, and surprise themselves when it hurts after they bit hard. Eventually babies learn that those things they are chewing on, toes, are part of their own body. So too with enlightened beings; they learn that the Others they see around them are part of their same body, a body much greater than the one contained in the skin. That is the real body, your Source being-body; and that is the real you. When you can hold that perspective as well as your immediate in-the-now perspective, you will be able to experience subjectness without it, as you said, all becoming soup."

Jerry leaned over and gave Maria a big hug, an embrace that melted their separateness as individuals into simply the act of embracing. She knew that he understood and that she could now begin formal preparation for the Welcoming Ceremony.

"Jerry, you will be introduced to the Sagrada community in a couple days."

"Great. I was beginning to think you were going to horde me here all to yourself."

"This is not just 'hi how are you.' You will have a Welcoming Ceremony, which is a sacred event, like an initiation, especially for someone such as yourself who has never experienced anything like this before."

"This sounds serious."

"It is, and it's not. It's not solemn serious, but it is something that we take very seriously to keep the integrity—the wholeness—of our community intact. We usually perform it for a new child who comes into this world, this strange world compared with the one they just came from. You have come into this world, which probably seems a bit strange compared with where you came from, so you must be welcomed just like everyone else. However, since you are no longer an infant, you must prepare for the ceremony."

"Why?"

"Because a baby does not resist what is new. You have lived long enough to build walls and defenses to keep you safe, to protect you from new experiences. So, one of two things could happen. You might resist so hard that you won't actually experience being welcomed. Conversely, when you have 200 people who are all intentionally creating a certain reality, if you are not absolutely grounded in yourself, you might be so caught up with the energy that you would literally lose yourself."

"Again? Does it help that I'm already lost? What do I have to lose?"

"Good, I will make arrangements. Our Leader will speak and then he will ask the community to welcome you. This will be the overwhelming part. You will be so welcomed that it might destroy you unless…."

"Whoa. Hold it. How can welcoming destroy me?"

"Unless you are sufficiently prepared for this kind of Welcoming, it could kill you."

"Kill me? It's that dangerous?" Jerry backed away from her.

"Not physically, but psychologically it could."

"How?" Jerry asked.

"In an ordinary welcome there is always some reservation, perhaps some distrust, perhaps some pretense. For example, when you visit someone and they welcome you into their home, it is with the unspoken caveat that you will not mess it up, damage it, take anything, and that you will eventually leave. Although you are welcomed, it is not complete. It is a guarded welcome, almost 'you are welcome here only temporarily and only if you don't express too much of your humanity.' Conversely, we know that you are human. We will welcome your humanity, your foibles, your irony. We will welcome you for who you are and who you are not. It will feel like being sucked into a whirlpool because the usual reserve of your kind of welcome will not be there to keep the distance and separation between you and the rest of You. To you, it will feel like you have lost your ability to choose. Hence, you must go into it with no reservation. You must be willing to release your need to choose how you think the Welcoming Ceremony ought to be. It will be however it will be, with no right or wrong, no good or bad. So allow yourself to be welcomed without reservation."

"Maria, are you saying that I should let go of all my beliefs about not deserving it and my fears of not being able to handle it all, and just go with the flow?" Jerry asked.

"That too. I'm saying that only when you relinquish the need to control your choices and those of others will you truly have the freedom to choose."

Jerry smiled at the paradox again. *I have to give it up to get it.*

"Yes, and one more thing, Maria added. "You will be tempted to preserve your sense of having free will. You will want to control the situation because the emotions will be overwhelming. Do not try to control anything, even your emotions. Cry if you want. Scream if you want. Don't try to resist because your intention to resist will be mirrored by the whole group, and your resistance will rebound back to you 200-fold. Your free will will not be gone. On the contrary, you will have a stronger will because you will be connected to our community. Your free will instead will be amplified by us, not constrained. You will see that free will isn't the important thing—it's a given—choice is the important part. You can choose to resist what is happening, but why would you want to resist being welcomed? Conversely, what happens happens, and you will find it more powerful to choose to accept whatever is happening how it is happening. Choose how you feel. Choose to be overwhelmed or choose to fly with it. You will be welcomed into a community that seeks for your intentions to be realized. So your first intention, I should hope, would be to welcome the community as they welcome you. It will complete the circle. A complete circle is very strong. Come, we shall practice."

"Practice? We have to practice this? Why?" Jerry resisted the idea of practicing.

"It's more conditioning than practice. This will be very strange to you. You will see." Maria looped her arm in his and together they walked to the west edge of the town, where they came to a stand of tall trees planted between huge monoliths together forming a large parabolic curve, like a U whose ends had been pried open somewhat. A parabola is unique because if energy or light hits it anywhere along the inner curve, it is reflected to a single spot near the bottom of the U, called the focal point. A parabola is a shape that can be used to focus and amplify energy. Across from that stand was a smaller stand of trees planted in a parabolic curve of smaller stones. The branches intermingled above their heads, as if the trees were joining hands. The monoliths were highly polished. At the focal points of these parabolas formed by the trees and stones, which were both in the same spot, was a boulder. Maria instructed him, "First, quiet your mind and be still. I know that this is very strange for you, and your mind will attempt to make sense of it, analyze it, and peer into every nook and cranny. Allow that to happen. Allow your curiosity to be satiated. Allow your curiosity full reign. Figure out whatever you want to figure out. Do you understand?"

"Um, I don't know. Do you want me to just be curious, as in, 'what the hell is this?'" Jerry asked.

"Yes, just like that. Look around. Ask questions. I will not answer them right now, but ask them anyway." Maria stepped back and closed her eyes.

Jerry began: "Okay, so let's start with that one. What am I doing here? How does it work? Why do I have to do this?"

At that point Maria focused on intending "curiosity." She used a breathing technique to send the intention outward.

"What are you doing?" Jerry asked.

"Very good, Jerry. Keep it up."

He felt a little jolt, like a hunger pang. Not only did he want to know the big questions, but he also found himself overwhelmed with all sorts of technical questions. *Why were these trees planted this way? What kind of trees are they? What were the stones made of?* He knew that he was at the focal point of a parabola, but it wasn't a parabola that reflected light, so what did it reflect? And on and on the curiosity went.

Maria increased the intensity. Now the items and issues were flying through his mind so fast and furious it was hard to stay present to them all. It was like being trapped in a small container with a swarm of bees. You want to keep your eye on each one so that you can make sure it doesn't sting you, but they are buzzing by so fast that it just makes you dizzy trying to keep up. All those questions in fact made Jerry so dizzy that he collapsed.

Maria stopped the intention and ran to him with some water. She shook his shoulders to wake him up again.

"What happened?" he said when he came to, still curious.

"This exercise was to show you first hand what happens when your ego tries to manage the effects of expanded intention. It becomes overwhelming and you shut down. You love being curious, yet when curiosity itself takes over you, it is too much to handle. We need to get you to a point where the intention can take over, yet you don't shut down. Otherwise, when you are welcomed into the community, you will shut down."

"That would be embarrassing."

"That's your ego talking," Maria pointed out. "Now let's try meditating, clearing the mind, and being still." This time Maria began at the same time with him, sending the intentions to clear the mind.

Jerry might have been astonished that his mind could become so clear. He usually had thoughts passing through with intermittent bursts of clarity. His mind was so clear that he didn't even have the astonishment. The experience was so calming he fell asleep.

"That was better, Jerry. You shut down in a more productive way this time. Get up and walk around. Stretch. Get some air back into your lungs."

"This is one powerful technology you have here."

"Yes, however it's really just a simulator of our technology. Flying a real airplane feels much different than a flight simulator. Right now, this is like hearing only the flute; tomorrow you will hear the entire orchestra. Are you ready for the final run?"

Jerry sat back on the rock.

"This time," Maria instructed, "try to keep two things in mind while having your mind clear. I know that sounds like a paradox, but you'll see what I mean. First, with the same clarity of mind that you just experienced, be open to what you experience—totally open. And at the same time, do not allow yourself to be carried away with it. It will be powerful energy flooding you, so you need to anchor yourself. Anchoring is not resisting. It might look like that when a boat is anchored and there is a current. And here's another paradox: anchor yourself *in the energy that is flooding you*. So, allow it to carry you and anchor yourself in that experience. I know it might not make sense, but try it. You'll see."

Maria explained more. "To welcome means to receive with pleasure and hospitality, to accept gladly." Maria accepted Jerry gladly into her life. The happiness he brought she gave back. "We perform the Welcoming Ceremony, as I mentioned earlier, for newborns. The child is handed from the mother's arms to each person, and lastly to the father. This way, everybody can feel like the child is hers or his, and vice versa. You will be handed, by hand, so make sure that you look into each person's eyes and heart and allow them to reciprocate."

Jerry nodded.

"We also re-Welcome those who have strayed from the community, who have gotten themselves into the delusion of being cut off from their Source being-body. When can a wave ever be cut off from the ocean? It is the ocean. Whenever—and it is very rare—someone has transgressed the codes of the community, we hold a Welcoming Ceremony for that person. There were two held recently, one for a young girl caught stealing from a neighbor and another for a teenage boy whose love for a girl was not reciprocated. He made himself out to be unworthy and isolated himself from family and friends. By performing the Welcoming Ceremony for them again, it erases any fears they may have about deserving to belong to the community. When someone loses the connection, whether it be to himself, the community, or to the planet, he feels justified in abusing that which he lost the connection to, even if he himself chose to cut the connection. It's the irony of the subject-object split. Every time we hold a Welcoming Ceremony, it solidifies the community even more because everybody gets to experience being welcomed, not just the one for whom the ceremony was being performed."

Maria sat behind Jerry and gathered energy from the infinite stores of it in the universe and sent it to Jerry. This was the practice run for tomorrow, so she sent him the strongest welcoming energy she could imagine and amplified it further with the help of the trees and monoliths. When it was over Maria asked Jerry, "What did you experience in this little demonstration here today?"

Jerry said, "I have never felt so wanted, so appreciated, so completely accepted, not even by my own family. It's scary how integrated I felt. I'm not used to it. There was no need to try to justify why I am the way I am, no need to prove myself, no need to impress. It was all okay."

He had felt that way only once before, except he did not consciously remember that moment. It was when the doctor put him in his mother's arms for the very first time. She gazed into his eyes with the love of the universe, and he gazed back at her with vast fullness and emptiness of the universe. Today, however, he also felt himself being carried away on a wave, so he grabbed onto it. Unlike being on top of a wave in a boat, where you go up and down, it was more like being in a three-dimensional wave in which you expand and contract. And if you position yourself at the source of that wave, you are not tossed around by its expanding and contracting. You are pulsing at the source. That must have been what Maria had meant by anchoring yourself. From there it felt like being at the source of the universe breathing—long, slow breathing. Refreshing, invigorating.

"Is that what I will experience tomorrow?"

"Only if you choose to limit yourself."

How much greater could it get? Am I really ready for this? he wondered. *Oops, that's limiting myself—of course I am.*

They walked back to her house without speaking, instead serenaded by the pinks, oranges, purples, and reds of the setting sun. Jerry didn't just look at them, they permeated him. Jerry unwittingly found himself crying at the luscious feeling of being inside the beauty of it all.

Chapter 21

Zero-Point Energy: Fact or Fiction?

By Helen Donellyn

Perhaps more powerful than nuclear energy, zero-point energy (ZPE) could be the next safe, environmentally responsible energy source. Conversely, misuse of it could be like putting a lit match in a baby's hand—he might just burn himself or he might burn down the whole city. Before deciding whether it's the next energy solution or fiasco, what is zero-point energy? Although scientists have been studying ZPE since 1909, there is still very little public knowledge about it because understanding zero-point energy requires some fairly technical knowledge.

Combustion, as produced by the burning of fossil fuels, has been the primary source of energy since the origins of humankind. With the exception of nuclear power, solar power, wind vanes, and water-driven turbines, we have burned things to keep warm, whether it be wood for a campfire, coal for a furnace, gasoline for cars, or even the methane from garbage dumps. Until the atom was split and nuclear power was harnessed, combustion had been the main method for generating electricity. A new revolution in energy production may be right around the corner.

ZPE does not rely on combustion or on splitting atoms, although it does work at the subatomic level. ZPE instead draws from the idea that atoms still have energy, even at absolute zero, when all thermal activity is believed to cease and the Heisenberg uncertainty principle no longer applies because the particle would have a velocity of zero. Scientists believe that ZPE taps the most fundamental energy of all. It is so fundamental that we are literally swimming in it. Moreover, we are made of it. ZPE is (part of) everything, from the air we breathe to the coffee we drink to the bed we sleep on. It's even our very bodies, since our cells are made of atoms just like everything else. So theoretically, the source is infinite.

The tricky part of using ZPE for energy is in harnessing it. Although it is everywhere, the forces are so small that currently it is thought that it takes more energy to extract ZPE from matter than it produces. Dr. Ian Stine, Chief Science

Officer at Sundial Labs, explains that "Zero-point energy is not a new concept. It has been called many things over the years—ether, vacuum energy, free energy, infinite energy, and so on. Theoretically we understand it, but right now it's like picking grains of wheat one at a time. We need to develop an effective and efficient way to harvest it."

Robert Gall, Chairman of Core Energy, Inc., one of the nation's largest suppliers of energy, claimed "ZPE is science fiction. When they can generate the gigawatts that are needed to power this great nation, then I'll believe, but until then—I think it's a total sham."

Although the large energy companies that supply most of the nation's electricity have not developed ZPE as a viable energy source, smaller, independent companies that have as their mission to find alternatives to fossil fuel are doing the costly front-line research and development. One such company was Energy Technology Assistance, Inc., headed by Jack Mason. This company had a working ZPE device in top-secret labs, until their efforts were thwarted by OWBs last month.

Many environmental groups are in full favor of the development of this form of energy. "If we can find a way to harness this form of energy, we can reduce the pollutants by as much as 90%," says Bob Washman of the Sienna Foundation. "Global warming could be halted, and the remainder of the precious fossil fuels will be conserved. I fully support such efforts."

Not all environmentalists are so supportive. Avery Thomas of Energy Watch cautions, "We don't know what the long-term effects might be. We could be trading one form of pollution for another. More research needs to be done before I jump on that bandwagon."

One thing seems certain: if zero-point energy is harnessed and becomes the norm, what will be the source? In this reporter's opinion, we will still be faced with many of the same issues of sustainability. Ethics will be more important than ever.

◆   ◆   ◆

Terrah rarely read the newspaper, but today she bought one because her instinct and curiosity told her to. It wasn't the headline that grabbed her, as it contained the usual sensational garbage. It felt instead like a treasure hunt. There is something inside she felt she must find. But what? She took it home and laid it out on the kitchen table. If she just looked through it, she knew that what she needed to read would jump out at her. Nothing in the first section, and nothing there that even remotely interested her. Governments and politics and wars and stocks did not affect her life much, a life that was closer to the wild kingdom than to the civilized one. Normally she got her news from the birds (e.g., winter is coming early this year), the squirrels (achtung!), and the flowers (this is a year of feasting rather than famine). She breezed over Helen's article on zero-point energy. Although interesting, it didn't jump out as something important. As she was about to give up looking, in the classifieds and public notices section a list of missing persons caught her eye. Usually it had the names of kidnapped children and runaways, but this time she recognized one of the names: Jerry Fowss. She drew in a sharp breath when she read it. *Jerry Fowss was that nice man that my granddaughter dreamed about. We went looking for bears.*

There was no reward money offered for information about his whereabouts, however, there was a phone number to call. Although she had no information, she called the number. It was a private answering service with a man's voice saying "Please leave a message." She hung up quickly, but the damage had been done. Her call could be traced. *What was I thinking? I won't be able to get information from a number where I'm supposed to leave information.*

Instead she went to her source of information—the woods. She found a spot that was neither too quiet nor too noisy. The stream in the distance provided calming white background noise. She closed her eyes and posed her first question to the universe—where had Jerry gone? When the words had congealed in her mind, turned from a fluid, fleeting thought into a palpable mass of meaning, she opened her eyes. The first thing she saw was a butterfly. It went up and up and farther up and out through the tree tops. Butterflies tell you about transformation. They transform from relatively ugly earth-dwelling, plant-eating caterpillars into beautiful air-dwelling, nectar-eating nymphs (they hardly seem like bugs anymore). This butterfly went up, so perhaps it was a transformation to a higher plane of existence. That might mean Jerry died. She closed her eyes again and asked whether he was alive or dead. When she opened her eyes a hummingbird flew toward her, hovered in front of her for a couple seconds and sped off. The hummingbird brings joy and ecstasy and is a messenger to the spirit world, so Terrah knew that Jerry was more than okay. She wasn't worried about him anymore, as it seems he was called to a spiritual purpose. But there was one niggling question in the back of her mind: why him? Ants crawled across her bare foot, biting her and startling her out of her question-asking reverie. "Ouch. You little buggers!" she said slapping them off her ankles. That was her third answer. The humble ant can build an empire one grain of sand at a time and can get creatures millions of times its size to move. Jerry was a humble worker ant. As she walked back down the mountain Terrah had a confident stride. She felt satiated from that conversation with the universe.

When she arrived back home, the phone was ringing, so she stepped more lively over the cats lying on the front porch.

"Hello? Is this Terrah Timbres?" asked the voice at the other end.

"Yes it is. What do you want?"

"Hi Mrs. Timbres. My name is Helen Donellyn. I am a friend of Jerry Fowss."

"Ohhhh." The afternoon's activity came into sharp focus now.

"Jerry has been missing for a week, and I am going through his contacts to find out whether anybody he knew might know his current whereabouts."

"Are you the reporter or the girlfriend he spoke so highly of?"

"Um, uh, both I guess," Helen sputtered, unaccustomed to people calling her that.

"Why don't you come over and we can talk."

"So you know something? Where is he?"

"I don't know his exact location, but I do know that he is all right. No need to keep worrying, my dear. Please come by tomorrow morning. I live at 430 Rio Rancho. I look forward to meeting you, Miss Donellyn. Bye."

Helen cradled the phone in her hand, stunned that she had just heard what she heard, and more stunned that she didn't get more information out of her. Helen was a master at interviewing people. The dots began to connect in her head. *This must be that batty old woman who took Jerry into the woods looking for bears. What would she know?* Her heart pounded from the excitement of having a lead. Or was it the excitement of simply connecting with someone who had a similar connection?

Chapter 22

Jack Mason slammed the newspaper and his fist down on the kitchen table so hard his coffee jumped out of the cup. His jaws clenched and he ground his back teeth as he considered his next move.

"Harry, this is Jack. Did you see *The Morning Sun* today?"

"No, why?"

"That bitch you let in here the night the OWB ship crashed was a reporter. Somehow she got wind of our operation and published it in the fucking newspaper! We're sunk, Harry, thanks to you.

"But sir…"

"You were the damn bleeding heart who wanted to help them, so now it's payback time. Take care of them, Harry."

"What do you want me to do?"

"Just take care of it—her and that guy. I don't want the possibility of any more trouble from either one of them. Understand?" Jack slammed the phone down and poured himself a shot of whiskey.

Chapter 23

On the day of the Welcoming Ceremony, Jerry felt that oxymoronic internal brew of excited anticipation and anxiousness from facing the unknown, like when you're going on a much needed vacation to a country where you don't know more than five words of the language.

Maria had prepared a large breakfast with many foods he had not had before. "These are herbs that have qualities that will support you today" was the only explanation she would give.

His curiosity had not abated. *What should I wear? Will lots of people be there? How will I know what to do? Will you be there to guide me? What if I goof up? Will it work? What will happen to me? Just how good might I feel?* He remembered what happened yesterday after allowing himself to feel such unbridled curious energy, so he stopped those thoughts and focused on being present every moment, whether chewing his food or putting on his socks.

"You might want to meditate for a bit," Maria suggested.

Jerry sat outside under a lemon tree and let the thoughts and anticipation come. Each time a thought popped up, he plucked it like a dandelion and blew it into the breeze. When the garden of thoughts, concerns, and worries was fully weeded, he knew he was ready. He returned to the house calm, open, and present.

◆　　　◆　　　◆

At the Community House, the Council met prior to the ceremony. "We have never had someone who was not born here undergo the Welcoming Ceremony. What if it doesn't integrate him? That could ruin everything we have accomplished. After all, this man is an adult who has never been Welcomed before. Previously all the adults who have undergone this ceremony had experienced it first as newborns," said one council member.

"What is your true concern, Emerson?" asked Jorn, the Head of the Council. "Do you think it will fail? Do you think it will kill him or ruin us?" Jorn looked at him as a father looking at a son who knows better.

Emerson explained, "Our community is grounded on the assumption that we are all one, and therefore we look after each other before we look out for ourselves. What if he does not share this orientation? It takes only one person to elevate himself above the community for all that we have worked so hard for to collapse. If this ceremony does not integrate him completely then we all will pay the price."

"It is good that Jerry showed up in front of Maria's house, not yours," Jorn chided.

"Yes." He lowered his eyes, indicating acceptance of the reproach.

"Therefore, Emerson, I invite you to take the responsibility of leading him in the procession and then seeing to his enfoldment."

"Shouldn't Maria do that? After all, she was the one who found him."

"The Visitor should feel as if he has two parents here. Maria has weaned him, and now you should guide him as a father does. It is up to you to see that your concern is addressed. Although you expressed doubt, it shows me that you care deeply about how this goes for him and for all of us. You want it to succeed. Do you accept this responsibility?"

"I accept."

◆   ◆   ◆

The members of the Sagrada community gathered in a grassy area reserved for this ceremony only. Since space itself can be conditioned, they conducted sacred ceremonies only in spaces that had been conditioned for such purposes. There was much talk and excitement among the people, as many had not heard about the coming of the Visitor until they received the call to the Welcoming. The children were especially active, some playing games, others pretending to put on the ceremony themselves. Some played musical instruments, but not together—a joyful chaos, compared to the precise coherence that was to occur.

When the sun was almost at the apogee, Maria took Jerry by the hand. "It's time."

They walked arm in arm to the welcoming grounds. The community members formed a single line, and Maria handed Jerry to the first person, who handed him to the next, and so on, like a receiving line. Emerson, the man Jorn had appointed to be Jerry's guide was at the end of the line. Emerson led Jerry around the perimeter of the stone circle, and when they had gone almost all the way around it, he spiraled into the center. As they were spiraling in, the people positioned themselves in the shape of a parabola. Emerson led Jerry to the focal point, which was in the center of the inner circle of stones—in the reflecting pool. From behind Jerry, the members of the Council stepped forth from the larger parabola and formed a smaller one behind him, again with him at the focus. He was now at the focal point of two parabolas, only these were formed by people, not stones and trees.

Jorn, who stood in the parabola directly behind Jerry, spoke: "Today we Welcome our brother, Jerry. We are honored to receive him into our community, into our selves, into our energy. Let us now focus our thoughts and words and Welcome him into our presence." He spoke some unintelligible words softly to himself then signaled the drummer to start a slow, steady beat. "Wel-come. Welcome," he chanted in rhythm. Jorn had the voice of the mountains—solid, deep, strong, and rich. The people picked up the chant with Jorn, who like a conductor, signaled the intensity to become greater and greater until the sound was nearly deafening and the rhythm had taken everyone over. Jerry's heart beat in that rhythm, his breathing synchronized to it; probably his very cells were dancing in that same beat. Then slowly Jorn brought it down to pianissimo. The sound transformed into intention, silent energy sent out to the universe for fulfillment. Some people had their eyes closed. Some held their hands out. Some clasped their chests as if holding a baby. The beat continued inside and among.

This is what Maria had prepared him for the previous day. He stood before the entire community and opened himself to the magnificence of the ceremony—the hypnotic rhythm, the focused intention, the love of inclusion. The energy picked him up immediately, got inside of him. He wasn't riding on the wave, the wave crashed through him and took him with it. He no longer felt himself, only the energy. Unlike yesterday, this energy was dense and rich, with many different variations on welcome. He was welcomed as a playmate, a lover, a brother, a friend, a teacher, a son, a student, a mystery. He embodied all that, a symphony of possibilities. He was welcomed for who he is, who he was, who he will be, for all his failures, for all his accomplishments, for all he was still to achieve. He was welcomed for being just the way he was, in all his humanity and all his divinity. At that moment when the chanting ripped open the fabric of possibility, Jerry felt himself explode into light. He lost consciousness of all the people standing around him, yet he felt their presence. They were all part of him now. He had just reached the next layer on the cake. It didn't feel so burdened with heavy, fleshy slow movement and thought. Things happened at the speed of light. He had been welcomed so thoroughly that they had become him and he them. He felt an expanded sense of Being, floating formless, although he still perceived his body as being the same.

The community knew that he was now one of them and one with them. As their energy had enveloped him, his enveloped them. A woman with a clear, beautiful voice sung out the joy felt in the hearts of all present. She sung in a sacred language of sounds, not words. Her voice took the energy of the group and focused it like a laser, transforming the evenness of the beat into flowing, liquid ear nectar that stirred together all the melted hearts in the crowd. When her song ended, the celebration began. Food was brought out. Children played. Adults danced. Music gave beat and harmony to all these activities. The solemnity of earlier transformed into exuberance. A little girl with blonde braids slipped her fingers into Jerry's hand "Will you play with me?" Jerry zoomed from spaciousness to her intense pupils inviting him into her world. He smiled and let her lead him into a game.

All day long he was given, as a gift, from one person to the next. With some he played, with some he danced, with others he spoke, with others he walked, with some he listened, one he kissed, with others he competed, but with each person he interacted in some way that brought together each of their spirits. He sampled food from all the households. For it being such a small community, the diversity was tremendous. Jerry was home, more home than ever.

The last person he was given to, a young man named Royce, walked with him back to Maria's house. Royce was apprenticed to the Energy Conservateur. He told Jerry that it was an important position to have.

"Royce, what do you use as an energy source here? How do you generate energy?" Jerry asked.

"Why would we need to generate energy? It is already everywhere. We just conserve it. There is no making it or destroying it, only routing it or channeling it to one purpose or another. It's like creating an extra loop in an already existing loop. Energy goes through different forms in natural cycles, and we just redirect it for a bit into our cycle and then put it back into the greater cycle. Energy is sacred, the cause of all and the result of all."

Jerry listened intently. What Royce said made perfect sense, but he had no clue how they might do that. "May I see how this is done?"

"I will create the intention that you'll be able to meet with the Conservateur."

They had arrived back at Maria's house. "Thank you. I'm so glad to have met you, Royce." Jerry shook his hand in deep appreciation.

Jerry sat in the garden looking over all the flowers and vegetables. Such simple abundance, which he saw with different eyes than he did that morning. He had become conscious of the plants' consciousness and regarded them now as friends. Even the plants seemed to welcome him, to enjoy his presence among them.

As he touched their leaves with the curiosity and freshness of a child, he pondered Royce's words, "Energy is sacred, the cause of all and the result of all." *Could he have been referring to zero-point energy? This would be the perfect community for it. They know their interconnectedness to each other and to all life. And they're not using zero-point energy, as in consuming it, but as in breathing.* In a split second, Jerry's understanding of zero-point energy shifted from the theoretical to the concrete. Gone were ideas about velocity and position and uncertainty, Casimir plates, getting enough to do something useful like power a light bulb. It was all around him and it was real. Jerry had the experience again of holding two perspectives at once, only this time he was in the aquarium looking out at himself looking into the aquarium.

Chapter 24

Helen's trip to 430 Rio Rancho to see Terrah began and ended on an eerie note. The sun was already high and bright, but the road to Terrah's house wound through a cavern of trees, making it dark and surreal where the sunlight pierced through the thick canopy. Helen took a blind corner a little fast and swerved to avoid hitting a ray of fierce sunshine as she came around the curve. Realizing what she had just done, she pulled the car over and took a few deep breaths to regain her composure. Her heart beat quickly and she breathed in short bursts. Now she knew just how anxious she really was. This was her first real lead in the Case of the Disappearing Boyfriend.

The small cabin where Mrs. Timbres lived was deep in the woods. Potted plants lined the front porch, and several cats lounged in the shade underneath the porch. As Helen drove up the driveway, a short and plump gray-haired woman came bouncing out the door and down the steps. Before Helen had even emerged from her car, Terrah said, "You must be Miss Donellyn. Come with me." Terrah's momentum kept taking her down the hill that was her driveway.

No handshakes, no small talk. Helen grabbed her Personal Secretary from the passenger's seat, put it in her purse, and hurried to catch up to Terrah, who had bounced down the driveway to a trailhead. Like a fox toying with the hounds in earnest pursuit, she turned and waited for Helen to catch up. Just as she had, Terrah disappeared into the woods.

Helen followed Terrah as best she could, all the while tripping on branches and getting burrs stuck in her nylons, on her skirt, in her hair. As that small, nimble woman got farther away, Helen's hesitance at pushing branches out of the way passed. She adopted the stride of a hunter pursuing the prey. She was a hunter of information, a stalker of facts. This game was her life, although the "woods" she usually scoured consisted of computer files and trails through cyberspace. It felt good to be out of that rarified environment, in one that, though more real, felt more elusive and unknown.

When Helen finally caught up to Terrah, she looked like she had gone through a gauntlet. Her hair was in an uproar, her nylons had runs front and back, there were burrs on her clothing, mud on her pumps, and sweat dripping from her brow. Helen breathed heavily, not getting enough of the thin mountain air into her taxed lungs. She bent over and took several deep breaths.

Terrah sat on a rock in a clearing. "Come, enjoy the view," she suggested. The valley gaped open on one side of the clearing. A light mist still clung to the trees in the valley, giving it a distant and imaginary character, which contrasted with the harsh brightness of their meeting place. "I do love this spot in the morning," Terrah mused as much to herself as to Helen. "The world below seems like a dreamland. This is more real."

"Mrs. Timbres,…" Helen began, but Terrah held up her hand to stop her.

"First, please call me Terrah. Second, please, sit down and close your eyes. Relax. Melt into the mountain; feel the sun warming your face. Breathe and relax."

Helen was grateful to be given a moment to catch her breath. Relaxing, however, proved difficult, as she was still hunting.

Terrah continued, "The question you were about to ask me, imagine instead asking it to these trees and this rock and this beautiful space in which we are. Expand your perspective then, and ask it to the universe."

Helen balked, contorting her face into a look that married suspicion and incredulity.

"Close your eyes."

She closed them.

"Ask your question to the universe."

"Okay. Wh—"

"Shhhh. To yourself."

Helen's reaction, unspoken but revealed by her furrowed brow, was *What did I get myself into?*

"No, the question should be the one you were going to ask me," Terrah corrected.

Helen opened her eyes and looked intently at this odd woman who commanded her to do many things now that she was quite unaccustomed to doing. She shut her eyes again, took a deep breath, and let it out defiantly. Slowly the question that had been running around in her head incessantly these past few days re-emerged. *Where could Jerry possibly be?*

"Keep repeating that question over and over until you feel it move from your head asking it to your heart asking it. It will slow down and feel heavy. That's how you will know. When you are ready, when you feel the universe has heard your question, open your eyes," Terrah instructed.

Helen decided that she had no way of knowing when or if the universe had "heard" her question so she opened her eyes immediately. Terrah watched for the first creature that made its presence known to Helen. For a long few seconds, nothing came. The air was still and the sunlight heavy. Helen looked down, and a glint of light in the grass caught her eye. Terrah noticed Helen's attention focus on something. "What do you see?"

Helen moved her head to the side, and from that perspective she saw the source of the glint. "There's a spider web by that flower, but I don't see the spider."

"An empty web," Terrah repeated. "How does that answer your question?"

"It doesn't!" Helen blurted in frustration. She did not like being the one questioned. She preferred to be the questioner. "This is ridiculous."

"Do you want to know about Jerry or not?"

Helen nodded.

"Have your usual methods worked?"

Helen shook her head, still sulking and fuming.

"Then you must try something different, right?"

Helen nodded, reluctantly.

"What do you do, Miss Donellyn, at night when nobody else is around to bother you?"

Helen looked at her sideways. "I write poetry."

"Ah, good. So you know that reading poetry is not like reading the newspaper."

Helen straightened and turned to face Terrah. She looked at her intently.

"Well, the good Mother Earth writes poetry too. You must learn how to read it. Most folks read her writing as if reading a newspaper—oh, there's a tree, and in it is a bird. How nice. And there's a flower, a *Chrysanthemum leucanthemum* specifically, a daisy. You know there's more to writing than who, what, where, and when. I will teach you to read her poetry."

"Okay."

"If you read a web like you're reading a newspaper, how would that be?"

"It's where a spider lives."

"Okay, good. As you know from your OWB friends, there are an almost-infinite number of ways you can interpret the same facts about a situation—with a positive slant, a negative slant, and everything in between. Now if you were reading a poem, how would you read a web?"

Helen looked away. She hadn't thought about the OWBs in a long time. "A web is something you get trapped in, killed, and die, like a web of lies, of intrigue."

Terrah leaned down and tapped one of the strands of the web. "What did you see happen?

"You touched one part and the whole thing moved."

"Yes, the parts are all interconnected. That's how the spider knows he has caught something. Now let's go back to your question. What was it?"

"Where is Jerry?"

"By reading nature like a newspaper, all you'd learn is that he is not home in his web right now. It is empty. Jerry is gone. Those are the facts. But how would *you* read this poem that Mother Earth has written?"

"I don't know." She thought about how she could interpret it as abandonment; she could also look at it as fate, pure and simple. She could consider that Jerry was being malicious or that he was the real victim in his own disappearance. She brushed those interpretations aside and answered, "Maybe it means that he has somehow escaped from the possibility of getting trapped and killed, or maybe it means that he isn't living in his own web of lies anymore. But Jerry was an honest guy. I can't see how that would be the case."

"My dear, I'm sure you know that sometimes you can't force a poem to mean something specific. Sometimes they just give you an impression or convey a feeling. Look inside at what's so for you right now, not how to analyze the spider web."

It was difficult for Helen to step out of being a reporter. She wanted to find answers her way, not the way of a woman of uncertain sanity. Nevertheless, she was willing to try anything, so she shut her eyes and focused on the image of a spider web and let the thoughts and free associations happen. As the images arose, she described them, "Each strand the spider had built, he wove his own web. Each strand was a choice, and it was connected to other choices, all of which together constituted one's life. Maybe it's my own life that feels empty right now, empty because Jerry is not here. The empty web is peaceful, though, too, glistening in the sunlight without the spectre of death sitting at the center. It's not just one's own life that is interconnected; everyone's lives are interconnected. What happens in my life over here might affect what happens in someone else's life, someone I might not even know."

"Now, how does that answer your question?"

Helen fought the urge to be short and flippant and say "It doesn't," but instead let words tumble out of her mouth. "If everything is interconnected, then it doesn't matter where Jerry is because we're still connected." Serenity settled in her cheeks for the first time today. Her muscles relaxed and she could laugh again.

"I brought you here to show you how I get my information. You would have thought me a crackpot if you hadn't experienced it for yourself. Maybe you still do think I'm cracked, but that's not important. What's important is that the universe knows all; you just have to know how to read her writing. The spider and her web, you know, were the inspiration for writing among some native peoples. You as a writer should look to the spider as your friend and guide."

Helen shuddered.

"In any case, your friend Jerry is all right. He is not here at the moment, but when I asked the universe about where he was, a hummingbird came to me, and hummingbirds are a connection to the other realm."

"What other realm?"

"The nonphysical realm, the realm of energy before matter."

"Where's that?"

"It's hard to say. It's nowhere in particular, but yet it is everywhere. It's the converse to our realm of matter before energy. They fit together like the two sides of a coin."

"If it's everywhere, is it like zero-point energy?" Helen sensed another puzzle piece falling into place.

"Hmmm. I don't know anything about zero-point energy."

"Somehow," Helen mused, "maybe Jerry got inside the world of zero-point energy while we are still on the outside, even though the entire universe is, essentially, entirely zero-point energy in all its myriad forms. Or maybe the OWBs took him, although they didn't seem the abducting type. Perhaps they weren't finished sabotaging the operation at the Mason Ranch and came to get Jerry to finish it for them."

"My oh my you have a fertile imagination Miss Donellyn. You should be very careful that you don't disappear too."

◆   ◆   ◆

Leaves

A leaf falls
   And the wind catches it
      And carries it

So that it never hits the ground.

Is it sad, the leaf, that it left
   The tree
Never reaching its destination?

Does it feel special, the leaf,
   That it didn't end up in a heap
     With all the other leaves
      That left
       their trees?

When will the wind stop blowing?
   If ever.

◆   ◆   ◆

Harry sat in his dark blue pick-up truck across the street from Helen's house. He had waited over two hours for her to return home. As she walked from the garage to the front door, he followed her in the side mirror. He dropped the newspaper into his lap as he watched her dig out her house keys from her over-stuffed purse. He snuffed out his cigarette in the ash tray and cursed himself for having to do this sordid work. He noted the time, 5:15 PM, as he drove away.

Chapter 25

The question in nearly everyone's heart, of course, was "did it work?" Did the Welcoming Ceremony truly integrate Jerry into the community? And if it did, how would they know? How much could one outsider shift the vibration of the whole?

The next morning Jerry awoke feeling light and content, the best he had felt in many, many years. He shared his experience of the Welcoming Ceremony and the festivities after it with Maria over breakfast. "I literally feel like a human spider web. There are faint fibers that seem to be emanating from my middle, and I can feel them move."

"Pay attention to them," Maria told him, "as that is your anchor and your pulse. You can read it to tell how things are. But remember to read it rather than internalize or become it. They can supply energy as well as drain it from you, depending on your attention."

"I met one man in particular whom I'd like to know better. His name was Royce, and he works with the Energy Controller."

"Conservateur," Maria corrected.

Jerry looked puzzled by her correction but continued, "I want to learn more about the flow of energy, the loops within loops that he mentioned." Then the door bird sang. It had bright orange and purple feathers and a long, curved beak. It nested above the door and sang whenever someone arrived. It had different songs for different people. The song she sang today was a low note followed by a high note followed by three intermediate notes.

"Come in, Royce," Maria called out. She turned to Jerry and said, "You are learning to manifest quickly, my friend."

What is she talking about? he wondered.

"Hello Maria, hello Jerry. You can assume why I'm here. Yes, Jerry may talk with Allan Beaupensee, the Energy Conservateur."

Jerry and Royce left immediately. Beaupensee was a small man whose skin was soft and supple for his years. His face beamed when he smiled upon you, like a kindly grandfather so proud of his grandchildren. He didn't shake hands with Jerry or even look at him much, yet he seemed to know just what to say.

"I think you were expecting to see some kind of device, a generator of some sort, or some mechanism by which we *extract or generate* energy in order to provide some sort of power. I studied the history of those techniques, which are considered ancient, highly inefficient, and some even dangerous, not just because of their mechanical properties, but for their theoretical basis. When you realize that everything—even the air you breathe—is energy, it changes your perspective—quite a bit, I might add. You don't have to generate energy as if it were something else, something to produce. That is a complete misconception," Beaupensee explained. Royce bobbed his head.

"But how do you heat your homes and keep them light at night?" Jerry asked.

Beaupensee looked at Jerry sideways, almost as if not knowing what to make of him. "First, my son and brother, you must forget about the paradigm of devices working mechanically. Everything works through you; you are the transformer. If you want to be warmer, then *you* intend to be warmer. Your home might not want to be warmer. Second, the energy is everywhere. You are energy and this chair is energy. The difference between your energy and the chair's energy is that you have the ability to alter yourself. That is a very important point. You do not alter other things; you alter yourself and because you are part of, interconnected with all else, the laws of nature follow through. You start the chain reaction by pushing your own domino, and the rest fall from there."

"How do you alter yourself? Jerry asked.

Royce looked at him as if asking *How can you not know this?* Beaupensee simply answered his question. "You start at the most basic level, which are your thoughts and feelings. Thoughts, certain concepts in particular, amplified by feelings set up a very powerful vibration. Sometimes I'm sure you have felt it in the form of anticipation. Or perhaps you get a sense of knowing when you are at the right place at the right time. Your chest vibrates; you can feel it in your solar plexus. These patterns of vibration do not stay inside you. As you know, you have many layers, and so they are projected first through your second energy layer, and now because you have been Welcomed, they project through your third energy layer to all of us."

"Does this mean that all of you know what I am feeling at any given time?" Jerry asked.

Beaupensee thought for a second. "Well, no. But really yes. If I wanted to find out, I would send my attention through the Source being-body, inquire about Jerry, and then look at how I was feeling. Because we are connected, we have access to that, but only if we 'go to the library and look it up.' Some lovers, for example, have more immediate access to the feelings of their beloved because they have chosen to access that third layer more directly and continuously with that person. May I demonstrate?"

"Certainly," Jerry said, uncertain of what he was agreeing to.

Beaupensee closed his eyes and concentrated. His right index finger carved curling lines in the air, as if he was tracing a path. Without opening his eyes, he spoke, "You are curious, excited, and skeptical. You want very much to be known but not to be found out, so you have grown a hard shell but are very soft, tender even, where the shell does not protect you." He made motions with his entire hand as if he was shifting something, straightening it up. "There. Now you try."

"Me? How?"

"Close your eyes and go to that place you found yesterday where you felt light as air."

Jerry did as told.

"Now follow aneh-mi-oh-nu to the one you want to tune into."

"The what?"

"The person's signature vibration, find her or his frequency, so to speak. Then just see what's there."

Jerry followed the instructions as best he could. He tried to sense Maria. "I don't feel anything unusual, just everyday cheerfulness."

"That's just fine, just fine. Probably a good thing, eh?" the Conservateur said. "So that's what I do. Not too difficult. Have any more questions?"

"Yes, thank you. How do these thoughts and feelings create the world that I experience?"

"Keep in mind, Jerry, that it's your experience. Someone else might experience the same thing entirely differently. Creating your experience from thoughts and feelings is not magic. You do not think 'I want some vegetable stew' and—poof—there it is. It is more subtle than that. You think 'I want some vegetable stew' and the energy goes out into the universe, and Anna, who is making vegetable stew thinks about you. She thinks 'I haven't seen Jerry in a long time. I wonder if he would like to come for lunch.' So she invites you for lunch. You show up, and voila, there is vegetable stew. Coincidence? No. The energy that radiates from you draws the situations and people who are in synchronicity with it toward you. You have seen what happens when two wave patterns are in synchrony, their amplitude increases in an additive manner. That is what happens at all levels. It's very simple, really."

Jerry rubbed his palms together. "I can see how that works very well for personal connections, but what about physical needs, like cooking your food, heating your home, those sorts of things?"

"Ah, yes. Layer 1. Combustion. Fire creates a special kind of transformation in whatever it touches. For the walnut shells, plum pits, corn husks, and so on, which desire to be so transformed, we have a ceremony to prepare them. Not all of them want to undergo such a rapid and radical change; some choose to return to the soil from which they sprang."

"Your garbage chooses…?"

"We don't use that term. Nothing is g-, gar, nothing is wasted. *Everything* is integral, has its place, and is necessary and wanted."

"So do you also decide what gets composted and what is burned?"

"Oh, no no, not at all. That sort of thing takes care of itself. I think you would say that my primary responsibilities are like those of a conductor, but not a conductor or music, a conductor of being."

Jerry raised an eyebrow.

"You see, because we are all aspects of one Source being-body, more complete and more grand than any one of us can imagine, it is important that we all keep the good of the whole body in mind. Now that's not to say that there are not individual wants and needs, like vegetable stew or to learn to dance; however, if someone is sending poisoned energy into the whole body, I locate and rectify it. Consequently, what I do is highly confidential, because I must constantly take the pulse of the community. I must tune into each person, as I mentioned before, and see that they are balanced within the balance of the whole. Balance, you know, is an incredibly dynamic process of up and down. Balance isn't flat, static. We still do have emotions, you know, and emotions are powerful. Hence they can be mischanneled or wreak havoc with a person if they're not felt and released. If I find someone who needs emotional assistance I create an intention for them to have it. Because this intention goes out to the entire community, the person whose energy matches the need will respond naturally. It is very effective. So, we don't have people who specialize in emotional problems. Sometimes the assistance can be as simple as a child picking some daisies for the person. Other times, if the emotion is so strong that the person becomes energetically disconnected from the community, it is necessary to perform a Welcoming Ceremony for that person. So, to summarize what I do, I listen to the symphony of being and help those who are a little flat or sharp retune themselves back into harmony."

"I am quite amazed. People must really put a lot of trust in you." Jerry said.

"Oh, yes, because most of them would not want to do it anyway. This is not for anybody. It happens to be my gift, and Royce's. We are like musicians, tuning the vibrations. It requires much intense training, much practice, constant testing of one's ability to make the correct choice, and constant diligence. But the rewards are tremendous. To have people come back into harmony and be whole again after being a little flat or sharp is the most beautiful sound in the entire world."

"Thank you, Mr. Beaupensee, for you time and patience with my questions. And Royce, thanks for arranging this meeting." Jerry went to shake his hand, but Beaupensee simply bowed his head.

On the walk back to Maria's house, Jerry pondered the Energy Conservateur's purpose and explanations. *Everything seems too neat and tidy. Where are the conflicts, the rough edges, the people who just don't get along, the bullies, the criminals, the police, the shady side of life? Here people are drawn together by the same intention; they're not forced together. What happens when people are drawn into different groups that have diametrically opposite intentions?* Jerry was like that baby who just discovered his own big toe and began sucking on it.

He looked up from his pondering to see some children playing in the field. They were playing a game with a spinning disk that looked like a Frisbee. Some of the children were more athletic than others and wanted the game to be one of physical skill and stamina, whereas some of the kids seemed more mentally capable of controlling the disk and wanted the rules to say "no hands." Clearly there were different desires competing for expression. In the schools Jerry had attended, this situation would likely have degenerated into violence and name calling, with the team that bullied the most getting its way. Given, though, that all these children were conscious of their shared purpose, namely, wanting to play the game, they decided to alternate quarters of hands on and hands off. Each side figured they'd be able to trounce the other side in the quarters of their specialty.

As Jerry watched the children playing, he realized that his question had been answered by what he saw. The kids gave their shared intention (playing the game) priority over their differences in how it was to be attained (using hands versus no hands). Winning and losing remained limited to the game itself, without it spreading into who controlled the situation. Jerry wondered how this simple technique of remaining present to a shared purpose despite having different paths for achieving it might apply to more intractable situations back home, such as the debate between pro-life and pro-choice, the tension between economic growth and environmental conservation, and other seemingly irresolvable political issues.

If I think a question to myself, it is answered immediately. Therefore, I must be careful what I think. How is it that everybody's thoughts don't cancel each other out? What if I have a negative or inadvertently hurtful thought? This immediacy between what's in my head and what's in my world is not what I'm used to at all. Maybe I should have Maria or somebody teach me about this culture. I like how it works, and who knows how long I might be here, perhaps for the rest of my life.

Chapter 26

The next day Harry arrived on Helen's street just after dawn. He sat in the truck reading the newspaper, occasionally watching the minutes disappear on the digital clock. The neighbors to the north left together at 6:22 AM. A man in a jogging suit strode by at 6:35. He noticed Harry sitting there and jogged into the street to look at the license plate number. Harry put the newspaper up higher to cover his face. *Damn, I'm screwed. I'll have to take the plates off.* At 7:30 Helen emerged from the cocoon of her house. That answered it: his window of opportunity was from 7:30 AM to just after 5 PM, when she returned home. He turned the key in the ignition and savored the low rumble of the engine starting. In all his years as a state trooper he had never killed anyone. *How did it come to this?* The perks for "helping" Mason, which once seemed so great, now paled in comparison to what he had to do. *I never thought I'd be murdering people for him. And if something went wrong, Jack will deny having ever said anything. Nothing can go wrong.*

As he got closer to his hotel, he recognized the older buildings. He thought briefly about his ex-wife, wondered if she remarried. *Doesn't matter.* Then he thought about his kids. Neither one had spoken to him in years. *It was all her doing. She turned them against me.* Now he understood why.

There was still the problem of finding the guy who had been with Helen at the ranch. During all of the surveillance, Harry hadn't seen him. The irony of having to exterminate the guy whose life he had previously saved didn't affect Harry. *If I kill her before I find him, I'm screwed. But if I don't kill her right away...I'm still screwed.*

Chapter 27

"Oh, you're the reporter who wrote that piece in last week's Science section. Not bad, not bad, for a…" and he mumbled something, obviously catching himself before insulting Helen. "Please, have a seat." Professor Steven Gilb was head of the physics department and fancied himself an expert on everything.

"Thank you Professor Gilb. I don't want to take up too much of your time…."

"So why are you here? Your article is done. Don't you reporters drop a story like a hot potato once it gets published?" he said as he filed some reprints in an overstuffed filing cabinet.

"Well, there are other circumstances that…"

"Get to the point please. I don't want you to take up too much of my time either." He sat down in his large leather chair behind a large desk covered with papers and large books with complicated-sounding titles.

"Professor Gilb, is it possible for someone to seemingly disappear from this reality and enter the realm of zero-point energy? Helen asked.

Gilb laughed loudly. He leaned back in his chair and scratched his beard. "Well, Miss Donellyn, what you are asking is utter nonsense. It's just not possible, like trying to put a galaxy under a microscope," he said chuckling to himself.

"Look, I didn't come here to be ridiculed. I came here because I thought you would have an open mind and be willing to stretch your imagination past the boundaries of the Received View. If you don't want to do that, then I'll find one of your colleagues to talk to," she said rising from the rickety chair she was given to sit in.

"Be my guest, but I assure you that they will all tell you the same thing. I'm sorry I couldn't be of any more help," he said, showing her the door.

Arrogant son of a bitch, Helen thought as she gathered up her coat, purse, and Personal Secretary. As she left, she shut the office door behind her a bit harder than is usually polite. Helen dropped everything on the floor in the hallway, out of exasperation and to get herself organized and put back together. First the Personal Secretary into its holder in the purse, then she picked up her coat off the floor and brushed the dust off of it, cursing under her breath. A young graduate student who was walking by stopped and helped her put her coat back on. He had a shock of bright red hair and speckled cheeks, not your usual stereotype of a physics student.

"Thank you," she said to him absent-mindedly.

"I, um, overheard what you were asking Professor Gilb."

Helen blanched. Embarrassment on the heels of humiliation was too much for one morning.

"Yeah, well if you're going to tell me I'm nuts too, then thanks again for your kindness and good day."

"No, I have a theory about that," he whispered to her.

Helen stopped cold and turned to face him. "You do?"

He nodded his bright hair vigorously.

Helen grabbed his arm and suggested they find somewhere to talk.

◆   ◆   ◆

Harry parked his pick-up several blocks away and put his lock pick tools in a plastic pen holder in the front pocket of his lime green and white striped shirt. He buried the nylon webbing in the bottom of the shoulder bag. His gun was in its usual spot under his arm. He put on a pair of surgical gloves. On top of the nylon webbing he put some brochures he had found for a lawn-mowing service. That was his cover.

In broad daylight, with his hands in his pants pockets, he walked up her sidewalk and rang the doorbell. Inside the protective cover of the screen door, he pulled out the first tool and shoved it into the keyhole and twisted it. Like a surgeon, he used the next tool to feel inside the lock barrel and push the pins into place, one by one. He had let many stranded drivers back into their own cars, but never had he used this skill for such an unsavory purpose. He felt a tad lightheaded. For show, he pushed the doorbell again, then looked around to see whether anyone was nearby. The lock was not giving way easily, so he kept feeling his way around the barrel, like a dentist checking teeth for cavities. Two pins were sprung. *This is an old lock, it should be easy.* A bead of sweat dripped from his brow onto the porch. The third pin fell into place. Only two more. The end seemed nearer. He continued glancing furtively to see if any neighbors were walking or driving by. He took a deep breath, closed his eyes so he could focus better and poked the thin metal tool ever-so-gently into the barrel. "Where's the g-spot honey? Show me your sweet spot," he said to the lock.

As he felt the last pin click into place, he turned the knob and walked in. He looked at his watch and scanned the room for a place to hide where she wouldn't see him but where it would still be easy to grab her from behind. There was a small table near the front door. The coat closet was around a corner; that might be a place to spin his web and wait. The kitchen was small, without even a walk-in pantry, only a round café table with a mosaic top in the design of a pink rose blossom and two matching twisted wire chairs.

Harry wandered through the house looking for something that would give him the name of her accomplice. He opened the desk drawers and rifled through her papers. Had he been a detective rather than a patrol officer, he would have scoured them for information. He only glanced briefly at them for obvious clues and found none. Although it was only 4:27, he still felt an internal pressure to get into position. There weren't many places for a man of his size to hide. He checked the bathroom. *If only she was a guy. I could get in the bathtub and nab her from behind as she took a pee. But girls face the wrong damn way!* he thought while relieving himself.

Finally he settled on her bedroom closet. It was less cramped than the coat closet. *She'll probably change out of her work clothes. I could hide there in the dark and pull her in so she can't see my face. As long as I get the strap around her neck quickly I can snap it and that will be the end of that.* He crawled in behind her business suits, looked at his watch—it read 4:38—and waited as patiently as a hunter in a duck blind.

◆   ◆   ◆

"We call him Professor Glib because he blows everybody off, even his own graduate students. He's more concerned with intellectual vanity than about pursuing science, so don't take it personally," the young man explained as they walked to the Student Union. "You know that there is a huge rift in science right now between those who think that our own consciousness or thoughts or mind—there are many terms for the same effect seen—influences the physical world and those who think that the world is the world, and we don't alter it, we only perceive it. Glib-boy falls into the latter camp. Sometimes we play with him by changing the pH of his coffee. He still has no clue. He thinks the janitorial staff is out to get him by pouring their cleaning fluids into his cup at night. 'Conspiracy!' he yells, and we roll over laughing, knowing that if he would only consider the physics of intention…"

"How do you change the pH? I thought that was something pretty basic, part of the chemistry of the water?" Helen picked up the crumb-clue Ben dropped.

"Voodoo," Ben teased, making wild gestures with his arms.

Helen glared. She wasn't here to be messed with.

"Oh sorry. Haven't regained your sense of humor yet, eh?" He leaned in close to her and squinted his eyes. "You're going to have to give up some of that seriousness if you want me to help you, because what I have to say is very serious but you just can't get too serious about it, otherwise…" He made the circular gesture around the ear signifying going crazy. "Got it?" he looked at her over the top of his rimless glasses.

"Yeah, now let's hear your theory." She leaned back in her chair and held her coffee cup with both hands.

Ben scanned the room nervously, to make sure that no one of any consequence was within earshot. He leaned in close to Helen, almost whispering. "I'm working on a theory which posits that matter, or what we think of as matter, is not made up of particles or charges but of standing scalar waves. It only looks like particles or charges because that is the center of the wave, the point source, so to speak."

"Great, but how can this wave theory of matter explain Jerry's mysterious disappearance?"

"Whose disappearance? What do you mean?" Ben asked.

"My boyfriend just disappeared a few weeks ago and I'm trying to figure out why and how. No, he's not a fugitive, and I doubt he was kidnapped or killed. There is no evidence whatsoever of his whereabouts. The police are looking for his car and keeping track of his credit card use, but in the entire time he's been gone, there has been no activity. The person who saw him last said that he appeared to be headed to work as usual. I have a mystery on my hands. And we had gotten tangled up with" she lowered her voice, "some men who had a zero-point energy device. I was doing some research into that—perhaps you saw my article in the Science section—and thought that maybe there was something going on with that ZPE stuff that caused his disappearance. But I don't know enough about ZPE to even begin to consider the possibilities, which is why I came to talk to Glib, I mean Professor Gilb."

"Right then, we do indeed have a mystery on our hands. Who can you turn to for answers to life's impenetrable questions? Aha, the Roving Physicist!" Ben spied a saucer on a nearby table and put it on his head like a hat then spun it.

Helen rolled her eyes.

Ben continued in parody mode, "What were the circumstances of his mysterious disappearance?"

"Are you toying with me?"

"Of course—not! Seriously, fill me in. What happened?" He took the saucer off his head, put his chin on his fist, and listened intently.

"He left for work one morning. It rained that day. He never made it to work and hasn't been seen or heard from since. It was like he disappeared into thin air without a trace. Zip. Nada." Helen got a little choked up. To regain her composure, she said, "So tell me about this theory of yours."

"Okey dokey. First of all, you know that most people think that atoms consist of electrons, protons, and neutrons, and these are like little billiard balls orbiting each other. Well, quantum physics figured out that that's all wrong. So the next generation of physicists realizes that they can't really pin down the electron; they can only give a probability of where it might be within this 'cloud.' But they still think that there is something, a charged particle buzzing around. Well, that's all wrong too. There's really only a standing wave, which is going in and out simultaneously. The center of that wave is what they think is the particle, because it looks like a point, like there's something there, but there's really nothing there."

"What's a standing wave?"

"Okay, suppose I have a circular pool and I drop a stone in the center. A wave propagates and goes out and hits the edge of the pool (assuming no loss of energy) and bounces back toward the center of the pool. Now these waves are the same frequency but they're traveling in the opposite direction and so they collide. If the crests both collide, you know they form a higher crest. If a crest and a trough collide, the amplitude decreases or they cancel each other out. So the resulting wave pattern formed by the interaction of these two identical waves traveling in opposite directions is the standing wave. It has a bouncy pattern that looks like it's not moving anywhere but just going up and down in place. If you give me your PS, I'll show you." Ben pulled up a link to an animated picture of a standing wave. "Except it's not linear like this, it's spherical."

"So you're saying that matter is made up of these waves." Helen said.

"Righto."

"Okay. So what?"

"I'm getting to that. We just poured the concrete, laid the foundation. Now we have to put up a wall or two. So the wave, in its very structure, contains information about itself, which goes out to other waves, and it gets information back from them. Truly the medium is the message. You have to figure that there are a whole bunch of these standing waves out there, in here, everywhere, bumping into each other. I mean the plutonium atom alone has 94 electrons. And they're all communicating with each other simply by being. This establishes the interconnectedness of everything at the most basic level without any extraneous mediating factors."

"No voodoo?" Helen teased.

"Nope. Next wall. How is it that a bunch of waves can look, feel, and taste solid? Or, how do we get from the subatomic to macro level?"

Helen shrugged her shoulders.

"Incoherence. Just as with light, where you have a lot of different frequencies simultaneously which gives you white light, you have that in matter, too. There is so much overlapping and bumping and interfering of these standing waves; it's such a jumble that it appears solid. In a sense, the waves weave themselves together to form what we know as matter, stuff. Even crystalline structures, which are highly organized, appear solid because the wave fronts are interacting with each other in an incoherent manner. There are a bunch of steps to be filled in there by experimentation, but this is my theory anyway."

"Tell me, Mr....?"

"O'Lannon."

"Mr. Ben O'Lannon. Are you just trying to impress me so that I write an article about you and your new theory?"

Ben got the deer-in-headlights look. "Of course—not. We're just getting to the good part and you want to get popcorn."

Helen rolled her eyes. *This guy is too much!* "Okay, so what does the Roving Physicist conclude, that if you throw a little more salt and pepper into this stew called Reality that it'll be more palatable?"

Ben twisted his face in appreciation. "We found it! Oh fabulous sarcasm, the lowest form of humor, but still better than that deadly seriousness of yours."

"Earth calling Ben. Come in Ben."

"Here I am, just about to solve the mystery, after this commercial break from our sponsor." He held up his empty coffee cup, got up, and refilled it.

When he returned he continued, "How might Jerry have disappeared? Well, what would have to happen to the waves themselves for such an anomaly to occur? Let's look in the most obvious corner. Suppose something happens that enables the standing waves to become coherent, you know, like laser light, all vibrating in the same frequency?"

"How is that possible?"

"I don't know yet, but I figure that if it can happen for electromagnetic waves it could happen for standing waves. They do tend toward entrainment, after all.

Oh yes, what's that? If you have two waves of almost the same frequency in the same field, they tend to synchronize. Did you ever notice when you're in bed with someone, snuggled up close, that if you're breathing out of sync, your breathing eventually synchronizes? Shall I demonst..."

"Don't even think about it." Helen pushed his hand away.

"We're coming into the homestretch now. Oh, wrong metaphor; I used that one with the last reporter who interviewed me. We're putting the roof on our neat little theoretical house. If a bunch of electrons/waves became entrained, i.e., coherent, then it would alter the very structure of space, and that particular form of alteration might not be visible to us. That is the mild version. The picante version is that the center, the source of the standing wave, tends toward infinity, but in normal circumstances has a finite amplitude. Now if there were enough entrained waves, the additive value of the amplitude just might get past whatever keeps the amplitude finite in normal conditions. In other words, he might have escaped to infinity."

"What does that mean?"

"That's your favorite question, isn't it? It means no more materiality. Poof. Disappeared. That's my best guess anyway."

"Death?" Helen asked, horrified even at the possibility.

"To be or not to be, incoherent, that is." Ben ignored her.

"For all your incoherence, Ben, you just might have something here. But I have a question."

"Oh no, not the dreaded 'what does that mean?'"

"No. Is this pulsing that causes the standing waves, the energy at the zero point, you know the stuff that's still there, even when there shouldn't be any because the velocity of the electron or whatever is zero?" Helen asked.

"Yes. That was easy."

"Where does it come from? I mean, what causes these waves in the first place?" Helen asked.

"Why God, of course," he said with uncharacteristic seriousness.

Helen burst out laughing. Ben smiled at seeing her finally let go.

"But seriously, folks," he said imitating Groucho Marx with an invisible cigar, "this theory points out the totally interdependent nature of the universe. Nothing can exist without everything else because the everything else is what creates the inbound wave. And that brings me to the second part of the theory."

"Oh god, now what? This first part has already stretched the limits of my credulity."

"Oh good, well this will snap it for sure then. Part two has to do with intention."

"What does intention have to do with physics?" she asked.

"Everything, actually. Intention functions as a generator of sorts. It organizes waves toward a particular pattern. It doesn't guarantee anything, because there are a lot of intersecting, interfering waves. Intention is what keeps everything from dissipating to a static state. Intention thwarts entropy."

"Okay, but how can Jerry get back here? Does he have to have that intention, or could we have it for him, or what?" Helen asked.

"I don't know. Let me think about that. In my wildest dreams, and trust me, I have some wild ones, some probably involving you even, I never dreamed that anything like this could happen, I mean, a person disappearing. Subatomic particles pop in and out of existence all the time, but what's possible at the subatomic level is nowhere near consistent with what's possible at the macromolecular level. People don't just pop in and out of reality. There's too much complexity for that to happen." Ben was stumped but already contemplating the next step.

Already Helen was formulating another article on this wave structure of matter theory, even though all this physics was making her head swim. She jotted notes into her Personal Secretary.

Both Helen and Ben were thinking to themselves, effectively stopping the conversation, so Helen concluded that it was over. "When you've thought about it and are ready to try something, give me a call," she said, handing him her business card.

"That's it? You're leaving so suddenly? But I haven't...'

"Thanks, Ben—I never thought I'd say this—for eavesdropping on my conversation and then stopping to pick up my coat. I appreciate your sharing your ideas with me. Let's see how we can make them work, okay?"

Ben bowed deeply and with great flourish, in the style of a Medieval knight. "At your service, M'lady."

Helen chuckled at his theatrics.

"Perhaps now that the formal part of our conversation is finished, you might care to venture into other realms of conversation, preferably over dinner."

"I probably shouldn't, but I am starving." She looked at her watch, which read 6:45. "Sure, why not."

◆   ◆   ◆

Helen pulled in the driveway at 9:20 that evening. As she fumbled for and dropped her keys on the front porch, she noticed some mud on the porch. Inside, she turned the lights on, dropped her shoulder bag on the floor near the small walnut table she inherited from her grandmother and put her keys on top of it. She walked to the answering machine and checked for messages. None. Next she went to use the toilet and, perhaps from fatigue, failed to notice that the seat was up. Mechanically she put it down and continued with her evening routine. By the time she got to the bedroom, she had her suit coat off and was unbuttoning her blouse. As she reached for the closet door, a loud nasally grunt, like someone snoring, came from behind it. Helen jumped back, adrenaline launched itself into her bloodstream, and yet she reached again for the knob, curious to find out about the source of this mysterious noise.

The snoring got louder and more rhythmic. She backed away from the door, one step at a time. Uncertainty and hesitation clouded her usual decisiveness. Torn between wanting to scream and run away and wanting to find out who was in her closet snoring like a jackhammer, Helen stood immobile, staring at the closet door. Rational thinking came slowly. *It's not a burglar. Could it be Jerry? No, he wouldn't hide in the closet. Who would hide in my closet? Nobody I know. Uh oh.*

The color drained from her face. The person behind the door began to stir. Helen turned on her heels and ran to the front door. She grabbed her keys and her bag and jumped in the car. Once in the car she dialed 911.

"There's someone in my closet," she told the operator.

"Get out of there now. Go to the nearest police station and file a report. I'll send a squad car over immediately." the operator said.

Helen tore out of her driveway. Inside, the man in her closet woke up from the sound of his own snoring. He looked at his watch and cursed under his breath. He opened the door a crack and peeked out. He saw a suit coat that hadn't been there before tossed on the bed. She was home! He listened carefully for sounds of the house's owner. All was quiet. With his gun in hand, he emerged from the closet, ran out the back door, through the neighbors' yards to where his truck was parked. As he sped out of the neighborhood, he heard the sirens in the distance coming in search of him.

The next morning he returned to his stake out. He wanted to see if she returned home after the police finished there. The neighbors left at their usual time. The jogger came by at his usual time and eyed him long and hard. But the woman never emerged; 7:30 came and went, then 8:00. At 8:10 Harry drove to the nearest grocery store and purchased a fifth of Jack Daniels. He needed some liquid courage to face Jack Mason.

Chapter 28

Jerry jogged the long way, up the hills and back down, along the river and through the town. He had taken to jogging very recently, never having done it before. People looked at him strangely, unaccustomed as they were to seeing somebody running for no reason than to run. He didn't care. It was freeing and exhilarating. There was no pressure to do it, no one to sneer, no one to ask how many miles he ran each day. When he arrived back at Maria's house, sweaty and out of breath, he realized that he had no other clothes to change into. "Maria, I need some more clothes. These are wearing out, and I'm getting tired of wearing the same thing every day. I jogged all around today and haven't seen a shop, a market, nothing. Do I have to weave my own? How do you get things you need around here?"

Maria smiled.

"Yeah, okay. Send out the intention. I should have known." Jerry closed his eyes and did so. "Done," he proclaimed. "What is the form of money here?"

"None."

"No money? What about bartering or trading?"

"No. I've never done that."

"So how does the economy survive?"

"Economy?"

"The exchange of goods and services. Surely everybody doesn't know how to do everything that everybody else knows."

"As I told you, we create intersections. When I am doing something, say, harvesting herbs from my garden, if I have a thought about giving some to somebody, then I do it."

"You just do it without asking that person, 'hey do you need some basil?' What if the thought you had about them had nothing to do with herbs, like you thought about that person because you saw her with your boyfriend and were suspicious of what's going on between them." Jerry liked making up hypothetical situations.

"It sounds to me, Jerry, like you don't trust your thoughts. You second guess them, like your own thoughts are trying to trick you. You won't need to do that anymore, since you have been Welcomed. Your connection with yourself and with everyone else is strong now. You will know what you have to do, like the hand knows what to do when the leg itches."

"Yeah, you're right. I just don't understand how you can have such certainty about an intuition."

"Perhaps you need to experience it more. When you operate from the assumption that everybody is separate, I can see how you wouldn't trust your thoughts. But we are not separate, and now neither are you. So you must trust yourself."

Jerry said nothing. He had that far-off look in his eyes from looking inward rather than outward.

Maria continued, "All I know is that when I send out an intention and someone else has a complementary intention, then our intentions interact and are fulfilled. It's not about wanting or needing. Those are inverse intentions for the lack of what you truly desire. They carry a vibration of unhappiness, which is repellant. If you barter or trade, then you are setting up an exchange based on unhappiness."

"Unhappiness? But buying gives you a sense of power, accomplishment, control, which makes you feel good. You feel fulfilled at having gotten something that was lacking." Jerry argued.

"If you are happy with things as they are, then you don't need to alter the situation by buying something in order to attempt to regain a sense of happiness and contentment. There isn't a sense that anything is missing at the moment. So there's no need for buying and selling," Maria replied.

"But," Jerry began.

"Take this desire of yours for clothes. You feel like something is missing. You really want to get out of these sweaty, smelly clothes, but you have nothing else to wear."

"Yes. There's nothing wrong with that."

"Correct. How you deal with it makes all the difference, however. If you focus on not having something, that's the intention you send out. Thoughts are energy patterns. If you focus on the perfect suit for you, your wildest, most luscious dream clothes, that's the intention you send out. If you imagine these two situations, which one feels better?"

"The second, obviously." Jerry began to see clearly the connection between happiness and materialism. Material goods were supposed to feed the unhappy beast inside, and they do feed it, they just don't satiate it. And the beast's hunger only grows. "Uh oh, I better send out a different intention. I sent out the intention of needing new clothes. How about this instead: I intend to have new clothes."

"That's an improvement," Maria said, "but it's still a weak intention. Try this: 'I love my new clothes' and picture them in your mind, especially if you prefer to have pants rather than skirts!"

Jerry took a moment to imagine his new clothes. They would be in the style native to this community—loose white trousers and a colorful hand-woven shirt.

"When your intention manifests for you, you must address the other person or animal or plant in a specific way. This honors the mutuality of the intention and acknowledges your connectedness." She taught him the words to say in the various situations that might arise.

"Thank you, Maria. What would I do without you?" He hugged her.

"You are smelly and wet. I double your intention for more clothes!"

"It's amazing how much lighter and clearer I feel now, having rephrased my intention. I wasn't aware of how empty I felt when I thought I needed something. It was so normal to feel such lack before I came here," Jerry mused to himself out loud.

"I have a long red tunic. You can wash up and put that on."

While Jerry was bathing, the door bird sang out a cheerful melody unlike any other Maria had ever heard.

"Come in to the garden," she called out. "Jerry, you have a visitor!"

Jerry emerged with wet hair wearing Maria's tunic, which only reached to about mid-calf on him.

An older woman carrying a parcel waited for him in the garden among the riot of blossoms. "Greetings neighbors, other versions of me. My name is Arborea. I was cleaning out my son's room, as he is marrying and moving out, when I found these clothes of his. He grew so quickly that he did not use them for long. I didn't know what to do with them, and then I thought of our visitor whom we Welcomed not long ago. Perhaps they will fit you." She extended the parcel toward Jerry.

Jerry looked at Maria. She smiled knowingly. He received the parcel with bowed head (as Maria taught him to do) and gave her a hug, saying, "I am honored that our intentions danced together to create this gift. We are all One." That was the protocol for receiving the fulfillment of one's intention such that the other person knew it.

And a protocol for acknowledging receipt: "I am a mirror of your kindness," she replied. Thus the circle was complete.

"Please join us for tea, Arborea," Maria invited.

Chapter 29

♦

Helen's Journal

I am homesick and scared to go home at the same time. And I am tired of living in a hotel. I've had to work from the hotel, too; the police don't want me going to the office, because if he knew where I lived, he also probably knows where I work. The police have searched the entire house looking for evidence. They dusted for fingerprints. They vacuumed the closet for hair and fiber. Nothing was found but the powder from surgical gloves. This guy was a pro. Apparently Ian saw someone that morning and the one previous sitting in a blue truck reading a newspaper. I am damned lucky he was a tired and incompetent pro, or they say I would have been dead.

They questioned me incessantly about who might want me dead, so I told them what happened when I covered the OWB story. I don't know if they believed me. At least there was the article to prove that I really was there. It has to be Mason. What was I thinking when I exposed his operation in the ZPE article? I should have known he'd do something like this.

I became a journalist because I love the thrill of the hunt for truth. I do not like being hunted. Maybe this isn't the career for me. Then again, just because there are some people who want to hide or distort the truth doesn't mean I should give up. If anything, it should make me want to take up the torch even more. I just don't like living this close to the edge. Nobody should have to have a police escort to go grocery shopping.

I don't know what I want anymore. My own hunt for an explanation of Jerry's disappearance has been fruitless so far. Except for a strange theory by an even stranger grad student, I have not found a shred more evidence. I have been reading up on that wave theory, and it seems a little far-fetched, especially that stuff about intention. But then again physics has never been my strong suit. However, as the Bard said, "There are more things in Heaven and Earth, Horatio, than are dreamt of in your philosophy." Who am I to judge? This is truly a mystery. Without Jerry coming back to fill in the gaps, it seems like a mystery that will never be solved.

I regret that I dragged him into the fiasco at the ranch. I feel like it's my fault that he's missing now. I don't know what to think anymore. I don't know what to feel anymore. My insides have been through the wringer. What is left to do?

Nothing. There is absolutely nothing left to do.

Now what? It is time to close the book entitled *Helen and Jerry's Almost Fabulous Life Together.*

Today is the first day I'm back home. I refuse to shut closet doors anymore. I'm going to be an eccentric old lady if things continue like this for me. Anyhow, I woke up this morning to a crow outside my window, cawing and cawing, with this plaintive tone in its call. I wanted to throw a rock right through my window to shut the damn thing up. But instead I got up and looked outside. It was sitting in the maple tree on one of the bottom branches (right at the height of my window). I looked around to see what it might be cawing about, and there it was, on the ground right below my bedroom window, a dead crow. I burst into tears. This bird is now going through exactly what I have gone through with Jerry. I felt I had something in common with this poor, grieving creature. If I could make such a plaintive sound, I would too. I wanted to reach out to it, but when I opened my window, it flew away.

I gave its mate a proper burial. And all the time I was digging the grave, that same crow (I presume) sat silently in the maple tree watching me. When it was over, I told it that it was okay to find another mate now and to let the past be complete.

Amen.

Maybe Terrah's method works after all. I mean, what happened with those crows was kind of creepy—not scary creepy, but weird how that event mirrored my own life, and by attending to its loss I completed my own. She said that we can ask the universe questions, but that was more like the universe telling me something. Funny, I've asked everyone but the universe…

Believing is Seeing

Look around you
inside
over
beyond

In seeing,
you know what is there
in your mind.

When perceived,
perceiver becomes part of the illusion.

When understood,
appearances seem truer
than highest Truth.

But fool yourself not,
for fools, they say,
have but senses gone astray.

I dreamed last night that I was at the circus. I assume it was the circus because I was in a Hall of Mirrors, a room which was almost, but not quite, a perfect circle made of mirrors about a foot wide. I was the only person in the room, so my reflection should have been in every mirror. Yet, as I looked around, there was a different image of me in each of the mirrors. They were all me, but not identical, as you would expect in such a room. In some I am well dressed, in others naked, in others a slob, or a homeless person. I can tell that in some I'm a teacher, a scientist, a Vegas showgirl, a transvestite. In some I'm black, some I'm oriental, and some native. But they were all clearly me. The one thing is, I didn't see any that were definitely male. It's like I was looking at all the different possibilities of Helen Donellyn—360 degrees worth.

I felt an internal pressure to choose one to identify with, but I didn't want to. On some level I knew that they could all be me or already all were me. I woke up to find myself screaming, "I am all of them! Why do I have to choose only one to be?"

Chapter 30

When Maria went to work in her garden, she found Jerry sitting under a lemon tree looking rather sour. "What has you feeling so contrary to your sweet nature, my Cherry blossom?" she teased.

Jerry lifted his head from his hands. His brow was furrowed and his skin sallow. His face was tense from restraining the sadness and fear. "It looks like I really am stuck here for good, aren't I? And I feel like I ought to be doing something productive, but I don't know what I can offer. All the skills I developed before are useless here. There are no computers for me to program..."

"Isn't that what you wanted to stop doing?"

"Well yes."

"It's a good thing, then, that there aren't any," she stated.

"After talking with the Energy Conservateur, I realized that I know very little about how the physics works here. To make matters worse, I don't have any practical skills, like farming or building. I feel utterly useless," he wallowed.

"Nobody is useless, you know that, Jerry." She put her arm over his shoulder. "Come with me. I will show you where I go for inspiration when I have these kinds of tormenting thoughts. Come."

"Now? Weren't you going to do something else?"

"The intruding plants will still be there when I return. I really didn't want to relocate them right now anyway. See how things work out?"

Jerry smiled, and they walked towards the center of the community. People who were outside waved to them. "Good day, Maria, Jerry! You must come by to visit when you would like some raspberry cake," said a blonde woman who was weaving at an outside loom tied around a tree.

"How is our Guest enjoying his sojourn?" asked Biryan, an elderly man also walking in their direction.

"I am enjoying it," Jerry smiled.

"You must not toy with me, young man. I have the sight," he said wagging a long bony finger at Jerry.

"The sight?" Jerry asked.

"Into your heart. It is pained right now. You are not seeing what is right before you. Open your eyes!" he said as he walked ahead of them more quickly.

"It is difficult to hide myself from others," Jerry said.

"Yes indeed. Why would you want to?" Maria asked.

"To hide my pain."

"Why? Do you think they have never felt pain before? There is nothing wrong with pain. It's a message. This way." She pointed out where to turn.

"Beaupensee told me that anybody can tap into how anybody else is feeling. At first I thought that was an invasion of privacy. But that's the only way to have a whole and integrated community, isn't it? If someone is cut off, unavailable, then the integrity of the whole is compromised. It's stupid to hide because it puts everyone at risk, not just yourself."

"When you're hiding is when you most want to be known," Maria said.

"You're right."

"Here we are. This is where I come to ponder the big questions," she gestured to the grove of fruit trees surrounding them. "Abundant beings whose arms are filled with great bounty, may we share in your copious nourishment? Inspire us to fruitfulness and sweet plenty," she said to the trees. Their leaves shook, though Jerry didn't feel any wind. "When I have a problem for which no solution is forthcoming, I come here to the orchard, and I try to think of a different solution for each piece of fruit I pick. It makes for slow harvesting but forces me to think prolifically," she said to Jerry.

At the base of each tree was a basket. Maria picked up the basket at the base of an apple tree and climbed into the first V in the trunk. She reached into the leaves and plucked juicy ripe fruit. Jerry watched in awe. He had never seen a woman her age climb a tree. He wandered from tree to tree, looking up at the crop in some and leaning against the trunk of others, still wondering what he might be able to contribute to this community. At the far end of the orchard, he saw a small, gnarled tree that was bent over from the weight of the fruit on its branches. It was an old tree that had blossomed profusely in the spring sun, and now it called out to Jerry to relieve it of its burden. He picked up the basket and plucked bright red, crisp apples from its boughs. He filled the entire basket yet still hadn't unburdened the tree, so he took a basket from another tree and filled that one too. The tree was small enough and Jerry tall enough that he could reach most of the ripe apples. Only a few remained out of reach. Taking a third basket, he studied the tree as if it were a complex equation, then put his right foot on a low branch and pulled himself up. Only two feet off the ground he was, and the world looked so different from there! He wedged his back against the thickest branch and plucked the interior apples. The trepidation gone, the apples picked, Jerry relaxed and saw all that he had accomplished. He smiled and felt the tightness in his chest and head go away. He picked up all three baskets and walked toward Maria. Half way he turned around and saw that the apple tree had sprung back to attention. He felt the lightness that the tree felt. *I am the mirror of your kindness,* he found himself thinking to the tree, as if it had acknowledged the intersection of intention. Perhaps it had.

"What shall we do with all these apples?" he asked Maria.

"If we don't need them, we take them to the Community House for others." Maria saw the changed expression in his face and body. It worked. There is always room to feel useful when the orchards are bursting with their cornucopia. She climbed out of the tree and helped him carry one of the baskets.

When they arrived at the Community House, a group of people sat laughing and drinking tea. Emerson broke away from the group and came over to help them carry baskets. "Maria, Jerry, it is good to see you both."

"We've brought apples galore. I hope someone wants to make pies," Maria said.

"That would be me!" said a young brunette. "My husband loves my apple pies. I am honored that our intentions danced together to create this gift. We are all One."

"I am the mirror of your kindness," Maria replied, while elbowing Jerry to do the same.

"What brings you to the orchard today?" asked Emerson.

Jerry looked at Maria as if asking whether it was okay to reveal the true reason. She encouraged him.

"I was feeling rather useless earlier, and she showed me that there are always ways to be useful. I unburdened a heavily weighted tree today."

"She's truly grateful, she is," said an old crone, "as I was when my breasts were gorged with milk and my boy was thirsty from playing."

"You haven't had gorged breasts in centuries," said and equally wrinkly man in the corner.

"In your dreams, I have," she replied, and the group burst out laughing again.

Emerson pulled Jerry aside and walked with him away from the group. "Did you notice today, Jerry, that at the very heart of your anguish there was a kernel of hope?"

"No, I didn't."

"I see. Well, shall we look at that now?"

"Sure." Jerry was one to go with the flow.

"When you examine your feelings of uselessness, don't you feel that way because you really do want to feel useful?"

"Yes, of course. I just lack the means to do so or the imagination to devise a way to be useful."

"So whenever you feel that way again, it helps to recall what is at the heart of it. This is called fu-an-gu."

Jerry knitted his brows. "Few what?"

"Come, I'll show you." Emerson led Jerry out of the Community House to the circle of stones in the grass nearby. "This is the most sacred space in the village. Whereas the ancient Greeks had pillars holding up the Parthenon, these are the pillars of our culture."

Jerry contorted his face so as not to laugh out loud.

"Okay, so they're short pillars. What I mean is that the concepts carved into these stones form the basis of our way of being."

"And what is that?" Jerry asked. They walked around the circle, and Jerry looked at the carvings in the rocks. They were ideographic, like the hieroglyphs of ancient Egypt; however, they were less pictorial and more geometric.

"We call this one ✹ fu-an-gu. Its meaning translates roughly as the deeper you get, the less it looks like itself, and when you reach the core, it looks like the opposite of what you started with."

"That's how hope can be at the heart of dejection," Jerry commented.

"It's not saying that it is one or the other or is one and not the other. It's saying look completely; look beyond the surface; don't judge until you have the whole picture."

"So how does it function as a foundation of your culture?" Jerry asked.

"You can apply this to whatever you want to investigate. Take your skin, for example. It is the first boundary between you and the external world," Emerson explained. "When you look at it with your eyes, it seems solid enough. It holds your organs and muscles inside and protects them from the elements. It shows you where you end and the rest of it All begins. It seems like a pretty definite boundary between you and not-you. We think that boundaries are hard and fast because language has given us that assumption. However, we also know that skin is permeable because sweat comes out and chemicals are absorbed into the body through the skin. Despite its permeability, it still looks and functions like a real boundary.

"As you move from the outside into the skin itself, it becomes harder to differentiate the actual boundary because all you see is the constant interaction between inside and outside molecules and photons being exchanged in both directions. Not only are the boundaries permeable, but there is constant motion, process, sunlight being converted chemically to vitamin D, air being taken in and mixed with blood, delivered to the organs, water mixed with chemicals (sweat) being released into the air. From this perspective it is difficult to determine where the skin ends and the environment begins. It's all process; skin is a process, not a thing. What looked like a boundary superficially is actually far from it. So, Jerry, what does that tell us about boundaries, demarcations, distinctions, and so on?"

"It tells us that language gives you your boundaries between one process and another, which makes it seem sometimes like there is a real boundary between one 'thing' and another," Jerry answered.

"Good, so let's use this concept to investigate language itself. If you take an abstract idea, such as love or justice, all the way to its core, you see that it is grounded in substance, in the material world. Love, for example, is grounded in what happens between two people. It boils down to actions, very physical actions—a helping hand, a kind word, a meal prepared with care. As a concept it seems abstract, but at its core love does something very physical. Conversely, if you take a concrete thing, like matter, and look deeper and deeper into its core, you see that it is insubstantial, vibrations in space. If you look at the continuity of space you will find that at its core is discontinuity," Emerson added.

"Foo-an-goo, it's an elegant concept," Jerry remarked, "a relatively complex idea which you boiled down to a single symbol. It removes the temptation to think something is one way or another. It invites you to look at how seemingly opposite things are related. It also shows me that everything—everything—is completely connected, so much so that it is impossible not to know that we're all part of one enormous body called the universe. Already I can see its many applications. In psychology it applies to people's personalities. On the outside, for instance, a person might appear to be highly self-confident, even to the point of arrogance, but when you look deeper into the workings of such a personality, you find that such people are often highly insecure.

Emerson continued, "This concept of fu-an-gu—note the sounds are more abrupt, not so elongated—is not a quality, like something being red or smooth, it is more like a context, a space for investigation, a process itself," Emerson explained.

"When you perceive something, do you really see all that stuff going on at once, the interrelationship of something and its opposite? For example, when you look at me, do you see into the molecules of my skin?" Jerry asked.

"No, that's not how I see you. It's more like the way an herbalist looks at a plant. Not only does she see the plant itself, but all the uses for the plant, all the good the plant can do. That's how I see you."

Jerry nodded. "This concept of fu-an-gu gives me a new vantage point from which to see what I already know. In 'seeing' the processes going on in my skin played in slow motion, I saw past the abstractness of it all and saw how they shared electrons, how one molecule transformed into others, how all the processes going on were so vastly intertwined. The complexity was both beautiful and mind-boggling, not to mention difficult to describe in the precise, linear, non-recursive language of science, which has difficulty conveying the sense of the whole, the web of interconnections and interdependencies in all their biotic beauty. The oneness that is fundamental to the manyness is lost. However, I still have some niggling uncertainties, questions. For example, if we are all one, what is the point of differentiating, of becoming different personas, different beings?

"That *is* the point exactly!" Emerson replied.

Jerry still looked confused.

"Imagine having only one finger. How much could you accomplish with one finger?"

"Not much. Anything other than pointing would be hard."

"Now imagine having twenty fingers. Just think of how many shoelaces you could tie at once, how rich the chords you could play on musical instruments. We are like the fingers of the One. We accomplish. We create. We do. We experience. Everything experiences. As you experience this flower, it experiences you in its own way. The fish experiences the ocean, the other plant and animal life there. The grass experiences the sunlight and the rain and someone walking on it. The water experiences the waterfall. Each being contributes its experience to the whole. Isn't it magnificent to think about from the perspective of the whole?"

"I never thought of grass as experiencing someone walking on it. It might not be a self-conscious experience, as I have, but it is an experience nonetheless," Jerry thought out loud.

"To be distinct within unity is life. The One implies the Many, and the Many imply the One. The point of differentiating is to be able to experience both simultaneously, which is wholeness, which is fu-an-gu. The One can appear to be its opposite because they are ultimately One. To experience oneness without differentiation, without twoness or threeness or millionness—yawn—wouldn't be terribly exciting. It would be rather static, no movement, no development. To experience separateness without oneness would be—I shudder to think it, too frightening, too frightening. The isolation, the loneliness would be intolerable."

"How do I experience both then?"

"You do all the time."

"I do?"

"Of course," Emerson smiled. "You have not succumbed to the crushing isolation nor have you lost yourself in the hypnotic vastness. We all dance on the edge between them. Like the skin, each of us is a permeable membrane between Individuality and Allness."

"I never thought of it that way. I always felt caught between them, in the middle of an epic struggle."

"It's easy to feel that way if your perspective has been stuck on the side of Individuality for a long time. From the perspective of Oneness, all of the experiences are valuable. There are no wrong notes, only notes, and the symphony score is being written as it is played, as it is experienced in every moment," Emerson said.

"This is tricky, given the way my language works. Like the Zen masters, you sound like you are talking in riddles, or worse yet, out of both sides of your mouth."

"Yes, I know. These words are like, like being on one side of a war only. They are limiting. I struggle with them. Our concepts are complete; they convey that it takes two sides to have a war in the first place and that both sides are integral to both war and to peace." Emerson smiled and added, choosing his words slowly and deliberately, "So long as you think that you are the only note, there will be cacophony. But even then you wouldn't notice it because you're unaware of the song of which you are a part. Once you become aware that you are a note in a grand symphony, you can begin to create a harmonious melody, if you so choose. There will always be those who create dis-chord, disharmony simply because they want to. After all, discord is fun for awhile, until you realize that it keeps you alone and separate. I'm not saying conformity is good, just that there's inherent pleasure in being part of something bigger than yourself and contributing to it in a way that is meaningful and harmonious not just to you but also to the others."

"Emerson, this is all very abstract. You said earlier that even abstractions are grounded in reality. Can we look at that? How does this concept apply to my life?" Jerry asked.

"Your inquiries are wonderful, Jerry. What kinds of things do you take for granted vis à vis being separate versus being One with everything? What sort of things do you assume are yours and yours alone?"

"Well, I have my own dreams, not yours. *As soon as he said that, Jerry remembered Terrah's granddaughter, the one who dreamed his dreams.* What I eat doesn't affect your weight. My thoughts are private, my desires are private, my pain is private, although not here I found out. I get paid for the work I do, not the work someone else does. I pay my taxes, not someone else's. It seems that there are lots of elements of my life that support the notion that I am separate."

"Yes, that is very true. Now consider what you assume about being connected or One with everything else," Emerson instructed.

"Well, we all have to eat, sleep, and breathe. I assume there will always be air to breathe, water to drink, night time to sleep. Let's see…I assume that even if you can't experience my emotions, you do feel the same types of emotions I feel, like sadness, grief, joy, satisfaction, etc, and I can generally tell when you're feeling them. This is more difficult. My context isn't set up for reinforcing my interconnectedness. I barely recognize it in my day-to-day activities."

"Yet you know that it is true, correct?"

"Oh yes, even more so now."

Jerry expected Emerson to continue talking, but he didn't. Jerry looked sideways at him, expecting more explanation, but it didn't come.

After a long silence, Jerry's thoughts caught up with him. "Oh, that's the problem! There's little infrastructure either in the world or in language to enable me to live from knowing that I am One with everything. We don't take it for granted enough. My infrastructure is grounded in the perspective of Individuality, whereas your infrastructure is grounded in the perspective that sees both Individuality and Allness and their interplay."

"That's an excellent deduction for having learned only one 'letter' of our alphabet, one foundation stone on which the edifice of our culture rests. Let's now look at the complementary concept to fu-an-gu. Nothing exists in isolation here, not even our concepts; there is always balance. This next concept is based on another fundamental structure of the universe, which you might know as a Klein bottle. Do you know what that is?" Emerson asked.

"Yes, I'm very familiar with it. A Klein bottle is a topological surface, an abstract geometric shape invented in the late 1800s by a German mathematician, Felix Klein, that kind of looks like a bottle, except that it spirals in on itself so that the outside becomes the inside and vice versa. It's not a true bottle in that it holds nothing." Jerry rattled off this description from memory, then started thinking. *There must be something to that. Terrah said something about the Klein bottle too.* Jerry's memories triggered a cascade of pleasant thoughts and feelings, from which Emerson jolted him.

"Yes, indeed." Emerson was pleased that he already knew. "Felix was a Visitor here, like yourself. This 'bottle' he invented using his mathematics is a sometimes-adequate metaphor for the paradoxical nature of the universe at is most basic form. Unfortunately, it didn't seem to interest many people outside the world of mathematics."

"Klein was here?"

"Oh yes, others too—Escher, Lao-tse. You're not the first Visitor we've had, although we haven't had any in quite some time."

They have all contributed great works to our culture. Is that what I'm supposed to do? Is that why I'm here? Jerry wondered. "They all went back," Jerry challenged.

Emerson smiled one of his characteristic enigmatic smiles. "You might say that. However, with fu-an-gu you saw that boundaries are illusions. The boundary between your body and the world isn't distinct; there's a permeability between inside and outside of your body, between Individuality and Allness, and between many other concepts, which I encourage you to think about. There might not be a difference between here and there," Emerson suggested.

"How can that be? There certainly seems to be tremendous difference—different people, different culture, different language…"

"Those differences exist between countries. They are insignificant. Perhaps this will help you understand." Emerson showed him the design carved into the rock directly opposite, at the western point in the circle. "The complementary

concept to fu-an-gu is mu-ishi-wa, and it is represented thus: . Mu-ishi-wa translates as 'there is only one side that serves as both sides.' Sort of like a Klein bottle," he said tilting his head and raising his eyebrows.

"Close your eyes, Jerry, and imagine being on a roller coaster that is a Möbius strip. It starts up normally, you go up a big hill and then down; the ride turns upside down, and your hands are waving in the air, but being a Möbius strip, it goes on and on, and the scenery changes with each revolution. Where did one lifetime begin and another end? Where does night begin and day end? Just keep imagining being in a world where there is one that is both."

Jerry saw himself in night and day at the same time. (It looked like a Magritte painting that he had seen, in which the streetlights were on as if it were night but the sky above the tree line was blue as day.) In the next revolution the scenery changed, and he was on the earth and the moon at the same time. In another revolution he imagined himself at the center of the universe and at the edge of the universe as if they were across the street from each other. In the final revolution the scene shifted again, away from the notions of space and time and physicality. Jerry found himself staring into what his grandmother might have called "the face of God." It was awesome to behold, as all the things that seemed to be separate, such as light and dark, here and there, even Jesus and Satan, were all Möbius strips. The entire universe was only one and it embodied both.

"Wow! That was powerful. I never would have imagined that imagining something could be such a mind-blowing experience. I came face to face with the divine."

"If you manage to drop all your preconceptions, this is how it is here, everyday. Mu-ishi-wa is also very mundane. Perhaps you do not see it this way yet because you still only see what you believe. There is more, so much more," Emerson said.

"Like what? Give me an example."

"Do you believe that egoism and altruism are opposites?"

"Yeah, pretty much."

"How?" Emerson probed.

"Egoism is about self-interest and altruism is about helping others."

"Might it also be said that egoism is akin to self-love and altruism is akin to loving others?"

"Okay," Jerry said.

"Is it possible to love others without loving yourself?"

"Well, I don't know. You're starting to pull a Socratic thing on me, aren't you?"

"I'm merely pointing out that love and self-love are the two sides that are one, because the individual is merely a finger of the body. Love the body, others, and you love the finger by default," Emerson said.

"Yes but it doesn't go the other way. Love the finger does not imply love the body. You could hate a toe."

"Perhaps that might be so if the finger thought it was separate from the body. When the finger knows, as you know from having been Welcomed, that it and the body are one, then loving the finger extends to the body because they are continuous. Where is the boundary? The finger is connected all the way to the toe. That is mu-ishi-wa."

"I see how that works now," Jerry said.

"Fu-an-gu ✳ and mu-ishi-wa ◎ are the first couple, the male and female, the yang and yin of our culture. Separately or together, they allow you to begin to hold more than one perspective in your mind at the same time. If you are looking at the glass as half empty, it prompts you to also look at it as half full," Emerson continued. "If you look at it one way for too long and you begin to think that it will always be that way, these concepts remind you otherwise."

Maria emerged from the Community House carrying a small basket of fruit, not just the apples that they had picked. She joined them near the mu-ishi-wa rock. "Do you feel useful now, Jerry? If you weren't so useful as a student, Emerson would not feel useful as a teacher, which is something I know he loves to do."

"In all my years of going to school, I never once felt that I was being useful by allowing someone to do what they loved to do," Jerry said.

"Maria, you flatter me," Emerson said, continuing the good-natured ribbing.

"I guess it doesn't matter whether I'm teaching or learning, speaking or listening, writing or reading, each is necessary to the fulfillment of the other. Mu-ishi-wa, correct?"

"Very good, Jerry," Emerson said.

"I'm headed home. See you later, Jerry." To Emerson, she lowered her eyes and curtsied, a symbol of respect to someone you know well.

"She seems to like you," Jerry said to Emerson.

"Indeed." Emerson had a dreamy, far-away look on his face.

"What next, professor?" Jerry asked.

"I think that will be all for today. But on the topic of usefulness, as Maria carried away a basket of fruit from your earlier activities, what will you carry away from this?"

"A pop quiz." Jerry thought for a bit. The day had been rich, not at all what he expected while sulking under the lemon tree. "I learned that the way I look at things determines what I see. If I look one way, I see only one side, and if I look another way I see only the other side. I should look beyond the superficial, to the core of whatever I'm investigating. So that's a method to use. My perspective determines not only what I 'see,' but also what is possible to 'see.' If my perspective remains tied to that of my body, then it will always be limited in what it is possible to see. However," he mused, spinning ideas off the top of his head, "if I could suspend such unidirectional observation and see something—not just visually, but with all senses and the mind—if I could see from all perspectives at once, wow, I might get to what's really real. It is where all possible perspectives coexist simultaneously. And it's what the OWBs showed Helen and me. If I can get to that space, then I am not tied to a single perspective; I can choose among them or choose all of them at once. This is incredible!"

Emerson challenged him further: "It's easy to imagine this if you are looking at something simple, like one of the apples you just picked. It can be challenging to maintain this meta-perspective in social encounters. Can you maintain it when someone is criticizing you? Can you simultaneously entertain not only your perspective, but his perspective and a neutral observer's perspective as well? Can you maintain it when there is a terrible disaster? Can you see all perspectives at once when you are upset, including the perspective of the person who upset you?"

"Before I came here, I would have said no automatically. I shall presume that I can do all those things. After all, I have been Welcomed." Jerry played in his mind with the geometry of the multiple perspectives. A certain picture came to mind, in which each point on a circle is connected to every other point. He began

to trace it on the ground, like this.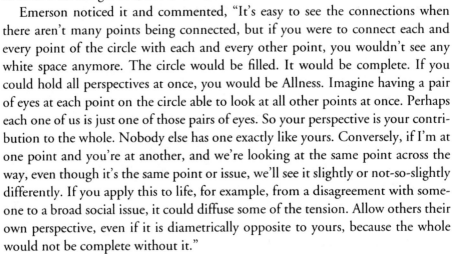

Emerson noticed it and commented, "It's easy to see the connections when there aren't many points being connected, but if you were to connect each and every point of the circle with each and every other point, you wouldn't see any white space anymore. The circle would be filled. It would be complete. If you could hold all perspectives at once, you would be Allness. Imagine having a pair of eyes at each point on the circle able to look at all other points at once. Perhaps each one of us is just one of those pairs of eyes. So your perspective is your contribution to the whole. Nobody else has one exactly like yours. Conversely, if I'm at one point and you're at another, and we're looking at the same point across the way, even though it's the same point or issue, we'll see it slightly or not-so-slightly differently. If you apply this to life, for example, from a disagreement with someone to a broad social issue, it could diffuse some of the tension. Allow others their own perspective, even if it is diametrically opposite to yours, because the whole would not be complete without it."

When Jerry looked up from his drawing, sitting before him was not Emerson, but a woman, a striking blonde with enchanting hazel eyes and a sexy smile. Jerry jumped, startled, which shifted his perspective ever so slightly, and now he saw Emerson sitting there. Jerry adjusted his perspective, internally more so than externally, so that he could see both genders of this person simultaneously. Slowly, Emerson's male side emerged merged with her, almost like a Harlequin.

"Emerson?"

"Yes, Jerry, this is still me."

"How do you do that?" he managed to sputter.

"Do what?"

"Turn into a woman."

Emerson broke into a hearty laugh. "That's like saying 'how do you have brown eyes?' It's the way we all are. I didn't turn into anything, you just allowed your perspective to shift."

"Well, how come I couldn't see *her* before now?" he said pointing to the gorgeous blonde.

"You thought you only had one perspective. Once you realized that it was possible to have more than one, you were able to see more than one."

"I suppose you're going to tell me that I have both male and female sides too."

"Yes, you do. Come, look," Emerson pointed to the reflecting pool at the center of the circle in which Jerry could see his reflection.

Jerry looked at his reflection and gasped. On his right side he saw a statuesque brunette who had an air of authority about her. She was well-proportioned, with high cheekbones and piercing brown eyes. He waited for him/her to say something, but s/he didn't. Of course not! If it was him, and he was waiting, of course s/he wouldn't say anything. He had never thought of himself that way before, as male and female, so he shifted his perspective to get a better look at his female side. He was the Klein bottle looking at himself as the Klein bottle. *Not too bad,* he thought. Jerry had never expended much energy getting in touch with his "inner woman." It had seemed like a waste of time. He was a guy. He knew he was a guy. He liked guy things. He didn't like girl things. Why waste time finding out what he already knew? Today, however, he saw the woman in him. She wasn't a little girl, and she was amazingly attractive.

"Is this the first time you saw your female side?" Emerson asked quietly.

"Sure is."

"We have been able to see her since you arrived. She is beautiful, don't you think?"

Jerry nodded enthusiastically.

"Although the gender we mostly manifest is primary, which means that it does the work, physically performs the actions, the other gender has supremacy, which means that it calls the shots, makes the decisions. It is the power behind the throne, so to speak. However, you can intend which to manifest."

"How do I do that?"

"Knowing that you are both male and female, you get to choose which one or both to manifest physically. When you know all that you are, in your bothness, intending is nothing other than choice. When you know all that you are, in your *allness*, again, it is nothing other than choice."

Jerry had a heavy, contemplative look. A lifetime of cultural conditioning had resulted in his unequal gender expression, namely, suppression of his female side, and now it was visible for all to see.

"Perhaps this should be all for today. You are going to have to adjust to the other perspectives you can now perceive." Emerson patted him on the back.

"No, oh no. This is incredible." Jerry flooded Emerson with more questions. "How do I address people? How do children know who their father is and who their mother is? What words do I use instead of 'him,' 'her,' 'he,' and 'she'?"

"Instead of identifying people by their gender, as you do with your pronouns like he, she, him, her, we identify people by their connection to the One," Emerson explained.

Jerry cocked his head, not knowing what Emerson was referring to, and thinking, *how can you not use pronouns?*

"Each person is a unique emanation from the One, so that is what we use as the referent for that person. Perhaps you have not seen this connection yet."

Jerry shook his head.

"Okay, relax your gaze and look at me. Look at the solar plexus. What do you see?"

"When I look head on, all I see is a kind of void, like a black hole."

"Okay, now shift your perspective."

"Oh wow, now I see a golden rope."

"Now look at your own. What do you see?"

"I see a multicolor braid, like a twisted rainbow."

"Okay, so if you were talking to someone about me, you might say something like 'Emerson is a great musician. Golden Braid played beautifully in the concert last night.'"

"You must have memorized everyone's connection," Jerry inferred.

"When you perceive the connections as a young child and can see it from the very beginning, it is as second nature to us as gender and names are to you. I wonder why you lost the ability to perceive each person's connection to the All. It's so fundamental to who you are."

"Is this like an umbilical cord to the source of life itself?" Jerry asked.

"Exactly."

"What about person-to-person connections? I'm extrapolating from that little diagram of multiple perspectives. Are there any little threads between us manifested beings?" Jerry asked.

"The second connection you will notice is one coming from the heart and going to someone else's heart. You should watch the older young people; it is very strong in them, so you can see it easily. Also, some older couples have a very strong and visible connection. This connection can change color, size, and shape from day to day, whereas the connection to the divine is constant. It is like your signature."

"Even if you forget about it?" Jerry asked.

"How could you possibly forget?"

"If you don't know it's there and don't see it every day, like me for example. I rarely look in the mirror…"

"Yes, even if you forget, it is still there."

◆   ◆   ◆

Before returning to Maria's house, Jerry sat under a tree near the Community House and watched people. Interactions took on whole new levels of complexity as he watched people's masculine and feminine sides deal with different situations in life.

One teenage couple in particular intrigued him. The one whose primary body was male shared a voluptuous female aspect who seemed to be more interested in the male side of the young girl with whom he was walking arm in arm than his male side was interested in her female manifestation. The one manifesting a female body was rather plain looking, with straight blonde hair and unremarkable features, but she had a rather handsome auburn-haired male aspect. The two primary genders looked ill-matched next to each other, but the supreme genders were hot together. *Maybe that's why that girl doesn't play up her outward femininity. The women who are ultra-feminine, I wonder if that's to hide a wimpy unmanifested male aspect.* Jerry looked around at other people to test out his hypothesis. It didn't hold. There were all variations of combinations—women who were both very feminine and very masculine, men who were very masculine and very feminine, men whose feminine side seemed growth stunted, others whose feminine side seemed much older than his chronological age, and the same types of variations were present in women. There were not very feminine women whose supreme gender wasn't very masculine and a young girl whose masculine aspect was a wrinkled old man.

I wonder if that's the way attraction really works. I thought I was attracted to what I saw—physically or emotionally, but it seems we're actually attracted more strongly to what we don't see, to the unmanifested gender of the other person, the one with supremacy. It makes sense, because that's the aspect making the decisions. Maybe that explains Helen's attraction to me, too, because she surely can't be much attracted to this body. It's funny, though, because I wasn't very aware of her male side until now. She can be rather masculine—assertive, bold, courageous. My female side admires her courageousness. I wonder what he looks like. And to think all this happened under the radar of awareness.

It seems, too, that my supreme female aspect's attraction to the hidden qualities of her supreme male aspect is in some ways stronger than the attractions of the primary manifested genders. I wonder if that holds for negative qualities as well, things that bug me about her. There's a lot more complexity to this than I realized. My female side hates getting her hands dirty, which is probably why I have always abhorred that kind of physical labor, whether it's fixing cars, planting trees, or plumbing. Maybe that's another reason why I went into more thoughtful fields. Theoretical physics and information technology are still very masculine but you don't have to get dirty. I guess I don't feel so bad about not being a "real man" because I have a drop-dead gorgeous female side. I wonder if my father would have treated me differently if he had been able to see her/me.

◆   ◆   ◆

Later that evening, Jerry lay in bed pondering the day's events. It had been rich, and the implications still needed to be fleshed out. Emerson was an adept teacher, asking just the right questions that made him go beyond what he realized he knew. *How is this all possible, suddenly being able to see things I have never seen before? Is it me or is it this place?* As he fell asleep, the dream world afforded him a glimpse of the richness of seeing from multiple perspectives nearly simultaneously, something he was not accustomed to doing in waking consciousness. He dreamed of being four people at once, seeing from four sets of eyes.

"It's coming now!" I shouted as I lay on the bed, convulsing in pain, feeling the contractions almost continuously now. I screamed more loudly hoping someone might hear and come to me.

"Get some clean towels!" I shouted to the housekeeper, and ran to her side. "Breathe deeply," I told her. "Steady and deeply."

"Here the towels you wanted, ma'am," I said to the delivery nurse.

"Good. Stay here in case I need an extra pair of hands. Your hands are clean, aren't they?"

"No ma'am," I replied, scared, not wanting to look at the pain.

"Go wash them quickly!" I yelled.

I ran away, glad to be away from the agony. *Everyone talks about what a beautiful experience birth is, but it is excruciatingly painful,* I thought on the way to the wash room. *I don't want to look at it.* I dallied in the washroom, not wanting to return.

I do not want to come out, so I recoiled from the bright lights and cold air of the outside world. "Turn the lights off, please. It's blinding out there."

"Oh, right," I said getting up. I turned the thermostat up, too, while I was at the environmental control panel.

"Thank you. The baby doesn't want to come out. You'll have to sing her out."

I hated singing the birthing song. My voice doesn't naturally go that low, but I tried anyway.

> Welcome, welcome, oh unnamed one
> Honor us now with your radiance
> Oh spirit, oh body, join us, join us
> Here in life
> (roughly to the tune of Dona Nobis Pacem)

I sang it over and over, until I felt the movement, the relaxing of the little body signaling that she wasn't scared anymore.

In the distance I heard a lovely sound, so different than the bump-bump bump-bump that had been constantly in the background. It called to me. I wanted to hear more of it, so I started climbing toward it.

"Uh oh, here we go." (pant, pant, pant)

"Girl, aren't you done washing your hands yet? The baby's coming! It's coming now!"

"I'm comin' mama," I shouted from the bathroom. *Oh god, I do not want to see this.* But I ran back to the birthing room. I saw the top of the head sticking between her legs, and then everything went black. I felt the floor give out on me and the walls cave in.

I fell in slow motion, being squeezed out of my home, into an unknown world.

"Aaaagggghhh!"

Chapter 31

◆

Helen's Journal

The detective working on my case called today. He said that they found the guy they think was my sleeping assassin—dead—assassinated. He was found at home, shot in the head likely by someone he knew well. He had a blue truck and was a state trooper. It must have been the guy who revived Jerry. They also picked up Jack Mason. He's going on trial for the trooper's murder, but they don't have anything to pin him to my case. With the trooper dead, there's no one to testify against him.

I asked the detective if they shut down the zero-point energy operation, and he didn't know what I was talking about. "That's your next case," I said. "Search every inch of that property, because it's there somewhere."

Even though Mason is behind bars, he said I should still be careful. If Mason really wanted to, he could order someone to finish the job, meaning kill me, even though he'll be in jail. But the gig is up, his dirty little secret is out. He doesn't have to protect it anymore. I imagine the OWBs would be glad that Mason is gone—if they're keeping track of these things.

◆　　◆　　◆

Helen looked at the number of the incoming call. It was Ben. She hadn't expected him to actually call her when she gave him her card. *Do I really want to talk to that clown?* "City News, Helen speaking."

"Helen, it's Ben. Meet me in the park near the model boat pond. I have to show you something very important. Oh, and wear shorts, you might get wet," Ben told her over the phone.

"This better be good," she said. "If my boss finds out why I'm skipping out on a staff meeting, he'd…I'd rather not think of what he might do."

◆   ◆   ◆

"Here, take this," he handed her a stick with a wad of gum on the end, "and wade out into the middle of the pond."

She looked at him like he was out of his mind.

"No, I'm not joking. Moi, joke? C'mon, c'mon, hurry," he said while splashing his way into the middle of the model boat pond. "I hope there's nothing in here that will eat me. Just think if people had model sharks what a hazard that would be to the model boats."

"Oooh, it's warm," Helen said as she dipped her feet into it. The boat pond was less than three feet deep, so the sun warms the water quickly.

"We have to be very still now, to let the water get back to being calm. So, did you miss me?" Ben said while they were waiting for the ripples to fade.

"No, I did not."

"Good. You're a woman of character. We're going to make some waves," he raised an eyebrow. "Touch the gummy end of the stick on the water to create circular ripples."

Helen tapped it in a regular beat.

"First watch what happens when I tap in the same beat." It formed a regular interference pattern. "Now watch what happens when I have a slightly different beat." He tapped his slightly faster. The pattern didn't change a little, it changed a lot. "See how the waves themselves carry information—about how fast I'm tapping, how hard I'm tapping? Now tap yours in a slightly irregular beat, with different intensities with which you hit the water, and I'll do the same." It was like the water danced to jazz music. "So imagine this happening in three dimensions, not just two."

"This is very cool, but what's the point?" Helen asked.

"To get you wet!" Ben splashed her.

"Aarrrggghhh!" Helen ran to shore in slow motion through the water. She didn't want to let on that she enjoyed his playfulness.

Ben splashed around more and got his whole body wet, head to toe.

Helen was all dried off when Ben got out of the water. He shook his head rapidly, like a dog shaking to dry off, spraying her with more water. Helen huffed. "Sorry about getting you wet again," he apologized.

"Yeah, sure you are." She wiped the water from her face.

"But that was a demonstration of a different kind of wave front, a less tidy one, one that seems to be more particles than waves. If you took a picture of the spray pattern, it would probably look a bit like a galaxy."

"Yeah, so?"

"You remember what I was telling you about standing waves? Well, last night I was looking at a picture of Hokusai's The Great Wave, and it struck me that my theory treats waves as nice clean, neat things, as sine waves are, but in real life they're not nearly that neat, like Hokusai's pseudo-fractal wave or a heartbeat pattern. How do you get a standing wave out of a messy waveform like a heartbeat? That was a little demonstration of what happens when the wave patterns aren't nice and neat. I wanted to see what happens, and I needed someone to help me."

"Couldn't you have found an unsuspecting undergrad or modeled it on the computer?"

Ben ignored her. "So that little demonstration was part 1. Part 2 is an idea I found today while I was at the library. That last bit we did there was random. Well, randomness doesn't support life. The orderly randomness of chaos doesn't sustain life either, even though we see fractal patterns in organic things, like ginger, the structure of fern leaves, and so on. However in systems from the quantum to the human to the cosmological, there is a type of order that is both chaotic and orderly. This form of complexity is called "bios" meaning "life," and it even shows up in certain musical compositions by Mozart and Bach! I'd be willing to bet you could find it in The Beatles' music too. This bios pattern is at the heart of creation, novelty, and life itself!" Ben exclaimed, as if he had discovered it himself.

Helen shook her head and rolled her eyes. She had never seen anyone get so excited about a theory. Ben's explanations were like performances, science theater, so she crossed her arms, sat back, and watched.

"Bios requires that there be bipolar feedback, positive and negative, synergistic and antagonistic, not just a recursive equation with unipolar feedback, like the kind that produces chaos."

"Ben, English please."

"Okay. Let me see. A recursive equation is like a generator. You put something in it once, and it keeps giving you more and more."

"How?"

"Say you have y = x +3, and you start solving this using x = 1. So, the first value of y is 4. Now, to make it recursive, you plug that 4 in as your next x. So the second value of y is 7. And you do that over and over."

"So, the third answer would be 10, right?" Helen asked.

"Exactly. That wasn't hard, now, was it?"

Helen shook her head.

"But we're not looking at just any old number. The variables, x and y in that equation we used, represent an action at a specific time, call it A_t for x and A_{t+1} for y. The next part, which is crucial to bios, is bipolar feedback. I know what you're thinking."

"What am I thinking, Mr. Smarty Pants?"

"You want to ask, 'what's that?'"

Helen snuffed at him.

"Do you have kids?" Ben asked.

"No."

"Well, you'll have to pardon me as I tap dance across orders of magnitude for the purpose of illustration." He got up and pretended to tap dance. Helen mocked clapping for him. "The interaction of waves is at the subatomic level, but it's easier to think about bipolar feedback using a more accessible example. Suppose you had twins, Gus and Billy, and you were the worst kind of parent, a behavioral researcher. You wanted to see the different effects of praise and criticism, praise being positive feedback and criticism being negative feedback. So Good Gus gets only praise and Bad Billy gets only criticism. Gus can do no wrong and Billy can do no right. So even when Gus spills his food or takes his brother's toys, he gets praised. And when Billy does well in school or wins a game, he gets criticized because he could have done better. Well, Gus grows up to be a narcissistic s.o.b, and Billy grows up to be a depressed and addicted loser. And you're left with the conclusion that neither praise nor criticism was effective feedback. Of course. You need the interaction of opposing forces for healthy life and growth. A plant needs both light and dark. Nerve impulses need to be stimulated and then shut off. Do you see the importance of positive and negative feedback?" Ben explained.

"Yes, but what does that have to do with waves?"

"Another good question. If we wanted to add a term to our equation that gave us bipolar feedback, we would add a sine function. You know the sine wave," he drew the regular up and down motion of a sine wave on the ground with his bubble gum-ended stick. The crest of the wave is positive feedback, and the trough is negative feedback. And now, maestro, a drum roll, please, for our grand integration" Ben said with his usual theatrical flair. Helen drummed on her thigh. "For part three of our three-ring science circus, we shall combine the brilliance of the wave structure of matter with the novelty of bios theory to obtain the greatest theory of all time!" Ben could not hold a straight face and broke out laughing at himself. Helen joined in because his laughter was so contagious, and he did look ridiculous spouting science as if he were a circus announcer.

When he regained his composure, Ben continued, "These biotic waves, think of a heart beat pattern, are the key players in a massive positive and negative feedback system which is created in and by the interactions of an action, let's call it the outbound wave, and the feedback, the inbound wave, which together form the standing wave, all of which gives us the world we live in. Every bit of the universe is a constant information out-information in feedback system, not billiard balls crashing into each other. When there's a certain dynamic, this biotic disorderly order, among the inbound and outbound waves, there can be novelty, life, evolution. The chaotic aspect keeps it unpredictable, sensitive to perturbation, and the orderly aspect keeps it from spinning off into never-never land. Isn't that beautiful? It's so simple, yet it generates such complexity. Maybe that's how your friend ended up someplace else, some newly created realm that we don't have access to because we weren't part of the same conglomeration of wave patterns at that particular time when he disappeared."

"Bravo! Bravo!" Helen shouted and clapped as Ben took a deep bow. She whistled a few cat calls and called for an encore.

Ben looked sheepishly at her as he sat back down next to Helen. "You think I'm ridiculous, don't you?" he asked with true modesty.

"I understand your enthusiasm and your sincerity. And if you weren't so entertaining, I would probably get bored and fall asleep, so thank you."

"It's a brilliant explanation of why Jerry seemed to disappear, isn't it?"

Helen's face went blank.

"Don't you get it? The waves just create what we can perceive in this world. Do you perceive the water at the bottom of the pond? No, but nevertheless, that water is as necessary as the stuff on top, and it's all connected, all just water. So what's going on at the surface even affects the water at the bottom even though you can't see it from your perspective. If I had a way to show you in 3-D, it would be immediately evident, but I don't, so you'll have to use your imagination. You still have one, don't you? That didn't fly away with your sense of humor, did it?" Ben ribbed Helen, who was becoming more morose by the second.

"Oh, so you're saying it's all interconnected, aren't you, even when there doesn't seem to be an obvious connection, one we can't 'see' and might not even know about?" Helen asked.

"Deeply, profoundly interconnected," he said in a melodramatic manner, then shifted to light and almost-flippant. "So apply that to the situation with Jerry, and voila, what do you get?" he grinned with a sweet and sinister smile.

"I don't know." Helen sighed. All the theories in the world couldn't bring Jerry back again. "This is all just empty speculation. Besides, it doesn't really matter any more, does it?" She turned away from him.

Like a rooster whose comb goes limp when the excitement is gone, Ben's eager ego was crestfallen. Her quest and questions had pushed his theory farther than he could have pushed it on his own, and for that he was energized and apprecia- tive, but he recognized that she was right: theorizing didn't change the situation. "You're absolutely right, Helen. In this case, knowledge does not confer power. Knowing won't bring him back, so accept the unknown, embrace the mystery rather than try to solve it; only that will empower you. Neither theories nor facts score points for the emotional football team," Ben said in a rare moment of sobri- ety.

"It's not that. It just seems that, because Jack Mason is behind bars and his operation is being shut down, there's no reason to keep searching. Kill or no kill, the hunt is over."

Helen sat silently on the edge of the model boat pond, dangling her feet over the edge into the water, her thoughts turned inward. She recalled what Jerry had told her about zero-point energy, that it was the most fundamental aspect of the universe, but was it the wave or was it the water in Ben's model? The wave and the water are not separate; there wouldn't be a wave without the water. And the water is the metaphor for space or whatever the waves propagate in. And there aren't any boundaries between this space and that space. There's just space and waves, and that's it. Space and waves. Maybe they're not separate either. As this realization sunk in, slowly, imperceptibly at first and eventually with the force of a thunderstorm, her face lit up like a firecracker went off inside. It all came together, the sense of connectedness with the relief of knowing that, because everything is connected at a level beyond seeing, beyond even awareness, she need not search any more. There was no need to explain Jerry's disappearance. He was wherever he was, and wherever that might be, there was still a connection. *He's still a part of the whole of which I am also part, regardless of whether I can see, feel, and touch him.* The connectedness hadn't disappeared because it is always there. Right now, he was like the water at the bottom of the pond which she couldn't see. Helen jumped up and threw her towel off. "Yes! That's it!" she said, jumping back into the model boat pond and splashing around it haphazardly. "That's it, that's it, that's it!" Ben joined her immediately, unable to resist the possibility of a water fight on a warm evening. They splashed each other and chased around like 4-year-olds. Something snapped in Helen, where she didn't care what onlookers might think, didn't care how silly she looked, and didn't feel the necessity of being sad or serious. She chased Ben and tossed water in his face. He picked her up in a fireman's carry and spun her around until they both collapsed with dizziness, laughing and laughing in the middle of the model boat pond.

Through wet hair dripping in his face, trying to catch his breath from the laughing, he said, "Enough speculating. Let's do something useful. Would m'lady care to sup with me? No place fancy, of course, as I'm soaking wet and on a graduate student's budget."

"I'd love to." She put her hand in his and pulled him up.

Chapter 32

Maria was already working in the flower bed in her front yard when Jerry awoke. He was still unsure of his new ability to see both male and female aspects of a person (it was as disconcerting as having double vision), so he watched how her male and female aspects were accomplishing the tasks of gardening. The female side was caressing the ground and the plants, handling them gingerly, looking for bugs, caring for them as she would her own children. Her male side was keeping them in order, lining them up just right, balancing the tall ones and the short ones, and removing any "weeds" that hindered their growth.

This doubleness fascinated him, so he watched for awhile and wondered. *Do your own male and female aspects ever conflict with each other the way men and women often do?* Hers seemed so coordinated compared with his own. In comparing her two aspects, he became aware of how his male and female sides perceived differently. By experimenting with intention he could switch back and forth, first perceiving through the eyes of his male side then through the eyes of his female side. The male side was exquisitely aware of details, of the color variations in the flowers, of the different species she planted, of the angle of the light hitting Maria's body, of the smell of the freshly turned ground, of the bugs darting about. Each new perception replaced the previous one, and although they occurred one after the other, each perception was like the next bead on a necklace, the next number to be summed. Jerry was comfortable with this mode of perceiving. It had been his primary mode most of his life.

Then with intention, he switched to perceiving through the eyes of his female side. At first it was difficult to stay there; like a ball on a slope, his perceptual tendencies wanted to continue rolling down to the familiar ground of his typical male way of perceiving. He found that he had to give up trying to control the experience in order for his female side to "have the floor." When that happened, however, immediately he felt the field of focus widen, like he could look at more than one thing at a time. He saw the scene as a whole—flowers, bugs, Maria, and sunlight—and was struck by the complexity of interactions within this miniature ecosystem. He could "see" that the flowers were happy for the attention and care they were getting, and the bugs were excited about their new source of food.

Maria's contentment amplified the sunlight as she admired the beauty of the life she was caring for. Jerry noticed that he actually felt softer, more integrated, and awed as he looked at the world through the eyes of his female side. The stirrings of a warm, magnetic affection arose from deep inside and caught Jerry off guard. In the whole time he had stayed with Maria, he hadn't unbuckled his emotional cinch. And now, simply from seeing through his female eyes could he allow the blossoming of reverence and love he felt for her.

She stopped for a moment and smoothed her hair, as if making herself more attractive for an unknown, unseen admirer.

I wonder how long it will take me to be adept at switching between my male eyes and my female eyes, or better yet, be able to see both ways simultaneously.

Without saying a word, he left and let her continue working undisturbed. *She and Emerson still seem to have an unexpressed liaison. I shouldn't interfere.*

◆   ◆   ◆

"Those concepts you showed me the other day," Jerry questioned Emerson, "how do you write using them? They don't seem like the kind of thing from which you construct sentences."

"You are correct. They're not words in the sense that we are using words right now. We stopped the practice of writing many eons ago, as it tended to foster aloneness, which led to many problems. People were forgetting their connection to the All and to each other. Male aspects grew stronger than female aspects, and some people became violent. Fortunately, the Energy Conservateur was a brilliant woman who saw the pattern and the solution."

"What are these symbols, then, if they're not words as I know them?"

"They are more like your national flag and what it stands for. They are the foundations of our culture, much like Liberté, Egalité, and Fraternité are the foundations of the French culture. They are the assumptions upon which all else rests."

"So if you don't write, how do you record your history or the day's news or compose poetry?" Jerry asked.

"Every choice is already recorded, all possibilities, even the ones that didn't occur; those are sometimes more important than what did occur. The first love, the one you didn't marry, the children you didn't have, the fight you walked away from, they're all in your third layer," Emerson explained. "To consider history, as you call it, you only need to look to that occurrence. It will *all* be there, from all perspectives, not just one person's perception of it."

"Even the things that didn't occur?" The look of puzzlement on Jerry's face prompted Emerson to continue.

"If you never forget that as a wave, you are still part of the ocean, you will always be connected to the entire ocean. If you forget that you are a part of a much bigger body and think that you are a droplet of spray, then you might think that you've lost your connection to the ocean and all that it holds, including access to all of that."

"So you don't write things down because you never forget anything?" Jerry asked.

"No, because we never forget our connection to the All, which gives us access. What is history but interactions among specific waves on the ocean? For those who suffer from the illusion that they are disconnected, writing history or news is a way of making up for that forgotten connection," Emerson said.

"Oh? How? That's a bold claim."

"If you think you are an unconnected droplet, then you hold the illusion that what is in your mind is accessible only to you and to no one else. So to get what's in your mind into the mind of someone else, you use language."

"Well, it's true, we don't have access to what someone else is thinking."

Emerson ignored him and continued, "The difference between your language and our use of these symbols is in intent. We use these concepts to remember the nature of our reality, to remember who we are. You use language to shuttle information between 'droplets.' It's very clever, actually. You package the information in meaning-packets called words and send them through space-time, either in the form of sound vibrations or optical patterns. The words have been sufficiently systematized so that the person who receives them can adequately decode them and infer the information or meaning intended by the sender. Language is the way that information (or meaning) travels between seemingly disconnected droplets. This kind of travel occurs in the old Einsteinian worldview, that is, at less than the speed of light. There is no provision for instantaneous communication in that worldview. We, however, remain ever present to our profound interconnectedness, as you have experienced also, so ultimately the type of language based on the travel metaphor is useless because there is no need to go from point A to point B, from my mind to your mind, as if they are separate places, because everything is connected."

"Does this mean that everyone knows what everyone else is thinking all of the time?"

"Oh heavens, no. That would be more than we could handle. It's more like, when you're thirsty, you open the spigot and allow the water to come out."

"How do you know you're not getting random thoughts from just anybody, but the thoughts of the person you want to communicate with?"

"Ah, yes, the spigot metaphor was too broad, wasn't it? Perhaps, then, it's more like tuning a radio. First you have to turn it on, like a spigot, then you have to tune it to a particular vibration, which could be another person, a place, a 'thing' as you call them. Similarly, sometimes radios play words, sometimes they only play music, sometimes there is just static. There are many layers to tune in."

"How do you know where and how to tune?"

"It's an innate ability." Emerson fidgeted, not knowing how to continue, as there was still an important part of their reality that Jerry did not know yet, and it was not time for him to know. "You have it too, but perhaps you have forgotten how to use it. Perhaps it is easier for you to understand how it applies to emotions rather than thought. You can tune into how someone feels, regardless of whether they say anything."

"Yes, but there is usually some physical clue that gives it away—a tear, a smile—we have become adept at reading facial expressions and body language, even though we are never taught explicitly to do so."

"And when do you learn that?"

"I suppose we learn it as infants. We fixate on faces and learn by mirroring our mother's face."

"It is similar here." Emerson's tone was more abrupt than usual. "As you saw in some of our foundational concepts, fu-an-gu and mu-ishi-wa, and in our physical being both male and female," Emerson continued, "there is a built-in cognizance of the balance or interdependence—of the twoness or manyness within oneness."

"Yes, that's the beauty of those concepts. I love how those symbols are like mystical poetry boiled down to a single concept, a single glyph. Potent. Powerful. Intense. For some reason, the language I learned lacks that duality-within-singularity. It expresses the separateness but has lost or maybe never had the expression of the underlying unity or co-creation of opposites," Jerry said.

"Indeed. Your language, and the culture built on its foundations, has cut you off from your true nature, so that you were literally unable to see the female part of you. You are both male and female. Your words and the logic that organizes them have you believe that you are one or the other, but not both."

"Emerson, you keep saying 'your language' as if you have a different one, but I've never heard anybody speak anything other than my language. What's going on? If your native language isn't English, then why do you keep using English?"

Emerson looked at Jerry like a deer caught in the headlights of a car that is about to run him over. Jerry was broaching topics that would require complete destruction of truths he believed to be self-evident. "Hmm, how do I explain this," Emerson thought aloud. "Well, Jerry, in all honesty, we don't really have a verbal language either, and so we use yours because we think that it would make you feel more comfortable during your visit. We certainly would not want you to feel uncomfortable, since it would overemphasize our differences and only enhance your tendency to think that you are a droplet. It would estrange you, which is contrary to how we want to feel. We are you and we want to feel as at home as possible." He smiled, thinking that was a very satisfactory answer.

Jerry's eyes grew wide as he tried to understand what Emerson meant when he said that they didn't really have a language. How could they not have a language? It sounded like utter nonsense, as fu-an-gu and mu-ishi-wa were wonderfully rich notions.

Before he could formulate a question, however, Emerson realized his error and diverted the conversation. "What do you see for yourself, Jerry, about how mu-ishi-wa applies to you directly, not just as an abstract idea that is nice to contemplate?"

"How it applies to me or how might I apply it?"

"Either," Emerson breathed a sigh of relief.

"First let me see if I remember it correctly. Mu-ishi-wa looks like concentric circles that were a little off center, so it appears to vibrate back and forth," Jerry recalled.

"That's the one, the female of the pair," Emerson said.

"What this concept says to me is that paradox isn't something to be resolved, abhorred, or circumvented—as it has been, especially in science—rather, it is to be embraced as the very foundation of our reality. It's what connects the Many parts of the One. It's the universal glue, not a wedge that divides one thing from another. Except in rare cases of oxymoron, like bittersweet, we have expunged it from language. Like the ostrich hiding its head in the sand, we think that doing so will make it go away, but it doesn't. Mu-ishi-wa embodies the paradox, as the seed embodies the tree. From it, the flora of your culture grow and bloom."

"That's very good Jerry. It was such a moving sermon that it almost makes me want to shout hallelujah. But what about you? How does it apply to Jerry Fowss?" Emerson asked.

"Me? Just me alone? How am I one side that serves as both?" Jerry asked, to stall for time while his mind went searching for answers. "There's only one me, yet I am both male and female, body and spirit, rational and emotional. I can do both good and evil, be both poor and wealthy, live in the here and now or the there and then. I can love and fear the same person. I can feel both happy and sad, say when a dear friend who has been dying a long and painful death finally passes on."

"You forgot to add that you are both here and there." Emerson smirked.

"How do you mean?"

"You, your individuality, is here," he said pointing to Jerry's body, "and your Source being-body is there," he said gesturing to everything else around him, "and there, inside." He pointed back at Jerry. "That is how you are the one side that serves as both sides. All those distinctions that you mentioned, rich and poor, rational and emotional, those are just dust, obsolete concepts. You must be willing to allow those concepts to become obsolete in the same way as you allowed your rotary telephone to be obsolete. Those concepts served you for awhile, but no longer. Imagine, Jerry, what would happen if all of humanity stopped pretending that there are two separate sides."

Chapter 33

✦

Helen's Journal

I don't know what happened. One minute I was having an overly serious conversation (despite Ben's attempts to make me laugh) about an overly serious topic
and then, perhaps like a guitar string tuned too tightly, I broke, and suddenly
everything seemed hilarious. There I was in the middle of a model boat pond,
soaking wet, trying to understand some post-quantum-theory theory about why
someone who used to be in my life isn't anymore. It was like being in the Monty
Python version of Waiting for Godot, which might go something like this:

"What are we doing here?"
"Do you mean 'doing' in a postmodern sense?"
"Yes."
"Nothing."
"No, we're not doing nothing, we must be doing something. We're at least
being, you know."
"Oh, yes, but that's not the postmodern sense, that's the existentialist sense."
"You're right. I must not have been thinking."
"If you'd have been thinking, it would be the Cartesian sense, then, wouldn't
it?" (hits him)
"So what are we doing here?"
"Hell if I know."
Both exit.

The absurdity of it, all of it. The absurdity of trying to know something so ridiculously speculative. The absurdity of trying to keep Jerry in my life by knowing where he is even though he disappeared! The absurdity of thinking that I could get him back if I just understood what happened to him in the first place. I just shake my head at my own silliness, silliness which prevented me from being truly *silly*!

And to think I was so judgmental of Ben for being fun. Yes, just plain fun! He's a stitch. I haven't laughed so hard as I did yesterday over pizza and beer. He loves to solve mysteries as much as I do—the fundamental mysteries of the world we live in, no less. And he manages to keep in perspective that he's just a fly investigating flea shit (as he put it). And to think that I thought he had an over-developed sense of self-importance. He uses the drama to make fun of it, push it over the top, so it spills to the bottom.

Sometimes I think that God sits up in heaven watching us, kind of like Marlon Brando in *Apocalypse Now,* and instead of saying "the horror, the horror," I see him belly laughing and saying "the irony, the irony." It's right under our noses all the time, and we fail to laugh at it because we're not watching ourselves play out our silly little ironic dramas called Life.

All my life I have been searching. Searching became my life. Being a reporter is a kind of sublimated searching. What was I searching for? Answers to what?

Who…am I?

What…am I doing here?

Where…is my proper place?

When…will it end?

Why?

Those questions are the tools of the reporter's trade, the technique, the means by which we craft a story. I became a reporter because I was enthralled by those questions, because I wanted answers to the entire question, not just the first word. Unfortunately, I severed the head from the body and set about answering these questions only as they applied to others (Who committed the crime? Who is the victim? What happened? Where did it occur? and so on), not as they applied to me. Although I wanted to, I never turned them on myself. I didn't have the courage to. It's scary to ask yourself who you really are. It's scarier to answer it for real, not a glib aren't-I-clever sort of way. I suppose that's why I courted a job that keeps those questions always in my vest pocket. It's easier that way. So what am I afraid of? It's time to turn the reporter on herself. After all, the answers aren't independent of me. I AM the answer to each of those questions.

I'm the answer. It's not out there. It's not abstract. It's not hypothetical. It is funny, however. There's that irony again. I hear God laughing.

So, here goes…

Who am I?

"And who are you?" said the spider to the fly.
The fly flew away.
Aha!

What am I doing here?

On Fridays we dance
We dance around
And round the room
Only we two

On Fridays we dance
We dance no other day
Other days for
Other things

On Fridays we dance
We dance to hide
For hiding in motion
Silences the words

On Fridays we dance
We dance arms entwined
Hearts entwined nowhere to go
But around and around

Where is my proper place?

Space
that's not
not-objects
And space

to breathe
not-breath
And space
to think
not act
I am
myself
And give
to you.

When will it end?

when the leaf that falls from the tree hits the ground.

Why?

A fickle trickle
Of mud blood
The water of sorrow
The sand of time
Together drop
By prolongéd drop
Into the cup
Of death's sweet wine.

Chapter 34

"I was lying on a table, like an examining table or gurney," Jerry told Maria about the dream he had, as he helped her relocate what he would call weeds, which she called interlopers. "The lights were dim, but I could see the outline of a man standing over me. He was big and muscular, like a wrestler. He put his hands on the top of my head and searched in my hair for something on my skull. When he found it—I don't know what 'it' was, perhaps a flap of skin—he took a deep breath inward. As he exhaled, he blew on me, starting at the top of my head and going straight down my face to my chest and abdomen. His breath was warm. My body melted like butter where he blew on me. With his strong but gentle hands, he spread open the fissure. None of this hurt. It was more curious than painful. Like a baker working with bread dough, he widened the cut and, working very professionally, like he was trained to do this, turned my flesh inside out. It wasn't literal, you know, like my lungs and spleen and everything were now on the outside; he just turned me inside out. And lastly, he pushed my head down through the opening in my chest and pulled my arms through, like you turn the sleeves of a coat inside out. He kneaded my muscles around, making sure they settled into the right place. Then he took another deep inhalation, made some gestures with his hands, and blew on me in the opposite direction, like he was now zipping me up again, closing the gap with his warm, healing breath. Then he put his hands over my eyes, blocking out all the light. Energy flowed from his palms into my eyes, filling me up like I was a flat basketball. I felt lighter than air, like I was going to float away. He instructed me to breathe in and send the breath out my back and then breathe it back in through the chest, the heart chakra. So I did that and the process was complete. The next thing I knew I had woken up. It seemed so real, not like a dream at all."

"Hmmm, you got turned inside out," she mused. "Did you feel any different when the procedure was over?"

"I don't know." Jerry thought about it. "I didn't feel physically different. I felt like it was the same old me, only lighter, as I said."

"That is probably a good sign. If you hold things inside, afraid to express them on the outside, then you would feel more vulnerable or exposed by such a procedure. It would be extremely uncomfortable." She pulled and pulled on one plant that didn't want to move. "Jerry, could you come over here and help me pull this one out. It doesn't seem to want to come willingly."

"Maybe you should ask it why not," he said while digging up plants and putting them in a large rectangular tray to be taken to a special place where they can grow without interfering with food crops.

"Yes, good idea."

When she was through negotiating with that plant, he asked, "Maria, if dreams are the mind's way of understanding or processing events that happened during the day, especially if they were challenging or confusing," Jerry said with the determination of a scientist hot on the trail of a new theory, "that dream might be my way of making sense of what Emerson and I discussed yesterday."

"Perhaps."

Jerry stood up and paced the length of the garden now, excited by the blossoming of ideas that was occurring. He knew that he was on the verge of something. He just didn't know what. His fingers, arms, and legs were beginning to tingle just thinking about it. His blood felt bubbly like champagne ran through his veins.

"The man in my dream told me to shoot the energy out my back. Why?"

Maria grinned and patted the disturbed soil back into place. "Sending the energy out the heart is like plugging into the unlimited source of energy. We have the chance to leave the third dimension and be re-sourced by the All-dimension," Maria explained cryptically, not wanting to give away too much. "And another thing," she continued, "if you don't stay in motion, you die. There are different ways of being in motion: there's motion through space, motion through time, motion through space-time, and recursive motion, which is what that is. It's the wave that falls back in on itself, it's the motion of growth and development, the fundamental motion of the universe. Because there really is only one side, mu-

ishi-wa , the motion only *seems* to go from one side to the other."

"That's why in my dream, inside became outside and vice versa, but there also seemed to be no difference between the two," Jerry caught on.

"Yes, you have felt your own infinity."

Emerson's words came flooding back into Jerry's consciousness. They had seemed so abstract before—talk of Klein bottles, which are just a mathematical construction—but now they were real. He had experienced it in the dream. *I became a Klein bottle, folded in on myself, recursive, self-reflective, a miniature ver-*

sion of the universe. He imagined everybody as a little Klein bottle, all within a larger one—a Klein bottle fractal, of course, which replicated itself all the way to the quantum level. Like a Möbius strip, which is a two-dimensional object that requires three dimensions of space for its recursive shape, a Klein bottle is a 3-dimensional mathematical "object" that requires a fourth dimension for its recursive properties, for its ability to have inside and outside be one and the same surface.

Aha! Like fireworks, ideas burst forth in all directions in Jerry's mind. *If my model of a fractal universe composed of Klein-bottle entities like myself is correct, then every level of the universe requires the next-higher dimension for its existence. Every particle of every cell of every molecule of every substance bordered on a higher dimension. And if you've ever meditated, when you watch your thoughts you find that there's always one watching the one who's watched, and one watching that one, and so on. Even consciousness requires a higher dimension!*

Jerry's imagination jumped from flower to flower, extracting nectar from each blossoming thought. When he thought about the actual words to describe the inside-out condition he experienced in the dream, the next idea-explosion erupted. For example, to say that his "inside" turned out implies and necessitates that there be an "outside." Similarly, "top" implies and necessitates "bottom," left and right, and so forth. As he dug up rogue plants, he realized, *Most of our ways of expressing opposition come from the way we experience ourselves in our bodies. Up and down, front and back, left and right are all grounded in our embodiedness. Perhaps that's why the architecture is so disorienting here. I want it to be either concave or convex, but it isn't one way or the other, it's both! If I was a purely energetic being without material left-right, front-back form, I wouldn't have that basis of comparison. The ways of expressing opposition might instead be grounded in the opposition of faster and slower vibration or expanded versus contracted energy field, like a ball of light or a vast cloud of charge. That would certainly change one's perspective on the world.*

Nevertheless, the traditional contraries in our language—hot and cold, good and bad, right and wrong, here and there, acid and alkaline—imply and necessitate each other. But that's not how we think of them; we think of them as being opposites, as radically different as you can get, as being mutually exclusive rather than as giving rise to one another. And it certainly is not how we use them in everyday talk. How strange it would sound to say, "my coffee is hot and cold, but mostly the hot is manifesting right now." It might be less strange to say "that guy is good and bad, and the bad side manifested temporarily in his committing a crime." Inside, it was as if Jerry's male and female parts shook hands, at said in unison, "it's about time he got that!" *Jerry realized that such connectedness—the tension and the harmony—which is often for-gotten, is the key to intentional creation. You cannot create one without the other; when you create love, you create fear with it.*

In the old system, for a new form to appear, the old one must seem to be destroyed. Most of the time this happens naturally, that is, below the level of consciousness. The warm air of summer is destroyed by the cold fronts that come in during autumn. Youth is destroyed by the seeming passage of time. We think or believe that we have no say over those processes. Perhaps we do. And our say is in how we "say" it. The words and their accepted, standardized meanings prevent us from grasping and expressing the true reality, which is an oppositionally based, co-creative flux, not a series of fixed states. How do you express a flux without destroying the flux itself, without turning it into an object? he wondered.

"We had better get these replanted before their energy reserves run out." Maria's practicality and focus on reality pulled Jerry out of his world of thought and ideas. She picked up the two shovels, and he carried the box full of interlopers to their new home on the north side of town, opposite of where the crops were grown. Maria and Jerry replanted them in this specially designated area, where they are not considered weeds but are the honored residents.

"Just why are we replanting these weeds, Maria? Couldn't you just put them in the compost?"

"Would you like genocide to be committed upon your kind?" she asked.

"No, but this is a bit extreme, isn't it?"

"Some people do not favor their vegetables over other plants. They believe that the variety of species makes for more flavorful crops and that those plants have come together by their own intention, like a party with many different types of people makes for richer conversation. However, I prefer to give my vegetables more room to grow, so that they do not have to compete for space, water, and sunshine. I think they taste better when they are more relaxed and feel secure that there are enough resources. We have come to this mutual arrangement to trans-plant the interlopers to their own field, because each has value in its own right. This plant here," she held up one with lots of little yellow flowers, "is the favorite food of that green and yellow bird whose song you enjoy so much. And this one is the only type of plant the larva of the Royal Orange Butterfly will eat before it makes its chrysalis. And this one has beautiful blue flowers in the fall, which I just love. Shall I go on?"

"No, I understand." A warm feeling of satisfaction welled up from inside, a contentedness tinged with excitement from knowing that he contributed to enhancing the life-experience of fellow beings. Jerry smiled to himself as he realized that this simple task of transplanting "weeds" out of the vegetable garden was vastly more gratifying than writing computer programs. In his previous life, he would have scoffed at the thought, but now he realized that it wasn't necessary to win the Nobel Prize or make millions of dollars to feel useful, valuable, and satisfied.

◆   ◆   ◆

Jerry loved to learn. Learning was being, doing, and having all rolled into one. Finding out not just new things, but also ways to connect them was reward enough. When he was a graduate student in physics, he kept a list of things that he knew he didn't know but wanted to learn. It was a game to add to the list and then be able to cross things off as he learned them. One of his lab partners challenged him to a bet: who could have the most number of completions minus the number of incompletions by the end of the year. Although Jerry lost the bet by only one point, it had been the best part of graduate school.

Emerson was like a custom-made teacher, the kind Jerry had dreamed about having as a child, who leads you to your next discovery so gently that you think you got there on your own. Before Emerson arrived at the stone circle, Jerry walked around it and looked at fu-an-gu in the east and mu-ishi-wa in the west. Their shapes and their sounds even conveyed the male and female qualities. The stones at the north and south nodes had unique designs carved into them as well. Jerry presumed he would learn about them today.

When Emerson arrived he told Jerry, "You learned about fu-an-gu and mu-ishi-wa yesterday, so now I will show you how to learn through them. Jerry wasn't sure what he meant, but he trusted Emerson and followed his lead.

"Fu-an-gu does not just tell us that if you investigate something deeply, you will fill find its opposite, it also gives us a methodology. It says, the deeper you get, the less it looks like itself, and when you reach the core, it looks like the opposite of what you started with. So, we must look inside. It's not about cutting up or cutting open, looking at something from the outside, or finding smaller and smaller components. Rather it's about going inside and shining a light in the corners of that small, dark room. Tell me, Jerry, what shall we investigate today?" Emerson asked.

"Let's look at the brain-mind distinction. Can we get to the mind by investigating the brain deeply?" Jerry had his doubts.

"Let's find out if that is possible. We will look into the brain and see what we find. It might or might not be your quarry, the mind. Sit comfortably. Close your eyes. Imagine a small movie screen in your field of vision. On this screen, see your own mirror reflection."

"Male and female?" Jerry asked.

"It doesn't matter, whichever is easiest for you to imagine."

Jerry found it easier to have a mental picture of his male self, as he still was not that familiar or comfortable with perceiving through the eyes of his female self.

"Now, Jerry, bring the image closer and closer, like you are in a tiny ship which you must fly into the pupil of the person on the screen. This ship passes through the iris, travels up the optic nerve, and stops in the brain. Get out and look around in your brain. Watch the exquisite dance of your own neurons firing."

He watched the cells giving bundles of elixir to each other, dancing with each pulse. It was a beautiful dance, an undulating, sexy tango, as the neurons fired their chemicals to waiting receptors across the synaptic divide, the way a tanguero looks across the room to catch the eyes of his chosen dance partner. Sometimes the receptors were receptive and other times not. As in a crowded dance hall, there were many variations of this happening all at the same time. In addition to the neuron show, peptides were released and received, transporting information to and from all parts of the body. Jerry was clear that it wasn't random. It seemed like the processes knew which other cell they needed to aim at, undulated appropriately, and aimed with perfect precision. Other cells remained stiffly aimed in one direction at one other cell, their freedom restricted by some unknown force.

Unbeknownst to Jerry, Emerson had stepped next to him and poked Jerry in the thigh with a small thorn from a rose bush. It was a small poke which didn't hurt much, but it altered the neural dance entirely. The sinuous undulation turned to sharp crystals instantly, and the sparking between neurons turned to arrows. Interactions sped up, and the entire color, mood, and tone switched from reds and blues and greens to white and steel blue-grey. Next Emerson took Jerry's hand in his own and stroked it lovingly. The oranges and reds returned. The crystals melted, but something else happened too. Each cell developed a glow, as if a light had been turned on inside, and a fullness, like the satiation you have after a good meal. The rhythm of the dance slowed to more of a blues beat, but without the minor key. Jerry could tell that his cells were responding to Emerson's. He had no idea how, but there was a definite coordination and interactivity.

Jerry's awareness then landed on the surface of a cell and was instantly sucked inside through an ion channel, like being on the type of amusement park ride where you're spinning and then the floor drops out from under you. He landed in the cytoplasm, which resembled being on the beach, with dogs going this way and that and Frisbees flying past your head and all manner of activity all around. He sensed that he was automatically getting smaller and smaller, in proportion to the structures he was looking at. As he approached the nucleus, he could see what looked like a factory inside. The smooth dance that was going on outside between cells was not present inside the cell. Here things were orderly. The DNA double helices in the nucleus were systematically unzipping, being replicated in pieces by RNA, and the carbon copies were then transported to needed sites elsewhere in the body, now most likely to heal the thorn prick on Jerry's thigh. Muscle tissue, skin, nerves, and blood vessels would need to be repaired; damaged cells would need to be broken down, salvaged for reusable proteins, and the unsalvageable ones discarded. New phagocytes also needed to be created to scavenge the damaged cells. Here was headquarters, where the commands were issued and instructions given in sets of three-base codes: Adenine-Thymine-Adenine, Cytosine-Cytosine-Guanine, Guanine-Adenine-Cytosine, and so on. Jerry watched, fascinated as he saw how his body worked at its most fundamental physical level.

How did these pieces of genetic code know where to go? There didn't seem to be any subcellular police directing traffic in this protein manufacturing plant. Each piece was encoded with a homing device (of sorts), which was like that device to put on your car that guides it through the highway system, so you don't have to drive. It knows its destination, and the system is set up to get it there. The body's peptides inform all the different systems of what is happening in all the other systems. Whereas the nervous system can be likened to electric circuitry, with wires running throughout the body through which nerve impulses travel, this other system was decentralized and chemical in nature, so that when something happened in the toe, the index finger also knew about it through chemical information exchange. Jerry was fascinated to learn how the body has both centralized and decentralized information processing systems. He made a mental note to think about how their two purposes and two different efficiencies could be applied to computers. How could the chemical system be mimicked?

Jerry saw that not only did his whole body respond to the thorn prick through both the centralized and decentralized communication systems, but when Emerson put his hand on Jerry's, Emerson's body was responding too. How? It had something to do with the light! When Emerson took Jerry's hand and Jerry's cells lit up from the inside, that energy and information from billions of cells enabled Emerson to establish cellular communication with Jerry's information physiology. Emerson thus could help Jerry's body heal itself, because communication was established and energy given. Jerry saw that, at the subcellular level of information, all beings are connected with one another through a light-based connection. Perhaps coincidentally perhaps not, that insight shrunk Jerry even smaller and sent him to the next level down, the nucleus.

Into the factory Jerry went. It was like stepping into a symphony hall in the middle of a concert. He couldn't say precisely that he heard music; rather, the power and orderliness of the vibration inside the nucleus made an impression on his awareness. It was like being at a concert where the music reaches inside of you and makes your own body vibrate, not because it's loud but because it resonates with you, touches something deep within. He couldn't tell where the vibration was coming from. It didn't seem to be part of the DNA replication, but it was there. Was this the beat that the neural processes and dendrites were dancing to?

As Jerry stepped into the vibration, everything went black. There were no more parts of cells to look at; he was at the foundation of life, inside the eternal pulse. It was vast. First he felt his source pulse inside this atom of this cell, originating from nothing and vibrating nonetheless. It radiated outward in every direction. And then he sensed, ever so slightly at first but then more strongly, the pulsing of other presences coming in toward him. Each cell of every being was pulsing. His vibration and their vibrations collided, a richness of presences, each distinct and each a note in a grand symphony, sometimes in unison and sometimes not, like wind chimes. At the source of his being, Jerry realized, was an interaction, a coming together of his own vibration and the vibrations of all other beings, including the nonhuman ones. It took both vibrations, his going out and theirs coming in, to make him who he was, to give him substantiality, existence. Is this the mind?

By being in this experience of pulsing, pulsing, and watching himself experience it simultaneously, he felt entirely connected to his fellow humans at this most basic level of vibration. The door was opened to all life in the universe. Never before had he felt such a sense of belonging, of being integral to the whole, from the inside out. When he was Welcomed into the community that had been from the outside in, the Many welcomed the One. The process of connecting this one, Jerry, to the One/Many was complete now. Never again could he feel alone. He was certain that he was indeed connected in his very Being to everything in the Universe. There was no going back to feeling alone in the world. It was a luscious spot there at the center of his own being, where he could stay forever in its warm vast hug. But Emerson's voice woke him from the meditation.

"How did you like experiencing the process of fu-an-gu, of looking deeply into your brain/mind?"

"Mmmmm, ooooooh" Jerry uttered, coming gradually out of the trance, trying to maintain that heaven of connectedness while also returning to his individual awareness.

Emerson let him take his time, as a radical break from such harmony can cause great trauma. Conversely, the temptation to remain there is great, as it feels better than anything else to be embraced by the All.

"What did you find at the core of your brain, Jerry?"

"A vibration, a pulse. Nothing else. It combined with other pulses. That's all there was, a great ocean of amplitudes."

Emerson explained, "In this state of connected wholeness with the void, the fundamental vibration, the light, you experienced the source of life at the very core of your cells, not just your brain cells, all the cells. We represent it like this, ᵒᵛᛜᵒᵛᛜᵒ•. Emerson showed Jerry the symbol on the southernmost rock in the wheel. It is pronounced aneh-mi-oh-nu, which translates approximately as 'the snake of light that moves through all.' It is the model on which many other structures are based, such as the double helix of our DNA; it is an electromagnetic wave, which is simply vibration. It is the motion of the energy through the chakra system. The two helices, one in the male direction and one in the female direction, carry life-source energy throughout the body, keeping it healthy and balanced. It is a golden rope, a multicolored braid, each person's signature vibration, the frequency at which they and the All are connected. It is this uniqueness that connects each of us to each other and to the whole, the One. It is through your uniqueness that you are connected to the Many. It is the bidirectional vibration that is the very source of All. Do you see here," he pointed to the wave emanating from the leftmost circle, "this is the vibration from you. And on this side is the vibration coming to you from all else. When they meet, you get that version of reality."

"This light that moves through all—do you mean it literally?" Jerry asked.

"Yes, why?"

"Something happened to me when I was young. My hands had the light. That's how this whole quest started, because I needed to understand that experience."

"Congratulations, you found the answer you've sought all these years."

"Perhaps. But now I want more. I have more questions. I want to become light. I want that snake of light that moves through all to move through all of me."

"It always has and always will, Jerry. Aneh-mi-oh-nu is the third foundation of our culture. It is the root concept, the most profound of the three. It integrates

fu-an-gu 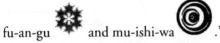 and mu-ishi-wa ."

"How does it do that?"

"First, Jerry, you saw that the body isn't separate from the environment, that the boundary is permeable, fractal, that there is only a fuzzy distinction between inside and outside, which ultimately breaks down. Then you saw that distinctions such as male and female, rich and poor, inside and outside are specious. Everything on this single reality-plane is interconnected through this information-light system grounded in the body's DNA, which is the same DNA in all living things."

Emerson walked from fu-an-gu to mu-ishi-wa to aneh-mi-oh-nu, intoning a different frequency at each symbol. When he had completed that, the images on the stones came to life, each pulsing and vibrating on its own and in unison with the others. Fu-an-gu grew like a flower opening over and over. Mu-ishi-wa pulsed back and forth, like a heart beating, and aneh-mi-oh-nu bounced like a wave, up and down, vibrated like a stringed instrument, and spiraled on its axis.

"Our concepts are not static; they are as alive as you and me," Emerson swept his arm around to the three concepts as a magician sweeps his cape.

Jerry stared in awe at how the symbols brought the rocks to life. They no longer resembled the insentient lumps of broken earth that most rocks appear to be. Similarly, these symbols were not like dead letters on a page, stacked one against the other in a heap of meaning to be made. They were a living symphony, which together activated the fourth symbol on the northernmost stone. Jerry walked from the southern stone to the northern stone to see how it glowed, with what it glowed.

"What do you see?" Emerson asked.

"It's incredible!"

Chapter 35

◆

Helen's Journal

Wouldn't you know it, I finally let go of my need to know what happened to Jerry, and I immediately dream of him. I stop searching and an answer comes to me. There's that irony again. In the dream, I was watching him but he couldn't see me. The more I watched, the more transparent he got. I could see all his organs. I could especially see his heart. It was getting bigger and bigger. It looked like it was going to burst his chest. And it did. It exploded like a supernova. It didn't kill him, though, not like a heart attack. It was more like a heart expand. After his heart exploded, he filled the universe and was no longer transparent. He had substance. Jerry is everywhere, if I just look. But there was something different about him, a lightness. Then "they" said that was all for today, and I woke up.

This dream was so vivid and seemed so real. It was almost like the image communication that the OWBs used. Could they be communicating with me through dreams? I want to believe that this dream is a sign from the universe (and not my unconscious toying with me) and that it's telling me that Jerry's all right, even if something happened to him which transformed him into something unrecognizable, something that isn't how I knew him to be. I don't know who "they" are, but I definitely had the sense that I was being shown this for a reason.

I saw his kindness in a boy picking up a glove dropped by an old arthritic woman.
I saw his curiosity in a puppy who wanted to meet everyone on the street.
I saw his generosity in a man who picked a rose with his bear hands to present to his beloved.

I saw his intelligence in a cab driver who knew every street in town.
I saw his reliability in the shadow of a building as it moved across the grass.
I saw his perseverance in a dandelion growing in a crack in the sidewalk
I saw his indecisiveness in the flickering of a candle.
I saw his resignation in the water running downhill after a rain.
I saw Jerry everywhere today.

I felt his touch by the afternoon sun.
I heard his voice in the rushing water.
I smelled his richness as I passed the spiced almond seller's shop.

It was William Blake, I believe, who wrote, "To see a world in a grain of sand, and heaven in a wild flower, hold infinity in the palm of your hand, and eternity in an hour." That's what the day has been like for me.

Chapter 36

"Allan, what is the status of our Visitor? How is his integration coming along?" Jorn asked. Jorn's interests as Council Head were the mirror image of Allan Beaupensee's. Jorn oversaw activities from the outside, the material perspective, whereas the Energy Conservateur monitored them from the inside, from the energetic perspective. They conferred regularly as a form of check and balance.

"Oh, it's coming along. I've been keeping an eye on him. He's not fully woven in yet. The thread is not fine enough for the intricate weave of our society. It is getting jammed because his lower energy channels are polluted and clogged. He keeps it well hidden, but the toxins are there nonetheless. Emerson is doing fine work with him, but it's not..."

"What is necessary to..." Jorn began.

"A fear-erasing ceremony to clean out the emotional debris."

"But that might unbalance others," Jorn pondered.

"That is a risk. And we can't force him," Beaupensee reminded Jorn.

"Do you think you could enable him to want it?" Jorn asked.

"I'll see what I can do, but I might have to break a few rules."

"Not too many, please."

◆   ◆   ◆

The northernmost symbol in the circle glowed and pulsed with its own pattern. The center kept the same pulsing beat as the other designs, and the petals or arms gesticulated like a luminous flower.

"Wow, what is this?" Jerry asked.

"What do you see?" Emerson replied.

"It's life itself! A flower of life. It has the male and female embedded within it, but clearly it is more powerful than a picture of a simple flower." This was his male side perceiving, naming, classifying.

"What do you mean by 'more powerful'?"

"It's more than a picture. It seems to convey something, like the other symbols you have shown me."

"What does it seem to convey?" Emerson asked.

Jerry looked at it longer, switching to his female side to perceive it. "Its vibration is contagious. It makes me want to burst. It makes my heart sing it's so beautiful."

"What would you call that inner singing?"

After thinking for a second, he blurted, "Joy!" However, there was another feeling lurking in the background—a longing, a missing.

"What does this show you, Jerry?"

Jerry inhaled slowly, which gave him time to think. He chuckled at the irony of the answer that came to him. "This symbol affected me at the immediate, visceral level. There was no thought necessary. I understood it in the blink of an eye. Whatever your meaning is for this symbol, I didn't need to ask because I understood it directly. I don't know if I could have done that with the other three that you showed me, but this one is marvelous how it speaks directly to you. That doesn't happen with our words—not by looking at them anyway. There are some words whose sound might connect on this level, but not the written word."

"Precisely. The vibrational signature of the concept is immediately evident. The 'word' speaks itself. That is how these fundamental concepts came to our understanding. We noticed certain designs that appeared spontaneously in malleable substances and saw a pattern to their appearance. Eventually we figured out which experiences produced which designs, so we transcribed the vibrational signatures of certain important experiences," Emerson explained.

"I wonder whether that is how our ancient languages were born." Jerry mused. "If so, their vibration must have been diluted over many centuries. Eventually the signatures were probably simplified and turned into pictograms or glyphs and then lost entirely in alphabetized languages. That would mean language went from being an intuitive, visceral process to a rational, mental process. The female element was lost."

"Shall we use the fu-an-gu process to look inward and see what effect this vibrational signature has on you?" Emerson asked. Jerry nodded. "Close your eyes. I am going to hold it up to your third eye, but instead of looking at it, I want you to look at yourself, go into your cells as we did before, and describe what you see."

Jerry reported, "I have become a point of awareness, and I'm going into the heart. I see it pumping automatically. I hear it beating in a soothing rhythmic pulse. I feel the moist warmth of it. I'm going through the pericardium and into the muscle cells now. The cells themselves have a pulse, too, almost like each of them has a tiny heart beating inside. I'm inside a cell now, and it is beautiful! How did I not notice this beauty before? The cell wall looks like a cathedral window with the petal pattern repeating over and over. The mitochondria cluster together in a hexagon-shaped structure at a pulse, and then go on their way; then others do it, so it seems like there is a shower of 'snowflakes' that come into and go out of existence at each pulse. I'm going into the nucleus now. Wow! Even the DNA mirrors that pattern. All parts of the cell came into alignment with that pattern. Why is that? What power does that concept have?" Jerry asked, opening his eyes.

"It is not unique to this vibrational signature; every single one has that effect. The vibrational signature pattern influences everything around it because it brings its vibration to the space. To be more specific, it crystallizes matter in a certain way according to its signature. Because of its molecular structure, your DNA is crystalline, a malleable crystal, in fact. That is why this vibrational signature could rearrange the crystal structure of your cells. That is why they looked like cathedral windows. Consequently, cells influenced by the vibrational signature of joy literally have a different material structure than, say, cells influenced by the vibrational signature of anger," Emerson explained.

"I see, too, how this concept can only be understood in light of the last one you showed me, what was it? It had a long name."

"Aneh-mi-oh-nu."

"Yes, the interaction of my vibration and this vibration is what causes the feelings of joy to occur, correct?" Jerry asked.

"Very good, Jerry."

"What is this one called?

"We call this one akra-na. We recognize that feeling it causes, which you call joy, as the outcome of the union of the material and the divine," Emerson added. "It happens at conception. This is the point from which every being develops, and it continues to happen whenever the physical you remembers its connection with the divine you, which is mu-ishi-wa, of course."

"It kind of looks like a big bang. I can see conception as being like a big bang. Hmm, maybe that's what happened when the world began, was conceived, too, the material united with the divine," Jerry mused. "I get it. Joy is what happens when your physical nature is aligned with your spiritual nature."

"It is not a state to get to. It is your foundation, your birthright. Perhaps if you allow yourself to get out of alignment, then joy is absent; otherwise, it is always present," Emerson said.

"I don't doubt that we all start that way, but it seems like there's always something that ruins that primordial bliss. You might burn your hand and conclude that the world isn't a safe place anymore. For me, it happened when I was 10, and my mother got that horrified look on her face which made me think she didn't love me anymore. Joy disappeared from my life at that moment, and looking back, I don't know what I or anybody else could have done to restore it. I don't think I ever got it back fully. Although I can recognize joy and think about how it feels, it's like standing in a chocolate shop looking at the candies but not knowing how they taste. I know what they probably taste like, but if joy is a chocolate bon bon, I have not eaten one in a long, long time." He took a deep breath. "That's the sort of thing that the Energy Conservateur handles, isn't it? He'd identify that misalignment and send corrective energy."

"Yes, that's precisely what he does.

"Could he help me so long after the fact?" Jerry asked.

"Time matters not." Emerson smiled and bid him adieu.

◆   ◆   ◆

Jerry resolved to go see Allan Beaupensee again. *I wonder how your connection to the divine can be restored when you don't have an Energy Conservateur looking out for you? How is the connection to the divine different than the connection to the All? How do you know if you have lost your connection? How can you tell when your child experiences this disconnect? How was my mother supposed to know that's what was happening? She didn't, obviously. What can I do to reestablish the connection?* Jerry's questions troubled him. Despite the understanding he had gained about the interconnectedness of everything and the profound connectedness he felt through the Welcoming Ceremony and again in these meditations, he was certain that something was still out of balance within himself. That disconnection which occurred when he was 10 had never been truly reconnected and healed. He felt he could not be truly interconnected with others if he was still disconnected within himself. *How did I lose that inner connection?*

Since the Energy Conservateur helps people stay in balance, Jerry went immediately to talk to Royce, to get another appointment with the Energy Conservateur. This was the first time ever that he asked for this kind of help, but something had to be done. Never before had there been this sense of urgency, knowing that it was personally unacceptable to be cut off from the divine, the Source being-body. Jerry wrung his hands and pulled on his beard as he walked through town. Worried thoughts cracked open a door of despair. He hadn't felt such uncertainty and discontent since he had arrived in Sagrada. The limbs of the cherry trees reached down, welcoming him into their comforting, fragrant arms. He fantasized about being hugged by someone who had as tender a touch as the delicate cherry blossom. Out of the corner of his right eye he caught some move-ment behind a tree in the distance. He looked in the direction from which it came, but there was nothing. But now he caught some movement in his periph-eral vision to the left and turned his head over there. It was as if he was seeing the wind whistling through the trees. This time he thought he saw color, too, a pale sea green. The third time he saw it, it was two trees over. There were two colors, the sea green and a light mauvy-pink. He watched them dance around the trees for awhile, flying in circles and chasing each other like squirrels would do if they could fly. It was a graceful dance of color reminiscent of ribbon dances. After watching them for about 40 seconds, he sensed that they knew he was there, and in that instant, behind the tree, the color-whooshes materialized into a little boy and girl.

"Hi Mr. Jerry," the boy looked away and guilty.

Jerry stood there, eyes wide, in shock. His world shook. Everything he thought he knew about this place and these people vanished. That sense of awe and panic he felt at age 10 returned. He leaned against a tree to steady himself. This kind of materialization was something he had only seen on TV. *Who or what are these people? Are they people at all?* Jerry faltered at regaining his compo-sure. "I'm sorry to have disturbed your fun," he said, "but how do you do that?"

"Do what?" the boy asked.

"What you just did—change form, materialize in front of my eyes, shift from being immaterial to being material."

"I don't know. It just happens," the boy said.

"It can't just happen. There are complex processes that have to occur for energy to become matter."

The boy looked up at him, panic in his eyes.

"I don't mean to frighten you. I spent years trying to find out how to do what you just did. I never succeeded. And here you are, able to do it," he snapped his fingers, "just like that." The children's fear eased. Jerry squatted down so that he could talk to them at their level. "I want to try that. Please, would you show me how you learned to do it!" Jerry hadn't been this excited since he arrived here.

"You just jump out," the girl chimed in.

"Jump out of what?" Jerry asked.

"Yourself."

"How do I do that?"

"I don't know," she said, crestfallen, realizing that her help wasn't enough.

Jerry playfully tried jumping a few times and fell down every single try. The boy and girl laughed harder every time Jerry tried jumping and falling. The last time they laughed so hard they melted into the grass as their color-whoosh forms.

After all three regained their composure, the girl added, "you have to jump your inside out of your outside."

Jerry surmised that first you must become unselfconscious. That's perhaps what she meant by jumping out of yourself. But the paradox was this: how do you consciously become unselfconscious? *It happened too while they were laughing, so maybe if I laugh hard enough, I can induce it that way.* Jerry started laughing hard, really hard. He rolled in the grass, kicked his legs up, flung his arms around. The girl and boy stood by, watching, confused. They looked at each other in that way that meant "adults are weird." When that didn't work, he gave up and said, "Okay, that's enough silliness for now. Can I just watch you for a little while longer?"

Jerry watched the boy and girl play at their game of tag until he felt the urge to continue his intention to visit Royce and Allan Beaupensee. His walk had a springiness that was missing before, and the despair had lifted. Jerry knew that he had experienced Beaupensee's work in action. "I am honored that our intentions danced together. We are all One," he said under his breath.

Chapter 37

◆

Helen's Journal

I had a strange dream last night in which I was looking at a ladder, a colorful ladder that was made of pieces like Tinker Toys. It seemed like half of the ladder was female and the other half was male. The female side had all kinds of ribbons and sparkly things decorating it, and the male side was rather stark but sleek, with lots of greens and blues. The rungs of the ladder were like couplings, and these also alternated between male and female. Something happened and the ladder twisted itself up like a candy cane. Then from the top the couplings started to come undone. It stopped at eye-level to me, then there was a hail storm of Tinker Toys, and they attached themselves to the broken halves of the ladder, essentially forming two identical ladders instead of one. The female half of the ladder added parts that were male, and the male half added parts that were female. And those ladders also twisted up like candy canes. Then I woke up.

I felt an intense desire to call that woman who took me into the woods, but I didn't. This is the strangest dream, and I don't know what it means. She'd probably think I was nuts. Oh hold it. I used to think *she* was nuts because she was the one who told Jerry about dreaming of bears. Okay. Done. We meet this afternoon.

◆   ◆   ◆

"It's so nice to see you again, Miss, um Jerry's friend."
"Helen."

"Oh yes, now I remember. Have you asked the universe any more questions?" Terrah asked.

"No, no I haven't."

"Okay."

Helen was stunned that it was actually okay. She had expected a reprimand.

"But it seems to be giving me answers anyway," Helen added.

Terrah smiled as if saying of course! "You said you had a dream that was troubling you."

"Yes, I did. I…"

"Before you start, I'm sorry to have to tell you that the dream expert, my granddaughter, isn't here right now. She's at college." Terrah beamed. "But I'll see how I can help. Tell me the dream as if you want me to experience the same dream."

Helen recounted her dream while Terrah closed her eyes and listened, trying to see the images as if she herself were dreaming it.

"I've seen this image before." Terrah got up and left the room. When she returned she had a high school biology book. She flipped to the page showing DNA replication.

"I dreamed about genetics?"

"My apologies. This was a distraction. Always look to the dream itself for your answers. It's unnecessary to know that your dream images resemble this, what does it say, DNA replication." Terrah closed the book and looked at Helen to see whether she was going to say anything more. "You used an interesting word to describe the rungs of the ladder. You said 'couplings.' Look at the root of that word: couple. What couple do you know that was recently separated, un-coupled?"

Helen first thought of which of her friends had broken up. The obvious answer is always the last one thought of. "I can't think of…"

Terrah gave her one of those motherly looks that says "I can't believe you don't see it; it's right under your nose!"

"Oh, you mean me and Jerry! So this is a dream about Jerry and me…" she crossed her fingers and then uncrossed them.

"In the dream, look a little harder at what happened after they uncoupled, after you and Jerry…" Terrah made the same gesture with her fingers.

"Each side of the ladder added parts and became an identical copy of the original ladder. There were now two complete ladders."

"So the female side, and I would imagine that represents you, gained some 'male bits' and the male side, Jerry, gained some 'female bits.' Each is now whole. So, *is* that what happened?" Terrah challenged.

Helen looked wistful. "I guess so, for me anyway."

"So in the bigger scheme of things, what does this dream now tell you?"

"This answers the question I had the last time I was here, the question about where Jerry is. I was expecting a certain kind of answer, like 'in Kansas, with the lion, scarecrow, the tin man, and Dorothy,' but that wasn't the answer I got. Even though it's just a dream, it feels like a definitive answer." There was hesitation in her voice.

"How do you feel about that?" Terrah asked.

"I never would have searched for any answer or information in a dream. I wouldn't have trusted it. I guess I'm still wondering whether to trust it. Maybe it was just a coincidence."

"Everything you will ever need is in there," Terrah pointed to Helen. "Sure, you can look out here for answers, but they're harder to find because there are more smoke and mirrors for you to get lost in, but what's out here is just a reflection of what's in you. Everything out here exists more purely in there."

"Really?" Helen was skeptical.

"How else could you write? How could anybody invent anything? Because it exists first here, then you bring it forth into the world."

"Oh, yeah."

"Try looking inside sometime. But mind you, you have to be quiet. Turn off the talk radio show that's always blasting in your head," Terrah scolded her.

"Yes, ma'am."

"Tell me, Miss Donellyn, when you were young, say 6 to 10 years old, what did you want to be when you grew up? Do you recall?"

Helen thought for awhile. "My father would read *War of the Worlds* to me, and I loved how much fun we had pretending. Then, when it was on the radio and all those people panicked because they thought it was real, we had a good laugh because we knew it was just a story. That's when I think I first became conscious of the power of words. I wanted to have power like H. G. Wells to create fantastic worlds in the imagination."

"Hmm, isn't that interesting," is all Terrah said.

Helen let out a short laugh, recognizing the irony in her own life, which she had not seen before. "How did you know?" she asked rhetorically as much as to Terrah. Patterns in her life emerged before her eyes. "I've been going about it backwards. I've been looking out there in the world thinking that's where the power of words was. And that's why I seem to be attracting so many physicists into my life. And that's maybe even why I was so fanatic about covering that story on the OWB crash. There it is, there's the material for my first science fiction novel. They spoke to me, you know, without words, directly into my mind. I have to write about *that*. They told us some amazing things, and then their ship healed itself. I saw it, it grew back together. It was amazing, and I've been sitting on this information this whole time because my editor just wanted the usual dry, lifeless facts called 'news.' Ugh, I've been so stupid!"

Terrah watched as the insights flooded Helen. She smiled to herself as she realized that her purpose was being accomplished. Terrah saw herself as a spiritual ophthalmologist, someone who asks you to read the letters in the bottom line of your eye chart called 'Life'—in other words someone who asks the necessary questions to help you see clearly on the inside by healing your inner cataracts, your inner myopia, which prevents you from seeing your ultimate goal or purpose because it was too far away and too fuzzy. When you lose sight of that core purpose, all you can focus on is what's in front of you at the moment, so you forget, and in forgetting you lose your way in life. When you can focus on the end achievement, see it clearly, getting there becomes easy.

Helen gave Terrah a big hug. "Thank you. You are truly an angel. I'm so sorry that I thought you were a little…" Helen was so embarrassed she couldn't finish the sentence.

"Wackier than a barrel of pickled ego-nuts?"

Helen nodded, laughing at the image that conjured up.

"That's okay dear. Now you have some work to do, so scram," Terrah told her as if she were talking to one of her cats.

Chapter 38

Jerry ran from the orchard. Gasping for air between breaths he asked, "Royce, what is going on here? I just saw two children who...I don't know what they were doing. When I came across them they were like colored energy whooshes. They had no particular form, just color, and they zipped around the orchard like the wind. When they realized that I was there, they changed shape back into human form right before my eyes! Is that your real form, as colored energy? Why didn't anybody tell me that? Is this 'reality' all a big charade? I don't know what's real anymore."

In a calming voice, Royce explained, "What you saw was a particular game, and the form for playing it is what you called a 'colored whoosh.' Different games require other forms."

"I was just starting to feel like I fit in here, like I wasn't such an outsider, like I understood your culture a little better. And now I...I don't know what to think anymore. I feel so...alien."

"When you start dating someone new, do you find out everything about her on the first date?" Royce asked.

"No, of course not."

"I know you're feeling shocked and perhaps even betrayed, like we misled you. We did not. Our culture is rich in nuance. You will continue to learn the nuances." Royce's compassion quelled Jerry's agitation.

"Yes, okay. Are they going to be as shocking as that?"

"We'll see," Royce answered. "We weren't sure how you'd react if you knew about that form or any other. Those children weren't supposed to be playing that game, but you know how children are. Besides, if you truly weren't ready to learn that about us, you wouldn't have aligned your intention to be able to see it."

"So now that the cat is out of the bag, tell me about it. Why do you switch forms? How can I do that?" Jerry asked.

Royce changed himself into a light purple whoosh and circled around the room and landed on Jerry's shoulder. *You're so full of questions, my friend. It doesn't really matter why we do it, does it? Funny word, there, matter. Why don't you say 'It doesn't really energy?' We adopt whatever form we need, given the beings and the circumstances. It's a bit like playing dress up. We simply shift our vibration to take whatever form is necessary, whether it be material or musical or simply colorful, as I am now.* Jerry "heard" this communicated by Royce directly to his mind.

"Does that answer your question?" Royce asked as he took human form again.

"I think so. And you do it by intention, right?"

Royce smiled, pleased.

"The little girl said that you have to jump out of yourself. The inside has to jump out of the outside. What does that mean?" Jerry asked.

"That was a child's understanding of something she doesn't really know how to explain yet," Royce said. "Here is another way to think about the type of intention it takes. Imagine that you are a facet of a large diamond. You look around, and you can see some other facets near you. You can tell that they are different facets because they don't see things from the exact same perspective as you. You have no idea that you are part of this great diamond, and you have no idea that there are other facets behind you, because you can't see that way. And you especially have no idea that you're all made of the same stuff, carbon atoms, because as the light shines through the diamond, it refracts as one color through your facet and as other colors through the other facets around you, so you think that you're all different because you're refracting different colors."

"Oh I see, but just because I understand that I'm a part of this greater whole doesn't mean that I can intend to become a fox and poof, there I am. It's like saying that I can choose to be a different facet."

"You're still stuck in 'facet-consciousness.' One facet cannot become a different facet. Shift instead to 'diamond-consciousness' and put your focus first on Jerry-facetness. Then put your focus on fox-facetness. Then try flower-facetness, or whatever you want to try. When you realize that you are the diamond, perceiving through any particular facet is simply a matter of where you direct your focus."

"And each facet has the capability of doing that?"

"Only the facets that know themselves as the diamond can. It makes for a very alive and vibrant sort of being, doesn't it? But again, it is only possible if you know yourself as both at once, the part and the whole, a facet but more importantly the whole diamond."

"Do those children know themselves that way? Are they cognizant of all that you just told me?"

"To them it is second nature, they have always known themselves as part and whole, energy and matter. That's your concern, is it not? Well, you just witnessed it in action."

"But *why* do you play this game of part and whole, facet-this and facet-that? Why have you concocted this whole other reality?"

"Because our intention intersected with your intention. Why did you create this other reality, Jerry? We want to make a difference as a community," he winked. "What difference did you want to make?"

"Ironically, I wanted to find out how to do what those children did so naturally. I wanted to figure out how to willingly, spontaneously, and consciously shift from matter to energy or energy to matter. You are living the answer to my question. That's what Emerson has been trying to teach me."

"Now you know why you are here," Royce said.

Jerry's whole life, which had been like a big, undifferentiated blob of uncertainty bouncing from one situation to the next, a search for answers to unreasonable questions, in this moment crystallized, revealing the whole structure from birth to this moment. It reminded him of when he watched his mother make rock candy out of sugar water: the crystallization process seemed like a miracle, like the creation of life. The true form and beauty of the sugar revealed itself in that moment. Similarly, the reasons for everything he had done became evident; the answer to his question spread out in front of him in the form of the people and place of Sagrada. This was it, this was how matter became energy and energy became matter. It was so incredible, the realization that he finally did it, he cried. Royce rematerialized and hugged him.

"The light of understanding that we turn on for ourselves shines more brightly than any candle held up to someone else's knowledge," Royce whispered to him. "You just recognized the asymmetry of perspective. You can look at the world as mostly matter with rivers of energy running through it in electrical wires and things like that, or you can look at the world as mostly energy with mountains of matter here and there. Neither is right and neither is wrong; they just have different constraints."

"How," Jerry sobbed through his tears, 'how do I become part of this? How do I master this ability to shift from one to the other? I want that now more than anything else in the world. I understand that the key to living as you do—as energy—is to both shift your perspective and use intention. Only, how do I get it to work? It feels like trying to learn to play the piano with both hands. I just can't find the coordination. I want to live as you do, but I can't seem to get past my own materiality. How can I develop that coordination? What else must I do to be able to become an energy being like you?"

"Before I can answer you, Jerry, I must speak with Beaupensee. I don't know enough about you to be able to tell you. Excuse me for a minute."

When he returned, he told Jerry, "Meet me here tomorrow, and we will work on that."

Chapter 39

Secret Lives of the Creators by Helen Donellyn
Chapter 1

Zorn fashioned his creation from the scraps left after the last destruction—some iron, a bit of phosphorous, and a lot of carbon from the charred remains of the now-destroyed planet. He put a seed at the center of this new world, a seed which he could ignite with a word, like lighting a candle. The ignited seed would cause an alchemical reaction that would bring it to life. That was the theory, at least. He had worked very carefully to get the proportions exact, as that was the most important step in the creation of a new world. Your raw materials could be procured from almost anything; its purpose could be whatever you chose; the rest boiled down to getting the mutual relation of the constituent parts in the proper order and arrangement to form a coherent whole, which demanded patience, attention to detail, and unbridled perfectionism. He had all those qualities, which earned him the reputation as the most gifted Creator in the Universe.

This new world would be different than the rest, which is why he worked in secrecy and solitude. It would have a quality about it that would result in nothing short of a paradigm shift in worldmaking. He would not reveal the secret to anyone, not even me, his closest and most trusted friend.

I met Zorn eons ago at the Universal Institute for World Creation, the UIWC. I was there pursuing a course of study in Remote Planetary Healing. I don't have the personality for more hands-on kinds of interventions, as Christ and Buddha like to do. I tend to work from deep space, like a coach, not on the field like them. Anyhow, Zorn showed up for Ways of Worldmaking 101 not with a blank canvas but with a multidimensional tapestry equal in quality to the final projects of the best students in previous millennia. The professor gave the rest of the students to his laboratory assistant and took Zorn under his wing as an apprentice.

I met Zorn, unofficially, at the trash dump in the outer reaches of the Arutian Galaxy where we deposit the remains of failed experiments, imploded worlds, and cometic spew. He was looking for raw materials, and I was looking to trap one of denizens of the Arutian dump for an experiment in evolutionary nutrition: I was investigating whether something that feeds on waste can evolve to a higher consciousness if it is given more ephermeral nourishment. Just as the beast was being lured into my trap, Zorn appeared out of the left arm of the galaxy and scared it away. I was about to curse him out and throw thunderbolts, when I realized who it was. He apologized profusely, not expecting to find anyone else bold enough to face the stench of galactic refuse. The next solar cycle, I was awoken by the cries of the beast I sought to catch; he was gravitationally bound to a planet in my front yard. I never forgot that act of kindness from Zorn.

Officially, I met Zorn at the Upper Paradise party. It was an enchanted lunar cycle, with the music of the spheres playing softly in the background and generous dispersement of the Elixirs of Love and Creativity. I was bedecked in my finest comets and shooting stars, like a tiara framing my vast countenance. He saw me from afar and recognized me straightaway. As I spiraled in closer to him, he caught the scent of my perfume, Flora di Sol. Without going into embarrassing detail, we danced together for the rest of the lunar cycle. He escorted me to my galaxy and then disappeared into a higher dimension to get home before the solar cycle commenced.

Zorn's brilliance lay in the fact that he observed astutely and applied his observations precisely. He wouldn't just see a star going supernova, he would see all the forces at play, the acceleration of gravity, the warping of space, the chemical reactions in the pattern and colors of explosion. And then he would say "what if…". What if there were more sulfur? What if the gravitational constant were changed? And one day he asked a very peculiar what if—what if I shifted the configuration of space so that as it exploded, the shrapnel circled back into the core and continuously refueled the explosion? It was brilliant, but nobody knew what would happen in the long run. Because of its radically different nature, he couldn't get a permit to create it near the Galactic Center. They granted him a Creator's Permit for a remote planet far from where it could affect anything. It was quite a blow to his ego, as he had been the Golden Boy at the Institute for ages.

Chapter 2

I was surprised to receive from Zorn a distressed plea for my services. His paradigm-shifting creation was wobbling, causing it to be off-key in a way he hadn't anticipated.

Chapter 40

"Is this going to hurt?" Jerry joked.

"Of course it will, if that is your intention," Royce replied, taking him seriously. He looked intently, with a narrow, laser-like focus at Jerry as if he was looking inside. Then he looked with a wide focus, as if looking at everything but Jerry. After a long moment of silence, Royce said, "There are slow vibrational patterns keeping you stuck in your materiality. We will have to uncover them and release them."

"What does that involve?"

He explained to Jerry, "Do you remember the symbol akra-na, the union of the material and the divine? To change form, that union must be present and strong, but yours is weak. Akra-na represents a very pure vibration. However, not all concepts vibrate at such a pure frequency. Fear and anger, for instance, pollute one's vibration with impurities. Matter already is energy, as you know, but it has a lower frequency than other forms of energy. Frequency and matter resemble the relationship between temperature and water. At lower temperature, water appears more solid than at higher temperatures. Fear, anger, anxiety, and their ilk are much more suited to materiality, the slower vibrational states than the one you wish to attain. Jerry, some parts of your body are stuck in lower vibrational states because there is pollution."

"What must I do?"

"For us, being in a body is like steam turning itself into ice. You, however, are like ice and must turn yourself into steam. When ice turns to steam, it loses its familiar structure, the way the molecules bind together in a particular, very uniform way. Your familiar structure is more complex than ice, but it too is bound in a particular uniform way. It has a pattern, and that pattern is held together not only by the molecular interactions—those are weak—but also by your thoughts. Fearful, angry thoughts hold molecular patterns in place very strongly. Those must be released. Even the fear of losing your familiar molecular structure must be released. It can be rather disconcerting to lose the left-right, front-back shape and consequently the unique perspective that you have identified yourself with for all these years."

"I understand. I still want to do this." Jerry made his intention clear.

"Fine. In that case, you must conduct a teacher-student mu-ishi-wa rondo."

"What does that involve?" Jerry imagined aboriginal practices in which stuck emotional energy was practically beaten out of the patient's muscle memory.

"It is a fu-an-gu practice of looking deeply into your heart as both the student and the teacher, much like you have done with Emerson, except that you guide yourself."

"How do I do that, if I don't know what I have to do?" Jerry asked.

"I will get you started. Sit comfortably and close your eyes for now. Breathe deeply 13 times, starting at the upper chakra. Breathe into each one. After the thirteenth breath, feel the connection to sky all the way through your body to the ground. Now walk through the door that is at the heart level. What kind of door is it—a revolving door, the door to a vault, a doorless doorway? Is it locked? Do you need a key to get in? Inside the door there is a curtain, a veil, behind which sits your inner teacher. Ask your teacher whether you may enter now. If the answer is yes, walk through the veil and sit at the foot of your inner teacher. You will know whether you are supposed to close your eyes or keep them open. Some teachers do not like to reveal themselves right away."

Jerry inhaled sharply.

"You're safe. Your teacher, no matter how frightening he looks, will not harm you. What does your inner teacher look like?" Royce asked.

"An enormous eagle with wings spread, like in a coat of arms."

"When you are ready, you will hear the voice of your inner teacher. Just answer the questions."

Jerry quieted his mind by focusing on his breathing. In, the cooling breath, the balloon filling him with life. Out, the cleansing breath, releasing all impurities back to the universe. Twelve more times. A brief moment of stillness, where all was quiet, was interrupted by a deep, resonant, soothing voice that spoke through every cell in his body, not just in his head as the inner critic does.

I know you're afraid. Fear itself will not harm you; it is only a vibration in your middle. How you respond to fear is what can harm you. You will survive if you relax and let go of any concerns, but hang on to the process, as you rode the wave in your Welcoming Ceremony.

I will survive. Relax. Release. Jerry repeated that as a mantra to quell the apprehension. He could feel and hear his heart pounding and nerves twitching. The voice didn't speak again until the physical sensations subsided. This time it was softer, more feminine.

You are storing your unresolved fears as if the threat that created them never went away.

How do you know that?

Feel your side, right under your arm.

Jerry felt a pinch when he pressed a particular spot toward the front under his arm.

Your residual fear is a by-product, a stored memory of a fear that was never resolved. After the threat leaves, the fear should leave, too; however, sometimes if we perceive someone close as the threat, the fear doesn't leave, as it should. We will revisit the experiences that generated the fear so that they stop releasing the toxic fumes of fear. Go back to an experience that shaped who you are today, an experience that caused you to make a decision or a judgment about yourself. What is the earliest memory you have?

When I was 4, I fell on the playground and hit my head so hard I blacked out. My poor mother thought I had died. She was so distraught that she then fainted. When I woke up and saw her lying there unmoving, I thought she was dead. I didn't know what to do. I called out "Mama" over and over, but there was no one around to hear me. I was alone and scared. I finally just put my head on her chest and cried. I cried so loudly that it woke her up. After that, she wouldn't leave me alone to play. I used to hate that, so I always tried to sneak away when she wasn't looking. At first she'd get steaming mad, but then it became a game.

What did you experience? Feel the way you felt then, the terror at not knowing why your mother was not responding to you, the terror of what seemed like absolute aloneness.

I was so young, I hardly had words for what I felt. My head hurt so much. I was scared when she didn't wake up. Why wasn't she fixing the boo-boo? Why wasn't she talking to me? It was crushing me, the anguish was so strong that I felt suffocated. I couldn't breathe. I was confused. Mommy was there, but she wasn't there. I couldn't bear it any longer. I thought I was going to die too.

That's when you thought you disconnected from the Divine. It's not going to kill you to feel it again because you know you can never be disconnected. It's a trick of the mind. You must feel the fear fully in your body in order to release it. Feel the tightness in your chest, in your muscles. Feel the nausea. Feel the constriction in your throat. Hold it for a few seconds. Now imagine, in your terror and aloneness, reaching up and grasping a strong hand. Pull it into you. That hand can pull you out of any fear. Now you have that strength inside. In your helpless state, feel the help that is always there. You realize that you are not alone. Feel the love that you felt pour into you at the Welcoming Ceremony. Feel wanted and embraced by all. How does that feel in comparison to absolute aloneness?

Jerry's entire body tone shifted; his shoulders dropped, his face softened, his arms and legs unclenched. *I feel full, like a fountain overflowing; powerful, like I have a mountain there to support me; safe and secure, like sitting in Dad's lap during a thunderstorm; and complete, like the satiety of a good meal.*

What did you choose so that you wouldn't have to feel scared, helpless, and confused again?

Although I kept trying to sneak away, I didn't go very far. I didn't want to be scared like that ever again. And I didn't want her to be scared either. I guess I chose to stay close, to protect her so that she would protect me, and I'd never feel abandoned and alone again.

How did you feel when she woke up?

Relief, indescribable relief. I didn't want to let go of her, so I didn't—for three whole days. I clung to her hand, her leg, her skirt, whatever I could grab.

Your clinginess to her was your way of protecting her and feeling protected by her mere presence. Feel the warmth of protection. How does that feel?

I feel like a cake in the oven. Warmth is all around me, allowing me, encouraging me to rise, to bake.

Relish that feeling for at least 20 seconds.

I feel done, cooked.

Good, but we're not finished yet. What happened later, around 6 or 7 years old?

I don't know. I don't remember anything that traumatic.

What did you want to be at that age?

I wanted to be a space traveler.

And what did your parents think about that?

Mom thought it was cute, but Dad couldn't stand it. He thought it was frivolous and had no benefit to humanity. He wanted me to take up a trade, like he did, and do something useful with my hands, but I wasn't coordinated and hated messy things. I couldn't do things like he did—fix engines, build furniture, repair broken stuff. I was much better at thinking up ideas.

So what did you do to avoid his disapproval?

I kept to myself. I stopped talking to him about things that were important to me. I avoided him because I didn't want to get into any arguments. I wasn't strong enough to defend myself against his booming voice and overpowering fury. I was no match for him, and I knew it.

What do you fear about him?

Though I consciously chose not to follow in his footsteps, I fear his disappointment, his criticism. Either way I was doomed: if I did what he did, I'd fail because I didn't have the talent, and if I didn't do what he did, I failed him in his eyes anyway. I hate the way he'd slide in a dig here and there, make fun of what I do, find some little way to criticize me about anything and everything. And if I reacted to it, then he'd get really upset, sometimes even beat me. I feared his power over me.

Feel that fear of being too small, like David facing Goliath. If you knew you could say magic words that would stop him from hurting you, what would you say?

Abracadabra alacazam! Please just love me for who I am.

Feel him loving you the way you are. He really did. He was proud of you because you could do things that he couldn't do. There he was, a grown man whose young son was better than him. He too felt like David. He feared being eclipsed by you. What would you like him to have said to you?

Good job.

Good job. Now make it really juicy. Don't hold anything back.

I'm so proud of you, of all the interesting things you can do, things I'll never be able to do. You'll be the best space traveler there ever was. I admire you for the difference you want to make in the world.

Reconnect with him. Imagine giving him a big hug and telling him all about your life, while he listens with rapt attention. Feel his love for you like rain soaking you through and through. His love and your love are mu-ishi-wa, two sides of the same thing. When you fully appreciate his love of you, you will truly love yourself.

What was the next incident, the one that set the path for the rest of your life?

When, oh god this is…when I was 10 and saw my hand fuse with the sheet, I tried to ask my mother what happened. She looked at me like I had just turned into a monkey or something. Her face contorted from fright and panic, but she didn't say anything. That look of horror scared me more than her silence or more than Dad's angry words could have. The look said "you freak, you alien; how can you be my son?" I stood mute before her, my blood running from my heart onto the floor. Deflated, defeated, I couldn't look at her any more. I turned away and ran and ran—down the street into the neighbor's corn field. I lost my breath three miles away. The owners of the farm called my parents, and my father had to come get me with the car.

And what did you decide in that moment when you saw her reaction?

I don't know. I was so frightened. All I knew was that I never wanted to see that look in her eyes again. She had been my protector, and now she was the one who lowered the guillotine on the connection between us. I remember seeing her in an apron and thinking that it wasn't the right clothing for a she-bear who could uproot your sense of being with a single, mighty glare.

Who really did that, killed off the relationship?

She did. She looked at me like she didn't want to admit that I was her son.

Could she have been scared of what she couldn't understand rather than horrified at you?

I suppose so.

So who really drove the wedge in?

Jerry closed his eyes and grimaced. He knew what the true answer was but didn't want to say it. Saying it would mean giving up his story in which he was the innocent victim. *I guess I did. All she did was look at me. She was scared and didn't know how to react, but I was the one who made it mean that the bond had been severed.*

What did you decide about how or who you were going to be from then on?

Hmmm. I think I feared that I lost her love, that she was so horrified that she didn't love me anymore, that I was someone to be feared. But I didn't want to be that way, so I wouldn't do anything ever again to make her fear me like that. And I assumed I had lost her love for good, so I tried to be good and do things that might win it back, all the while convinced that I had ruined it—the only person who really loved me—I scared her away.

Do you think now that your mother stopped loving you because of that incident?

No, she didn't stop. I wanted to think that she did.

If you could say magic words to her, what would you say?

Mom, I'm still the same person. What happened wasn't a bad thing. It was miraculous. Please don't be scared anymore.

What insight have you gained from seeing them newly?

I see that I don't have to be afraid of losing their love anymore. I never lost it. I simply couldn't see it and refused to feel it. It has always been there and always will be.

Can you forget everything they have said and done, look at them as strangers and love them for who they are, like you would the old lady walking her dog in the park?

Just as humans, you mean, strangers even.

Exactly. Take your old fears and your judgments and pluck them from you and deposit them in the cosmic waste basket.

To forgive them would be like falling from an airplane without a parachute. There's nothing to hold on to, nothing to keep me safe, nothing to.... The tears, reluctantly at first, congregated in the corner of his eye. He blinked them back. They came anyway, defiantly rolling down his cheeks.

I'm scared. By forgiving them I'd lose the only connection I have. Granted, anger and bitterness are not the bases of an ideal connection, but it's all I have. Once that's gone, there would be nothing...

It's a connection that doesn't nourish you, however; it poisons you. There is no nourishment in fear and anger. When you release that connection, it will create a vacuum, forcing you to establish another kind of connection. You get to choose what kind of connection you want from that point on.

But how do I do that?

Imagine an umbilical cord made of chain connecting you to them. See that it doesn't serve you; it enslaves you. Cut it off. Stop the flow of poison. There will be a brief moment of shock, as if you've fallen off a cliff, but the wind will catch you.

Jerry inhaled sharply, as if he had a visceral reaction to the imagined severance.

There is always love there to support you. Feel their love for you. Just let it in. It's there, pounding at the door. Open the door.

Okay. It was like opening a kiln door. Warmth and light flooded in.

See your mother and father as you know them now. Imagine them getting younger and younger. See them as newlyweds, as teenagers, and children, now as infants. Hold them in your arms. Look into their newborn eyes. All you see there is pure love and joy. Akra-na. Remember that that's who they really are, and that's who you really are. Do you forgive them? Do you forgive yourself?

Yes, I forgive you. Jerry had wet cheeks. He realized how unfair he had been to them, shutting them out for having a natural visceral reaction to something they couldn't explain. He saw how they felt inadequate because they couldn't explain it, how afraid they were that something bad had happened and yet they could do nothing to prevent it. *I forgive myself, too.*

What do you want to say to them now?

Mom, Dad, I'm in a place where the walls between you and me don't exist. The boundary between us, well, there is none. All these years I have set myself up in opposition to you, only to find out that you and I are one, like different facets of the same diamond. I am you and you are me. How can I hate you? I would be hating myself.

Jerry came to understand the cycle by which fear is propagated. Their simple fear triggered his fear, which resulted in him fearing them. Love was derailed. In looking at this, the seeing pulled it apart, crumbled the fear, broke the cycle, tore down the hard walls that had kept him isolated from their love and them from his. It all turned to mush. His body itself turned soft and limp as he slumped over involuntarily. With the fear gone, he felt hollow inside, like something was missing, the something that gave structure and meaning to his life. What would it be like now, without that fear propping him up?

"Open your eyes," he heard Royce say.

There, standing before him were his mother and his father.

"How—?"

"Shhh," Royce signaled.

However this happened, Jerry was so grateful for the chance to release the past. He grabbed them both into his arms, his mother on his left and his father on his right, and sobbed out the grief and regret of decades. Mr. Fowss patted him on the back and Mrs. Fowss stroked his hair. "I'm...so...sorry," Jerry stuttered.

"We are too, dear," his mother said.

Jerry felt the frail, elderly man he called Father in his strong arms. His arms could now crush this man who had once so overpowered him. He stroked his mother's hair, gray and thinning, and looked into her sunken eyes. The horror was gone. There was still a small blue light in them that reached out, questioning, to him. He held her tightly, swaying back and forth like teenagers at a prom. *What took me so long to do this?* he wondered silently as he kissed the top of her head. *Why couldn't I see the real Mom and Dad as other parts of the real me?*

His heart jumped, like it has received a shock and beat excitedly. The internal floodgates burst, and all the pain and anger and sorrow that he had been holding onto all these years poured from his eyes, his heart, and his throat. The rivulets of tears turned to a flood. He could barely catch up to his breathing. His body expanded, filling the universe. The image of akra-na flitted through his mind, and he wondered whether now he'd be able to experience akra-na, joy.

Chapter 41

◆

Helen's Journal

I forgot all about writing science fiction until Terrah reminded me. How could I have forgotten all those years? Oh yeah, I remember what happened now. I was in fourth grade. We were doing book reports, and I did one on *The Earthsea Trilogy*—lots of magic and dragons and things like that. I loved those books! Children were wizards and had power, real power. When I had finished giving my report and other kids were allowed to ask questions, Timmy shot his hand straight up, and with a smug look on his face asked, "Why do you bother reading about dragons? They're not real anyway. Only real things matter." I was crushed. The fire of my passion in life was extinguished by his righteous sputterings. He said it with such authority. I felt chagrined and embarrassed, so from then on I stuck to real things, because after all, according to another 9-year-old, that's all that matters.

I had even forgotten that I found out years later that Timmy's parents had sent him to a kiddie shrink because the only friend he had was an imaginary friend and he wouldn't talk to anyone else. I took the brunt of his "therapy." By then the die had been cast. Funny how such stupid little incidents can change the course of life.

Maybe that's what the course of life is, one stupid incident after another, until we stop being bumped this way and that by stupid little incidents and decide what the course is really going to be. Oh there's my big fat conscience saying "Okay, so what course is it going to be?" I'm going to pick up where I left off in fourth grade. I'm going to be a science fiction writer.

There's a buzzing in my chest right now, like I've had too much caffeine. Ben has shown me that if you get too serious about things that are really, really important you stop having fun doing them. I think that's what happened to Jerry, why he ultimately gave up on his dream. It got too serious.

Chapter 42

For several days after the meeting with Royce, Jerry stayed to himself. His body felt different, like his clothes, in this case his skin, didn't fit quite properly. He had to get used to feeling like he was overflowing the cup he was in. So he helped Maria in the garden because it got him moving and using his hands. So much lately had required concentration and thought that it felt good to do something physical. He thought of his father as he transplanted the interlopers and pinched the unwanted growth. For once, the thoughts didn't have a hard edge to them; he simply thought about his father's life and how it overlapped with his own. His father would be pleased that he was doing something with his hands. Jerry, too, lost some of his hard edge, his constant questioning, his need to understand.

"There is a special gathering happening tonight, Jerry," Maria mentioned while planting tomatoes. "Usually there is music; sometimes there is food; but always there is a ritual called the bakala, which is a kind of synchronized movement. It is a way of sharing our joy directly with others. You should try it. It is most exhilarating."

"Okay, I'll go," Jerry said. Jerry got the distinct impression in a mental image that he should also bring a food to share. He surmised that he might be starting consciously to receive others' intentions and know them as that rather than as stray thoughts.

◆　　◆　　◆

It was usually pitch black at night, but this night, there was light coming from the center of the village. Several tents had been erected near the Community House, and music was coming from the southernmost one. Jerry was drawn to it, but Maria wanted to socialize with the women in the tent to the west. He put the vegetables from the garden with the other food and was pulled toward the music, which had a beat that was strangely familiar and not entirely regular.

In the tent with the music, Jerry saw couples dancing, or so it seemed. Some were cheek to cheek and others elbow to elbow, forearm to forearm. Royce saw

Jerry and waved him over to his group. Emerson and Allan Beaupensee were there, as well as some other women he didn't know yet.

"Jerry, you have a tremendous opportunity here tonight to experience one of our supreme pleasures. The bakala is a cultural treasure. Notice how it is done: the man and the woman move together as one unit, one body with four legs. The heart is where the bakala originates," Beaupensee explained, pounding his fist on his chest. "The partners connect at the heart, and the movement arises spontaneously between them, that is why each couple's movement is different; there is a different dynamic between each pair. I find it as fascinating to witness as it is to do."

As Jerry watched, he noticed the sensuality between some of the couples. The subtlety of a movement of the leg or an extension of an arm. In other couples, the joy each was feeling was so magnified by the other that the energy spilled over to the couples nearby. Royce left the group of men when his wife entered the tent. They moved into the center slowly at first, carefully, but they too could not contain their joy, and soon their movement became a frenzy of spins and flying hair and arms and legs. Jerry could see clearly, however, that regardless of the intensity of activity, the heart connection was not broken. This was not like swing dancing, where the man leads with his arms, it was more like tango, where the lead comes from the heart or chest, the difference here being that there was no leader and follower, just a mutual creation of movement. "When you are that connected by the heart energy," Beaupensee explained, "it is possible to move without spinning apart because the movement arises between you. That is the secret, the betweenness. The bakala is where the logical distinction between individuals is dissolved, where the I-that-is-you merges with the you-that-is-me."

"How do I learn to do this?" Jerry shocked even himself by asking. He usually thought of himself as socially challenged when it came to dancing. But this, this was not mere dancing. It made his chest pound, his whole body vibrate. He felt more connected to himself than he had ever felt, and he hadn't even done the bakala with anybody yet.

"Learn? There's nothing to learn. Just feel. Here, bakala with Monica." Monica Silverstone had wanted to make Jerry's acquaintance, and this was the perfect chance. "Close your eyes for now, so you don't get distracted. Feel the beat of your heart in your chest. Feel the energy it is sending out. Feel the energy that she is sending out. Just do what feels right," Beaupensee nudged them out into the center. Their energies connected, they didn't have to touch each other to move in synchrony, which is not the same as doing the same steps, like waltzing.

What a heavenly state! He relaxed into the movement, did not think about it, and just let his body do it. It was like being in a trance. This was not the self-conscious rocking from side to side that he remembered from the high school prom. In fact the point of the bakala is to lose *self*-consciousness entirely, to merge with the source of consciousness.

"The ability to let go of control is very important for what you came to see me about recently," Royce told him privately. "This is a good way to practice that, to just be the movement rather than trying to do the movement."

The bakala: people moving together in synchrony with their heart energy. How simple and elegant. What a relief to Jerry. He didn't have to think about words anymore, but he knew less about movement and dance than he did about language, orders of magnitude less.

"Come to my house tomorrow, Jerry," Emerson said, "and we can explore this more."

Chapter 43

"I would enjoy the bakala with Emerson again," Maria said as Jerry was leaving for Emerson's house.

"Why don't you come along, then?" Jerry suggested, oblivious to her sadness.

"No, perhaps not."

"Why not? It'll be a lot of fun," Jerry encouraged.

"Jerry, I must tell you something. Emerson and I were to be married when we were young, but he altered his intention when another woman caught his eye. It was enough to dissolve the certainty of our bond in his heart. He married her, and several years later she died very unexpectedly. Emerson has not courted since then. Nor have I."

"But you still feel very connected to him, don't you?"

She nodded.

"It sounds like your intention isn't clear either. Is it sheer coincidence that both you and he have adopted me, taught me the ways of this culture, made me feel at home?" Jerry left immediately for his bakala lesson.

◆　　　◆　　　◆

Jerry had a spring in his step and whistled a tune as he made his way to Emerson's house. During a pause in the tune, Jerry heard footsteps behind him coming closer. Monica Silverstone, the children's teacher, nearly walked into him. "Hello Mr. Jerry. Shall we walk together to the bakala lesson?" Monica was tall and blonde. She had an athletic build, toned from interacting with children—running with their games, picking them up for hugs when they fall.

Jerry blinked and thought *How does she know where I'm going? Does everybody know everything about everyone else?* "Oh, right. Yes, let's walk together," Jerry said, remembering now where he was headed.

"I saw you last night and my heart leapt to be your partner, as the bakala works better with a man and a woman than with two men," Monica explained. "I am honored that our intentions danced together to create this moment. We are all One."

Jerry quickly searched his memory for the response to the acknowledgment of the creation of an intention intersection. "Oh yes, I am the mirror of your kindness." He bowed his head to her. "But tell me, Miss Silverstone, aren't we all both male and female anyway? Why does it work better this way?"

Jerry noticed her male side shoot him a "you better believe it, pal" look. He was rather tough in contrast to the sweetness of her female side. "Indeed we are, but the balancing of primary energies is one of the purposes of the bakala," she said.

As they walked the rest of the way to Emerson's house in silence, Jerry's mind spun with questions, *What else is there to learn? Is it the access to a mystical experience, like the practice of the Sufi dervishes? Will I be any good at it? I was never a good dancer. What if I step on her toes?*

"I'm a little nervous about this," he admitted. Jerry caught himself doing what he always did when confronted with something new—questioning incessantly—but this time he stopped the questions from overpowering him. He also felt a little intimidated by Monica's brawny male side.

Monica gave his hand a soft squeeze.

Emerson greeted them heartily. "Welcome, friends, welcome. This way please. Miss Silverstone, it is a delight to see you again. I thank you for accepting my invitation to assist Jerry in his quest to learn the bakala," he said as he kissed her hand and turned to face Jerry, continuing, "although he will come to see that there is nothing to learn. There is only to feel. Maria did not come with you?"

"No, she…"

"Ah, so our intentions did not intersect." Emerson led them to a large room with a wooden floor. It opened into a beautiful garden that reminded Jerry of Zen gardens. It conveyed a sense of serenity, which seemed to contrast with or balance the exuberance of the bakala.

After providing water and snacks, Emerson gathered them together. "Place your right hand on the other's heart. Your heart has a strong field around it, many times stronger than the field around your head. Feel the beat of the heart, the beat that is life. Feel how quickly your hearts come to beat in unison simply by becoming aware of the other's heartbeat. Now Jerry, move your hand slowly from about four feet away toward her heart. What do you feel?"

"I feel the energy field getting stronger. There seem to be layers, rather than a smooth transition." After feeling her field and his own heart's field with his hand, then Emerson instructed Jerry to feel her heart energy with his own heart instead of with his hand. This was trickier because he had to learn how to sense her heart energy with his own.

"Heart-to-heart energy interaction is much stronger than hand-to-heart. It is like a magnet," Emerson said.

Feeling that magnetic pull himself now, Jerry realized that this is how the couples stayed so connected while moving at such a frenzied pace and with such complicated patterns.

"How does this heart-to-heart connection manage to keep people spinning away from each other from the centrifugal force?" Jerry asked.

"Theory later. Just do. You must experience it to truly understand it. You cannot do the bakala up here," he said pointing to his head.

Next, so as not to pull the heart's energy field in different directions, their bodies and energies needed to feel how to move together, so Emerson pulled a large round mushroom about a foot in diameter, like a puffball, from the garden. He instructed Jerry and Monica to stand close together and to move so that the mushroom would neither fall to the ground nor be crushed between them. Jerry found this to be harder than it sounded, and it fell several times before he developed the sensitivity to move in synchrony with Monica. It fell whenever he began to move on his own and forgot that he was doing this with her. The key, he realized, was not to think about his movement, just to feel what was happening between them. Old habits and stereotypes of wanting to lead, to control the movement, died hard. However, when he shut his eyes, he could do it better. His skin and the sensitivity to the heart field became like an ear, and he listened with his body to the movement of her body. In these moments, Jerry discovered the complete joy that occurs in moving in synchrony with another.

"The bakala harmonizes the body and spirit with the Source being-body," Emerson explained. "It requires the body to do, but the effects are felt by the spirit. We developed it because we are not accustomed to being in physical form for such extended periods of time, as you now know. For us, being in material form is like everything happening in slow motion for you, Jerry, or like choosing to be depressed. This slower vibration can get tedious after awhile. So we invented the bakala to enable ourselves to feel the bliss of living as energy while we are living as matter."

"Another way to look at it," Monica added, "is like a tuning process. Musical instruments need to be tuned. The body is like a musical instrument that needs to be tuned back to its true frequency in order to stay in harmony. By becoming attuned to another, the bakala enables you to stay tuned. Both are necessary to create this physical existence."

Oh, this is why I'm finding out about this only now, now that I know they're energy beings, not just physical beings.

Monica continued, "The bakala recreates ●॰ೲ೦ೲ●● aneh-mi-oh-nu, the snake of light. Two separate beings become one, winding around each other in an energetic embrace."

"It's the core energy source and generator which keeps the body-machine alive. Jerry, do you remember when you first saw our cords?" Emerson asked.

"Yes."

"It's the same thing—your cord inside your body, connecting it from head to toe. But also from cell to cell. Where the ●॰ೲ೦ೲ●● enters the body, it is visible as the cord you see, the golden braid or the twisted rainbow." Emerson clarified. "Enough talk. We have more to do. Now we will play some harmonious vibrations—music. If you do not get distracted by the music, it heightens the effects of the movement because now there are more elements in harmony, and the more elements in harmony, the higher the state of bliss and Oneness."

Listening to and feeling the music vibrate in unison with their hearts, their cells, and that eternal pulse sourcing their very lives, Jerry and Monica touched hands, then hearts, and pulsed, legs and arms keeping the heart's beat. The inner beat coursed up and down the spine. They swayed together, chest to chest, sideways, forward and back, whichever way the music took them. The heart connection grew strong; hands touching or chests touching was no longer necessary. Connected as one body, merged in spirit and being, yet moving as individuals they swirled around and around, like dolphins playing in the waves. No longer aware of identities, of time, of place, moving as if animated by some unknown force, they spun until they lost themselves. The pace increased, the beat hastened. Their energy ascended, and their bodies evaporated into a whirling funnel, like a tornado, right in Emerson's house. They whirled up off the ground, bodies blurred into spinning colors, moving so quickly that forms were indistinguishable.

Jerry left the physical, material world behind, transformed into pure energy, and became a colored whoosh just like the children in the orchard.

The music ended, and Jerry thudded to the ground, stunned and unaware of what had happened. The ground moved under him, spinning him through the galaxy. Ever so slowly, the whirling sky slowed down, enough now to lift his head up and look around. Jerry looked up expecting to see the usual stars, galaxies, satellites, and moon. They weren't there, but what he saw was teeming with life, like a drop of water under a microscope. It wasn't more matter, it was more like waves rippling across space, flutterings of light, ghostlike, joyful, and serene.

Monica made the transition back into material form more gradually, coming down by spinning back down slowly. She and Emerson went to Jerry's side.

"How was it, Jerry?" Monica asked. Emerson beamed expectantly.

Jerry sat up, dazed, and as he realized what happened he rose and hugged Monica and Emerson. "I did it, didn't I?" His face shone with a combination of ultimate ecstasy and pure serenity. "That was akra-na. I know it was."

"Tell us your experience," Emerson said.

"I saw myself as the Source of all Being, the One that is Many. It was like being inside of an enormous creature, like a huge jelly fish, an amorphous, pulsating being. I have a single, all-seeing eye at the center of my body rather than on top and in front. As I looked in all directions, from the center of each cell of this body is a thin thread going out to every single being. At the end of each thread is an identity, a different consciousness, like you, me, an insect, a tree, a river, a cloud, each doing its own thing but still attached to the source through an umbilical cord-like thread. Those are the threads I learned to see not long ago. I could watch each identity from the perspective of being inside all of them or from the perspective of any one of them. I saw my own identity-body and how I/it used to think that I was alone and separate, having forgotten that I was actually connected to the Source Being-body. And I saw others as well, thinking they were alone and separate, fighting against each other as if it mattered. It was hilarious to watch, these, my own extensions that have forgotten their Source Being-body.

"I lost my sense of time; I lost my sense of place, of being here; and I lost my sense of identity, my individual perspective, and became the movement itself rather than Jerry doing the movement. When I was pure movement, that's when I merged with the Source being-body. There wasn't emptiness even though everything about me was gone. There was still a pulsing in me. I was the pulsing, expanding outward and inward at the same time, vibrating at different frequencies. And like before, I wasn't alone. I felt Monica's pulsing, your pulsing, the pulsing of everything, which was just there, constant, and I was no different from it. Being at the source of everything, a point that expands to infinity, the nothing from which all is created—oh, now I see—I got to the zero point, became zero-point energy."

Slowly, seeing the pieces fall into place, Jerry laid them out, one by one. "I had to experience being zero-point energy in order to answer my own question. I couldn't understand the matter-energy equivalence from the outside looking in. I had to get to the inside so I could see that there is no difference. One is the other. That's why I'm here. I couldn't see, even by living in your culture, watching you, and learning your 'language' how you created your reality from intention, and that you were, in fact, being the proper and ethical use of zero-point energy. I couldn't understand it from learning your concepts, the very foundation of your culture. I had to become capable, myself, of living from that proper and ethical place. I had to become All within myself so that I could realize that there is no 'using it' like it's outside of me. I *am* the question and the answer to my own question, the ultimate Klein bottle. The answer is not out there or in here. Thank you both for leading me to this point." Tears streaked his face, and gratitude filled his heart.

Chapter 44

"I had this dream last night," Helen told Ben,

"Last night I dreamed," Jerry told Maria,

"of Jerry."

"of Helen."

"He was coming towards me from a long way away."

"She was far off in the distance so I ran toward her."

"And about half way his body started evaporating, disappearing before my eyes."

"And I couldn't get there fast enough by running so I changed from my material body to my energy body."

"He was just this orange ball of light."

"I became an orange whoosh, as I did during the bakala."

"He encircled me and then there was this poof and the color was all around me like a cloud."

"I didn't have arms to hug her so I enclosed her within me."

"I felt warm and loved."

"I could read her thoughts and tell her mine directly."

"Then the orange cloud was sucked inside through my navel, like water going down a drain."

"It wasn't enough to hug her from the outside in. I wanted to hug her from the inside out, so I entered through the third chakra."

"It was the oddest sensation of feeling Jerry's presence inside of me, like we were both in my body."

"It was eye-opening, literally, to see the world through her eyes, from her perspective.

"Then I woke up, but it feels like part of him is still there. I can feel it in my heart."

"Then I awoke to a strange feeling in my legs and arms, as if I weren't there, no more solid bones giving me upright posture, no more muscles holding the bones in place, no more nerves with which to feel pain, and no more eyes to view the world. Yet I didn't feel blind. Instead I could sense all happening at once but not 'out there.' It was all happening to me. I was being shot, stabbed, fed at a mother's breast, hugged, tortured, sat bored in school, was begging for scraps of food, was mesmerized in front of a television, was working working working, in backbreaking labor, in dehumanizing conditions, in plush over-air-conditioned office buildings, in front of millions of computers; I was being born and I was dying thousands of times each moment.

"There was no place to go, nothing to do, only to be, to experience all this variety of experience. At rare moments, the cacophony of it all melded into harmony, some of the experiences being attuned, like when the orchestra is warming up, yet amid the dissonance you can hear faint strains of a melody, briefly from a violin, then briefly from a trumpet, then punctuated by the piccolo." The identity known as Jerry Fowss blurred into the abyss of life itself, like the wave that sinks back into the undifferentiated waters of the vast ocean.

Epilogue

I have tried to convey what it is like being the One and the Many by telling you a story about one of the waves of the vast ocean of existence that I am—and how this wave interacted with other waves, with the shore, with the air. I hope that you read this not as a story about a fictional Jerry Fowss, but as your story, so that you too may know the awesome magnificence that you are. You are One that is Both.

Resources for Further Reading

Abram, David. *The Spell of the Sensuous*. New York: Vintage Books/Random House, 1997.

Andrews, Colin, with Stephen Spignesi. *Crop Circles: Signs of Contact*. Franklin Lakes, NJ: The Career Press, 2003.

The Graphic Work of M. C. Escher. New York: Gramercy, 1984.

Gangadean, Ashok. *Meditative Reason: Toward universal grammar*. New York: Peter Lang, 1993.

Gangadean, Ashok. *Between Worlds: The emergence of global reason*. New York: Peter Lang, 1998.

Gibson, Walker, ed. *The Limits of Language*. New York: Hill and Wang/Farrar, Straus and Giroux, 1962.

Hicks J, Hicks E. *Ask and It Is Given: Learning to manifest your desires*. Carlsbad, CA: Hay House, 2004.

Hyde, Lewis. *The Gift: Imagination and the erotic life of property*. New York: Vintage/Random House, 1983.

King, Moray B. *Tapping the Zero-Point Energy*. Provo, Utah: Paraclete Publishing, 1989.

Lakoff G, Johnson M. *Metaphors We Live By*. Chicago: University of Chicago Press, 1980.

McTaggart L. *The Field: The quest for the secret force of the universe*. New York: HarperCollins, 2003.

Narby, Jeremy. *The Cosmic Serpent: DNA and the origins of knowledge.* New York: Jeremy P. Tarcher/Putnam, 1999.

Ogden, C. K. *Opposition: A linguistic and psychological analysis.* Bloomington, IN: Indiana University Press, 1967.

Pert, Candace. *Molecules of Emotion: The science behind mind-body medicine.* New York: Touchstone/Simon & Schuster, 1987.

Prechtel, Martin. *Secrets of the Talking Jaguar.* New York: Jeremy P. Tarcher/Putnam, 1998.

Prechtel, Martin. *Long Life, Honey in the Heart.* Berkeley, CA: North Atlantic Books, 2004.

Rasha. *Oneness: The teachings.* San Diego, CA: Jodere Group, 2003.

Rosen, Steven M. *Dimensions of Apeiron: A topological phenomenology of space, time, and individuation.* Amsterdam/New York: Rodopi, 2004.

Rosen, Steven M. "What is Radical Recursion?" *The SEED Journal.* Vol. 4, no. 1:38-57.

Sabelli, Hector. *Union of Opposites: A comprehensive theory of natural and human processes.* Lawrenceville, VA: Brunswick, 1989.

Sabelli, Hector C. *Bios: A Study of Creation.* Singapore: World Scientific, 2005.

Schlain, Leonard. *The Alphabet Versus the Goddess: The conflict between word and image.* New York, NY: Penguin Compass, 1998.

Thomas, Gerald H. and Kane, Keelan. "A dynamic theory of strategic decision making applied to the prisoner's dilemma." Presented at the New England Complex Systems Institute, Boston, June 25-30, 2006.

Tiller, William A., Dibble, Walter E., and Kohane, Michael J. *Conscious Acts of Creation: The emergence of a new physics.* Walnut Creek, CA: Pavior Publishing, 2001.

Watts, Alan. *The Book: On the taboo against knowing who you are.* New York: Vintage Books, 1972.

Wolff, Milo. *Exploring the Physics of the Unknown Universe*. Manhattan Beach, CA: Technotran Press, 1990.

Websites

Haselhurst, Geoff. www.spaceandmotion.com

Sabelli, Hector. www.creativebios.com

Valone, Thomas. http://users.erols.com/iri/ZPEpaper.html

Wolff, Milo. www.quantummatter.com

978-0-595-39490-6
0-595-39490-6

Printed in the United States
144095LV00004B/36/A